OF THE ELEMENTS BOOK 1

BORN OF
WIND

J.B. LESEL

PRESS

Published by Vulpine Press in the United Kingdom in 2021

Cover by Claire Wood

ISBN: 9781839193439

www.vulpine-press.com

To my beloved father, Dov

My deepest thanks to:
David, my delightful editor.
Helene, Rachel and Ben L., and Saskia C., my supportive cheering team
Ulf Anneken, shedding inspiration via diligence and craft

In memorium, M. Boehm and E. Tarvyd, beloved teachers and guides

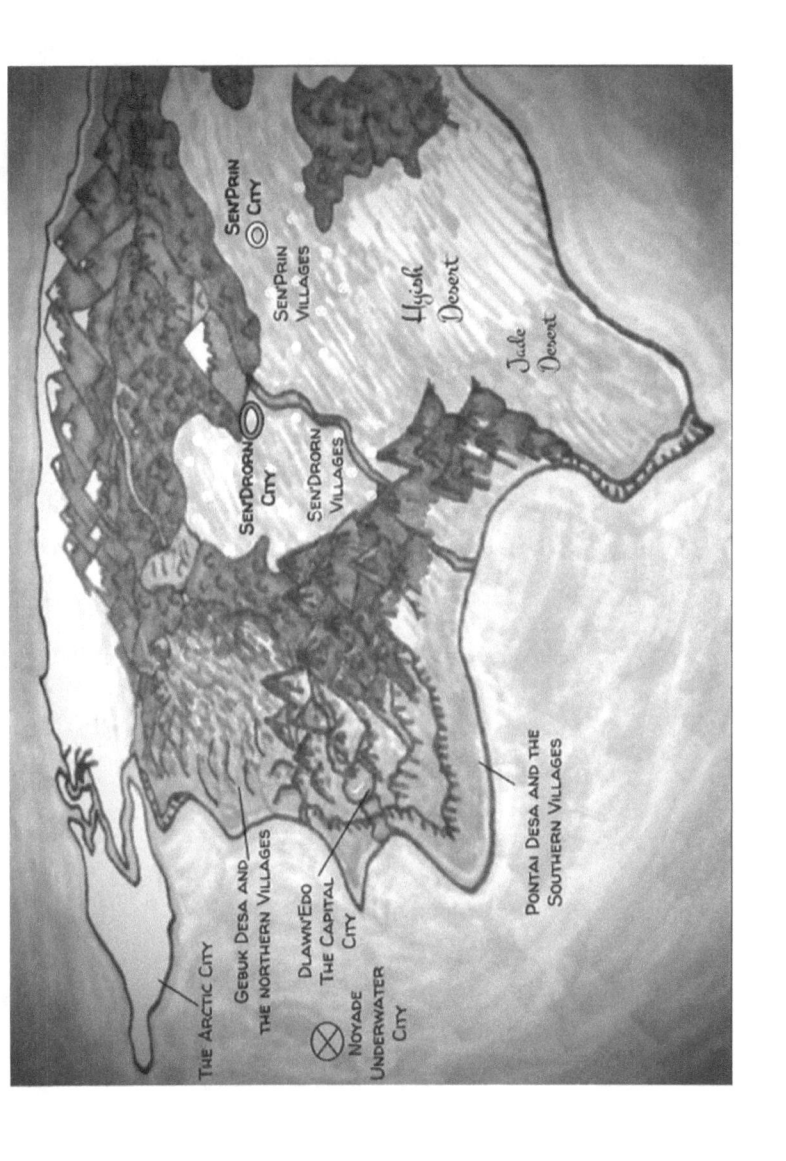

CHAPTER ONE

The bulbub trees were the best in the forest because their bark glowed green at night, their sweet-tasting roots bated animals, and their vines hung in sheets that could be pulled back and hidden behind.

Two creatures stood between two such trees, digging deeper into the muddy soil in search of the tasty roots, unaware they were being watched. The image of these creatures took form on the page of a journal, not far away. From their shiny scaled hides and wide-set, golden eyes, to the mossy tufts like fur that grew wildly on their stumpy legs: these creatures had no names, so Meleena, who hid behind the bulbub tree curtain, called them muul'dre as she hurriedly sketched the details of these creatures inside her precious journal. She was the first person ever to do so, to her knowledge.

Her notes about the muul'dre's behaviors crowded the margins: one couldn't bother with neatness in these rapidly changing settings. The pages were bound with thread to a clamshell cover, broader than the span of her fingertips, and squashed in the pages were flattened seedpods, leaves, feathers, and tufts of moss.

Meleena kept aware of the croaking, the blooping of birds and the patter of raindrops which echoed through the forest canopy like a pulse, telling her there was peace in this moment as she held her journal aloft.

She flicked away the odd pesky strand of seaweed-blue hair from her face. They floated in the air as if underwater, which was always a bother on land. Then again, she welcomed the warmth as the tendrils soaked up the sun's rays, energizing her and staving off hunger. It was forbidden, of course, during school hours to be out here, alone, but who would ever know?

The sounds of the forest stopped, causing Meleena's writing hand to tense. A crash shook the leafy canopy as what looked like two bushes crashed through, bulbous yet pointed at the end: a green beak. The beak separated, then snapped together like a clamp over the muul'dre's torso. The muul'dre let out a long cry as blue blood oozed out of its side and it lifted, up, up, up…

The beak connected to a long, rope-like neck, covered in moss, and a plump body atop two gangly legs, which Meleena had previously mistaken for sapling tree trunks.

Meleena's eyes widened. The giant bird blinked a tiny eye in the center of its leaf-beaked head and drew up, gulping its prey down whole. It happened so fast, the muul'dre's beetle-hide hadn't even shimmered as it normally did when alarmed.

A second later, its companion's did, but the muul'dre's rainbow jostling of scales came too late.

"*Ruuu!*" The alarm cry rang from the second muul'dre as it attempted to flee towards the undergrowth. Meleena tried her best to sketch the face of the bird, but her hair kept getting in the way and her glasses kept sliding down the bridge of her nose.

The gangly legs of the great bird were swift, its plump green body covered in moss rather than feathers, shining in dappled sunlight.

Meleena's fingers tingled. Being so close to danger caused adrenaline to flow through her veins. Her sense of safety shattered as a rustling from behind sent her stumbling off balance, tipping her headlong into the wet leaves and landing in a startled heap.

"Meleena!"

Fear jolted inside Meleena, which soon gave way to anger as the familiarity of the voice hit her. How could her mother have found her, *here?*

The woman who staggered from the bushes and pulled back the bulbub tree curtain had similar features to hers, though streaked with worry lines. While Meleena's hair hung in strands and had become riddled with twigs, her mother's similar blue hair sat high in a neat bun.

"Impossible! You've really been ditching your last year of school to hide in the forest!"

"Mama, what are you doing here? It's not safe for you!"

"Safe for *me?* No Meruyan belongs out here, where the unknown animals of the land can hunt us! We are a foreign entity here and easy targets!" Her mother looked around and shuddered at the trees. So dense, anything could be hiding behind them. "And I can't believe you ditched class again!"

"I know, I'm sorry..." Meleena was looking around too. Her ears perked up, something really *was* amiss. The forest had gone silent: the bird and frog songs had ceased. Meleena's heart began to race. With the pulse of urgency she whispered, "But now isn't the time—"

"I'm confiscating this!" Her mother snatched her journal and slammed it shut.

A low and hollow trill filled the forest. If something happened to her mother out here, she'd never forgive herself. She was already shaming her parents enough by being out here.

Without a spare moment, Meleena gripped her mother by the arm and pulled her into a run, "Hey—", just as the giant bird barreled towards them on its gangly, sapling-like legs.

Her mother's eyes widened, and she slipped from anger to horror.

"The bog, it's the best way to lose a large predator!" Meleena shouted as she pulled her mother along.

"Careful!"

"Mama, please!"

The beast was quick and swiftly dodged the trees as Meleena hop-dashed between wetter, more decrepit logs—they couldn't outrun this bird for long. Its neck feathers splayed and its beak snapped aside vines to clear its path.

"Yeoch! My leg!"

Meleena caught a glimpse of blood, her mother had scraped it badly on the underbrush.

"It's not much further!"

What at first seemed to be a patch of straw grasses, Meleena knew to be a subtle sign of water.

Meleena snatched the journal from her mother's quivering hand and slammed its two shell halves shut, sealing its pages inside its watertight lips, before she jumped into the patch of straw grasses. They were actually startled lily pad creatures the size of dinner plates, retracting grass-like hairs from their backs and gliding away so rapidly that Meleena plunged into the freshly revealed water's surface.

But it was the giant water striders who lived here that Meleena was counting on for help...

"Jump!" employed Meleena from the murky green bog water.

Her mother's turquoise skin had gone pale and blood oozed from her scratched leg as she stood at the edge, stuck between the decision of staying dry or becoming a wild creature's lunch. Hollow clicking rumbled loudly behind them. The bird's head appeared, its long beak snapped off her mother's hair bob. Her mother screamed and fell into the green bubbling water. The bird's beak skimmed over the water, snapping and searching as Meleena pulled her mother deeper into the bog.

Then the giant water striders came. Sleek and black-bodied, they glided on needle feet over her head to crowd the shore of the bog. *"We-wah-we-we-we-wah!"* They spat acid at the bird's beady eyes, hissing with distress as they defended their hidden eggs, laid under the edges of the muddy water.

The bird retaliated with terrifying clanking, the sound so close that it reverberated in Meleena's bones, until it finally turned and its gangly tree-like legs disappeared, though it was hard to tell it apart from other trees, especially from under the surface. But Meleena knew: she'd had previous experience.

Her mother climbed first out of the bog, covered with muck. Once on her feet, she sloshed algae and water from her hands. On her forearms, her sea fins had sprouted because of her contact with water. Her face contorted in what could have been any number of bitter emotions, all of which spelled trouble for Meleena.

Dordin plants grew along the lake's edge. Meleena picked one of their round, fruit-like bulbs, which she alone among the Meruyan knew contained medicinal qualities. It took some strength to squeeze the bulb until its juices flowed over her hands. Meleena lowered onto her knees to make certain each drop fell into the wound on her mother's leg. The bloody cuts sealed as her mother's leg returned to normal, though it didn't do much to ease her mood.

Meleena handed over the journal, safe from the muck in the shell binding, and resigned to her capture.

***

Dinner was tenser than usual that evening. Sure, Meleena hadn't been doing well in school lately, ditching more than usual in her last year. But what was the point? In the village of Pontai'Desa, nothing was ever going on. The Meruyan villagers were all about fishing and farming, both on the shore and in the underwater parts of town.

Meleena entered the kitchen, the only common room of her family cottage, where her father stood over a pot of simmering pon-urchin and bean stew, looking himself like a giant string bean with his lanky green features. The smell of pon-urchin meat, salty and savory, hung thick in the air. The giant sea urchins were land-farmed proudly by many villagers in the town. She'd soon have to pick a job like this to apprentice for, to become trained in. The very thought of apprenticeships made her arms droop down by her sides.

Peering over his glasses, her father pleaded silently with her, disappointment showing behind his kind eyes. He was the guilt-sort of parent, whereas anger had always been her mother's game.

Her father rubbed the steam from his glasses. Most Meruyan needed glasses if they wanted to see clearly above water. She'd always cursed it, like they didn't really belong here, in the shore world. Underwater, she couldn't keep a journal. She hated the thought that if she'd grown up underwater, she'd have never aspired to do something more than fishing or farming.

A moment later, her mother came into the room.

"I like the haircut," her father said and kissed her cheek. "Dinner, Vivia?"

She'd bathed and put on a fresh dress after their dunk in the bog. Though all Meruyan clothing was made from kelp-weave and therefore could be worn in the sea, it was not meant for swamps.

Her mother took a seat in a chair opposite her, saying nothing.

"Er… when can I get my journal back?" It was the wrong question, but was better than letting the silence fester.

"How can you go into the jungle? Alone? I suspected you were skipping school but I had no idea the danger you put yourself in! This is about your safety! Loroh, back me up on this…"

"Your mother is right, the jungle is no place for a Meruyan."

"I can handle myself in the forest! I have cataloged and named everything in there!"

Her mother cupped her hand to her mouth.

Oops, too much. Meleena spent more time than they knew in the forest, often ditching class for days at a time.

Her mother's expression softened, melting into a pleading concern. "You're so smart, Meleena. I just want you to be successful. You can't make a living on your little drawings, you know that. You need to focus on getting a good apprenticeship next year. Tell me how I can help you."

"They aren't just little drawings! This is valuable information that could provide discoveries to help our community! I could be, like, a naturalist."

Her father focused on stirring his soup, her mother put her hands to her face and rubbed her eyes. This was a daily argument, going in circles. Meleena had heard it enough many times, *"That's not a trade-skill I've ever heard of…"* and her rebuttal, *"I know what job I want. I can visualize it. Why can't anyone else?"*

Meleena sipped the pon-urchin stew and glanced out the window, though it was now too dark to see anything. She couldn't help the sinking feeling, as if the forest wasn't there to back her up. It left her each night— forced her away, to spend time with the people that didn't understand her.

Her father said, "Your brother Tomiyan has a great trade skill. And a family! Maybe follow his example."

Tomiyan was all right, they had always been close, but since he married and moved out, she was the only child left to bear the brunt of her parents' worry. Still, what example? Marrying young and becoming a fish trader was definitely not her path.

He continued cheerily, "If you want something bigger, maybe join the Meruyan Council, like me and Kelrick."

Kelrick, her other brother, was not all right. He was a mud-sack. Once, on a tour of the local council center, he'd run off while chaperoning her class visit in order to put in a good word for the coveted annual Council Apprenticeship. Meleena's classmates teased her for the rest of the school year about it.

This had been her only experience with the local council and the kind of people who joined it. Though she didn't truly know what they did, she assumed it had to do with managing fish-related trade issues. Kelrick now lived in the Meruyan Capital, a city she'd never been to, but she assumed he now dealt with a wider scope of those same fishy issues.

Her father was the village Historian, so he kept an office library full of strange artifacts and recorded noteworthy local incidents. There was no room for a similar vocation involving plants or animals.

"There's the underwater district. Why not study sea creatures? You could work for a seaweed farm." Her father's glasses slid down the bridge of his nose as he smiled, pleased with his own idea.

"Yes, lots of wildlife there, you could revolutionize the lobster industry," said her mother, with a face dreamy with the pride it would bring.

Meleena, trying to be respectful, laughed it off. "That's not what I had in mind. And I don't want to live there, under the sea in caves! They live like octopuses scared of reef sharks!"

Her mother picked up Meleena's journal from the table and drew it into her arms. "I'm sorry, Meleena, but if you want a good one, you'll have to decide on something soon. If we can't help you choose, then think on it this week without the distraction of your journal. You'll earn it back next week if you go to all your classes! You have until the end of the week to select an actual apprenticeship you wish to pursue."

"What! The week is halfway over! How could I even pick..." Meleena narrowed her eyes.

Her mother knitted her eyebrows, pain and anger under the surface. "It hurts me to do this, but we want to help you. To guide you towards a bright future."

"Alright, fine..." Meleena's face was hot with anger.

Her parents exchanged exacerbated looks as Meleena drew herself back from the table and excused herself from the evening.

***

General Malotus felt the wind ripple over his body as he soared in the sky at the center of a tornado, the wind bending under his control. His assistant, Yulah, flew at his side driving her own tornado forward, while a dozen of the General's lower-ranking men followed behind.

Soon they would reach the ridge just over the horizon. From there they would see the speck that was Pontai'Desa. Full of silly Meruyans. Gill breathers living out of their element, living simple lives.

Malotus and his team were not coming to the Meruyans on official business tonight. They weren't even here at all, officially. He would count on Yulah to stop his penchant for destruction from uprooting the entire town. What they needed would be inside one of those wooden onion cottages, anyway. Information from their hostage had yielded this lead—their only lead.

Wind Goddess be praised! Pontai'Desa, a silly little fishing town. Of all places! Malotus's heart beat with fierce excitement as he squinted into the wind.

***

In the morning, Meleena slunk into the kitchen for breakfast. She wouldn't dare ditch school today. Her mother's threat was serious. She'd destroy her journal if Meleena didn't pick an apprenticeship to aim for by week's end. Meleena was surprised then, to see her older brother Tomiyan sitting at the family's old oak table.

Her parents had obviously not believed she could not be trusted to arrive at school herself. They had called for backup.

"So, I heard you've been acting up again." He smirked and sipped blue root tea, his glasses opaque from the steam. The morning light streamed in through the open windows, bathing the kitchen in a soft glow.

She tucked her kelp-weave dress under her legs as she sat on the bench. "You know I do it so I can see more of you." She was half smiling but feeling lousy. "How's the wife and baby?"

"They're well. But, no distractions! We're running late," he said, checking a copper-geared object on his wrist.

"Whoa, shiny contraption you got there." Meleena came over and took his arm for a closer look.

"Birthday gift from our dear brother in the capital. New Warix technology, they call it a wristcom," he answered, slowly standing up. "It has a compass, can tell the time, and can dial in to communicate with someone else. Though Kelrick is the only other person I know with one."

"Never heard of it. Maybe it's the next big thing." Meleena stuffed a potato roll in her mouth, slung her pack over her shoulder, and nodded. Tomiyan poured her a cup of tea, which helped her choke down her large mouthful of food.

"Well, now I'm ready." She smiled, then stuffed the rest of the pastry into her mouth. He stood up from the table, looking stately in his brown kelpweave tunic and trousers, with a smock tied in front—for the day's fish guts, soon to come.

As they walked to school, Meleena recounted to her brother the lively dinner discussion of last night. They passed the wood- and onion-shaped cottages of the town, enclosed by sapling trees forming fence posts, entangled with strings of kitten's ear ivy. She made a mental note to draw that later, when she'd gotten her journal back.

"Well, it sounds like you really should go visit Kelrick in Dlawn'Edo. I know he can be... difficult, but there's more to the Council than just him."

She made a face. "Why didn't you follow Dad and Kelrick's footsteps and join the Meruyan government?"

"I've seen their world, but I'm happy right here. Plus, I have a wife and daughter of my own whose future I must protect, but if adventure interests you, I wouldn't write off the Council so quickly." He adjusted his glasses.

They passed the main square, where the day's bustle had already begun, with Meruyan holding baskets to collect fresh foods from the marketplace; sea-beast drawn wooden carts traversed the streets, led by farmers bringing fruit from farm to shops.

They rounded a corner leading down the lane to the old schoolhouse, built like a conjoined ring of wooden onions—an onion-cake, frosted with moss from years of exposure to the moist coastal air. Other teens were visible from all directions down the stony lanes.

They approached the doors and Tomiyan opened them to let her in. "Just ask Dad for a tour of his study tonight," he said and left it at that.

School went as expected. Talla, the only overachiever of the class, shot her hand up and answered every question with ease, while Meleena and the rest of the students sighed, groaned, threw paper birds, sometimes at Talla's head, and did everything else bored students do. Everyone except Joru, Talla's twin brother. He sat beside Meleena, always looking at her.

A gill breather. What a hokey place this was. Meleena tried to ignore him, leaning on her elbow and facing away from his batting eyes.

He was shy, but his intentions were clear. She had already told him it would never happen. For this, Talla especially despised Meleena. "You broke his heart, you flirt!" she would howl at any occasion.

But Meleena couldn't make herself love the guy, or blame herself for existing. And that was that. Whatever. Just one more year putting up with this and she'd be free, but free to do what? Her family was right, there were no options anyway.

After school, she slunk home, hands in pockets with nothing to draw and no ideas for an apprenticeship. In her room, she dropped her backpack on the floor, flopped onto the bed, heart sinking. No journal to scribble her thoughts, or her way through problems.

A knock startled her and she uttered a noise muffled by a face-full of bedsheets.

Her father spoke through the door, "Meleena, I wanted to show you something. I spoke to Tomiyan, he said you seemed down."

She sat up. "I'm fine."

"Well, he suggested I show you my study."

"I've seen it."

"I just thought…" His voice trailed off. "I could help you pick an apprenticeship."

The wooden floor creaked as he stood outside the door. Her heart sank further at the thought of his judgment.

"—Maybe I can convince your mother to give your journal back sooner…"

Meleena opened the door. Shadows danced on his face from the luminous worm-shell candles that lit the hallway at night.

"Sounds like a deal."

She followed her father to the room she scarcely visited. Books lined the walls from floor to ceiling, and glass cases pillared the middle. He lit the worm-shell candles and led her to one particularly large case to the left of his desk.

"This is where I keep the most precious artifacts."

Meleena lifted her glasses and inspected rolls of parchment, metal-plated shells, dusty leather-bound books, broken copper gadgetry, and inscribed parcels.

Her father opened a dusty book titled *Gifts of the Warix: The End of the Wet Ages.* "This book contains everything the Meruyan have learned from the Warix about how to live on land. Everything wooden, from homes to paper, land-farming, fire for heating and cooking. Wouldn't you like to meet a Warix someday?"

Meleena ignored him. He was trying to get her to apprentice for the Council, but it wasn't going to work. But she was running out of time and ideas.

"There's more to the council than you think…" Her father handed her a scroll to read:

Legend of Peoples.

1–Meruyan: Aquatic people of the Water Spirit. Government: Meruyan Nation, Run by the Council. Capital: Dlawn'Edo

2–Warix: Forest people of the Earth Spirit. Government: Two Enemy Nations.

Sen'Drorn Warix: Name meaning "loyal to the state." Centuries old, run by Emperor Ryogrim and advisors. Capital: Sen'Drorn City.

Sen'Prin Warix: Name meaning "loyal to the people." Small, split-off nation, run by Governess Arenay. Capital: Sen'Prin City.

3–Hyish: Reptilian people of the Fire Spirit. Government: many clans, trading-based hierarchy, Mayfee clan most prominent. Capital: none, no-madic.

"What is this?" Meleena ran her fingers over the waxy scroll. It appeared there was more going on outside her village than she realized. "A Hyish?" She'd never even heard of that.

"Yes—reptilian people who live in tribes all over the world—be it forest, grasslands, or desert. They invented glass, you know, like those in your glasses."

The thought of sketching and documenting their culture piqued Meleena's interest. She'd love to meet a reptilian person one day. Outwardly, she merely shrugged and returned the scroll.

Maybe the council idea wasn't so bad, after all. Not like she had any better ideas.

"What else is here?"

Her father handed her a horn. Turning it over, she ran her finger over the etched markings running along its surface. "I've never seen a horn like this… it's like the farmers brand on pon-urchin spines, but this seems… daintier?"

"A Warix horn. Far away in the Arctic City, where both Warix and Meruyans live, it has become trendy to brandish Meruyan symbols. You could visit if you joined the council's apprenticeship. There is a reason your mother and I raised you here, it's safe. But there is more to the Meruyan nation than fishing villages. I promise it."

As Meleena took the horn into her hands, a tangible part of a creature from a distant land, the world outside the village felt real for the first time. She wasn't excited about the idea of working for the council, but it was starting to look like the best option at least as an apprenticeship. A chance to leave the town, at least she could sketch wildlife, and quit later, maybe run away to live in the forest... yes, great ideas were forming.

"Fine, I'll sign up the council apprenticeship."

She helped herself to an object. A small box with a golden frame caught her eye. She held it flat in her palm, opening it to find... a wooden bauble, shaped like a droplet.

"Well, you can't simply join. The council is the hardest apprenticeship. You will need recommendations and diligence in your final year of school."

He almost had her there.

"Maybe it's not worth it then; I'll just clean out pon-urchin carcasses. Why was this junk in here?" Meleena turned over the trinket. It was crudely whittled into the shape of a ram's head, with gleaming white eye holes. The light seemed to be emanating, curiously, from within.

Before her father could answer, a deep rumbling began. Rolling thunder. They looked up, startled. A baby cried somewhere in the distance.

Hurried footsteps pounded, getting louder—Vivia and Tomiyan appeared in the doorway. Vivia gripped the doorposts, panting. "A flash storm has broken out!"

"There's an evacuation to the underwater community already underway," said Tomiyan through bated breath from the hall. "My family is waiting in the kitchen. We have to go, now!"

The rumbling continued.

Loroh furrowed his brow. "That's strange, it seemed so clear earlier this evening."

"Does that matter?" Tomiyan said. "A tornado has sprung up and has already smashed some cottages at the edge of town!"

Meleena's heart pounded as she ran behind her parents and Tomiyan down the hall. She had forgotten to return the carving and had absent-mindedly shoved it into her pocket. *I guess I'll return this when the storm passes. Can't exactly go back now.*

Tomiyan's wife held a restless infant and stood as they entered the kitchen. Something crashed on the roof.

Meleena and her family ran through the village towards the beach, their straw shoes slapping the stone pavement. The wind pushed them, though there weren't any storm clouds above. Stars winked at her against the boundless darkness.

As they reached the beach, they saw other Meruyans wading into the ocean. As the waves lapped at their bodies, fins sprouted on forearms and calves. Some plunged in headfirst, arms extended. Meleena had experience with this: a steep drop not far offshore.

Still, there hadn't been a night evacuation in years. She barely remembered the last time. Storms this bad didn't come along every season. Meleena spotted their village elders who ran the community. She spotted Talla and Joru. Joru blushed, then faced away from her, and Talla scowled in her direction.

Meleena shivered in the cold night air. More Meruyans dove straight into the crashing waves and out of sight. Meleena, like most, stashed her glasses in a pocket: she wouldn't need them again until life on land resumed.

Trembling under the weight of her world falling apart, Meleena stole a blurry glance toward her village being torn asunder. At least this bought her some time to decide on apprenticeships. Then she, alongside her family, dove into the dark waves.

CHAPTER TWO

A falcon fought against the winds as he flew into the empty village of Pontai'Desa, his mossy mane blowing in the breeze.

The storm was abating such that he could now enter the orbit of the village. He swooped to avoid paving stones as they came loose and shattered cottage windows. A tornado spun: cottages burst apart as the tornado crashed through them until at last, the falcon swooped as the tornado dissipated at the village square. The form of a man replaced the spot where the tornado had been, his eyes shining silver pinpricks.

The falcon landed on one of the remaining cottages with a soft plop as soothing straw cradled its talons.

His master lit a torch, illuminating the square enough to inspect his surroundings. The silver of his eyes dimmed to their natural green, matching his military attire.

"Grimley, come here," the man beckoned. The falcon known as Grimley screeched and took to the wind, landing on the outstretched forearm of his master before the echo of his own screech had abated. Grimley's right wing brushed his master's thick black mane, which flowed over his master's shoulders. On his master's head were two protruding steer horns growing out from his temples: the falcon's favorite perch.

A creaking door caught their attention. The falcon could feel the tensing of the muscular perch under his feet as the master turned to face the door.

A slender woman stepped out. She was of his same race, a Warix, yet instead of ashen grey skin, she had the purplish hue of a velvetus tree. The falcon knew her, they served the same master.

She pouted her lips. Her youth brought insubordination. "Was it really necessary to destroy all those cottages, General Malotus?"

Malotus shrugged. "I can enjoy being destructive as long as it is also effective. As I predicted, Yulah, the Meruyans fled into the sea during the storm. We can search without interference."

Yulah's sharp-boned, foxy face shot upward in indignation and she combed her long purple hair into a twist with her fingers. "We're here to search the cottages, not destroy them! How am I supposed to look for the Pendant if there's nothing but rubble!" She swept her thin arms over the sight to indicate the damaged village. Loud wind still whipped around the edges of town as Malotus's men held the storm in place.

Grimley's mossy mane tingled from the breeze. The master and his servant continued to argue, and the falcon was transferred to perch on the level steer horn atop Malotus's head.

"They need to believe it was a real storm."

"Thanks for trying to cover our tracks… and yet again you've gone too far. And we've yet to find the Pendant. Maybe the villagers knew we were coming and took it with them?" She nervously ran her fingers through her hair, twisting it behind her curling horns.

"What? These fish-peasants? No… I think it is more likely our hostage was lying to us. Let's keep searching, and if we don't find it tonight, we can go back to headquarters to deal with our duplicitous little informant some more," the irked General Malotus commanded.

Several Warix soldiers appeared, their dark green uniforms matching General Malotus's in style. Malotus's soldiers appeared from the outskirts, showing signs of fatigue from powering the storm, and searched the remaining cottages.

"This is the cottage? Let me see." Malotus followed Yulah into the round cottage, ducking to enter the low doorway with Grimley the falcon still perched on his horn, who also ducked, his long tail streaming in behind them. Yulah led him down a hall and into a small library, where she had just been, candles still burning on the walls to light the way.

"I can't see any evidence you were even here!"

"I didn't want them to know, obviously!"

"Well, you don't expect them to leave it in plain sight! Come, let's get our hands dirty!" He grabbed a decorative chair from behind a desk and sliced open the stuffing with his clawed hand. He rooted around inside, letting the insides burst out, then chucked the chair aside with a sharp clack as the wooden legs met the floor.

"Malotus! What did you just do? Now they will know someone was in here!"

Malotus looked at her for a second, "Relax," then shot his arm out, palm facing the ceiling. As he did, a wind blast came forth from his core, like a shudder. Though Grimley the falcon was familiar with the sensation, the crash startled him and sent him lurching. He screeched as the straw ceiling burst open.

"Shhh, relax, Grimley." A hand came to stroke the moss-wrinkles on the falcon's chest, relaxing him. "Now we're good... A bolt of lightning from the storm did it. Ah what is this?" He lifted a scroll lying on the desk in a neat curl. "This scroll seems to indicate a list of items in this library."

His eyes flitted along the page, holding it to the dim candlelight. "It lists what we are looking for... So, it must be here somewhere."

"I for one am shocked it didn't get blown away."

"Just get to work," he snarled.

Yulah groaned and resumed searching through the rubble.

Their efforts continued late into the night. As they worked, Grimley the falcon lifted off and watched the figures at the edge of town control the winds, holding a stormy wall up, raging to outsiders, but calm for those within.

***

Meleena and her family, along with the rest of Pontai'Desa, descended into the dark chasm of the ocean. Their finned legs streamed behind them, heads facing the depths as they descended into the unknown, only a tiny pinprick of green light in the distance guiding them. What was it? She didn't know, only that it was their unified goal to reach it. She sensed from the tinging of her hair that the underwater community still lived well within the depths of the sun's energy-giving rays.

The sensation of breathing through neck-gills was always a surprise as the cold water rushed in and curled through. After several minutes of total immersion, the less sensitive finger and toe webbing extended, making the padding much easier, though a chill ran up her spine as the endless depths expended on either side of her, the other Meruyans so small in comparison. It was easy to imagine a beast of boundless size emerging to swallow them up: they'd be totally powerless to stop it.

She squinted and tried to focus on the beacon below, which radiated from a bioluminescent orb. It could only be the underwater village square.

She scarcely visited, and couldn't recall how long it had been since the last storm that had brought her down there. As they drew closer, small flickers of light exposed the caves all around them—the homes of the underwater villagers. She had never seen it at night.

As Meleena and her family floated into the square, surrounded by the rest of Pontai'Desa's shore-dwelling villagers, she realized they were not alone. The Underwater Village Elder held a staff aloft, its end illuminating the stone pavement of the square with a glass orb, in which swam a brightly glowing jellyfish. The green light.

Long fins streamed from not just his limbs but his cheeks: barnacles lined his hairline, looking more like seagrass inlaid with more critters calling it home. Snails, crabs, brittle stars, tube worms—all crawling freely or sanctioned to his kelpweave robes. It was hard to tell what was alive and what was decoratively inlaid, such as pearl and shell, though perhaps that could be said about them all. He must have been down here for a long time.

"Welcome, shore guests. I have received word about your descent from the shore Elder. Our volunteers will bring you to the great hall shelters so you may get some rest." He spoke in native Meruyan, a language comprised of a series of clicks, or short sound pulses, interpreted as words. Meleena was as fluent as anyone who only comes to underwater on market day once a week—agreeable, though imperfect.

Meleena followed her parents, as the shore villagers collectively followed underwater villagers with luminescent jellyfish orbs to light their way. They made their way into the large cave-dwelling system, a wide cavern set up with rows of beds of algae to sleep on.

It was easy to distinguish the underwater villagers from the shore dwellers. Firstly, the shore dwellers had more decorative inlays on their kelpweave, which Meleena knew meant more expensively made clothing. While both sported kelpweave clothes and varying shell types twisted into long hair, only the underwater natives had anything alive skittering in them, from live sea stars to barnacles in patterns. Perched crabs pinched as their hosts extended an arm to hand out additional kelpweave blankets to shore guests. Meleena recoiled at the plump lobster the size of a dog beside a boy about her age, who handed her a blanket with a shy nod, avoiding eye contact before moving on. The lobster notedly did not avoid eye contact. Strange boy, she thought, how kind of him to volunteer in times of crisis.

Would she do the same during an underwater emergency, in which the underwater community would come to the shore for safety? He must be earning points for a desired apprenticeship, she figured.

Meleena feigned sleep while glimpsing her parents conversing with adults nearby, about whether their cottages would still be standing in the morning. She assumed they would stay up long into the night, but there was nothing to be done. She closed her eyes and passed out.

In the morning, after a simple seafood breakfast from the generous underwater community, Meleena learned they were still not cleared to go back to the surface, so she left her parents to their continued discussions, and swam out to poke around the undersea life.

Children glided between rocks and coral exploring the park's sea life, supervised by more adults discussing the storm. They bobbed up and down in a circle nearby. She overheard her brother Tomiyan suggest sending someone to scout the surface, and report back when it was safe to return. Meleena shook her head to herself. If there was nothing to be done, why keep picking at it?

Darting fish became targets of interest, so she followed the shimmering scales of the school, twirling around them in a three-dimensional study of their movements. Maybe her father was right, Meleena decided. It wasn't so bad here, life was carefree and simple in the ocean.

She pulled the wooden pendant from her pocket and turned it over in her hand. She had kept it close—among the algae nest bed—as not to lose it during the night. She touched the wooden eye socket, hoping to uncover the source of the strange glow, but felt no gems. It was like a pinhole, the source of the light seemed to come from within the thing itself. What was this thing? She let go of it for a moment. It floated, dancing with the motion of the undersea current, like a dandelion in a light breeze. How strange... Wasn't wood normally supposed to float? It must be denser than normal wood.

A sudden sting jolted the back of her arm, breaking her thoughts and wrenching her back to the moment.

"Yeouch!" Meleena turned, now face to face with her schoolmate Talla, who was holding a struggling jellyfish by its crown.

Talla laughed and said, in a broken version of the underwater dialect, "That's what you get, inattention of surroundings! The sea, dangerous swamp, Smell-eena!" Her long hair swirled around her like an outstretched octopus.

Another stinging surge spread through Meleena's flesh.

"Didn't my sister just warn you to be more attentive Smell-eena?" Her twin brother, Joru, laughed kicking up sand with his legs.

Meleena scowled and shook her head. She wasn't going to let them win by getting angry. She spat sand from her mouth and shielded her eyes from the dust. She had totally forgotten about the pendant in all the commotion. Meleena shoved herself up from the boulder and lunged forward, grabbing Talla's left leg fin, pulling the startled girl down. The opposing reaction propelled Meleena upward in the other direction, away from them.

"Hey!" Talla screeched. "Come back here, you!" But Meleena was already darting away, aiming to lose them in a grove of bull kelp.

She swam with swift intention, darting between the tall strings, around, then hiding low to the ground, kicking her legs to stir up some obscuring dust of her own as they swam above, distancing herself from Talla shouting, "Apologize to Joru, he's the only boy who would ever like you!"

"Hey!" Joru protested. "I don't!"

Their voices grew distant, Meleena veered off and out of the grove in the other direction, only to collide with an object. She pushed back and realized she had swum into the biggest lobster she had ever seen.

She pulled back with her arm-fins to propel away, but as the silt cleared she looked around to realize they were in a sand bed full of even more such lobsters with rippling hard shells of rusty marbled browns, like polished sea stones. They brandished huge pincers and with their long bobbing eyestalks stared her down, making her back away nervously.

"Don't worry they're harmless!" came a pleasant voice. Meleena looked up to see a boy around her age cradling a lobster in his arms.

"Woah, what is that?" croaked Meleena, regaining her balance and noticing the skinny boy in front of her. He wore kelpweave overalls and looked familiar. "Hey, you're the boy from last night. The one who handed out blankets in the town hall."

Meleena looked down at the oversized crustacean in his arms.

"My name is Deemayan, but you can call me Deem. And they are Rock lobsters. This is my family's farm, where we raise them." The blue deepened on his cheeks as he blushed. "Oh yeah, I volunteer at town hall during storms. Swim this way with me and I'll lead you out of here," he suggested in a kind tone.

"Cool." She introduced herself as Meleena from the shore village. "What do you do with all these lobsters?" was all she could think to ask, keeping her fingers and fins close to herself. "Why are they so big… Do you eat them?" More pincers opened and shut around them. "Use them to crack coconuts?"

"Oh no!" he gasped. "These are a Rock lobster variety, who regularly shed their carapace, which we sell at the market. They're used for all sorts of things. Shoes, combs, I dunno what else. Lucky for me, I suppose. If we had farmed an edible breed, I'd have been miserable. I only eat plants myself. Though we can't afford much seafood anyway."

Meleena soon noticed that Deem was a natural with handling them, petting and nudging them as they moved towards a cave-front home.

She followed him to a small, corralled area near the cave entrance, where he gingerly placed the lobster from his arms into a kelpweave bedding. The corral contained a few droopy-looking lobsters. The lobsters seemed to perk up at his presence.

"These are sick," he explained, kneeling, and pulling a mossy clump from his pocket, then shredding it to feed to the various inhabitants.

The cave door opened and a Meruyan woman came out, followed by three young girls who came swimming out of other cave crevices to greet them.

"Deem! Lunchtime!" clicked one of the children.

"Well, I best be heading back home," Meleena said, getting ready to swim off, and realized she didn't know where she was. "Eh, if you can point me towards the town square…"

"Would you like to join us for lunch?" his mother asked.

"No, that's alright…"

"Join us for lunch!" screeched the young daughters. Meleena shrugged. She had nothing else to do. "Why not."

She followed and cupped the cave walls as she swam into the low cave entrance. The room was sparse except for etched out shelves, many holding clay or glass jars held in place with rope. Carved coral crates cluttered the corners. Meleena had expected sea glass to cover the windows, but here it was merely kelpweave curtains.

Meleena was curious about what lunch would be, since cooking and fire couldn't exist underwater. They floated around the table. Red coral link bracelets drifted on the woman's wrist in front of Meleena's face as Deem's mother placed bowls with different types of algae salad greens on the slab, which slid into divots to lock them down. She broke scallops on a rock with a repetitive crack and floated them into bowls for the taking.

"So, Deem was it? The volunteering, was it to get selected to apprentice for the Council or Aldrok's Journey?" Meleena asked.

"No, I... I Just know what hardship is like, and want to help where I can."

"Oh, come now," his mother said, drifting into a seat at the table slab, beaming. "I know you have bigger dreams than staying here with the lobsters, Deem. You don't have to stay here just to support the family." She turned to Meleena. "He's shy, but always does well in school. I bet he has a chance."

"Mama, don't get his hopes up," said a sister, an orb-eyed child with purplish hair streaming around her.

"He has big dreams for the underwater community," said another. Deem sat in quiet embarrassment, looking mortified.

After lunch, Deem walked her out, and insisted to swim her the whole way back to the city hall, to make sure she got there safely.

It was afternoon when the scout approached the town hall to report that the storm had subsided and it was safe to return. Since there could be no bells rung underwater, the Elders released dozens of spotted yellow eels from Town Hall. This was in accordance with local tradition, to signify when there was an announcement. By evening, they had gathered the whole town. The residents of the shore community readied themselves to resurface.

It was nearly nightfall when the people of Pontai'Desa finally reached the shores of their village, only to discover the extent of the damage. Many cottages were destroyed, curved wooden panes littering the ground, some onion-shaped houses burst open. The mayor called for everyone to return to their homes to assess their damage, and officially report back if they could host or needed hosting. A rider set off to the capital city to deliver the news and request aid.

When Meleena and her mother found their cottage still standing—though disheveled inside—they returned to the town center to offer their home for hosting.

"Our home!"

Meleena winced as she turned to the commotion. The yowling cries came from Talla's mother, who came dashing up the cobblestone road ahead of her family to deliver a report. Talla and Joru raced behind their parents, the color flushed from their faces.

"The back half of our cottage is gone!" her mother cried to the elder. "Everything seemed normal from the outside! I even started preparing dinner!"

Her husband caught up and panted, "When the twins tried to go to their rooms, we went down the hallway to see it was only rubble!"

The village elders had assigned a scribe to record the damages, who scribbled his parchment. "I'll add it to the list of damages. Looks like you will need a host family until it is fixed."

Talla had tears in her eyes; Joru turned away and pretended not to look.

Their parents exchanged smirks. "You know, our bedroom is still intact... the damage is only the twin's room."

"But mama, why don't we all stay together?" Talla whimpered.

"Shush now. Your father and I need some time to ourselves too sometimes. It's not all about you."

"Very well then." The scribe nodded and looked around the group. "Ah, Vivia! You have a daughter their age and extra room, you would be a perfect host for these two until their place is up again. Is that all right? It could be a few weeks, we're severely short on materials and manpower."

"No!" Meleena couldn't help but belt out in disdain.

"Meleena!" Vivia snapped. "Certainly." She bowed her head to the scribe. "Anything to help those in time of need."

Vivia glanced down to her daughter with a tight lip and furrowed brow: duty above personal feelings.

Blood rushed to Meleena's temples, she thrust her hands into her pockets, and at that moment realized with a jolt that they were empty. The ram head trinket! She had totally forgotten about it until now, and now it was gone.

CHAPTER THREE

Meleena wrote in her Journal, which was finally back in her possession.

To rescue you from the sharks, dear journal, I told my parents I would join the council. There's no way I'll qualify for their apprenticeship, but I've resigned to whatever miserable choice the elders will make for me at the Light of the Meruyans Festival, at school year's end. Or maybe I'll train forest beasts and start a traveling circus.

Also, I lost the strange wooden trinket from the study. I hope that doesn't count against me. Oh well, nobody's noticed. I must have lost track of it somewhere underwater when Talla came by. What an oyster-brain!

Father will be leaving soon, to report to the capital and request aid for rebuilding. As part of the grooming process for the council apprenticeship, he wants me to come with. To keep up appearances, I had no choice but to agree. Oh well, perhaps it would do me some good to get out of this town for a little while.

Meleena closed the cover of the clamshell-bound journal. That morning she was up early. As she entered the kitchen, the pungent scent of blue root tea wafted. She slipped into the bench beside her father.

"I've made day packs for your journey," her mother said softly. That perked Meleena's attention. She thought her mother would be beaming for her 'finding her path,' but her apprehension told Meleena her mother felt conflicted. Perhaps she had misjudged the weight of this.

Her father stirred his tea. "You are in luck, Meleena. When we arrive, we will attend a meeting about the storm, where I will submit my proposal to the Meruyan Nation regarding the storm and damages."

"Why am I in luck?"

"The Meruyan Nation doesn't have the funds or resources to rebuild Pontai'Desa by itself, but our allied nation, known as the Sen'Prin, have heard about what happened and their leader will be attending the meeting."

"And?"

"They are a Warix nation."

Meleena nodded in understanding. "I'll meet a Warix."

"Yes."

She puffed her lips together and nodded, trying to look impressed, but not too excited. Her pulse, in truth, beat a lot faster. She couldn't keep herself from getting hopeful about this whole thing. Perhaps there was a chance she would find something greater there?

"Can't wait to show you around, teach you some history!" Her father gave her a goofy look, sad and nostalgic. He pulled her close to his side in an awkward side hug so that their shoulders touched.

"Aww, history!" she moaned but settled into the embrace. "Thanks, though."

***

Flax was seventeen, and his heart was thudding with anticipation for tomorrow. It would be his first outing since the draft, six months ago, into the Sen'Prin defense forces. He would be joining Governess Arenay at the Meruyan capital—and oh yes, there was homework.

Like most Sen'Prin Warix, he'd never even been outside of Sen'Prin City. He stooped over the parchment and chewed his pencil absentmindedly, trying to focus on the assigned reading that was pertinent to review before the upcoming meeting.

He scratched his left horn and closed his left eye. *Why did I wait until the last night to read this?*

The scroll in his tawny hands read: *The Warix and the Legend of the Wind Goddess.*

According to the old legend, the four elemental spirits helped shape the planet. Of the many beasts, the elements desired more: a nation to worship and love them. Water Spirit favored sea creatures, who dwelt in her realm, so she shaped the Meruyan, an aquatic people. Fire Spirit favored reptiles, with cold blood needing her warmth, so she gave the scaly Hyish tribes her spark. Earth Spirit held affection for mammals, who built their dens and burrows in her soil, so she made the Warix, a tribe to build homes of brick and mortar.

Wind Spirit, however, was quite content drifting the planet, without a creature to worship her. In time, the other three elements grew tired of watching their tribes, and retired to passive worship. Only Wind Spirit enjoyed observing the creations of her sisters.

One day, while drifting over the landscape, she came across a Warix tribe. They were an inspired mix of the mammals from Earth Spirit, and appeared like a forest in autumn: skin the shades of tree bark, vulpine ears under hair the colors of leaves in fall, small horns and eyes like drops of tree sap in angular caprine cheekbones.

She heard them fighting, as a lone Warix man was ejected from his tribe and sent out alone. She watched as he stomped off alone into the woods and hunted with a makeshift spear. She followed for days, but he failed to hit any marks. On the brink of starvation, it appeared his tribe had forsaken him.

In a moment of empathy, she graced him with some of her power, to help him survive. His horns became translucent, he could now sense the wind through them, and his eyes glowed silver like hers when he channeled his first gust.

The thankful Warix carved her a gift out of wood, a pendant in the shape of a ram. He called the Wind Spirit "Nushenyu," "My Goddess" in his language.

The two became close. They experienced the joys of the new world together, roaming without bounds. Although the Warix man's wind abilities were small compared to hers, he could whip up a tornado and soar alongside her.

Soon their bond led them to love.

One day, the pair were strolling through the woodlands, arm in arm, when they happened upon some other Warix— his former tribe. Despite all that had changed in his life, when he saw his former kin on a hunting party he flung into a rage. Shouting, he confronted them, using his wind powers to shove them against the trunks of trees. "Stop, my love! You're hurting them!" the Wind Goddess cried quietly. "Stop this cruelty!"

He did not stop. This unbridled display of revenge disturbed Nushenyu, who derived only pain from in her lover's vicious soul.

Nushenyu held a soft spot for all peoples, and in her desperation to end the cruelty, she did all she could: she blessed the tribe with wind powers too, so they might defend themselves. She hoped her partner would flee, clearly outnumbered, and the encounter would be over.

But his anger was too strong— he stood his ground. The tribe's use of teamwork held their true strength, assaulting him with wind-propelled spears until they managed to draw him out of the woods, and to the edge of a fjord.

He stood with his back to the rapids. Rushing waters pummeled the rocks far below. Wind Spirit Nushenyu blew above the canyon behind her trapped lover. She wept over the mess she had caused. They all looked up at her.

Around her neck swung the Ram Pendant. In her sorrow, she blamed herself for all the trouble and declared she would leave the physical realm and not return to meddle with the affairs of mortals anymore. She focused all her energy into the wooden carving and became obscured in a flash of light. The eyes on the little wooden ram glowed white, as the object now floated alone in the air above the fjord, then plummeted into the rapids below.

The lone Warix, devastated by the result of his petty actions, plunged into the fjord after her, into the tumultuous waters, and was never seen again. The surviving Warix kept the legend of that day alive and their tribe began to worship Nushenyu. Over many generations, the remaining Warix without wind powers faded from existence or bred into the tribe, leaving none of Earth Spirit's original creations.

The other elemental spirits never regained their interest in the mortals: The Meruyan, Hyish, and Warix nations. All expanded territories, farmed, built villages, and eventually made contact with one another.

The Legend of the Ram Head Pendant, as it was known, kept a special place in Warix culture. Was it still out there somewhere, washed out to sea? What if it was found, would it hold immense powers, or invoke the Spirit of the Wind Goddess? These questions motivated early Warix explorations and led them to take a special interest in the Meruyans, the nation of the sea.

Flax's eyelids were heavy. He folded his arms on the desk— just a short nap. Next thing he knew he was being jabbed in the arm. He awoke with a snap, opening his eyes to strain against the rays of the morning sun.

"You forgot something," said his friend, Thian, already dressed. A sensation suctioned Flax's cheek as Thian peeled the scroll off his face and handed it to him.

"Yeah, at least I did the reading."

Thian shrugged. "True, I didn't even try. But I am here! Making sure you are on time. That must count for something."

"It does." Flax smiled gratefully and rushed to get ready.

***

Assistant Yulah marched beside General Malotus through the fortress corridors, open on one side to overlook Sen'Drorn City. Yulah gazed at the caramel sky of dawn silhouetting the sloping roofs of the volcanic stone buildings between the pillars. While most of the citizens of this capital city slept, its leadership was hungry for news of the recent events that took place at the Meruyan shoreline.

A beetle landed with a clack on one of the copper slates that hung over the terrace, causing her to jump and momentarily lose step with Malotus. She lifted the sides of her colorful wool dress and trotted to catch up with his strides.

"How mad do you think he will be with us?" she kept her voice at a near whisper.

Malotus didn't answer. She watched the inner wall of the hallway, lined with portraits and murals, telling the stories of a long military history. As the chamber doors of their destination shared the same wall as the portraits, it was invisible when peering down the corridor, so she kept track of how near they were using the pictures.

"Uncle?" She turned towards Malotus, probing a reply from her uncle, the General. His face was hidden at this angle by his black shaggy mane of hair, his hands locked behind his back.

"You are meant to call me General Malotus, at least on official business, no?"

Her cheeks flashed hot. "Oh uh, sorry... Er, General Malotus!"

He turned to her, grinning. "'Sir' will do nicely as well."

"Don't smile like that, your smiles scare me."

"I appreciate the flattery." He puffed his chest, making prominent his pressed black military regalia, just like the rows of portraits of Sen'Drorn war heroes behind him. "I'm just taunting you, Yulah, don't look so nervous. At the meeting, just stand behind me, I will do the talking."

His eyes fixed on a point straight ahead. *He must be nervous*, she worried, *he won't even look at me.*

Malotus grumbled to himself as he trailed in and out of thought. Yulah caught part of, "...shouldn't have been us to retrieve it in the first place."

Yulah would have retorted by reminding him that he volunteered for the task, that he liked flexing his wind powers and inflicting damage on those poor Meruyan villagers... but she held her tongue. Now was not the time, right before his defense of their failure.

They passed a painting depicting a bloody battle scene. They passed to the bug-eyed Ranfaf the Second portrait. The meeting chamber was close. The sun had now fully broken through the distant horizon, drenching the corridor in morning light.

Malotus extended a finger without slowing his stride, and callously scratched the side of the final portrait as he passed. The bulky Warix in the painting stared out as he posed in traditional Sen'Drorn General's regalia.

Yulah recognized the face, his broad nose sporting a gold ring in one nostril, the bald head: thick black ponytail sprouting between curving horns.

Inside the large meeting hall had high vaulted arches tracing an open ceiling, with tilted copper turbines to let in and trap wind from the ceiling areas. This enabled maximum wind power use inside the emperor's chambers, as copper was a known Warix wind amplifier.

The room consisted of a stone amphitheater, upon which the council was already seated. A bald, hulking, wrinkled Warix man with faded-silver eyes and a gray ponytail sat on a black-rock throne, peering down at Yulah and Malotus as they approached. The large gold loop in the Emperor's left nostril did not do more than accentuate his sagging cheeks and chins.

Behind the throne, a large silken tabard, green and gold, depicted the Sen'Drorn sigil: The flower-maned-lion, a noble but ferocious beast in gold, stalking on a green backdrop. Their forest heritage.

"Ah, General Malotus! *Nushenyu be praised.* Tell me you have good news," boomed the husky Warix. The large, empty eyes of the old man widened. He gave a hungry, prolonged stare at the sight of Yulah, who shuddered and crossed her arms over her chest.

"Emperor Ryogrim, we turned the village upside down but the pendant was not found. Either the Meruyans anticipated our arrival, or our confidant was untruthful. My apologies, sir." Malotus's words contained an air of indifference. Yulah's heart rate sped up as she cringed behind Malotus.

"Do you realize how long we've been waiting to hear anything about Pendant of the Wind Goddess from those swimmy little Meruyans? We can't lose an opportunity like this! And you, General Malotus... I'll have your horns cut off for treason! Maybe some time without your wind energy will put you in your place until I'm ready to let them regrow!" Emperor Ryogrim's nostrils flared, spitting as he barked the words.

Malotus held calm, hands behind his back.

Yulah watched Ryogrim's wrinkly temple bunch up with rage at the start of the defense.

Malotus lifted his chin high and his ears went back like a cat challenging a large dog on its turf. "If the pendant was not there, what can we do?"

The Emperor huffed and puffed many disheartened noises before managing to spout, "Treasonous backtalk!"

A shot of adrenaline made Yulah's heart thud, but she had to say something. It came out as a whisper that made her cheeks flare with heat at the sound of her own voice. "I… I don't see why we don't just attack the Sen'Prin outright, sir… We could probably wipe them off the map even without the pendant."

"A good question, child," Ryogrim answered, his face softening. She kept her arms up, her fingers tightening around her arms. "Their city is built on the old ruins of a mountainous fortress. With such a strong natural defense, we've been assured by the War Tactics team that we could never get up there with an army. If the Pendant provides extra wind power, then it might be feasible."

"We could torture more out of the Meruyan official we have chained up in the prison…" Malotus offered. "Perhaps he is behind the Pendant disappearing. I think he knows more than he's telling us."

"Yes, good." Ryogrim grinned and waved a hand. "Follow up on any leads we may have missed there. You are dismissed. Wind Goddess blessings."

"Wind Goddess blessings," echoed the council.

Yulah let out her first deep breath since they'd arrived.

***

"What a waste of time," remarked Malotus as he and Yulah strolled side by side through the cobblestone streets of town on their sunny day off. The black-stone city remained empty at this relaxing hour.

"I thought it went okay," Yulah reassured, mainly herself, finally letting her shoulders drop.

"Yes, but I still wish the Emperor would just drop dead…" Then he added in the same flat tone, "Come, let's go get some sweetbread at the bakery."

Yulah's eyes widened and she looked around desperately.

"What? I thought you liked sweetbread." Malotus blew bushy hair out of his eyes and laughed. "Old Ryogrim already goes along with everything I say. I'm his best advisor. Selecting the most decorated warrior as Emperor is clearly a flawed tradition." He shook his head and smirked.

Yulah gasped. "How do you get away with such brash talk!"

They turned a corner to the street scented of freshly baked bread. Malotus said, "Simply put, I cannot be replaced while the Sen'Prin are still our main threat. I have intel of a… personal nature… on their leader."

"What does that mean?" Yulah cried. "You never told me you had a personal connection to the Sen'Prin!" She thought for a second, relative to his age. "Did you know Governess Arenay?"

Malotus's expression changed, it looked as if he had stepped on broken glass with bare feet. She should have known better than to ask about his past. They walked in silence for the rest of the way to the bakery.

Malotus pulled open the door for her and smiled. "What would you like? My treat."

CHAPTER FOUR

The ride up the mountain to the capital had been so bumpy that Meleena had to take care not to nip her tongue when she spoke. It was always to ask questions about some animal she had witnessed.

After a long ride through the jungle, Meleena and her father trotted into Dlawn'Edo from the south gate atop his kelpie. Her father let the reins drop as he lifted his arms to the view opening at the hilltop before them. "Welcome to Dlawn'Edo. Ahead is Crescent island, but most of the city lives under the lake."

Meleena was in awe, trying to take it all in. But the moment was short-lived. Her father pulled the reins aside, and they rode over another wooden bridge, which led to the back of a huge waterfall.

***

Arenay briefed Flax and Thian on what to expect on arrival at Meruyan capital city, Dlawn'Edo. The city was essentially a fortress, in a lake fed by a gigantic waterfall, atop a steep mountain surrounded by forest. There was no simple spot for a Warix to land. The city's only entrances, the North and South gates, allowed narrow passage by foot from a lower altitude.

Flax could see the blue speck from a distance. Inside a tornado of his own making, he flew alongside Thian, in toe with Governess Arenay as they headed for the North Entrance.

In a gust of released wind, the Governess landed at the center of the dirt road, blowing soil and leaves from the forest in the energy torrent. She stuck the landing in the narrow opening between the tree cover.

Flax wasn't so graceful, nor his aim so true, on this problematic landing as his sight clouded at the peripheries. As best he could, he reduced his tornado's intensity, but miscalculated descent speed as the dense forest blocked any wind to draw from.

The ground rushed at him. His heart thudded. In an attempt to prevent face planting, he blew wind energy directly down, causing him to fly back at an angle and slam into a tree.

"Ouch!"

Branches cracked between his various joints as he slid. The bitter taste of dried leaves filled his mouth, and he spat them out and winced from the pain before struggling to his feet and brushing leaves from his military issue clothes.

"Boys? Where are you?" A distant cry from Governess Arenay. His ears perked up.

He rubbed the silt from his eyes. His sight unclouded as the focus drained from sensing the wind. He knew their outward appearance would be changing from silver to their natural brown now. He'd never seen it in a mirror on himself but knew from looking at it happen in other Warix.

"Follow my voice, boys!" Governess Arenay called again.

Crunching leaves and snapping stalks told Flax that Thian must have landed nearby in a similar style to himself. Sure enough, a brawny form came out of the brush to join him.

"A perfect landing!" Thian grinned broadly, his shaggy bangs covered his eyes. "And the rucksacks are still intact!" He turned and slapped the rucksack on his back. It was crawling with ants.

They high fived to a job well done.

Soon they burst forth into the clearing. "There you are," Governess Arenay gave an exasperated sigh. "I hope you haven't damaged our provisions on your lousy landings."

"No, Governess!" Thian said proudly. Flax joined him, the large rucksacks sliding up their backs.

"Let's go. And brush yourselves off, boys, you're covered in plants from your hair to your boots."

She turned and led them up the path towards the dazzling mountain peak.

Thian groaned. "Why did we have to land so far down the mountain?"

"We have to be respectful of our hosts and enter their city correctly, as not to startle anyone. We're already strange enough to them."

As they marched, Flax and Thian dusted off their similar, lower-ranking uniforms, gray, lined with scarlet, the reverse colors of Governess Arenay's. Flax pulled a twig from his chestnut hair. Thian shook a multitude of fire ants from his shaggy hazel locks.

Flax jumped back from the onslaught. "Ah, come on!"

Thian shrugged. "Sorry! I landed in a nest!"

The Governess smacked Thian's pack to rid it of ants. She tried to remain stoic but was clearly suppressing a laugh. At nearly twenty years their senior, she was old for a soldier, but youthful for a leader. She had been just eighteen when she started the revolution that led to The Great Split and founded the Sen'Prin nation.

Governess Arenay updated them as they ascended the mountain. "You will both one day, hopefully, advance in our ranks of the Intel Department, and I am counting on this field trip to broaden your understanding and aid in your growth. We are here because the Meruyans reported a curious storm a couple of weeks back, at one of their small villages. They called us here to help finance rebuilding, but I believe there is more to the story… Perhaps the work of the Sen'Drorn Warix, snooping around and up to something. Today we will hopefully find out more, and maybe understand what our enemy is up to. Now behave and don't make me regret bringing you along. Hopefully, you both did the required reading, and it is at the forefront of your mind."

Governess Arenay combed her fingers through her auburn mohawk, causing the copper beads in her hair to jangle. She turned to look at Flax and Thian. Those eyes like liquid amber that instilled a sense of trust for a promise of a better future. "Trainees: Flax and Thian, welcome to your first outing. The Meruyan Capital, Dlawn'Edo."

Flax, Thian, and Governess Arenay stepped onto a stone bridge that marked the north entrance to the city. The bridge connected them to a broad crescent island, crowded with buildings adapted from the Warix architecture style, but river reed in place of wood.

Blue-skinned Meruyans crowded the streets. The patchwork of greens, blues, and purples of the Meruyan looked like a tangled river of kelp. More structures and swimming citizens filled underwater streets in the lake bed, visible under the transparent water. Creatures jumped, breaking surface, and circles of fish farms covered areas of the water like great lily pads.

Flax's ears filled with the rushing of water and his lungs with the refreshing air. Water droplets teased his arm hairs, and gusts of wind conveyed the power of the waterfall, pouring water from the peaks into the lake basin.

His home, Sen'Prin City, was also in the mountains, but under a different sort of forest canopy: it didn't have any views, nor waterfalls like this.

His anxious muscles urged him to race ahead, but Arenay's next words kept him and Thian in check. "Remember to be on your best behavior as we walk through their fair city."

Thian pressed a palm over his face, mimicking a starfish. The two laughed and punched each other in the arm.

Arenay pointed to the tremendous waterfall in the far side of the cliff face. "That's where we're headed."

***

Meleena and her father dismounted in the cave under the magnificent waterfall, and she inhaled the aroma of wet clay. Loroh tossed a squid to Peela, the kelpie, and she sucked it into her tendril-mouth.

"Kelpies hydrate through their skin, so we'll leave her to swim in the lake. She knows to meet us here on our way out."

Peela galloped right through the falls, breaking its curtain with her body. Her iridescent green scales reflected the waterfall before she dove into the clear waters, leaving behind a trail of three-toed mud-prints. The inner wall depicted a colossal mural, etched from the mountainside. Images swirled around Meruyans and various sea creatures.

Her father explained, "I'll give you the full history tour after the meeting: how an old Meruyan oasis became our unified capital. But now we haven't got spare time—"

The echo of footsteps on the cave walls drowned him out. Three strange creatures approached them. Tall, with skin and hair like autumn leaves, adorned with copper jewelry. And atop their heads, horns!

"Excuse me, are you going to the Council meeting?" asked the finely clad Warix woman to Loroh. To Meleena's surprise, she spun her hand in the Meruyan greeting.

Loroh beamed and reflected the gesture. "Hi there. I am Loroh, Council Historian of the Southern Village, Pontai'Desa. And this is Meleena, my daughter. You must be our honored guests."

"Yes, Governess Arenay of the Sen'Prin. These are trainees from my intel department. Pleased to meet you, Historian Loroh of The Meruyan Nation, and Meleena."

Arenay smiled. Meleena simply nodded, and the two made eye contact.

Meleena, an ordinary Meruyan of sixteen, and Governess Arenay, leader of the Sen'Prin, regarded one another. She barely noted the two Warix youths standing behind Arenay, their presence overshadowed by their leader's glory. At double Meleena's height, Arenay stood with the stature of a soldier.

Meleena noted the emblem on Arenay's regalia. "I like that creature on your badge. What does it mean?"

"Oh, this?" she indicated. "It is the symbol of my nation, Sen'Prin. Scarlet Nectar-sprig on white background. The Nectar-sprig is a nectar collecting leafy fey-dragon. The Nectar-sprig is considered among Warix to be the bravest of creatures, because it pollinates the nectar of the flower-maned lion, a mutually beneficial act, at the risk of its own life. The white background symbolizes blank slates, new beginnings."

Meleena wished to see a nectar-sprig and a flower-maned lion. She'd be adding these creatures to her journal later.

As the group entered the grand hall and made their way up to the meeting room, they had some time to converse. Oil lamps lined the walls through the passageway that led into a wider space. Meleena kept staring at the Governess, overcome with awe at this tall, confident leader.

Her young company walked behind her, pointing and chattering about new things left and right.

They entered a square plaza surrounded by three-story balconies teeming with busy Meruyans moving between rooms and floors. It was the seat of Council: of all Meruyan government.

Arenay asked Meleena, "So, you are here to learn about the Meruyan Council. Will you join, like your father?"

Meleena rubbed her elbow. "Not really, I mean… We have this program in our final school year, only top students can get the Council apprenticeship. They travel the Meruyan territories and learn about history and politics, pass some tests before they can join. I probably can't qualify. I haven't been going to class that much…"

"Why not?'

"I, uh… spend time in the forest learning my own things. I am learning about the ways of the animals."

Arenay smiled, amber eyes locked on her. "Ah, well, perhaps your passion is worth something. Though, I would be impressed to see you qualify for the apprenticeship."

"It's still a few months away, we'll see."

"Perhaps you could join us someday."

Meleena's face felt hot. She nodded a little too fast and looked at the floor. A warmth like a kindling flame began to ignite within her. For the first time, a lifeline outside her village opened to her, that she never thought possible. If a Warix could find interest in her skills, perhaps, there was hope for a future after-all.

Loroh broke the silence as he ushered the group into the meeting hall.

Two Meruyan guards stood outside the doorway in tortoiseshell armor, wielding shark tooth spears. They nodded as the party entered, the Warix ducking under the small doorway into the cave-like hall. Meleena gazed up at the wooden ceiling with intricate carvings of sea creatures and waves, wood beams connecting down to reinforce the cave wall. Tall windows had a view of the inner waterfall with the city blurry behind. An oak table took up most of the chamber, with a dozen Meruyan Council members mingling in clusters.

"Ah, Loroh! Good to see you. I see you've brought our Sen'Prin guests," said an ancient Meruyan Councilman who bowed as they entered. He swirled his hand in traditional Meruyan greeting as they came closer.

"Elder Councilman Ives," Loroh returned the greeting, and Meleena hastily copied. She glanced at the back wall, at the mounted Meruyan Nation flag. Azure blue and green swirling together in the coexistence of land and sea.

Then she spotted her elder brother Kelrick, whom she hadn't seen in several months. At the sight of Meleena and Loroh, he came over and patted his father on the shoulder, then went around to give Meleena a hug.

"Little sis, what brings you to the capital?" He beamed. His hair was trim and came to a blue wave in the front, slicked back and smelling of kelp oil. His intense blue eyes locked with hers.

"Don't make much of it, Kel. I just came to observe." Meleena folded her arms.

"Fine, fine," he said, putting his hands up in mock submission. He strode off to the other end of the table, just in time to help Councilman Ives into a chair beside his own. Meleena sat by her father halfway down the table.

Meleena hissed and shook her head. "Such a fish-kisser!" Then regretted it as she realized the Warixes were sitting right across the table. She realized the apprentices, Flax and Thian, were about the same age as herself. They each had a sheet of parchment in front of them for notes. While Flax's quill was poised, his gaze attentive on Councilman Ives, Thian's quill twirled in his fingers, his attention on the ceiling murals.

When everyone had arrived and took their seats at the table, Councilman Ives addressed the room. "Welcome, Council. And welcome honored guests, Governess Arenay of Sen'Prin, and her two apprentices, here to offer aid during times of trouble. First, I am sorry to announce that there is still no word on the whereabouts of Councilman Lock, missing from this table now over one month. Does anyone have any leads to report?"

The Council members blinked, looking around at each other.

Arenay addressed them. "I might, sir. We will get to that. But first, please proceed with your next order of business."

There was a murmur in the Council, and Councilman Ives stroked his white beard and continued, "Alright—well. Next is the condition of the Southern Village, Pontai'Desa. Loroh, what reports are there on the damages?"

Loroh stood and announced, "Several homes were destroyed in the storm, and we can't afford the rebuilding costs without help from the capital."

Councilman Ives turned to Governess Arenay. "Warix of Sen'Prin, what aid could you offer?"

As Governess Arenay stood up, Meleena noticed a row of copper piercings on her pointed ear. "Hello, Meruyan Council, thank you for your warm welcome. Yes, it is true we want to lend aid, but there is more to this than lumber. Let's get right to the point. We have reason to believe your two seemingly distinct issues are, in fact, related." Her bright amber eyes looked almost electric against her auburn skin and short crimson hair as she paused for effect. "We think the storm that hit your village was not a natural storm, but rather a Sen'Drorn attack."

Confused whispering filled the room.

Meleena raised her eyebrows. Okay, so she knows how to command a room. "Who are the Sen'Drorn?" she whispered to her father.

He whispered back, "Other Warix... these Warix are from the Sen'Prin Nation, they have been at war with the Sen'Drorn Warix Nation for the better part of two decades."

She gave a puzzled look.

"Just listen. I can explain later." He hushed her with a finger to his mouth.

"Not a storm?" voiced Councilman Ives. "But why would they attack a tiny village? The Sen'Drorn have never had a presence in any of the Southern Villages."

"Our spies tell us the Sen'Drorn have a Meruyan in their dungeons. In fact, we think this is Councilman Lock. The Sen'Drorn kidnapped and tortured him for… It must be over two weeks now. I was planning to send an agent to alert you, but then the storm occurred, and I thought it better to come in person after what you reported over wristcom—Councilman Lock must have told the Sen'Drorn something important was in that village…"

Now the whole room wore a look of bewilderment.

Meleena was even more confused—*not a storm? Maybe that's why the clouds seemed so isolated in the village and the skies clear over the sea. Warix were in my town, possibly my home?* Only now did she notice the wrist device Arenay and her initiates wore, just like the one her brother had shown her.

She tried to process all this: Sen'Prin *and Sen'Drorn—two factions of Warix. The Sen'Prin are led by this Arenay, now at this table, and aligned with the Meruyans. So, there must be good ones and bad ones.* She tried to follow—*Sen'Drorn, bad, Sen'Prin, good. Why don't they like each other?*

"The only thing we could imagine is of any interest to them would be…The Ram Head Pendant. Meruyan Council, does this mean it really has turned up, and was being kept among your people? And if so, why didn't you tell us such a precious artifact had been recovered?"

The Council turned to one another in stunned whispers. Elder Councilman Ives answered for the group, "I'm sorry, Governess, your words have shocked us, we expected that you had come to offer only help and provisions, not such confusing news and talk of some fabled artifact."

"It's not *some* artifact." Arenay's cheeks flared with anger. "It is believed to possess the spirit of our Goddess. If we could obtain it, the Goddess would certainly join our righteous cause and ally with us to defeat the Sen'Drorn."

Ives answered, "The Meruyans are unfamiliar with this Warix legend, and this Council certainly does not know of such a thing in our midst. Loroh, you are the historian of Pontai'Desa, do you know anything about this?"

"Well, I don't know any stories. But, a ram head thing does sound familiar. My wife found a strange doodad last summer while preparing for a dinner, some other Councilmen were our guests. A wooden figure like a ram, with white gems for eyes, was clenched in the pincer of our dinner lobster," said Loroh.

"So, what came of it?" Arenay asked through piercing amber eyes.

"I thought it was nifty and kept it in my study."

Meleena stiffened. *No, it couldn't be...*

"Was Councilman Lock by any chance one of your dinner guests that night?"

"Hmm, yes, I believe he was."

"And your cottage, destroyed in the storm? Turned over?"

"It was puzzling... The cottage was fine, but my study was in complete disarray... Struck by lightning, we thought. I didn't consider checking if any small items were missing." He rubbed his neck. Flax and Thian scribbled on their parchments.

Meleena's heart pounded. She glimpsed the pages the Warix boys had been writing. Flax had scribbled, *Pendant lost, impending doom.* Thian was drawing cartoonish doodles of various Council members. Then his hand slid to draw something on Flax's parchment—a ram-headed symbol.

A shock ran through her. *That was it!*

Her heart thudded like it wanted to jump out of her throat, but she knew she had to say something.

But how...?

Arenay looked crestfallen. "Then... there is a good chance the Sen'Drorn have it by now... I'm also sorry to say in that case, your Councilman Lock is more than certainly dead. We can only hope if they use the Pendant to summon our Goddess, she will not fall to their whims."

Meleena squeezed her eyes shut and shot a hand into the air.

She heard Loroh's voice whisper, "Dear, what are you doing?"

"If it pleases the room, er Council, I have something to contribute." Butterflies fluttered in the pit of her stomach.

"Excuse her. She didn't mean to…" Loroh said, turning red in the face. Across the room, Kelrick's eyes bulged in her direction, and he ground his teeth.

"I want to hear from her," interrupted Arenay. "After all, she lives in the town in question. What do you know, girl?" She leaned forward so she could look Meleena in the eyes. Meleena shivered and swallowed hard. She tried not to let this matter. If only she'd never come here.

"Well… I don't know who the Sen'Drorn are, or why they are fighting with us, but…"

"You don't?" Now Arenay looked startled. "We've been at war since the Great Split eighteen years ago—Council, you really ought to teach this in your schools! The Meruyans were the root cause of the split!"

Councilman Ives scoffed, "Politics is none of the concern of villagers. Especially not the Southern Villages. Unless they become Council members."

Meleena was lost in her head, trying to work it out. *What is this "Great Split," and what does it have to do with the Meruyans? How could I have never realized the world outside my village is so complex? Or these other Meruyan villages and cities, do they all live like us?*

"But I just know I found that thing my father mentioned. I took it from his study on the night of the storm."

"Describe to us, what did you find?" Arenay would not avert her eyes—Meleena found it only made this harder.

"Er… this wooden thing might have been the object you are talking about. I put it in my pocket when my family fled to the underwater district, and, well…" She paused, watching the faces of those in the room.

"Yes? And where is it now?" asked Ives. When Meleena opened her mouth to speak again, only a hollow gasp came out. Her stomach turned over and she could feel her eyes holding back a bulge of tears. *Oh great, I'm not really feeling this, I don't really care about this! Why am I even tearing up! Ugh!*

Kelrick buried his face in his hands. Her father looked stunned. Meleena's heart flurried, she tried to hold a straight face. A chair scraped against the floor as someone stood.

Then, kneeling down beside her, Arenay's face suddenly came close to hers. Meleena's throat closed tighter.

She placed one hand on Meleena's shoulder. "It's alright. I know you are strong. Just whisper it to me if you want."

Meleena tried inconspicuously to wipe the tears away before they came out.

She grounded herself with a deep breath, then finally said in a small voice, "It must have fallen out of my pocket somewhere in the ocean… your grace!" Meleena's heart pounded upon the release. She wanted to leave the room before the deluge of tears broke through her weakening willpower.

Arenay whispered gratefully, "Thank you for your honesty…" and with a deep sigh of relief, took Meleena into a warm embrace. She stood up with Meleena and walked her outside the meeting room.

Once outside, Arenay nodded and smiled before returning to the meeting room. A sense of deep gratitude and admiration flushed through Meleena for this woman. She spent some moments alone in a cathartic cry, wiping away and washing her face, then hurried back into the meeting so it wouldn't seem like she was gone long.

Meleena slipped back into her seat. Arenay was standing and addressing the room. "—For now, our safety is assured. We can say for certain that the Sen'Drorn do not have the Pendant. But the Meruyans must now be vigilant for its reappearance, as the ocean currents are sure to carry it to you again. Spread word to all territories. Next time it is found, notify us immediately and we will come. If it weren't for us, stalling the Sen'Drorn's plans, they'd be taking an even bigger share of your crops. You need us as allies to continue to root for you."

This incited an uproar of chatter of mixed opinions. Loroh smiled at Meleena. She stared at her hands in her lap while Kelrick audibly released a long-held breath.

"In the meantime…" Arenay continued to address the room. "We will donate the rest of the materials you need to rebuild your town. Think of it as a promise. To better communication between our Peoples."

"Here, here!" Elder Councilman Ives answered.

~ 45 ~

"The Sen'Prin will also maintain an ear to the ground." Arenay turned to her trainees. "Flax, Thian... you have your next assignment. If anyone will find the Pendant first, it's likely the Hyish reptilian traders. You will spy on the Mayfee clan, the most prominent. If we get word, we can trade it from the Hyish before they sell to Sen'Drorn."

Flax and Thian high fived.

CHAPTER FIVE

As the summer approached, the long-awaited day finally came. As Meleena awoke that morning, a pang of stress and uncertainty hit her before she understood why. She stared at the ceiling, memory returning to her, and she knew. This was the morning of the Light of the Meruyan festival.

She thought back on that influential day at the capital where she had met the Warix and Arenay: people who believed in her, and her gifts. Hope for another kind of future, outside her village. She had spent the year studying and taking school more seriously than ever before. She had stopped ditching it for the forest, reserving her visits and journaling for after school hours. Later, even the journaling lapsed, as she prioritized bringing schoolbooks to read by her favorite ponds and glades. She wondered if she had done enough.

This evening, she and her peers would be assigned their apprenticeships, which would lead to a lifetime role in the village. Tonight would be the final test of whether that year had all been a waste or not. It was nerve-racking.

She sat up and peered outside her window. A fog rolled across the lush hills which surrounded the village, like a sheet of glumness over everything. Meleena reached for her journal on the bedside table, attempting to purge herself of the glum shadow of thoughts:

I found out the other day that Talla does all these extra activities on top of school grades. What was I thinking? I can't compete with her. Then again, the Council does take on a few students each year. The failure rate is so high on their council training journey that many of them end up in some meager job at the local Council.

I'm extra nervous because the apprenticeships are announced from least to most prestigious. The council journey apprentices are last to be announced, and anyone leftover without any assigned apprenticeship is really in trouble. They reassigned to apprentice elsewhere, in faraway towns perhaps. Nobody really knows where they go, but they don't return.

I have decided that if I don't get the council apprenticeship, I'll run. Before they call whoever is left, I'll be out of there. I'll steal my father's kelpie from the stables and ride into the forest, and keep going until I hit the Warix lands.

She thumped the journal shut and climbed out of bed, stretched, and dressed. She then filled a running-away bag with most of her other clothing and the journal, before heading into the kitchen for breakfast. She had the rest of the day to enjoy one last stroll through the village—her home until now, Pontai'Desa.

By that evening, the bag had been safely stowed in the stables, behind some barrels of chum for the kelpies. Back in her room, she changed into her pearls and seashell adorned festival gown, then went to find her mother.

"Oh, Meleena dear..." said Vivia from a makeup mirror, marking squid ink carefully around her eyes, turning as Meleena entered the room. "I am so proud of you for your improvements this year. I have faith you will qualify for something." She clasped her hands together and bowed to give gratitude to the water goddess. "After all the trouble, I will breathe a sigh of relief tonight."

"Thanks." Meleena tried to smile but cringed—really inspiring—as if she'd be grateful that any apprenticeship would do. "Where are Tomiyan and father?"

"Your father has gone early to help set up. Tomiyan and his family should be here any minute."

"I think I'll go on ahead and meet you there."

***

Meleena headed alone to the Town hall. Guilt clouded her head. This could be the last night she'd see her family.

It was easy to see the structure from a distance—a goliath seashell, with towering spikes and air holes for skylights, the main valve serving as the entrance—one of the few buildings of Meruyan origin and not the Warix influence. The village was loud with the chatter from excited Meruyan adorned in their best garments, flowing kelpweave dresses and robes of many colors, inlaid with sparkling shells, pearls, and fish scales. Everyone was heading to Townhall—children following their parents, elderly couples holding hands, and young lovers too. Nervous teenagers ready for assignments, their future masters of the craft, and last year's apprentices, one year wiser. They all came to join the festivities.

Inside the Town hall, the festival was kicking into full swing. The aroma of frying seafood filled the hall. She made her way through the crowded room of Meruyans, exchanging pleasantries, and wishes of luck from classmates and fellow villagers. She saw Meruyan she didn't know, from the underwater community, live starfish and barnacles clinging to cheeks and arms, fish bones braided with their hair.

Talla was right in the mix, chatting and laughing with the council members. A pang of envy surged in her, for Talla's knack for being charming when necessary. Trying to avoid her, Meleena navigated the crowd, which brought her close to Joru, standing in his parents' shadow. Meleena skirted by Talla's mother, overhearing part of her conversation. "You know, I could have been on the Council if I hadn't had the twins."

More Meruyan Council Members grouped in a corner by the sloping shell wall. They were clad in hand-crafted robes made from fine kelpweave and Warix silk. She recognized Elder Councilman Ives, the senior Counselor who presided over the meeting in the capital six months ago.

He approached the podium in flowing emerald kelpweave robes inlaid with lobster carapace around his shoulders and a rope of red coral around his neck. "Everyone, please take your seats along the long great-hall tables. We shall start the festival feast, a gorgeous bounty indeed."

Meruyans carried slabs of wood, piled high with seafood. Starfish, sea urchin, tuna, followed by clay bowls sporting local lobsters, oysters, and prawns, all farmed in the underwater part of Pontai'Desa. Some Meruyans were already seated at the long rows of wooden tables, decorated with flowers and seashells of all shapes. A massive conch shell flowing with more bountiful seafood decorated the middle of each long table.

Meleena found her family—her parents, brother Tomiyan, his wife, and her young niece—already seated at the long bench seating. She sat down by her father.

"Good evening, everyone," Councilman Ives began. "After our bellies are full, I will announce the internships for this year's finishing class, which they've worked hard for. The last apprenticeship to be called is our Council's very own. Council apprentices will go on Aldrok's Journey of Future Leaders, to learn about our brethren elsewhere at the tropical Northern Hilly Villages, the Underwater Territory, and the isolated Arctic City. There, they may earn qualification to sit on the Council. Remember, anyone whose name has not been called after this point will go on special assignment and will leave with the Council tomorrow."

Meleena's stomach flipped like a dolphin when she realized it would be her name called among them this year. She clenched her jaw. Oh, how she hoped that wouldn't be her. Not like she was expecting much better.

"Now, tonight is about Meruyan unity from near and far. While you enjoy the feast, and through the evening, we welcome our cultural dancers from all around the territories. First, welcome Arctic City dancers."

She eyed a festive octopus. Its glassy eyes stared back into hers. Her stomach turned. How could she eat at a time like this?

Her father caught her eye. "You know my trick when I'm nervous? I take off my glasses, so everyone becomes a fuzzy blur." He smiled and lowered his to the end of his nose. "Try it. You'll feel better."

"Thanks." Though a queasy feeling surged inside, she hesitated to lower her glasses as her father had suggested. *I don't need his tips.*

She had worked out her own trick from watching the sea lions at the beach—how they threw their heads back, their faces pointing up to the sun. They appeared to slip into a state of complete tranquility. She called it their sun surrender. Though she wished she'd perfected it before the council meeting, and this particular thing probably wouldn't work inside the hall, away from the sun's rays.

She focused on the Arctic dancers wearing lots of white and skins of creatures she'd never seen, and what she guessed was the fuzzy carapace of a giant starfish.

After a few minutes, when they left the stage, Councilman Ives returned.

"Now that you're fed and comfortable, it is time to announce the local apprenticeships for this year's finishing class."

Yeah, right. Fed? Comfortable? Looking around the room at her classmates, most had either lost their appetite like her or dealt with the anticipation by gorging on dinner. Now it felt like her entire life had led to this moment. She regretted that it had not occurred to her to take this seriously, sooner.

Oh oysters, what will happen? I need to calm down. The forest still waits for me.

"Bramble Sheepherder, woodcutter, pon-urchin farmer. Kerko, Palvo, Alekni."

Okay, so I'm not the very bottom. I really don't want those.

"Silk production... Gidi and Isender."

That's also crap... Every time I don't hear my name right now is a good thing.

"Shoemakers. Tuuli and Ismon. And the woodworker, crafter of furniture and other things. Roopin, Kall, Ervo."

I'm pushing my luck here. Maybe that one wouldn't have been so bad.

"And kelpweave tailors, Rejo, Amoneny. Leather tanner... Josia, Lupei."

These are getting better now... How much further can I expect to be?

"Tusk engraver... stone carver..."

And on it goes.

A few other names and apprenticeships were called, narrowing down to the final jobs. Joru was assigned lantern maker.

"Professions of study: fiber fruit... Tusk material... spider web development..."

Maybe I'd be okay with one of those.

"Aamu, Soll, Basmay."

Oh, fish. Basmay got that one? He's smarter than me for sure.

"Medics... Hoko, Rugger." Councilman Ives stroked his beard. "That's it for all local apprenticeships. Students, please approach your new instructors tonight, or by the start of next week."

Well... That's it. I have no chance. She buried her face in her hands. *Unless I get the council apprenticeship.* Even thinking it sounded ridiculous.

"Now, let's break for the Northern Village Dancers while the council finalizes their apprenticeship choice."

Meleena glanced over at them. Though they had sat down to eat, the Council members were again by their favorite wall. The local teachers now stood with them, all discussing together.

Then her bubble of concentration burst as a girl emerged from the crowd, heading her way. Talla... *Ugh, why now?*

Talla wore a gown of narrow red-and-white stripes, large spines protruding up the back like a glorious, poisonous fish. Her hair was tied back and held up by a ribbon of cone shells. She held a large roasted crab claw in one hand. Meleena was small and wiry next to Talla.

"I don't think I've ever seen you in a dress before, Smelleena," Talla smirked. Meleena didn't answer. "Your name hasn't been called."

"Neither has yours." The heat rose in Meleena's cheeks.

"That's because I'm obviously getting the council apprenticeship." Talla waved the crab claw around as she spoke.

"You're not even a little bit nervous?" Meleena's face rose to meet Talla's, who brushed the curls from her eyes and looked down her nose.

Clapping interrupted the moment as the Northern dancers finished. They bounded offstage, wagging their red coral headdresses. Councilman Ives thanked them and welcomed the Underwater City dancers. Not the underwater locally, but from far away, the last of the Meruyan nation's great underwater settlements.

Talla turned back to Meleena. She pointed with the half-eaten claw. "Look, Smell-eena, don't go expecting much from this. Only top achievers like myself make it for the council apprenticeship. You will probably be joining the misplacements tomorrow. Now *there's* a mystery of the natural world you can uncover."

Meleena didn't want to feed into her game. Trying to defuse it with another topic, she spoke through clenched teeth.

"Why do you want to be on the Council anyway?"

"To be at the top of society, obviously."

"Just get outa here," Meleena said through gritted teeth.

Talla smiled smugly and walked off.

More clapping erupted as the dancers finished. "Thank you, Underwater Dancers." The Councilman Ives' voice echoed. "And it looks like the Council is ready to announce. We have a few very close candidates this year. They've studied hard and cultivated special talents. They are unique of character. We only hope they have the grit for the demands we place before them."

He cleared his throat. "And now without further anticipation... From the underwater community, congratulations Deemayan!"

Meleena's ears filled with the sound of cheers and clapping from the crowd, especially the underwater community, whose children blew miniature conch shells.

One candidate down. Wait, Deemayan? Don't I know that guy? She looked over at the lanky boy in ill-fitting kelpweave robes, likely borrowed. He was squinting. Poor boy, he probably doesn't even own a pair of surface glasses. Since he spends all his time underwater, he wouldn't need to. Like her own, Meruyan eyes were only sharp under water.

"...Top of his class and highly recommended by peers and the local community. His caring nature and learning mindset have earned him this place today in the Journey!"

Of course! He's the boy I bumped into underwater.

"Now, from the shore community..."

This is it.

Meleena stared out at the colorful crowd and tried her best to avoid making any eye contact with anyone. Whenever she looked up, her throat closed as if there was a tight string around her neck. Her father tapped his glasses to her and smiled. *Taking them off won't help me now!*

Councilman Ives continued, "With a long history of good grades and volunteering all over town—congratulations, Talla!"

An uproar of claps and cheers hit Meleena like a wave. Talla stood and bowed from her seat.

Of course, it would be Talla. I hate that she's right, but I guess I can't be surprised, it's all she'd ever been groomed for. But Talla's parents' seats were empty. Meleena spotted them at the bar, paying little attention to the honor their daughter had just received. Meleena *almost* felt bad for Talla, until the pang of her own failure hit her.

Her breath came fast, chest heaving. Well, that was it then… no apprenticeship. But what did she expect? She looked at her family, tears forming in her eyes. The only option left was to escape into the forest. She wouldn't have much time before she'd be hauled off to who-knows-where. Councilman Ives spoke, but she barely heard him over her inner thoughts, like dim waves inside a shell. "…newfound dedication… brilliant mind… things around… final year… we are capable of."

Something soft on her hand. Her mother was holding her hands, and her family's faces around her reflected elated anticipation.

"Congratulations, Meleena!"

Her stomach dropped at her name. Her father beamed, and her mother burst into tears. The cheers of the room flooded into her ears. What was happening?

Whispers filled her, "*Is that the weird girl who goes into the forest?*" and "*how could she get in?*"

The gaze of so many direct onlookers was unbearable. As the growing awareness for what had happened sank in, Meleena pulled off her glasses, and immediately the crowd became with a mass of faceless, blurry colors.

"Congratulations to Talla, Meleena, and Deem," called Councilman Ives over the cheers, and they responded by bursting to full capacity. And yet the thoughts screamed inside her skull. *Me? Really? And Talla? Is this cause for celebration, or a nightmare?* Her head felt scrambled but couldn't help a sense of elation bubbling up from somewhere deep inside.

Councilman Ives held up a spiraling conch shell and blew it. The trumpeting resounded for some time before he ended with a blessing. "May the Water Goddess bless you on Aldrok's Journey." He swirled his hands in the spin of greeting and blessings as the crowd repeated the words of praise, and their hands copied the swirl in reply. Council members walked over to place crowns of colorful moon snail shells atop each victor's head, and a red ribbon-bound scroll into their hand—instructions, no doubt, for the Journey.

"Remember, any students whose names have not been called, please report to the Council before the end of the evening. You have the next couple of days to prepare and come with us."

Everyone in Meleena's class had been called, but a handful of students from the underwater district went pale behind blue cheeks.

Meleena remained in a dumbfounded delirium and she looked from the scroll in her hand to the room, and accidentally made eye contact with Talla. Talla mirrored her own baffled expression momentarily. Then the look changed to contempt.

Oh, shark-claspers!

Talla was at her side before she could run.

A sting hit her face, reminiscent of the jellyfish sting underwater so many months ago. "You pond scum! You cheated your way in, I know it! Your father or brother make any special calls to the Council in Dlaw n'Edo?"

"No, I..." Meleena stumbled back from the shock, her cheek stinging from the slap. Talla's eyes flamed, and Meleena raised her hands. "I... I didn't know about any of this."

Having missed the sight of the slap, Deem came over to congratulate them, beaming and squinting without a pair of glasses. Talla turned on him before he had the chance. "And who the hell is this?"

Deem flashed an awkward smile and held up his scroll. "Hi, I'm Deemayan. Deem for short. So, I guess we will be traveling together."

"Shut up, you," snapped Talla. "You're just another person weighing me down on this journey."

"But, there's always several candidates each year…" Deem corrected, smile fading. Meleena smirked and shook her head—he was just so unaware of who Talla was, it was actually funny.

"Now, to finish off the evening, the last group of dancers, from our very own community," Councilman Ives announced.

"Excuse me… I'm part of that group. One of my qualifying features, you know." And with that, Talla was gone.

Meleena apologized to Deem and excused herself too. She slipped into the crowd, gestured to her parents to let them know she was going home. It was enough commotion for one night. But she supposed this meant she could unpack the rations…

Talla's words echoed in her head as she ran through the warm night air in the empty town. Had it really been her grades and recommendations from teachers that had impressed the Council? *Your father or brother make any special calls to the Council in Dlawn'Edo?* What if Talla wasn't wrong in her accusation? It hadn't crossed her mind that Kelrick or her father might have been involved.

They both work for the Council, stupid!

Maybe Talla was right, that I lack the dedication for something bigger than myself.

Her heart pounded and her head spun with conflicting thoughts. The scroll crumbled in her clenched fist. When she arrived home, she buried herself under the covers in the dark where she could better settle the issue.

I should, if anything, do it for the excitement of journaling new beasts in distant lands. And I have to follow through and prove Talla and the others are wrong about me. Talla is going, and she isn't more mature than me! I must keep focused on my goals… If this is the only way Arenay can recruit me, I should at least try.

CHAPTER SIX

The same day Meleena awakened for the Light of the Meruyans Festival, in a faraway desert, two Warix spies hid among hooded Hyish. It was a busy market day at the Jade Hyish encampment, tucked in an oasis among iridescent green sand dunes.

Flax squinted out from under his hood, robed to match the locals. His eyes were the only exposed part of his face, not unusual here, what with the frequent dust storms and not a single cloud blocking the sun and its punishing heat.

He weaved between colorful stalls, many selling handicrafts, often made from jade or glass. The wafting scent of sugary street foods filled the air. Sellers occupied foldable stone-slab chairs, which collected the sun's heat, a fixture in all reptilian encampments.

Flax spoke into a wristcom under a long brown sleeve. "Fourth month following the Mayfee Hyish clan. Day six, Jade desert, land of the Jade Hyish clan. Still no sign of the Pendant."

As he and his comrade, Thian, followed Mayfee's clan to each new trading location, it was his job to record what the local tribes were selling, in the hopes of finding the Pendant among them before Mayfee's clan. His comrade, Thian, was to follow closer to Mayfee herself.

"The Jade Desert could fool one into thinking they had reached green meadows, but it's only an illusion. In this barren place, the only life that exists is hearty shrubs, a couple of insect species, and the ever-adaptable reptilian Hyish people, who subsist on those shrubs and bugs. But the abundant mineral jade found in the sand has been the true key to their survival. The Jade Hyish trade it to Mayfee and her clan in exchange for vital resources. The Mayfee clan then resell to other Hyish clans along their trade route. And like all Hyish, they have acquired Warix wealth by selling their superior glass products, which is due to their ability to spit fire."

He approached a Jade Hyish trader's stall to inspect the wares—glass dishes with sparkling specks of Jade inside.

"Warm Sands Welcome," the vendor said. The vendor eyed him, a little too long, his yellow slits for eyes fixed on Flax's every movement.

"Just passing through," Flax said in the hissing Hyish tongue.

"You have strange eyesss. Desh'ju?"

Are you...?

Before he could ask if Flax was a Warix, he spun on his heels, feigning intense interest in the next stall. He had to keep a low profile—it was better the Hyish didn't know there were Warix among them. The Jade Desert Hyish never interacted with his kind, and the less the Mayfee clan knew about how much the Warix wanted the Pendant, the better. Enough to stalk them for months, actually. If she did, the savvy trader could withhold the object and demand a much higher price when the time came. More than the Sen'Prin could accord. If the time ever came.

He wandered on, passing a straw mat where Hyish channeled fire breath down long tubes, glass blowing. Hyish children, hatchlings, weaved between stalls and over the dunes. They coughed out tiny fireballs, setting ablaze their treats—insects on skewers, and crunching away. Flax winced. It made him nervous how uncontrollable these young rascals were. They hadn't yet grasped the danger in their abilities, and although the flame came out in tiny, infrequent spirts from their small mouths, that was all it took sometimes to light something of consequence on fire.

Some of their flames missed the targets as one hatchling set a comrade's robe on fire. One squawked with laughter and the other with annoyance as they patted out the flames. Flax had seen burned market stalls and hissing parents, their slit eyes staring, fangs lashing out at their offspring in punishment.

"Heads up, Mayfee and her entourage are heading to the markets now. I'll wave to you," said Thain's hushed voice through his wristcom.

"Thanks for the heads up, buddy." Flax meandered out of range of the stall and slipped a hand into his sleeve, switching the device from record to transmit.

"Are you ready for a break yet?" Thian's voice whined, followed by a long static rumble.

"Thian, are you shaking your shirt again? My wristcom is coming in static..." Flax tapped the gadget nervously.

"I needed to air out! When will headquarters give up on the Pendant and send us for reassignment already? We've been following the Mayfee clan for four months—and nothing! Just nonstop ruffing it. I can hardly take this anymore!"

"Yeah, it's lame." Flax moved into a corner under a colorful tapestry and took out a spyglass from his pocket. He extended it and scanned the goings-on of the market in case there was anything new to report on.

"Thessse are rare, foreign fruit delightsss!" one seller from the Mayfee clan hissed through a thick Hyish accent to a Jade Clan passerby, who'd stopped to inspect the colorful striped melons.

"Hold on, Thian, I should listen to this..." he whispered into his wrist.

The fact that it was a *fruit* stall meant it could only be from Mayfee's clan—nothing like that grew here. Flax didn't even need to look at her emblem on the stall—the snake-hawk skull. It was just the sort of merchandise they brought in to sell at a premium. The seller said it himself, "Sssuch could never be grown in a place like thisss... it'sss only fair to charge a sssilver coin!"

"Uhn, ghha," *Yes, Okay.* The Jade Hyish, a teenager with a long face and webbed head spines, pulled a gold coin from his pouch and shook it expectantly out in front of the seller. The confused yet delighted seller gladly accepted the gold coin and handed over a hefty melon.

Switching a knob to record again, Flax spoke softly into his wristcom as the Jade Hyish customer wobbled away with his melon. "The Jade Hyish may not understand the value of coins yet, having been introduced fairly recently by the nomads like the Mayfee clan. Before that time, the clan traded in particularly large jade pieces directly for food and resources."

He switched it back to transmission mode. "Hey, Thian, I think the locals like the coin system…"

"Course they do! Hyish love shiny things!" answered the voice of Thian through the device.

No sooner had they exchanged these words, and the webbed-spine Jade Hyish juvenile returned to the stall, his mother in toe. Flax chuckled to himself and watched through his spyglass as the juvenile plunked the melon back on the counter, and his mother hissed, "I thhhink you charged my son too muchhh."

The vendor's eyes narrowed. "What are you sssaying?"

"Sssuhan!" *Dirty Liar.* The mother crossed her arms. "Sssuh'Ju nels!" *You cheated him!*

"Ahnn'yaeh!" The vendor waved him away. *Get lost!*

Flax spoke into his wristcom notes. "Uh oh, looks bad, the Jade clan is learning the value of money!"

A crowd was drawing, as others stopped to see what the commotion was about. The mother drew support from those around, while her son's head shrank closer to his neck. The atmosphere grew tense.

Flax felt a tugging sensation on the hem of his robes and put down the spyglass. A Hyish hatchling gripped a handful of his robes and stared up at him with a skewer of impaled beetles in the other. "Can you light my snack for me?"

The hatchling coughed several times at his skewer, tiny sparks missing their mark.

"I'm busy, go find someone else," he hissed in his best Hyish tongue.

The hatchling didn't move. He tugged Flax's robe again.

Flax shuddered, despite the heat of the day, and took a step away, tugging his robe free. "Off with you!"

The hatchling hissed, turned away, and continued spitting tiny sparks at his skewer, which dissolved in midair. Flax moved away and found a new place to stand out of sight, by yet another glassware stall. Intricate tubes rose from the table: Flutelike cups and pronged eating sticks branching like horns. Some had beadlike insects on them to accentuate their purpose.

He inched closer to the scene unfolding. The Jade Hyish mother pounded her fist on the counter, spitting furious sparks from her mouth with the words. "You Mayfee come here, with your fruit! You buy too cheap!"

The Mayfee vendor kept denying there was any problem. A crowd was starting to form around them, more opinions crossing in the air like the sparks from their mouths.

"You sell too high!" cried another Jade Hyish, siding with the mother.

Flax chuckled and inched even closer. "Thian, you're missing out on the drama over here." He hid by a stack of crates at a stall directly across from the crowd.

He overheard a Jade Hyish saying, "Nikil, go get Master Fang involved." The drama was mesmerizing.

Thian's voice came through his wristcom. "Nice! Looks like we're coming your way. I'll catch a glimpse."

Across the marketplace, a brown hooded figure, taller than the others, tried to look natural among other market-goers. Flax recognized Thian's tilted walk as he took up a post, leaning against a large barrel. Mayfee's procession had to be somewhere nearby, but Flax couldn't yet see her.

A higher-ranking tribesman, denoted by his feathered elbows and heavily jeweled body, had arrived at the vendor scene. "We will kick you out of here and refuse to trade with you if you don't grant us fair dealings!" hissed the Jade elder.

Flax started—a tugging on his robe. He flushed with anger and turned, the same hatchling tugged his robes again. "I can't get it to light!"

"Not now!" Flax hissed back in Hyish.

"It's because Mayfee trades to Warix! She inflates the prices!" shouted the crowd.

Just then, Mayfee and her procession came up the avenue, banners bearing the snake-hawk skull emblem. A slew of purple hair traversed her head, and piercings jangled all over. Her feathered elbows and clawed hands held the reins of a large beast with serpentine neck and bulging spiky limbs. It was a Netic, the living cactus-animal mount of the Hyish. Its beady black eyes stared, and a forked tongue probed the air as they ga-lumphed along.

She took one look at the crowd and smiled broadly. "Ah, all is fine, dear Jadeee. I will provide whatever you need."

"Don't trust her!" some shouted from the irate crowd.

Flax turned his attention to the drama, shooing the hatchling with a hand and inching away without much more thought until something tick-led his nose.

It was smoke reaching his nostrils. Was something burning?

He leaped into the air as small orange sparks flickered off his robe.

"For storm's sake!" Flax danced around, patting at the robes, failing to look where he was going in all the panicked jumping. He stammered back-ward into the glass stall, losing his balance. The crack of shattering glass marred the air.

That little sucker!

"My glass!"

Time slowed… Many Hyish turned his way. Thian's voice laughed on the wristcom.

Intricate pieces lay in glistening shards all around him while Hyish stared, horrified. The vendor hissed and yanked Flax's hood from his head.

"What is this?" he shouted.

Gasps erupted from the crowd.

"He's a Warix spy!"

Flax leaped to his feet and took off, pulling his hood back on to hide his brown hair and horns. He tried to slip into the crowd, but the glass vendor and others took chase. Flax slammed right into something spiked.

Yeowch!

He peeled himself off in horror—it was Mayfee's Netic!

"Flax! What are you doing?!" came Thian's voice, but it was too late. "We're supposed to avoid contact with Mayfee!"

The glass vendor caught up to him and pulled his hood off again.

Mayfee's yellow eyes shined. "A Warixxx!"

The shocked faces of the crowd turned to accusative repulsion.

Flax gulped, a shiver running up his spine. He was knocked to his knees by grasping hands and hissing Hyish. He stumbled to stand, but the mob pulled at him. He kicked his legs, releasing wind energy, thrusting them back. The Hyish winced from the pressure. It was just enough to escape.

"Run for it, Flax!" Thian's strained voice shouted from his wrist.

He clambered to his feet and ran, darting towards the sand dunes, the mob in pursuit.

"I can't take any more of this!" he panted into his wristcom. He switched to transmitting back to Sen'Prin headquarters. "I have been compromised, requesting immediate reassignment!"

Nobody at headquarters was standing by to answer. He turned around to the mob, chasing him.

Small bursts of wind energy propelled his steps into elongated glides. He was gaining distance from the oasis and outpacing the mob of screaming Hyish. They were losing ground, and the longer he ran, the more Hyish gave up and turned back.

A jolt of electricity pulsed from his wrist. He rolled up his sleeve. A message line on his wristcom read, "Agent Flax. Please stand by—orders to come."

He ran until the Hyish were specks, stopping and leaving sight. He was alone among the shrubs with the expanse of desert on all sides, unclear even from which direction he had come.

The wristcom buzzed again. "*Go to coordinates: 45, 37. Immediately.*"

Flax furrowed his brow, his heart pounded. This was really it, leaving the harsh climate finally to some new assignment. What kind was yet to be determined. He could only hope it wouldn't be as nomadic as this.

He stretched his arms, feeling the direction of wind through his horns, and pulled a blanket of air towards himself, wrapping it into a spiral to form a tornado. Well, here it was more like a dust devil of green sand. He spat the sand from his mouth and wiped his eyes as he pushed off with his feet, propelling his dust devil northbound over the dunes.

***

From his tornado, Flax watched the landscape change from the searing desert to rolling grasslands, and finally to a fairer, wooded climate. He landed near the coordinates, many miles north, where pine trees interspersed with Warix farmland—pens of bramble-backed sheep, their hides sporting polka dots of ripe ruby red berries, and green cattle chomping in the pastures.

At the sight of the nearing town, he took caution and switched from a tornado to quickstep. The coordinates were leading this way, but unsure who he was there to meet, he had to check his watch gadget for clues every few minutes.

He ducked behind the first building on the edge of town, a farmhouse with a barn beside it. The surrounding wheat fields separated the property from the town.

"*Go to the barn behind the farmhouse,*" the text strip now read.

Flax slipped inside the barn door. Cautiously, he looked out: the screen door to the farmhouse creaked just out of sight. Flax looked down, realizing he was still dressed in desert Hyish robes. He rooted for an explanation in case this visitor was not who he had come for.

Flax heard footsteps coming and put his arms up in a defensive stance.

A Warix dressed in farmer's linen clothes came through the barn doorway and met Flax's gaze.

"Agent forty-three, Flax?" the farmer asked before Flax opened his mouth to speak.

Flax's sleeve still rolled up, he presented his brass wristcom and its engraved contents. *Sen'Prin Military, Intel Division, Undercover Agent 043, Flax.*

"That's me. Who are you?"

"Welcome, Agent Flax. I'm from the Sen'Prin Territory Acquisitions Division, and I will provide the debriefing for your new mission." The farmer flashed his wristcom engraving: *Sen'Prin Military, Territory Acquisition Division, Logistics Coordinator 009.*

"I see. But if you don't mind me asking, where are we? What is a logistics coordinator? And why was I not sent back to Sen'Prin headquarters for my reassignment as is the general procedure?"

"This is a former Sen'Drorn village called Vendengire, whose allegiance we recently acquired. My team helps them, incognito, during the transitions. We redirect resources and try to protect them until Sen'Prin sends in more defense. So far, the Sen'Drorn haven't noticed our presence here, so headquarters have asked me to meet you, as Vendengire is on the way to your new mission location."

"…And where is that exactly?" Flax asked.

"Sen'Drorn City."

"What? *The* Sen'Drorn City?" Flax's eyes blinked in disbelief.

"Yes. You will infiltrate it."

"How am I supposed to infiltrate the wind walls of our enemy's city? They have a fifty-foot wall of storm, so I've heard."

"Come on, boy, think! We have found you a new identity, and a way in. You will be living undercover among them, as one of them. Do you accept this mission?"

This was better than he could have hoped for. Flax nodded. "For how long?"

"As long as we need you there. Or until your identity is compromised," the coordinator answered. "You will report any important information and frequently record notes. Just like your last mission." Then he handed Flax a folder. "In here is your new ID, personal history to read beforehand, work permit, and acceptance letter for the job which you will need to enter the Sen'Drorn city as a non-resident. Last week, the good people of Vendengire received a notice from Sen'Drorn City requesting an apprentice to work under a master engineer in the city. You will be that apprentice, a farm boy born and raised on this very farm. Have a walk around to get some concrete memories of this place for your backstory before you head off. Read the rest of your bio and memorize everything about it, and when you are ready to head out, in this barn you will find an old wind-powered motorbike. It's been yours since you were sixteen. In three days, you will ride it out of town, all the way to the gates of Sen'Drorn. The guards can see for miles down the road. They will see that you really did ride here from Vendengire."

The coordinator handed Flax a stack of clothes: linen workman's shirt and britches and a pair of leather boots. When Flax had changed into them, he handed back the Hyish robes, then took a walk around the farm.

Chickens clucked by, sporting leafy plumes as Flax came for a good look at the purple wooden farmhouse he now must pretend to have had grown up in.

He studied his new ID, chuckling at his name. "Flax of Vendengire." His new job title read: "Apprentice engineer, trade district."

Flax had never expected this. His heart boomed at the thrill. His mother had only told him a couple of years ago the truth about his father. Like all young Sen'Prin Warix, he was drafted into the military at seventeen, but he chose the spying division for other reasons.

He was born just after the Great Split, when many fled the once unified Warix capital city, in chaos and destruction. The rebels who left formed the Nation of Sen'Prin, his mother among them, but not his father. All he knew about his father was that he was a tradesman of some sort, who had chosen to remain in Sen'Drorn City and not go with the politically charged Odella, his mother.

And now he was going to Sen'Drorn City. A place the Warix of Sen'Prin could never enter. Except for a lucky spy.

Flax was not entirely sure what exactly an engineer *did* every day, but probably he'd have time to look around once he arrived. Maybe he could do some investigating of his own, elsewhere in town.

Maybe he'd find him? And meet him? And ask him why he stayed.

Flax remained in Vendengire for several days until the new assignment was ready. No problem there: he was grateful for the break and the ample time to perfect his cover story.

He slept in the barn and ate what the coordinator brought him. When it was time, and he'd gotten the go-ahead, he set off.

On the red dirt road, on the wind-powered motorbike, he rode. Brown overalls flapped in the wind over a farmhand's tweed shirt. The leather boots gripping the sides as he rode towards the infamous Sen'Drorn City. He passed meadows, farms, the occasional village in the distance in low hills, but eventually, this terrain was replaced by pine forest. The air smelled sweet and fresh, and the rush of adventure filled his head. What new things were to come, he could not know.

Then, over the horizon, it suddenly came into view. Flax took a deep breath as he saw it, nestled amongst the pine hills—a gigantic barrier of dark clouds moving in a flurry of circling wind, dominating the landscape. His first look at Sen'Drorn City.

The dirt road appeared to lead directly towards the enormous, calculated storm. "This is why we can't attack the Sen'Drorn directly," Flax whispered to himself as he leaned forward on the handlebars in anticipation. "Ranged siege of any kind would fly right off. Nothing gets over those walls."

The entry gates became clear as he approached, a single entrance unobstructed by the encapsulating winds. Up high on the ramparts, he saw Warix soldiers spaced every ten feet, standing with outstretched arms, each creating a little piece of the storm sphere. A wide gap in these posts above the blackjack stone archway gates allowed access to the city, where Flax aimed as he rode closer to the arch.

Five guards looked down from the ramparts above the gateway, and two muscular guards flanked the pillars where the road came to a stop. Trying not to draw too much commotion, Flax slowed the motorbike to a crawl well before the entrance guards.

"Hello there!" Flax called once within earshot.

"Stop. Dismount your bike and present your ID," the front guard on the left demanded.

Flax had his new ID at the ready and pulled it from his shirt chest pocket. The guard looked at the ID and then at the other guard. He came over. They both looked at it, at Flax, and then again at each other. Then they nodded to Flax and one said, "Inside for further inspection," as he stepped aside and indicated towards the inner gates.

Flax nodded back, heart fluttering. He walked his bike in as he entered the covered stone passageway. What if they saw through the disguise? If the forged paperwork was missing something? He suspected they would do far worse to him than just let him return to Vendengire if they caught him. The large double gates to the city were visible at the end of the hall, directly in front of him. He was so close. He turned to his left and saw a stone arch inspection booth. A scowling Warix with fat spiraling horns and almost greenish skin sat behind iron bars, inside a cave-like chamber.

"What is your business here?" he grunted.

"I have papers to get inside the city… I'm from the villages, coming to work here in the trade district." Flax slipped the paperwork and ID card between the bars. The guard scoffed at the papers.

"How do I know these papers aren't fake?"

Flax kept his cool, staring the guard right in the eyes. "Call the number and see… I'm expected at the engineering shop. For Borak."

The guard scoffed, then turned away, withdrawing into the cave. Flax could hear he was speaking to someone on the other end of a phone in a voice too low to overhear. Flax stood nervously, awaiting his fate.

The guard hung up, turned around, and coughed out the words. "Welcome to Sen'Drorn City…" The guard pulled out a map and drew a big red 'X' on one spot. "Central trade district. Don't get lost, farm boy."

He shoved the map through the bars with his muscular arm. Then he pulled a huge copper lever, using every bulky muscle to make it move. The double gates creaked, causing Flax to turn. Sunlight poured in from the other side of the tunnel as the gates parted and then swung outward with a view of the city and distant hilltop keep. It was built from black volcanic stone and loomed above the rest of the matching architecture of the city below.

Flax's heart raced as a rush of adrenaline hit him. He pocketed the map, remounted his motorbike, and zoomed inside.

CHAPTER SEVEN

After all the emotional drains from the evening at the Light of the Meruyan Festival, Meleena should have gone right to sleep. She was alone in the house. Her cheeks were sore from smiling, her wrists sore from spinning her hand in greeting to everyone who congratulated her.

She had stopped at the stables and collected her bags. The candidacy package lay unopened before her. *I guess I should open it and decide if I'm running away or not.*

She grabbed the large parchment scroll, printed on waterproof kelpweave, and unfurled it:

Itinerary:

1. (Four days travel) Travel on foot through the forest paths from Southern to Northern Villages. Camping overnight.

2. (One month stay) Northern hills, tropical climate, stay with host family in the village of Gebuk'Desa. Learning local issues with a guide. Restock provisions before departure.

3. (Day trips with guide) Underwater Territory, learn of their technology and ways, history, and politics, and Bio-dome project.

4. (One month stay) Half-day travel from Underwater Territory to Arctic city. Learn about political and social structure, accompanied by city mayor, and host family.

5. (Five days travel) Return home, direct via underwater kelpie carriage. To be arranged by Arctic City.

Total Trip: two months. Important Note: after the journey, the teens must complete an interview detailing what they have learned. Only upon passing this test and receiving proper conduct reports from hosts and guides, are they judged worthy and invited to become a junior member of Meruyan parliament.

After rereading it several times over, Meleena thumbed through some of the other documents, which included a non-responsibility clause in case of injury or death. To be signed and returned to the Council before the journey.

That night, she dreamed of wild adventures to come. In the meantime, she had a fortnight to rest and prepare.

***

The days grew longer, and the morning of departure arrived. After breakfast, she finished packing, giving her room one last look over for the foreseeable future. She dressed in a shirt and slacks then checked the windup-gear clock in her room. Her parents would soon meet her outside the cottage, where they'd go together to the goodbye ceremony at the forest trail at the edge of Pontai'Desa.

Taking care not to let the samples fall out, she scratched some last thoughts onto a blank page of her clamshell journal. *Why does everything have to be an "event"? I never thought of how annoying that must have been for the candidates of previous years. I also almost forgot about my companions. That sea worm, Talla. Deem seems okay, though.* Then she gingerly tucked her journal on her bookshelf.

It was too precious to take. She slipped a small, simple notebook into her daypack in its stead. A poor substitute, but it would have to do.

As she carried the bags to the main room, her mother waited, beaming with pride. "Meleena, we have goodbye gifts for you."

Meleena followed her outside the hut, where her father was waiting. His kelpie, Peela, was hitched to the wooden post, the aquamarine scales around her face glistened in the early morning light.

Her father clapped his hands together. "Peela will join you on the journey. She's old but loyal. She will carry your bags, and you will never lose the path with her by your side." He patted Peela on the neck, then fed her a dead squid from his pocket.

Peela tweeted happily as Loroh fixed Meleena's satchels to her sides. "With the extra weight of the bags, you can only ride her underwater."

"Meleena, I have something for you as well," said her mother. She presented a large book, with a cover of fired clay, inlaid with flat seashells and tiny pearls. Inside were ample blank pages. "A new journal for your trip."

"It's wonderful! Thank you!" Meleena embraced her mother. *Maybe she understands me more than I ever realized.*

As they walked to the western archway that marked the edge of town, her father, holding Peela's reins, explained her proper care and feeding, as well as the dangers to be aware of on the road. He counted on his fingers: "...Don't wander off-path. Read every sign you pass. Don't take any shortcuts..."

"She made it this far with enough common sense," Meleena's brother Tomiyan said. He had joined up with them in the town square. "I'm sure my little sis can fend off exotic creatures, both thieving and stampeding."

Meleena laughed. *He doesn't know the half of it.*

Beyond the stone archway, the cobblestones of town ended, and they came to a grassy clearing. A dirt path led beyond into the forest.

Many Meruyan townspeople were already in the clearing, awaiting the sendoff. Talla and her family were among them. With her hands on her hips, she stood beside her twin brother, Joru. Her parents had their backs turned, chatting in a ring of other adults.

Talla's eyes flashed at Meleena as she spoke to Joru, of which Meleena only caught part. "...Old sea cow if I ever saw one."

"Come over here and say that!" Meleena growled. She noticed Talla wore the necklace of silver and black pearls, which she had worn the night of the Festival.

"Pshh... I was talking about your animal, the old kelpie mare. My parents bought me a new kelpie steed for the trip."

Talla pointed to the large kelpie, with lustrous teal-green scales and strong physique. Under a dreadlocked seaweed mane, he rooted in the grass, indifferent to Talla's presence.

"Looks like he's not very loyal," Meleena said. "Peela and I will keep each other safe."

"Clover is strong, I can ride him, and he can carry my bags. I'll be way ahead of you by nightfall. Then you can be disqualified on your own merit, without any undeserved help from me."

Meleena's cheeks flushed hot. She turned away. The last thing she needed was to let her anger be seen in front of everyone.

A moment later, a crowd of Meruyans passed under the archway, many with live barnacles and starfish clinging to them—the underwater community. A boy was at the center of the crowd. Three young girls with silken blue hair followed close behind Deem, his sisters, whom Meleena had met that day underwater.

But Meleena's focus was on the enormous bronze-shelled lobster scuttling by his side. She, and everyone else here, from the looks on the faces, had never seen a lobster of this size before. Its beady eyes rotated atop its armored body. Rope-strapped bags clung to its sides behind the large, menacing claws which stuck out in front.

Deem, squinted as he approached Meleena and Talla.

"Ew! Is that your lunch, lobster boy?" asked Talla, mouth agape. For shore kids, assuming every underwater kid was a lobster farmer was an insult, but Meleena knew that in this case, it was actually true.

Deem took no offense. "This is Pinchy! He's a working breed and my companion. Careful, he may pinch if he doesn't know you!" Just then, a colossal claw swung, and Meleena jumped back to avoid it. He pulled out what looked like a hand-sized fingernail. "I keep this scale from his first molt. It's my most prized possession."

"Ew," said Talla. "That thing's going last." She indicated a wide circle with her finger, which encompassed both Pinchy and Deem.

Deem frowned. "His tail does get in the way I s'pose."

Meleena scowled. No way she'd let Talla be the boss of this trip.

Deem excused himself to join his parents, calling him over. They placed a pair of spectacles on his face and all embraced. Meleena had been right the night of the Festival when she guessed that he hadn't owned a pair.

"My family saved up some coins to get me my own glasses," Deem said when he returned, wiping a tear from behind his new glasses. "I can see on land! How wonderful!"

An elder Meruyan from the Council came over, swirling a hand in the gesture of greeting. Meleena, Deem, and Talla repeated the gesture in response. He was advanced in years, with faded gray-blue hair. "Hello, Future Leaders! I am Councilman Professor Levlos. I will be your educational guide when you arrive at the Northern Villages and beyond. Provided you arrive on time."

Their faces must have shown worry, as he added, "Just kidding around. I'm sure you will be fine my young navigators, it's a straightforward route through the forest." He pointed at the sloping trees that clung to the mountainside.

Councilman Ives, who had been the master of ceremony at the Festival, now approached. Meleena had not noticed him until now in all the commotion. "All travelers thus present, it's time to send you off." He handed each of them a gadget, a wind-up pocket watch with a built-in compass. Warix technology, for accuracy in finding their way.

***

Meleena, Deem, and Talla each hugged their respective families and friends, said their goodbyes, and headed down the road into the leafy jungle, pack animals at their sides. Talla and Clover first, followed close by Meleena and Peela, with Deem and Pinchy at the rear.

Meleena couldn't tell if the energy boost she felt was from her Meruyan nutrient-absorbing hair from the sun or the pure excitement of stepping into the open world. But her bliss was broken when, not long into the trail, her bickering with Talla began.

Deem tried to defuse with pleasantry. "I think both your kelpies are lovely." He kept screwing up his expression, trying to adjust to the new glasses.

"Don't get involved," Talla and Meleena said together.

Hoping to mend the mood and include Deem, Meleena said, "Pinchy looks ancient, can you tell me about him?"

"Very ancient!" Deem's face brightened, and his gaze lifted from the floor. "A hundred years, at least! Bronze lobsters can grow forever and live hundreds of years." He patted the glossy carapace of his companion.

"Okay, shut up, she didn't ask your life story," called Talla.

He blushed and looked at the ground again.

"Stop making the boy feel bad!" scolded Meleena.

"Stop managing what I say!" Talla shouted back.

"You are really a piece of work," Meleena sighed and led Peela past Talla, brushing past the fronds that hovered over the trail.

Only the crunch of footsteps and the calls of birds and insects resounded from the jungle. It was peaceful for a while until Talla's voice cut in with, "...Where's Deem?"

"I'm shocked you know his name..." said Meleena, glancing back. The boy and his oversized lobster were gone.

"He probably hung back because he couldn't stand listening to us..." said Meleena. "And you were so rude to him."

Talla merely shrugged.

They continued another half hour or so in silence, as noted by checking the pocket-watch. Then the tree cover opened to a clearing. Meleena recognized this clearing. It marked the fork in the road between going up the mountain, to continue to the capital city, or around it through the coastal wilderness. Meleena had stood here nearly a year before.

The wider, much steeper road led to Dlawn'Edo. The narrow one—which they were meant to follow—would eventually take them to the Northern Villages cluster. Meleena was thankful to remain on even ground.

Talla was already panting, gulping down water, and starting on some wheat cakes. Meleena drank, led Peela to graze by a pond at the edge of the clearing, then pulled out her new journal, she sketched the elongated leaves and ribbonlike bark around her. Talla had left Clover to sniff the dry surroundings, browsing the unknown foliage in vein.

"You really should lead him to the pond," Meleena said.

"What's it matter?"

Meleena sighed and collected a strand of pond grass to show her. She split the strand open, and white juice oozed from it, along with the pungent smell of salt. "See, this is related to their natural food. You need to keep your kelpie happy and strong for the journey ahead."

Talla still looked dumbfounded and glanced sideways at Peela, long mouth happily munching. She waved it off with one hand. "Sure, whatever." Meleena led Clover to graze beside Peela.

Talla got up from the boulder. "I don't know where the boy is, but I want to keep mov—" She froze as a rustle disturbed the foliage.

Deem parted the reeds, soon followed by the scuttling Pinchy.

"What took you?" Asked Talla.

"You were waiting for me?" Deem asked, surprised.

Talla made a face. "No."

Then Deem made a suggestion. "I have an idea. To keep things peaceful, let's count thirty minutes between each of us on the pocket watch. Each of us waiting before the next one goes."

"Fine by me," said Talla.

Meleena agreed. "Just watch out for vangrots."

"What's that?" asked Deem.

"A climbing creature with many arms and sensitive nose, which sometimes steals food."

They agreed: Deem would go first this time, followed by Meleena, and then Talla.

"Well, see ya at camp tonight," said Deem. "Oh, I almost forgot…" He unfurled a scroll from Pinchy's saddlebag. "I guess we are camping here tonight. I drew a red X on my map to correspond with the directions." He indicated to an outcropping in the land just north of a wide seaside valley.

His map was full of red ink, dotted lines, and notes he'd marked beforehand. He was prepared. Meleena's earlier review of the materials didn't seem like much now. Maybe she wasn't deserving of this journey after all.

Once Deem had gone, Talla and Meleena tried their best to ignore each other during the painful wait. A peaceful breeze passed over her, yet she couldn't calm her pounding heart or distract herself with her journal. She smacked away bugs flying at her face and took a deep breath, trying to get into the sun surrender relaxation. Luckily, Talla kept to herself.

After a minute of warm sun on her face, the fluttering in her stomach calmed. The journey was just beginning, and she had no idea what to expect.

At the half-hour mark, Meleena, brushing the grass from her trousers, waved an indifferent goodbye to Talla, and continued into the jungle with Peela. As the pulsing sounds of creatures grew louder, and a damp smell assaulted her senses, she was sure this was the densest jungle she'd ever been in.

CHAPTER EIGHT

Flax's motorbike hummed over the black stones as he entered the gates of Sen'Drorn City. Rows of ebony buildings rose in front of him, copper pipelines snaking up their walls, their tops forming spires like dripping wax. Second-story platforms enabled direct landing on doorsteps.

In order to use wind energy indoors, Warix used wind turbines to circulate in fresh air. He could already tell this was a prosperous city: all the spinning turbines were copper, which was expensive and a more effective conductor than bronze, which they used in his home city.

The broad street was quiet. Only a few Warix passed by, going about their daily business, some on foot, some on wind-scooters or bikes. The swift sound of swooshing wind passed his ears as some jumped directly between floors.

Flax passed numerous alleyways which spaced the main street's otherwise continuous wall of three-story buildings, until he reached a particularly wide alleyway, and turned right, doing his best to follow the map.

He soon found it impossible to keep a clear picture in his mind of where to go. He frequently stopped to check the map as narrow streets gave rise to narrow alleys. They jutted off from the larger streets at seemingly random angles, like branches of a tree. This was nothing like Sen'Prin, the city he grew up in—both in narrowness and business. Sen'Prin was much more spread out.

The handlebars of his motorbike nearly scraped the walls at certain points, and he had to stop frequently to avoid crashing into other Warix passing through. He squeezed through turns and down flights of unexpected stairs until he was fed up and ditched the motorbike in favor of walking. Tossing his pack over his shoulder, he looked back at the bike as he walked off—he hoped he would be able to find it again later.

After working his way through the disorienting maze on foot, Flax squeezed past a surprisingly crowded alley and emerged into a wider square with a fountain at its center.

"Wow…" he gaped, awestruck—the square lengthened into the busiest walking street he had ever seen. It was alive with people, cafés, shops, storefronts with interesting gadgets and wind-powered devices.

This was the old district. This was Fleeg Street!

No second-level entries on this level—probably too crowded to risk any collisions. He chuckled as he passed pedestrian signs reading, *Hold onto your shopping! No wind use on Fleeg Street!*

He walked into the chaos, passing waves of other Warix as the scent of heated copper and sugar filled his nose. The clacking of hammers on metal, the chatter of excited customers and ceramics scraping on teacups, all mixed together as he made his way past cafes, shops with signs like 'Best turbo-boots in town,' 'Blue's Blacksmithing' and 'Hone your wind energy, meditation and technique training.'

His mind buzzed with ideas for notes to record to his wristcom, as was his old habit. *We have busy areas in Sen'Prin City, but not so many choices!*

No, he thought, *forget notes to the gadget…* His excited thought shifted from his training as a formal observer to meet his indulgences— how much he'd like to brag to Thian the next time they met. *"You know how we have 'the cafe', which becomes 'the pub' at night? Well here, there are five separate cafes and pubs just on Fleeg Street! And they are all full!"*

But as he went, he saw more things to remind him that although this place was plentiful and clean, it was but built on treacherous beliefs. A stall selling 'miracle cure medicines' made from kelpie hearts made him shiver.

He nearly forgot he was looking for a particular shop. He stopped at shop windows. What gadgets had the Sen'Drorn created to hone wind powers that the Sen'Prin hadn't?

I suppose that's why I'm here to learn as much as I can about their lives and developing tech. Finally, an interesting job. He smiled at the realization, then a jolt ran through him as another thought struck him—*my father! If he is in Sen'Drorn City, he likely works on this block. This is the closest I've ever been to him...!*

Did his father work on this street? He had no clue where he might find the man, only that he intended to figure it out, somehow, during his extended stay here. Maybe he'd pick up some clues at the new job...Which he still had to find somewhere in all this.

He stepped aside and pulled the map from his pocket once more. The engineering shop, "Borak's Gears n' Gadgets" was apparently located back up the street, closer to the fountain square.

Everyone in Sen'Drorn City was familiar with Borak's shop, a truth Flax learned from asking half a dozen people for help in finding the place on the busy street. One Warix woman holding the hand of a small boy told him, "It's iconic! When I need my son's wind scooter fixed or parts for anything, I go *there*!"

Flax turned, scrutinizing signage back up the street until he saw it ahead of him—a large sign above a wooden door, bolted at each corner to the ebony stones. Words written in warped wrenches read: *Borak's Gears N' Gadgets.*

His new life for the foreseeable future awaited inside that door. Chest pounding from nervousness, Flax gulped hard, pushed slowly on the shop door, and slipped inside.

The shop proved smaller than its counterpart in Flax's imagination. An over-crowded room stuffed with aisles of hardware overwhelmed him. His eyes darted around the shop trying to take it all in at once. He inspected the narrow aisles—pieces of metal in every size, steel, copper and bronze spades, casings, rods, tubes and tubs—shapes he never knew before, decorative and otherwise. There were glass globes and tubes of various sizes. There was a leather and rope aisle, an aisle of nuts, bolts, and of course, gears: every size and shape Flax could imagine and more. There were wheels, lots of wheels, in every size—rubber, metal, tiny and large. Can't forget accessories—propellers, light bulbs, horns, and sails, ranging widely for gadgets of all sizes. The place was a playground for an open mind.

The room echoed with the clanking of customers browsing through tools in the shop. The place smelled of rubber and metal. A loud fan whirred, its blades spinning around in a failing attempt to cool the sweltering room.

That must be Borak, thought Flax from the doorway, watching the muscular Warix of early middle age tended to the customers waiting in-line. He was hunched over the counter, turning a delicate device over in his rough hands. Every so often, he shot a hand towards a clunky metal tube on the wall, unleashing wind energy to keep the momentum up, and electricity in the room.

A lanky teenage customer partly blocked Flax's view of Borak. The teen rubbed the back of his green Mohawk as Borak explained the fault in his broken wind-board. A Warix man in formal vest waited behind the teen, checking his wristcom every few moments and tapping his foot. Behind him stood a young woman with white-blonde hair wearing a cheerful expression.

"This broken motor will need to be replaced, and parts don't come free."

"I'm not paying any more for this! I barely crashed it!" scoffed the customer.

"What does 'barely crashed' mean? Either you did, or you didn't!" said Borak, shaking his head. "An' it doesn't matter how badly you crashed it. Smashed parts are smashed parts!"

The teenager folded his arms while Borak sighed heavily. His barrel-chest dropped. Flax watched uneasily from the doorway, shuffling his feet. The exchange reminded him of the Hyish markets all over again.

The Warix in formal apparel waiting in line sighed too, unfolded his arms, and pushed forward to the counter. "If this will stop your bickering so I can have my turn, then keep it! Some of us only get one lunch break today, you know!" the businessman barked, tossing several coins from his pocket onto the table between them. The coins rattled on the metal countertop. "There, problem solved!"

The teenager's eyes widened, dumbstruck. "Wow, thanks," gaped the teen, blowing a tendril of green hair from his face.

"Just get out of here." The businessman glared.

"Ye can pick up the fixed wind-board in two days," added Borak, turning his square jaw upward to meet the eye of the still dumfounded teen. The teen nodded and departed quickly from the awkward scene, trampling Flax's foot on his way out the door.

"Ouch!" Flax snapped out of his daze of observation, prompting him to move from the doorway into the aisles. He looked up, startled at the bellowed words from the counter, "Finally!" but it was just the businessman, now free to moan about a clogged something or other.

Not about me, Flax breathed, trying to look casual as he perused the aisles among other customers. *What am I doing?* He was treating his new mission like the Hyish mission, even though in this case, he was supposed to be making his presence known. At the realization, he sheepishly entered the line of people waiting at the counter, standing behind the Warix woman with platinum blonde curls and horns pointing downward.

Other Warix entered the shop. Some entered the line behind Flax, holding whatever products they had taken from the shelves or broken gadgets they had brought with them.

Flax was now close enough to hear Borak mutter some profanities after the businessman walked out. The Warix woman in front of Flax giggled. She leaned over the counter to whisper something inaudible to Borak, her perfect apple butt close to Flax's now blushing face.

Borak made an amused sound like 'harrumph' from his belly, and said, "Ye'…I can make that. Casings on aisle three." He crossed his arms, grinning, and watched her as she pranced off.

Flax was now face-to-face with Borak. At the sight of the man, Flax's thought verbalized as he murmured, "What was that about…?"

Flax's heart skipped a beat as he realized he was staring at the man who would become his master—the Warix who'd be in charge of dictating the course of his life for quite some time.

~ 81 ~

"Mind yers," scolded Borak, a peevish grin on his face, bulky arms still crossed.

"Sorry…"

Borak leaned forward. His bag-cupped stone-brown eyes looked into Flax's. Borak chortled, "She were lookin' for a toy…"

"For a pet?" Flax blushed as Borak bent back to normal.

"Eh?"

"Oh." Flax cleared his throat and straightened himself up to regain composure. He looked down on Borak's head of thinning gray hair, which surrounded the small horns, like calf's horns, which crowned his bald spot. "Master Borak…I…I have been sent here to serve you upon Sen'Drorn request. To be your new apprentice."

Borak looked Flax up and down. Flax handed over his new papers.

"You seem physically fit enough." Borak raised an eyebrow. "But we'll see about smart enough. What's your name?"

"Flax," he answered dumbly as the shop bell rang, and another customer came inside.

"Well, young Flax, I have customers and no time to train ye' now. What do ye' know about bolt sizes?"

He motioned for Flax to join him behind the counter.

Flax's mind raced. What if he gets turned away? He was in over his head here. For storm's sake, why had the Sen'Prin not provided him with some practical background information?

"Nothing really," he said with an air of indifference. *I hope I don't bump into anything…*

"It's okay, just observe for now." Borak slapped a hard hand on Flax's shoulder.

Flax nodded. "I can do that." *Okay, maybe we can do it.*

A silky voice interrupted them.

"Borak, isn't it nice to finally have an extra pair of hands around here?"

Flax looked up to see a young woman just a bit older than himself, beaming at Borak. Her long purplish-brown hair fell lightly around her delicate face, and was topped by two nubs of the horns which curved be-hind her head. She winked a violet eye at Flax as if to say, *"You're wel-come."*

"We'll see how it works out," Borak replied, then ducked under the counter and hauled up a large box. "Here's yer order for today, miss Yu-lah."

"Thanks." Her long hair swished as she turned away on delicate, toned limbs, carrying the box out with ease. She was wearing a silk dress. Flax's knees were rubber, his limbs suddenly locked in place. He couldn't speak or move, only stare in awe. He watched the back of her head until she left, two long horns embedded in the flowing hair like frozen waterfalls. Tran-quil energy washed over him.

He tried to make his voice sound normal. "Who was that?"

Borak glanced sideways at Flax. "Yulah? She's a regular. Comes in twice a week." He waved off any further conversation with the back of his hand. If only Borak would give more information than that...but Flax didn't push the subject further. Hopefully, she will come again.

After a few more customers, the afternoon rush was over. A sheet metal cuckoo clock hanging on the wall above the doorway struck two.

Borak turned to Flax. "I close now for a couple of hours, work on or-ders in the back room, my workshop, until late afternoon, then open again to cater to the after-work customers. I close for the night around seven."

"Okay, so I'm off from seven?" asked Flax, face brightening. His body drooped, heavy from exhaustion. He had been in the desert just this morn-ing, traveled hundreds of miles, and was now ready to drop.

Borak raised a bushy eyebrow. "Off at seven? Hah! That's when yer trainin' really starts!"

How am I going to get through this day? Flax thought to himself.

CHAPTER NINE

Meleena, with Peela at her side, moved along the dark jungle path. This time, for better or worse, without the company of the others.

She could no longer see the sky through the dense canopy. Tall trees and ferns entangled in vines and covered in lichen and moss. Broad leaves erupted from every which way, with the occasional lipstick pink honeycomb flower poking out. Unknown wildlife trilled. Meleena felt a strange mix of fear and wonder. She felt relief at the importance of keeping moving. For once, she was not in the mood to draw.

She walked with caution to avoid slipping in muddy patches or tripping on roots. Peela walked normally, with a perplexing grace. When she touched a tree for support, ants attacked her arm. She walked on, scratching at the burning, red blotches.

After walking on for what felt like the most of her life, and far too much for one day, she finally came to a fork in the path. But she wasn't alone there. A Meruyan, dressed in kelpweave overalls, lay snoozing with his back against a signpost.

Slightly annoyed at the need to think in such an exhausted state, she ignored the man and read the sign:

> *High road: use any time. Approx distance to main path rejoin: 3*
> *hours. Low road: floodplains for use only at low tide, when river*
> *pass is clear for walking. Approx distance to main path rejoin: 40*
> *minutes. Warning: floodplain area contains strong current, sharp*
> *rocks, and leeches. Do not swim.*

There was a small dial at the bottom of the sign, with a pin indicating six hours between the tide cycles. The pin was pointing to the end of the high tide cycle, not quite at low tide, but oh so close.

Did this mean high tide was finished, and the water was draining? Did this mean she could cross?

She looked again at the snoozing farmer and noticed the official Council badge on his chest. She could wake him and ask for help.

No, I don't need help! I am perfectly capable of reading a sign! What kind of Champion would I be if I asked?

She studied the sign again. The lousy thing was too unclear. If only she could see the river from this point. The path was too dense with jungle and winding to see anything.

It might take a few minutes, or an hour, to drain. Should I risk it?

Meleena certainly wanted to spare herself the extra hours of walking. She felt heavy. Her feet already ached. It had been nonstop all day.

She stared at the sign. No motion. Which way had Deem gone? There was no way to know. Then she startled, thinking about Talla. If Talla caught up and found her still here, she'd look foolish.

"Come on, Peela." She took the left path, the short path going down to the river basin. She glanced back for one last look at the sleeping Meruyan and could swear he opened one eye just for a moment.

The path was steep, leading through the last bit of jungle before opening finally to a query of boulders at the basin's edge. It was mostly sandy, a wide landscape ready to traverse—a ring of jungle on a raised cliff around it. There was only one problem. One last vestige of the river had yet to drain, and it was blocking her path. The water was rushing too rapidly for even a Meruyan to traverse safely. Worse, where the river opened to the sea, the current pounded against jagged rocks. That would pull her and chew her up if she attempted to swim.

Meleena cursed and looked back from where she had come. The path, so steep, looked exhausting to return to. Plus, more hours of walking the long path. Her legs trembled with exhaustion. She clenched her jaw. No, she would not go back.

She removed her boots, melting with the relieving pressure. With one hand holding onto Peela for support, she plunged one leg into the river, murky from the mixing sands, to test the depth. Her grasping foot failed to touch silt, meaning it was too deep for comfort.

She retreated to the boulders, clapping a palm down in frustration, her cheeks and ears were hot. *That useless sign! I could never have known how significant the difference in that pin would be. It's not my fault their design is flawed. I'm not an oyster-brain. I can figure it out from here.*

"Peela, stay." She stroked Peela's neck scales. "I'll scout upstream, where the river is narrower. Maybe we can cross there."

She left Peela and began climbing the boulders. Webbed with slimy moss, she soon discovered how slippery they were. She lowered each foot with intent, testing for grip before putting her weight down. Yet, even so, it was too slippery, and she fell. Her head traded places with her feet as both took a tumble. Her limbs met the hard surface. Waves of searing pain shot up and spread through her body.

Her forearms and legs sprouted fins as she got wetter, hindering motion further. Smeared with fresh mud, she trudged on. The better views upstream only showed that the river continued as thick and impassable as ever. Each time it deceived her into following further: it appeared easy, just ahead, a little further...

A sudden rustling in the canopy made her stop and look up, but she saw nothing. She lost her footing and slipped, slamming into the rocks and slipping into a deep, soggy crevice. Water dripped off her eyelashes and tendrils of hair. Her knees and elbows burned, skinned, and muddy. She breathed in the smell of damp, earthen minerals. Her heart pounded in her ears above even the roaring river.

What kind of Champion am I? Left alone, all I do is get myself into a deeper mess by the minute. Maybe my family did cheat to get me in. Maybe I'll fail too soon, and the Warix will never let me join them.

She needed to calm down, to take a deep breath and perform the Seal's sun surrender. She closed her eyes and tilted her face towards the sun. Her heartbeat slowed, and she filled with warmth from the sun.

Still in pain, she reached over the boulders and jumped until her hand grasped a dry grip, and pulled herself up.

She removed her glasses, thankfully not broken, and wiped her face.

She made her way back downstream towards Peela but froze as she saw *her*. Talla and her kelpie emerged from the jungle and stepped onto rocks. Meleena's heart sank—she had run out of time.

Meleena slipped between the rocks, trying to hide. Then, she realized the awful truth. She needed Talla now.

"Hey bozo, I see you. You left your kelpie here," said Talla.

Meleena blushed and got up.

Without another word, Talla turned and led Clover by the reins. She trudged the opposite way Meleena had gone, towards the wider mouth of the river, and plunged in without hesitation. Meleena's mouth fell open. Talla's calves bloomed to leg fins as she waded in, but the current didn't knock her down, as Meleena had expected. It rose not quite to her waist, which allowed her to hold her own against the moving waters.

How did Talla know to do that? Am I missing some basic instincts?

She watched until Talla made it to the other side. Part of her expected Talla to trip and get washed away.

Peela neighed and bobbed her head, eager to follow. Meleena led her, and they plunged into the wide river mouth. Since Meleena was shorter than Talla, she took caution as her feet sank into the gooey silt. They did finally stop sinking, and though Meleena was pretty deep, she managed to wade across without trouble. Her initial test of the water had not been bold enough or gone deep enough. She was sure that had she been braver, gone a little deeper, she too would have discovered it. She felt sheepish at the realization.

"How'd you fall behind?" Talla called from the shore, one hand on her hip. Her pearl necklace caught the light and burned Meleena's eyes.

The sand cradled Meleena's feet as she stepped from the river to the shore.

Talla waited, a smug expression on her face.

Meleena focused on the view. Even Talla couldn't ruin this place. The jungle ring that encircled the sandy basin, crowned by distant mountainous peaks, was mystifying. Meleena took in the sweet air and answered, "Thank you for showing me the way."

"Couldn't figure out a way to get across, huh?" Talla flicked her green hair behind her head. "You look awful. Have a drink."

Meleena was still caked in mud and bleeding from her forehead and skinned joints. They drank water from their packs and walked towards the ocean. Meleena washed the mud off at the beach, then took out her first aid kit. She applied bandages and salves to her aching wounds.

They walked along the beach without speaking for a time, a tranquil ocean on their left, with pillars of stone sticking up from the water offshore. "How could you be so certain you wouldn't get swept away?" asked Meleena.

Talla did a victorious shoulder pump. "I just asked the farmer, didn't you? He said to take the low path and stay downstream at the river—the current is stronger upstream, fish brain. The water is more concentrated."

"Talla, I'm actually impressed…" She was glad to be rescued, even though it had come from Talla. She made a mental note to find a way to show up Talla later.

"It was nothing," said Talla, smiling, in a rare moment of peace between them.

Tranquility swept in with the sea breeze. It soothed her stinging limbs, and the salty air rejuvenated a sense of hope within her. The sand beneath her feet streamed with flowing natural patterns, changing with each soft step.

As they headed inland into the basin, their peaceful moment came to a swift end. Soon, Talla walked far behind Meleena as they huffed through the endless sand, Talla cursing and muttering to herself.

The trouble started when Talla tried to ride Clover when she became tired, but he only neighed and flinched, not letting her climb on. She managed to get a good hop in, to which he responded by reaching back his head and nipping at her, which quickly escalated into braying and tossing her off, headlong into the sand.

"At least you chose a good place to fall off a kelpie, soft sand to break your fall," said Meleena, which of course, did nothing but irritate Talla further. She shouted profanities at Meleena, who kept pace ahead, while Clover dawdled far behind.

They arrived at the far side of the valley. A steep earthen slope led back up into the forest. Both Meruyan girls sighed as they looked up the steep, mud-carved staircase they were to follow out of the basin. The sun was low in the sky. It would soon be dark.

Talla let out another profanity and tried desperately to get on Clover's back once more.

"Told you he's not loyal." Meleena rolled her eyes.

Talla let out a muffled snarl as she slid off Clover's side. "Let me ride Peela then!"

"No! She can't take a Meruyan's weight on land." Meleena scowled at her.

"Oh yeah, I forgot she's lame."

"Gah! Don't be so spoiled! I'm sick of you bullying me, and for your own problems!"

They bickered between heaving breaths all the way up the cliff, taking their leg pain out on each other.

At the top, they came to a fork with another small wooden sign like one from earlier that day, faced back the way they had just come. This was where the long route met up with the short route. Another sign pointed them towards their first night's campground.

Meleena considered her decision to take the short path. Her burning leg muscles and pounding chest told her it had been worth it. Then again, if not for Talla, maybe not.

The coastal jungle was different here, less lush and more scrubby. Probably a result of the salty wind. The vegetation gave way to a bare, rocky outcropping. A fire pit lay at the center of the clearing, and a large log hitching post stood on their right as they came up the trail through the scrub. The ocean view beyond the rocks was vast, breathtaking, under an orange sky. They had arrived just in time for sunset.

"Guess we found the campsite," said Meleena as they entered the clearing.

"Guess you should shut up and set up," said Talla.

She wasn't wrong. Meleena rolled her eyes.

Meleena undid the ropes on her tent and bedroll, releasing Peela's burden. Talla was having trouble getting Clover to stand still long enough to do the same. Each time she tried to untie something, he'd move a few steps away.

Meleena laughed. Now it was time for her to show off. She approached them with an octopus in her open palm and said, "You have to earn his trust. If you spoil him with treats, he may eventually let you ride him."

"What! Why didn't you say anything earlier?" Talla grumbled and fumbled with her daypack for more treats. Meleena took that as a thank-you.

The sky became a brilliant pink. Once their tents were set up, Meleena took a crack at starting a campfire before the darkness descended. With the help of some hand-picked fire snails, which she plucked from a tree and held over some dry brush, she had a sizable blaze. Talla stared, eyes wide.

Inside her tent, Meleena ran her fingers over the clay and shell journal cover, then wrote in it for the first time. She drew anything she could recall from the day: creatures, plants, seed pods. It wasn't long before a knot in her stomach urged her to look over the schedule and maps instead.

A scuttling sound caused Meleena to poke her head out from the tent, her eyes adjusting to the dim firelight, now the only light source.

"Hey there," came Deem's quiet voice and Pinchy's scuttling legs on the sand. Their long shadows grew behind the glow of the campfire. Meleena crawled out of her tent.

Deem undid a rope and Pinchy was unburdened. He patted and thanked his beast, who scuttled out of sight, followed by a splashing sound.

"Did he just jump into the ocean?" She looked over the cliff's edge. Waves lapped at the rocks below.

"He'll be back soon, he's just gone to get dinner," Deem said, waving a hand at the sea. He set out his bedroll a few feet from the fire and laid down, arms behind his head, elbows out.

"Don't you have a tent?" asked Meleena.

"No," said Deem. "My family didn't have enough savings for a tent. But it will be nice to sleep under the sky. I've actually never done it before." Deem gazed up, and Meleena took in the brilliance of the night's sky. She had never paid much attention to it before, but now it was no less than glorious, lights twinkling in the vastness.

The three of them sat together by the firelight.

Deem grinned timidly, making light conversation. "You know, I didn't grow up with any of this stuff. Like these glasses." Holding his glasses aloft, he rubbed his eyes. "How do you ever get used to them?"

He polished his glasses on his shirt, then took out his prized carapace from his pocket, and polished the scale as well.

"Most Meruyans need them on land." Talla sat up straight with her legs to the side.

Deem said, "Doesn't seem worth it, just to live on land."

Meleena said, "it's worth it to live on land, we have libraries, fire, better food! Comforts you can't argue with." She kept her knees out in front of her in an arch.

Deem shrugged. "I don't see what I'm missing. We have our wall carvings. Delicious food like oysters and sea urchin."

"We eat those on shore, just…you guys do the farming and picking."

"Exactly. That's what motivated me to join the Meruyan Council, better living standards for the underwater village without the compromise of living on land."

Talla squinted and raised an eyebrow. "Really?"

"Yeah," laughed Deem, missing Talla's insulting tone. "So, what motivated you two to be here?"

"That's easy," Talla answered first. "To be on the Council is to be the most successful and influential in society. I don't know why Meleena is here, though." Addressing Meleena and holding out a branch with bulbous brown mushrooms to roast on the fire, she said, "You never seemed interested in anything until now."

"That's not true. I've always wanted to help society somehow, just not in the normal way..." Meleena stammered. "I can't really explain it, but changing things through observing and learning from nature somehow. I thought going on this journey would help me get closer to that. But I never wanted to join the Council to get there."

"So why go on this journey then?" asked Deem. "If you don't want to join the Council?" He leaned forward, genuinely interested.

"I was dragged to a Council meeting, but I met a Warix there. Going on the journey was the only way I could think of for them to notice me, to help them fight the Warix who attacked Pontai'Desa. I want to use my natural observations to help their greater cause."

"Why do you spend so much time paying attention to these things? It doesn't matter," Deem asked.

Tall shrugged before answering.

"It does matter. It affects you, your being. Involving yourself in nature, to understand the connection—it can also prove very handy. It could even save your life one day."

Talla shrugged again and removed her stick from the fire.

"Like that grilled poison mushroom you're about to eat," said Meleena.

Talla lowered her food and gave it a full eye-bulging stare before saying matter-of-factly, "I know why you hate the Council." She set her dish aside. "When we were twelve, on our school field trip to the Pontai'Desa Council, her older brother Kelrick chaperoned our class. And then he ditched us when he saw a Council Elder who he could cozy up to for a recommendation."

Meleena brought her knees up to her face. "I'll never forget the embarrassment I felt when the whole class laughed at me. I wanted nothing to do with him or the Council from then on."

Talla shrugged. "I dunno, I thought it was courageous of him, got him in, didn't it?"

"He's just an oyster-brain." Meleena crossed her arms.

A splash startled her from the nearby ocean, and Pinchy returned, dripping wet and came to Deem's side, who patted him. Moonlight reflected off his smooth carapace. It dropped something into his hand from its pincher.

"Speaking of oysters, I'm starved! Does anyone want some seafood?" Deem gulped, steering them away another fight. He presented some shrimp handed over from Pinchy, and opened a bundle of wrapped leaves, placing them to bake in the fire. "I don't mind sharing! If I had arrived before dark, I could have set underwater traps or fished for more, since we head inland tomorrow. It was my mistake taking the long route at the fork earlier. I was scared and went for the safest route, but I assume you both went the low tide route? Looks like it was the right way to go."

"Yeah, but it was the risky route, I scrutinized at the sign for ages before deciding. Plus, we still had to cross a river," answered Meleena, holding her tongue about how difficult it had been.

Talla looked at them. "What? It wasn't that bad. I didn't bother with the sign. I just asked the farmer."

Deem looked dumfounded. Meleena blushed.

"Am I the only one who asked the Meruyan farmer for help?" Talla said in earnest.

Deem shook his head, and blushed, red coming into his blue cheeks. "He looked like he was sleeping, I didn't want to bother him...Guess I should learn to speak up."

Meleena looked into the campfire. She knew her pride had kept her from asking.

"Well, clearly, Meleena didn't either. She was stuck at the river when I showed up," said Talla. Meleena knew she was right. She munched her dinner quietly, embarrassed.

"I am impressed, Talla." Deem smiled. He got up and brought them each a leaf of fish, grilled on the campfire.

Meleena only gazed into the crackling fire, letting them watch the flames dance and flicker. She took a deep breath.

Talla said flatly, "Meleena is too proud to ask others for help because she is trying to prove she belongs, when she knows she doesn't."

"What! That is not—" Meleena started, but Deem interrupted them. Pinchy hissed from nearby in the darkness.

He whined, "Is it too much to expect this means a little peace for to-morrow?"

Meleena's face was hot with anger. She poked the campfire savagely with a stick.

"Meleena?" His big blue eyes glowed beside her, and he smiled, disarming her.

She sighed. "I've just always felt like I'm naturally unlikeable. I stopped asking for help a long time ago. Not like my older brother or Talla, they've always been naturally charming." She caught Talla's eye, who nodded in agreement and it stung.

"You oyster-brain, just because I don't want to marry your brother!" Meleena ground her teeth.

"I wouldn't let you near him, sea monster!"

Talla jumped to her feet. So did Meleena.

"So, if you don't mind me asking, why do you two hate each other?" Deem stood and held his arms out between them.

"She's been teasing me in school since I can remember." Meleena stomped off into the dark. "I'm going to bed."

She went to her tent and tried to sleep. She'd had enough of trying to bond with these two. But sleep would not soothe her. She tossed and turned all night, plagued by dreams of being sent home. Professor Levlos, appearing from the bush and saying there has been a mistake, you never qualified, you must come with me, now! Next moment her brother was throwing a fishmonger apron and tongs at her. You work for me now! Joru came into the shop, planting a kiss on her cheek. I'm so glad to be your fiancé.

She struggled until the light of dawn filled the walls of her tent, when she woke up with an iron taste in her mouth, finding her bottom lip sore, chewed during the night.

The slow ambient sound of whistling breath signaled that the others were still asleep. The sweet scent of wildflowers drifted in, as if beckoning her. Though certainly not refreshed from her first night outdoors, she leaped up to begin packing, charged and ready to head back into the wilderness.

CHAPTER TEN

Flax's first day working in Borak's engineering shop was almost finished.

"I have hours of orders to fill. Sometimes I'm in there til midnight...Plus if there is a spare moment, there are my own projects..." proclaimed Borak. Then, glancing at Flax's deflated expression, added, "But...seeing as it's yer first day and all, and we've not yet agreed officially on terms, I'll let yer off at shop's close today. We'll start on workshop lessons from tomorrow. Now let me give ye' a tour o' the workshop."

He turned to the door marked *Tinkering Lab: Engineers Only* behind the counter.

Flax followed Borak into the back room. Borak pressed his palm on a pipe by the entrance, which blew energy into its mechanism to start up the generator, which turned on the lights.

In terms of gadgetry, what the front room had in quantity and organization, the back room doubled in the first and lacked in the second. The floor was littered with rods and spanners, wrenches and screwdrivers. The shelves that filled most of the room were more like huge trays full of everything thrown together. A tool wall came complete with welding gear and a fireproof suit.

Chains and conveyor belts full of half-finished projects hung from the high ceiling as copper turbines and tubes circulated in wind. In a corner, something large and mechanical lay under a grey blanket. An immense workbench was just as messy with half-done projects and piles of tiny parts, with a small spot here or there left for actual workspace.

In the back of the room, a huge fan with propellers through a grate awaited a Warix's wind energy. Borak blasted it with one arm, sending its blades spinning and bathing them in a fresh breeze.

Borak crossed the floor toward his workbench, kicking tools and metal out of the way with a loud clanking. Flax followed close, desperate not to knock anything out of place. A crate stood by the workbench. Flax peered inside—it was full of copper-plated gauntlets.

"Hey, Borak, why do you have so many gauntlets in here?"

"Mind yer own and listen here."

With a painful screeching sound, Borak pulled two stools from under the desk and motioned Flax to sit with him. He scooped a half-made device from the workbench and held it up for Flax.

"A series of pipes is at the base of all our devices. Wind power from a Warix, when blown through copper piping, will come out more focused on the other end. The finer the craftsman, the tighter he makes the coiling. That increases surface area to improve wind energy. Bronze also works, but it's a weaker conductor than copper. You can feel the difference when testing out gadgets."

Flax admired a loose copper tube cluster on the table. It was like a snail shell, or small leaves, spiraling with intricate designs. "You craft so beautifully. Intricate, like I've never seen. You're an artist."

Borak shrugged. "I s'pose so. A good craftsman must be creative. Experiment. Create new shapes. But let me explain. It's the wind blowing through turbines that's stored in a generator. Then the energy is converted to electricity to power a house. For bikes or airships, they are simpler, directly using wind power without the use of a stored generator. These are the basics of Warix technology."

Borak reached out and grabbed a screwdriver from a rack of overhead tools. With care and attention, he twisted the copper gears with the pliers. It was amazing to watch a man of such bulk working with such tiny, delicate parts. He placed a shell over the parts, screwed it tightly over the contraption, and held up a finished device.

"A gadget to dry hair. For the ladies." He bowed. "This is the kind of thing I work on back here for a customer. Soon enough you will learn how to make and repair simple things like this. But one thing at a time…"

He set down the hairdryer and screwdriver and turned to Flax. "Now that you've seen what it's all about—let's talk scope of the job. If you accept the apprenticeship, ye' will be paid ten silver coins a day, get half an hour for lunch break every day, and sleep in a spare room in my flat upstairs. Most nights we will work until late in the tinkering lab, fillin' the day's orders. I will teach ye' everything I can during these sessions. One day off a week. We may call it early some nights. I ain't aiming to work you to the bone here. It's important teh get enough sleep for a job like this. Does all that sound okay to ye?"

He had no idea. Working for Borak would only be one small part. Where would he even find the time to scout and transmit to headquarters?

"Yes, sir. I accept your terms," said Flax, though he had less choice in the matter than Borak even knew—nor could he quit the apprenticeship if things got hard.

They shook hands, making direct eye contact.

That afternoon, Flax observed Borak in the workshop and the store until closing time. At seven, Borak said, "I think that's enough fer today. As promised, I don't want teh overwhelm ya' on yer first day. Better you turn in early and start fresh." He yawned wide. "I'll show yer to the flat, and you can get settled in for tonight."

Not busy? I still have to find time to send a transmission. His eyes were already beginning to droop. *And I still have to retrieve my motorbike.* He picked up his pack from under the counter and followed Borak outside to a narrow doorway beside the shop, where Borak unlocked the door and led him down a dark hallway.

"Borak, do you have a place I can keep a motorbike, by the way?" he asked as they ascended a creaky wooden staircase at the end of the hallway.

"Ye' can keep it in my tinkering lab, if ye' don't mind me taking it apart and showin' ye' how it works." He winked. They had arrived at a door on the second floor. Borak stopped to unlock it and bowed for Flax to enter first.

Borak powered the light switch as he stepped into the flat, illuminating wooden floors and a modest living room, as sparsely decorated as the shop was full. It contained only an area rug between two leather chairs, facing a stone fireplace. A desk by the window faced Fleeg Street.

"I like to relax here, come up with new ideas by the fire, en all that. Without the sensory overload of the workshop," Borak said.

Borak's palm blew on the lights as he showed Flax a kitchenette, "Breky oats and lunch sandwiches there—" the bathroom, "—shower and toilet there," and two small bedrooms each containing a simple bed, desk, and window.

"Took me some time to clean out the second bedroom, what with the extra crap I kept in here—what's left is down in my workshop or in the garbage bins. I didn't know when exactly the apprentice job would be filled. Well, sleep tight, we start bright and early tomorrow. I'll be down in my workshop if ye' need anything."

Flax nodded as Borak closed the door, leaving him to the silence. He set his pack down on the bed and waited, listening to the chirping insects outside the window. Then he said in a normal tone, "Hey, Borak..." Then a bit louder, "Hey, Borak?" How much noise could he get away with?

The floor creaked, and Borak opened the door. "Ye?"

"Never mind...good night."

"Good night."

Well, that proved it. There was no chance of sending transmissions to Sen'Prin from this room.

He heard Borak's footsteps and the door to the flat close and knew that although Borak would be in the workshop soon, Flax needed to find a more secluded place to send back messages.

He stuck his head out the window and peered into an unlit alley below. He stepped onto the windowsill. Stabilizing himself on a copper utility pipe, he hoisted himself onto the sloping roof. The stone tiles clacked under his feet as he found a comfortable, secluded position to crouch with his wristcom.

He rolled up his left sleeve and spoke into his wristcom. "Agent forty-three, Flax, reporting from inside Sen'Drorn City. All went as planned, I was taken in as engineering apprentice, and am reporting from the roof." He sent the transmission, not expecting a reply right away, but seconds later, an incoming voice call. Flax switched the device to live feed, and a familiar voice shocked him on the other end.

"Sup, buddy!"

"Thian?!"

"Yup! I got reassigned just after you left transmission range! Arenay wanted to keep our little team together, so I spent my day training our replacements."

"In one afternoon?"

"Yeah—I said, 'follow the Hyish, take notes, don't get caught.' Then I hightailed it back to HQ. Couldn't get me out of that desert fast enough."

The two laughed.

"But how are you in signal range?" asked Flax.

"Turns out Sen'Prin and Sen'Drorn aren't that far from each other—not like the distances we traveled with the Hyish...Sand dunes blocking signals...Anyways, how's life in the enemy capital?"

"I was surprised, they live pretty lavishly, better than we do in Sen'Prin City, that's for sure." Flax relayed everything that happened that day, especially the wondrous details of the city which he knew would make his friend jealous. "But something was amiss. I saw things that made me uncomfortable...I saw kelpies hanging at the butcher's shop. Didn't we see those as pets in the Meruyan capital?"

"Their lavish lifestyle comes at a grim price, my friend. That's why you're a spy, don't forget it," Thian replied.

"Don't worry. I wouldn't say I can ever feel too comfortable here."

Soon an hour had passed, and Flax looked up at the starry night and decided it was time to go. They made plans, though the exact hours could not be set, for Flax to send transmissions from the rooftop each night. If Thian was standing by at that time, they could speak live. Otherwise, it would send a recording.

Late that night, Flax turned off his wristcom and peered over the roof into the alley below. No lights. He yawned but was determined to go find his motorbike before climbing into bed. He clambered back through his window, where Borak's snores met him through the thin walls. He tiptoed into the fireplace room and soon breathed the fresh air outside. Map in hand, he strolled the lonely, lamp-lit streets and took the opportunity to clear his head of all he had just witnessed. Was it really this morning, he had woken up in a hooded robe, spitting sand from his mouth, hundreds of miles away?

He crossed under a stone bridge and thought about how long it had been since he saw his mother, Odella. She had raised him alone back in Sen'Prin City. A woman who had fled this very city before his birth. Who gave up everything for what she believed in. And what was that exactly? A choice to no longer live as passive oppressors?

The echo of giggling children up ahead interrupted his thoughts. Flax came to a small courtyard where they played, chasing each other in the lamplight. A mother watched from a window and called for bedtime. What happened back then, between his mother and father, when she decided to leave here during the Great Split? What kind of man was his father that he wouldn't go with her? He must have known she was carrying his child. Or did she keep that from him intentionally? Maybe she didn't know, either. Maybe she would have chosen to stay, and he, Flax, would have been raised here in Sen'Drorn City, just like another one of these happy children. With an intact family. Was it even worth it to leave?

Not that growing up in Sen'Prin City was so bad, I guess. It was just a boring place, with enough resources to live modestly. He just couldn't help wondering what kind of man would stay, knowing the contention of the times. Meruyan oppression had just become public knowledge and gaining traction as an unacceptable source of Warix prosperity. From what he understood, the Sen'Drorn still used it to this day. Its current citizens, those who stayed back, therefore, must have been okay with that fact.

Though the people here didn't seem as terrible as he had always been taught, he had to find out more about them.

As he touched the black volcanic stone of the buildings, a thought came to him. Although this empire, which he now dwelt in, was always his enemy, it was harder to imagine from inside the walls. *Sen'Drorn itself seems like such a mild, peaceful place.*

He came upon the alley with his bike parked as he left it. He suspected a prosperous city like this hasn't got a lot of crime. Although, as he wandered, he came upon more Meruyan, picking trash from the streets and pushing brooms. He nodded in greeting, but they refused to meet his gaze. Were they compensated, and where did they live?

It took another hour to walk his bike home, not trusting to drive it in the dark, narrow streets, but eventually made it back to Fleeg Street in time to settle into an exhausted sleep. His first in the capital.

He found himself back in the desert, running free on a tornado cloud, until a Hyish Netic rider bearing a long spear came out of nowhere, swung at him, and launched him frantically headlong into a heavy face full of sand. A knocking sound penetrated his dreams, startling him awake. He opened his eyes to the unfamiliarity of his new room. His tongue tasted his mouth, relieved to discover it was not really full of sand.

He rolled over. The wristcom read seven thirty sharp.

Borak's voice called to him to get up. Flax stumbled into the only bathroom and had time for a rinse as Borak prepared hot oats at the kitchenette. Flax put on a fresh shirt, slacks, and workbooks, ate his oats, and took a wrapped sandwich from Borak. Then the pair thudded down the wooden steps and out onto the quiet morning streets. Flax took in the fresh air, the scent of baked goods, and caught a glimpse of some other shops beginning to open. Borak unlocked his own, and they stepped inside the rickety door.

For the morning shift, Borak started Flax on the basics—at first, only observing. Flax came to learn names of tools and parts, and their location around the shop, gradually moving on to doing simple tasks like writing down orders, or fetching parts, or stocking the aisles. He learned that the copper and bronze were kept behind the counter, in locked cabinets. They were still the most valuable thing in the shop, even with the active Meruyan mining it for Sen'Drorn.

At two, they closed, and Flax had his first workshop lesson.

"I do my best to fill morning orders for the next two hours, and anything I can't do is pushed off until after closing time, from seven until I'm too tired to keep going," Borak explained.

Flax stood by, watching Borak get to work on a stack of orders, slips of paper he brought in from the store counter. Borak seemed to know every inch of this crowded, yet glorious, mysterious place. When he needed a part, Flax watched as Borak plunged a hand into a shelf tray. His hand churned, and his finger emerged with the part he wanted.

"How did you do that?" asked Flax in amazement.

"I know this place well. It's mentally organized." He tapped his own skull. "I know what yer thinkin', how do I keep the front of the shop so neat?"

Flax smirked. Yes, that was going to be his next question.

"When I get shipments in from the blacksmith, I know where they go in the store, always put'n 'em in the same place. That'll be your job now."

"I don't know how I'll ever learn this...But maybe I can try to organize this room for you sometime?"

"Ah, ain't worth the bother."

"So, what's under the sheet?" Flax eyed the large sheet-covered thing in the corner of the room.

Borak's eyebrows parted from low on his forehead. "I'm workin' on a personal project—trying to invent something that never existed before—a flyin' machine."

"But why would we need that if we can use wind energy to fly in a tornado?"

"Ah, come on. First, not every Warix can do that. Second, it'd be much quieter, low key, and energy-efficient than all the messy hubbub it takes to fly in a tornado." He shot Flax a serious look and wagged a finger. "Don't tell anyone 'bout it though. It's not even close teh functional."

They continued working, Borak showing Flax how to fix basic objects. From a desk, Borak pulled out several pairs of gloves and fitted them to Flax. "Go ahead, test them out on that sandbag over there."

Flax approached the sandbag, swinging from a steel chain hooked to the ceiling of the workroom. Flax focused on his senses. Through his horns, he sensed the direction and strength of wind, filtering into the room from the outdoors through the pipes and rotating copper turbines. He focused, concentrated on absorbing, pooling, pulling it from where it entered into the core of his being.

It filled him like a whirlpool, the intensity growing until he released it by launching the directed energy up into his right hand, the limb coursing with it and through the gloved hand, where it whirled and reacted with the copper conch shells, finally released into the world again as a directed beam. It hit the sandbag like a fist, slamming it back with a bang that sent it spinning on its axis.

Then he tried with the glove he had crafted. The designs on it of copper nodes and spiraling conches were crude and were nothing near the level of intricacy of Borak's work. Flax bent his knees, prepared his posture. He gathered the wind, sending a pulse of energy through his right arm through the glove's conductive mechanisms. The bag barely stumbled.

Borak said, "It's okay. Your first creation. But er…We'll have to melt yours down and start again, though."

By the end of two hours, Borak had completed morning orders—including several pairs of men's wind-enhancing jump-boots. Though Flax was tired, the shop would reopen soon for the late shift.

At seven in the evening, they closed the shop and continued for the night workshop shift, not finishing until past ten, when Borak excused Flax and remained in the shop himself. Flax didn't know how long exactly, as he dragged himself up to his room and conked out in his work clothes. He awoke in a groggy state some hours later to the sound of Borak's door closing through the walls. Flax struggled out of his work clothes and dug himself under the blankets. No report to Sen'Prin would be given tonight.

He yawned all through the next morning. It stumped him how Borak had the stamina for all this every day.

On his third night, Flax tried harder to send a message out to Sen'Prin—lest they panic he had been exposed as a spy already. He let Thian know all was okay, of his exhaustion, and that he would send updates when he could—if he had something worthwhile. There was no energy to socialize, but Thian being Thian, that was unavoidable. On the fourth night, Flax shouted in frustration when Thian kept him on the line just to chat.

The routine continued through his first week. Borak's promise of '*not working him to the bone*' was, so far, not going as intended. Falling asleep at the counter halfway through the week, Borak slapped him awake with a hand on Flax's shoulder and said, "I know yer tired, it's hard learnin' new things every day, getting into the routine."

The sympathy was well-intended anyway.

The woman known as Yulah came back to the shop two more times before the week was out, a lovely consolation-prize—or it would have been, except she was so quick, and Flax had barely spoken to her. Her elegance lingered on his mind: her flashing eyes, her hair, her laugh, lavender perfume, and long, tanned limbs, swinging together in that gait.

A cat in the alleyway startled, knocking over some trash cans, and Flax nearly fell off the roof.

His respite came finally, on his day off, which he slept through entirely, but proved necessary for the weeks to come.

At the start of his first week, Borak was comfortable letting Flax, under supervision, work the customer line. Flax brightened up as Yulah came in and approached him at the desk. Digging below the deck, he found the box marked for her. It rattled in his hand. It could only be the boots and gloves, about two dozen, that Borak had made last week.

"Why is it you come in here to get orders so often?" asked Flax.

"It's for my job." She winked at him, in a *never you mind* kind of expression.

"You are…really beautiful," Flax blurted out. He handed over the box.

"Thanks, but you're too young for me." She flicked her silky hair to turn and go.

"I didn't ask you out!" he defended, blushing.

The next time she came, two days later, he thought of a better plan. "I'm new to the city. Maybe you could show me around some time?"

It was met with another half-smile, wink, but a rejection nonetheless. He was about to hand over the box when a loud snap cracked. Something smashed behind Flax. He had been about to reach under the desk when he caught sight of a shelf full of glass that fell from the wall and smashed into the ground. One shard flew off and lodged itself in the tip of his horn, breaking it off.

"Oh, fidget!"

"Flax! What have ye done!" Borak rushed out from the backroom to find the floor covered in glass. "Get a broom!" Flax hopped the desk, racing with a broom to the aisle he had, clearly improperly, stocked the hour before.

The other customers stood around, staring. Yulah's eyes fixed on Flax to see what he would do next.

Borak joined Flax at the wreck. "Damnit, boy! This is going to cost a wallop to replace!"

Flax felt his broken horn and winced. It would throw his wind energy askew for days before they grew back, but it didn't matter. He'd be too busy to notice the time flying by. Yulah cleared her throat, and he snapped back. She took her box from Flax, and he was barely aware of her exit as he got to work cleaning up the mess.

Another busy day.

More busy days went by. More responsibilities. More transmissions to headquarters from the rooftop.

At the end of his second week, they were closing up when Borak said, "Flax, note for ye."

Flax was puzzled. He didn't know anybody in the city. He opened a quartered parchment to find a short message scribbled:

"I admire the way you handled that accident with Borak the other day. You treated him with such respect even when he yelled at you. I know he can be rough sometimes. I feel partly responsible, as I am the one who insisted to commission him an apprentice. How about I take you for a little

tour of the city? Meet at Quail Egg Cafe on Fleeg Street, midday break, tomorrow. -Yulah"

CHAPTER ELEVEN

Meleena climbed out of her tent as the sun rose on the campground. Deem was up by then, rolling his bedding and strapping it to Pinchy. Meleena had breakfast from a satchel—bread and fruit—before Talla finally emerged.

The three of them secured the rest of the baggage to their respective animals in silence. Then they started down the trail, Talla and Clover first, Meleena and Peela next, Deem and Pinchy at the rear. This time, they would try walking together.

As they headed into the jungle, Meleena and Talla were already bickering about who could tie a better pack. Deem interrupted, "If we're going to walk together, maybe just don't talk to each other. I just want to get to the next town in peace. Take my ma's advice—when any o' my sisters are 'bout to start fightin'—she says, 'When you feel an urge to speak to one another, just swallow that breath back into your chest.'"

The frustration only refocused towards Deem. *How dare he think he's better at this than us*, thought Meleena. And after such a nice night bonding by the campfire. Despite the pleasant sounds of chirping birds and insects around them, they kept up a tense silence all morning.

The next couple of days played out in a similar routine. They were hiking all day, taking short breaks, and camping in the map's designated clearings, which they arrived at just by sunset each night. All three tended to avoid speaking to each other most of the time. Talla and Meleena would bicker if any conversation lasted longer than a dozen paces, and Deem was too shy to speak about much at all. Meleena and Talla took turns in the lead, Deem always bringing up the rear, watching the landscape intently. Colorful birds squawked overhead, a passing bust of pastels over the thick canopy. Has anyone ever cataloged the species that live here? She did so in her journal each time they stopped to camp.

The trail took them inland and always slightly uphill. By the fourth day, the seaside jungle finally fell away. The types of trees changed, thinned, giving rise to muggy grasslands. Meleena could feel the wet air was noticeably thinner. Her breaths became strained. They had reached a considerable altitude. A mist rolled over the plains, disrupting visibility in the early morning.

From the top of a hill, surrounded by yellow grass as high as their knees, they could see they were heading towards a distant valley, flanked by the outline of green hills partially obscured in the mist.

"Those must be the Northern Villages," said Deem, finally breaking the silence as he checked his map. "In that valley ahead!"

"Then, it's just through these grasslands," Meleena said.

"It must be close to lunch now." Talla threw her seaweed-green hair back. Meleena and Deem agreed they weren't ready to stop yet. "Well, we should eat it before we arrive at the villages, they will have food and re-stock of provisions. Man, I can't wait to be back in civilization."

They spoke of food and village, and lost track of the path, as it grew thinner and thinner, when Meleena looked up and noticed it had ceased to exist. The grass was up to their waists, unmaintained and overgrown. The weather didn't help them find it. The fog was still heavy as the sky darkened.

A storm was coming. Visibility beyond the tall yellow grass was limited so they could only see trees: fat, eerie trees with broad branches, but no leaves.

It was eerily silent here compared to the jungle, with no clear path ahead.

"Have we gone the wrong way?" Meleena asked. Mobility had become difficult. She scanned the yellow grass for any indication of where to go next: sameness in every direction. A vague sound, like munching, echoed as if the pastures were close.

Their footsteps crunched over dry, flattened grass, which was much shorter among the trees than in the open field. Areas were flattened before she even passed through: a good sign that people used this path.

Peela let out a nervous squeal. "Hush now," whispered Meleena, patting Peela on her long neck. She took out her compass to make sure they were still bearing northeast.

As they walked on, only the sound of their footsteps could be heard in the spiny thicket. Though the air was tranquil, the munching over silence was eerie.

The barrel-trunked trees were all around, with sickly grey bark and a thick jumble of leafless branches on top. Unlike an orchard, they weren't planted in clear rows.

"Is this even an orchard?" Meleena frowned. "Also letting them die like this…"

She stopped to inspect a ball of brownish material scattered around the orchard floor. "It must be the rotten fruit from the trees. Such a pity, so much left unharvested. I wonder what happened here…" When the sound of her footsteps ceased, the sound of distant grazing grew louder. Her heart skipped a beat in excitement. "The villages must be just beyond this dead orchard!"

They crunched among the barren trees.

Meleena reassured, "It must be just around the corner, just a few more feet forward, could be the village."

They kept on for a time, but there was no end to the sparse trees.

Deem cried out, "Ouch! My foot!" He pulled up a wooden plank almost invisible among the grasses. "It's a signpost."

"Ugh…another sign," groaned Talla.

Meleena let out a disgruntled sound of agreement.

Deem read aloud, even as the girls continued on. "The Quiet Forest. BEWARE: No sudden or loud noises. Do not carve or use cutting tools on the trees. No open food in the forest: Wild animals present. Trees have been known to shift."

Meleena could only offer up a shrug.

"That's not all," Deem said. "At the place I tripped, there was also a fence hidden among the grasses, but it was knocked down, totally decrepit."

Talla frowned. "So? Maybe there were farmers once who took it down."

"That might mean we are close to the villages," reasoned Meleena.

"No. More like it was trampled," answered Deem gravely.

"'Trees have been known to shift.' What does that even mean?" asked Talla.

Deem held up his hand. "Shhh, keep it down. Do you guys hear that?" he breathed.

Meleena stopped, slowing Peela, and listened hard for the grazing sound again. She could only hear it when standing perfectly still. It didn't sound any closer than before.

Deem breathed, "Maybe we are going the wrong direction...?"

They all looked around.

"Which way did we come from?" Meleena asked.

Talla folded her arms. "You jellyfish are so bad at directions!"

Deem tapped his compass. "Is this working?"

Meleena's chest constricted. Something was wrong. The distant hills were no longer visible in the dense grove. Just trees on all sides. Were they even still in the valley?

"Our scrolls say to go northeast after the jungle, and follow any Meruyan signs," Meleena offered, holding up her map.

Deem was frozen, listening for something. He placed a hand on the tree bark, rubbed the branch, and crouched low to inspect the exposed roots of the tree, then the rotten fruit.

"Okay, we don't have time for this," Talla declared, leading Clover by his reins and intending to march on without them. She nervously chewed the end of her pearl necklace, as if leading away herself as well.

Meleena sighed and continued walking close behind her alongside Peela.

Talla smirked at Meleena. "What? You really think the trees are shifting?"

Meleena said nothing. Something moved a few paces in front of them. A small creature swung between the exposed branches.

"Vangrots!" Meleena pointed. She'd previously sketched them in the forests outside Pontai'Desa.

It had large eyes, a face of whiskers, and a big grinning mouth full of sharp, tiny teeth. Deep green moss fur covered its delicate body, glider wings on the arms, and striped reptilian scales in patches. It gripped the trees with all four limbs and tail.

Deem whispered from behind, fear in his voice, "We really should stay close."

Despite this, Deem and Pinchy fell his several usual paces behind as they trudged on stepping through the thickening grass, now up past their shoulder. It was too dense to see more than a few steps ahead. Meleena lost track of Talla, just ahead of her.

Or at least she assumed Talla was just ahead until the sound of her footsteps vanished. The air stung with the bitterness of rotten plant matter.

"Talla?"

Her heart thudded.

"Where are you? Say something, so I know you are still ahead of me…"

Only distant munching.

"This isn't the time to ignore me…"

Meleena jumped as a vangrot popped out and landed on the ground in front of her. It grabbed a rotten fruit from the ground, stuffed the ball into its mouth, and launched out of sight in a flash.

Meleena picked one up and was struck by the odor of fouled grass.

"What…" She couldn't place the familiarity.

Deem's voice from behind startled her. "It's not fruit, it's dropp—" He was cut off by a bloodcurdling scream erupting among the trees.

Meleena spun around.

"Talla?" screamed Meleena, then corrected in a panicked whisper. "Talla?"

Again no answer.

Meleena took a few steps forward, lost among the trees. She spun around. Deem was nowhere to be seen. Just trees, obscured by mist.

She tightened her grasp on Peela's reins.

A sudden swoosh hit her in the back, and she was knocked to her hands and knees. The brown pellet had been snatched from her hand.

Peela cried out in panic. Meleena rolled the ground to see her overrun with vangrots, climbing all over her scaly body, pulling at her seaweed mane and pulling loose her saddlebags with their tiny hands.

Talla's voice echoed from an unknown direction, "My food! You mongrels!"

Chattering and shrieks of vangrots filled in the silence.

The ground trembled.

Meleena thrust to her feet and tried to shoo the animals off Peela, but they continued to grab and rummage, clattering defensively in response. Peela thrashed, bucked and roared in terror, which launched the vangrots into a screaming frenzy. Their claws caught as they struggled to hold on.

Meleena grabbed one with both hands and threw it off, but it came back with a vengeance and bit her on the hand, causing her to yelp out too. The orchard had become ablaze with a ruckus from several species fighting each other in an angry uproar.

Food was spilling everywhere—things being torn, tattered, and tossed left and right.

Then the floor itself seemed to shake. The branches of the trees rustled as if a heavy wind was passing through, but Meleena felt no such thing. If she was maintaining any calm up to this point, it was now shattered. She wildly looked around for the source of the rumbling, but there was nothing to lock her eyes onto. Short of breath, and in a dizzy confusion, she lost her balance. As she swayed, she saw the trees begin to rearrange themselves. Was it her imagination?

She spotted Peela's distant form: it was disappearing into the fog between the trees. Meleena clutched a tree for support, but it shuffled as she reached, dislodging her grip, or perhaps she was just dizzy? She nearly fell to the ground again, trying to hold onto something.

She bounced and staggered from tree to tree, hopelessly chasing after Peela's now distant calls. The vangrots and their horrid screeching continued assaulting her ears. She reached into her pockets for the compass, only to find them empty. Everything had been snatched—those lousy vangrots.

She stared at the ground. The trees must be gliding around on those shallow roots. The only way to avoid being trampled would be to grasp onto one of them, tight. To climb. She sprang toward the branches of one, latching on as it carried her away, goring her as she struggled her way to a stable spot at the top.

Meleena screamed from the branches, "Help! Deem? Talla?!"

The tree thrashed. It seemed to be…galloping.

Trying not to fall, swaying this way and that, she could see the jumble of other trees were, in fact, running around every which way, stumbling past each other in chaos in no particular direction.

Her tree was bumped around, trunk slamming into others, some defending with their branches, as Meleena fought to stay on with all her strength and burning muscles.

Her stomach twisted itself into knots. Peela, her supplies, and the new journal—all gone. How was she ever going to find them? Or Deem and Talla for that matter. She could see one tree over the tops of the others, with larger, fuller branches, impressive and sturdy.

If only she could get to that one.

Then something colorful caught her eye, distracting the thought. It looked like a scarf, caught on one of the branches of a passing tree. She didn't recognize it as one of their own scattered possessions. Her predicament sank in. It must have belonged to someone else, now lost to this place.

She was alone, with nothing, and probably going to be crushed to death in a mess of frantic stampeding trees. The vangrots bounced between branches, and their horrid screeching continued.

But now was not the time to fall to pieces! She reached out and snatched the scarf, curling it around her neck for safekeeping, then searched the thick, brambly canopy for anything blue, be it Meruyan or kelpie…

There, in the near distance, something blue was moving away.

"Peela!" she shouted in frustration, as if seeking sympathy from the trees. "Great!" she screamed to them. "There goes my father's beloved pet, and all my stuff!"

The tree trunk only shifted beneath her, forcing her to cling on tighter. It bent gradually to the side, creaking hideously from the tension. Like a catapult, it slung back; Meleena greeted a view of the roots, bulbous and churning like a mass of...hoofs?

The tree released the tension in an attempt to fling her away. In the commotion, she completely lost all sense of direction, but landed on another tree and clung for dear life.

The tree rampaged, but the lot of them seemed more aligned now, no longer crashing into each other, gaining a sense of order...more like a herd...fleeing. And Meleena understood. Two tiny leaflike structures at the base of their branches: ears! These were related in some distant way to the family of deer-tree creatures she had sketched before. Unfamiliar, and much more tree than deer. She closed her eyes to focus. At least she could think with them galloping in a single direction.

"Meleena! Jump!"

Meleena opened her eyes...among the trees was a creature highly unusual...A lobster?

Pinchy! Running alongside her tree, dodging lashes from the deer-trees as the forest ran alongside them. *So disoriented. Got to focus. Moving too fast for sun surrender.*

"Jump onto Pinchy's back!" shouted the voice of Deem, though she could not see him.

Did these deer-trees have eyes? They must be grazing from mouths under their hoof-roots...But...Stop—not the time to think the deer-tree kinship now. Her vision replaced with spinning again. The tree had bucked and flung her headlong from its branches.

She propelled towards the ground again, glasses flung off her face, and cracked under the endless stamping hooves as she shot her arms out and braced for pain. But then something jerked her back by her hair before impact with the ground.

The world was upside down, still moving. She scrunched up to see her body pulled into the embrace of two large pincers. Pinchy! Around the periphery, a sea of bounding root-hooves on all sides. And there, between a blur of scampering needle legs, was Deem, hanging onto the underbelly of the charging rock lobster, his hands and feet between plates of armor as if tucked into pockets.

Getting clobbered a few more times by roots and branches, Pinchy finally escaped the mess. Meleena saw stars. She lay on her side for a moment, just as the fall had left her, breathing heavily and trying to gain back her composure. Some cathartic curses later, she sat up with some difficulty, feeling very bruised, with arms worn out from clinging for her life.

Meleena and Deem rolled safely onto the floor in a patch of soft grass, Meleena trembling all around, gasping to pull the scarf tangled around her neck off her windpipe. She rolled to see Talla's unconscious body flopped onto the floor, delivered from the back of Pinchy's huge claws.

Deem gasped for air, then he finally said, "What do we do about Talla? She's out cold."

"She looks bad." Though Meleena couldn't really inspect her, with her own vision blurry.

A deep, sinking feeling flooded in. Her eyes welled up with tears. She failed to fight back. "Peela...I lost her. And my journal."

"I didn't see Clover anywhere either. Sorry...I could only do my best to save you two, and I lost track of the kelpies," Deem murmured, rubbing his arm and humbly ignoring his act of heroism.

Meleena fought to catch her breath. "No, it's okay...I think you saved all our lives..."

"Just glad to help." He smiled. "Look!"

She looked up. They lay on the edge of a narrow valley, leading to villages in the distance. The wide space in the valley, inhabited by the deer-trees, had tightened into a natural corridor, flanked by dense green hills covered in blossoming orchards. Meleena could tell through the blur. The cusp of the Northern Villages.

"Well, we better get her some medical attention." Meleena smiled as her body shot with pain, now overshadowed by hope.

CHAPTER TWELVE

As the days went by in Sen'Drorn City, Flax discovered the work in Borak's shop to be much harder than his previous assignment with the Hyish. The quality of his reports to Sen'Prin relied on the quantity of his learning. He learned as much as possible about the trade of engineering, and when he had extra time, about the daily lives of the civilians of Sen'Drorn.

The Quail Egg Cafe stood at the center of the bustle, exactly halfway down Fleeg Street, between a hair salon and a grocer. Charming tables and chairs sat on the street, perfect for those with leisure time to watch the passersby, sipping a tea or coffee. Flax was not a person with leisure time, but this meeting with Yulah was providing a valuable window to observe the everyday lives of the people of Sen'Drorn.

At least that's what Flax should have done, observe the passersby— but instead he focused solely on Yulah's violet, almond-shaped eyes. They drank tea and shared a plate of finger sandwiches, and basked in the scent of exotic fruit and tea. All this was exactly the sort of leisurely lifestyle Flax had never experienced in Sen'Prin City, as it didn't exist there.

Flax sat on the edge of his seat, leaning close to the table. His right hand patted his knee under the table to squelch his nervous energy.

"So, what do you do at your job?" he asked, thinking about how often she came to collect engineering supplies from Borak's shop. "You said in your note you are responsible for my position here?"

"Oh, it's nothing special. I just run errands," said Yulah. "I collect boxes from Borak, so I've seen Borak working hard there without any help for years. I put in a good word for him."

"With…wait, who is your boss?"

She said nothing, only shifted her gaze to her finger on her teacup.

Flax knew the paperwork that got him into his position came from the Council of Emperor Ryogrim, so whatever she or her boss did, they were *very* connected. Perhaps she could provide him with useful information for his nightly reports to Sen'Prin, although he sheepishly realized his primary motivation was for her to like him, and wanted to spend more time with *her*.

"So, what was it like growing up in the country?" asked Yulah, her eyes sparkling.

Flax gulped. How had he only now realized how hard it would be trying to date here? If this even was a date. He chose words carefully, not to say the wrong thing—to ruin both his hopes with this woman, and his position as a spy. He started off his "past in Vendengire" on a safe, factual note. About the chickens, the farm, the old purple house. He did his best to come off as shy, to avoid details where he could. Painfully, he had to describe the part about his two parents and big country family.

Of course, he had none of those. Of course, he couldn't talk about his life in Sen'Prin City, a small city, with a single mother and no siblings.

He directed the conversation to something true he could speak to—the contrast of Sen'Drorn to his previous life. It was genuine, to act in awe of this city, which he really knew nothing about.

In a slow, deliberate act, he finally turned, gaped up at the ornate buildings and at the busy Warix people. They seemed so happy and carefree. So much wealth here—so much copper and bronze jewelry. Back home, there was not so much material to flaunt. The bronze went to city piping, and copper to military gadget tech.

Yulah smiled at him. The ignorant country-boy act was coming off as charming.

He still had to avoid seeming totally unaware of the life and way of the Sen'Drorn nation, as he was playing someone who had grown up with its benefits, just outside the city life.

"We have it good, living in the best civilization that ever existed. Prosperous, with fresh food, clothing, everything," said Flax.

They had almost gotten through the whole lunch hour without getting into any talk of governments, when a server came by to take their dishes, and Yulah set three silver coins on the table as payment.

"*Nushenyu's blessings!* It's my treat!" she said, winking. "Better than to let a new apprentice pay."

Perhaps this was not a date after all. He still wanted her to like him, and to see her socially again.

Keeping up with the country-boy act, Flax reached over and held up a coin. It bore the face of Emperor Ryogrim, a Warix man with a grim scowl. Ryogrim, keeper of cruel policy, this warlord whose army beats and Meruyan exploits abroad, and locally too, apparently. Yet such a treacherous government was almost undetectable here, the impending war outside almost unbelievable, aside from small reminders that were only glaringly obvious to an outsider like Flax. Like the exotic fruit on his plate, cultivated from Meruyan farms and the consumption of Meruyan kelpies and other pets. The peace that existed here was only possible *because* of the exploitation of others.

Flax had, since he could remember, struggled with the dilemma—how could Sen'Drorn civilians be good people while living under a cruel empire? Did they know where their prosperity had come from? Flax found these people living in Sen'Drorn City, passing on the streets, no different on the surface than any Sen'Prin Warix he had ever met. They lived in ignorance or chose not to notice the truth around them.

"Flax? What are you doing?" Yulah asked.

She had caught him staring at the coin in his fingers. Flax scratched the base of his left horn, trying to look casual. He said, "Oh. I uh… just like to look at the emperor's face sometimes."

Then she leaned across the table and his heart thumped in his chest.

"It's okay. You don't have to pretend to love Emperor Ryogrim…" she whispered. "I hear he's a real jerk in person." She winked.

Flax let out a held breath and asked, "Oh yeah. So, does the military get involved in everyday life here a lot?"

"Not really. Why?" Yulah said, beginning to stand. He stood up as well, and they took a stroll up Fleeg Street.

"Well they patrol in my hometown, Vendengire. To defend against Sen'Prin invasions." He knew this was the case from his training.

Yulah gasped, then said something he was not expecting, "Oh, good thing! I bet that makes you feel safer!"

Flax tried to play along, "Uh, yeah." He wasn't sure where she was going with this.

He wanted to ask her more about her view of the Sen'Prin. But what could he say to get something informative, and still have it come off as something he already knew?

As they walked back up Fleeg Street together, he dug around in his mind to stop the awkward silence and say anything, and finally just said, "Yeah, those Sen'Prin, huh?" then looked to the floor, feeling stupid.

To his surprise, Yulah's face brightened, as she sprang to reply, "Right? Have you heard that they raid villages in the night? Killing families, taking their land, converting whole regions for their armies… what barbarians!" She crossed her arms and shivered.

Flax was shocked. He had after all grown up with the idea that his own nation, the Sen'Prin, were doing good work on that front. Like the Sen'Prin operative who had given him the assignment, who'd had said he was "territory acquisitions logistics coordinator" or something of the sort. Flax smiled—that face was the source of her fear, a 'barbarian.' And so was Flax.

But aloud, he sighed somberly in feigned agreement, as if recalling a shared history. "The Great Split! Crazy, right?" He wanted to know what she was taught regarding this.

"Oh yeah, what a crazy time to live in! I was just a little child, I hardly remember it myself. My boss was there though. He would remember. I doubt he'd tell me. But, rumor has it he…" Her words cut off. "Nevermind. Poor Emperor Ryogrim. He did the best he could to keep things together after the mess. Rebuilding the wall, cleaning up the city. Scrounging up people to go after the terrorists, but, they had a big head start, as you know. Only caught up with a few stragglers," she said. Flax swallowed hard, knowing they would have been killed on sight. He looked into a passing window and saw a butcher's heavy cleaver clap down on a hunk of leg meat, causing him to jump.

Within a minute they were back in front of Borak's shop. "Well Flax, here we are." She kissed him on the cheek before turning to go. "Until my next visit." And she disappeared into the crowd. Flax stood there, dumbstruck, and drew his knuckles to his cheeks to cool them.

***

That night on the roof, reporting to Thian, Flax recounted what he had observed about the people of Sen'Drorn.

"How was the first week?" Thian started them off.

"Exhausting."

"Aww, sorry to hear. What are the people like? Do they seem like a bunch of Meruyan abusers?"

"I went out with this girl, and she gave me this whole other story. She is our age but was raised in this nation. She has been totally brainwashed in her education."

"Or she just doesn't care."

"I don't think the average people here know a lot about where their food and metals come from. They are simply sheltered, ignorant. Fed lies by their government."

"Okay but anyone middle age or older must know! They would have been there!"

"Oh yeah." He lowered his eyes, thinking of his father. "I'll have to find out more, and ask older people, I guess. Maybe I'll bring it up with my master engineer if there's ever a good time."

"And this girl you talked to... tell me more about that."

"Thian! It's not exactly related to the mission. But, yeah." He blushed, unsure where to proceed. What if Thian judged him for getting too personal with the citizens here?

"Tell me! I'm your best friend!" his voice moaned playfully from the wristcom.

"She is pretty cool. Okay, gorgeous! With violet hair and eyes..."

"And she went out with you?!" Thian teased.

They both laughed.

Flax sighed. "It was just a casual meeting. But the way she speaks, so elegant and relaxed…"

"Woah, buddy. Don't go and fall in love! Remember? Temporary life! Maybe she can be useful though, but that's it. Give you intel about life there."

They continued to speak about the engineering job for the records, what he had learned, how to use this gadget and that, to fix this or that, for some of which items Thian hadn't never even heard of.

"Yeah, their tech is really more advanced here, there is some valuable knowledge I'll be bringing back to Sen'Prin. The master engineer has been at this for decades at least. A real pro."

"It's all those rare metals they can mine from the Meruyan sites! I'm tellin' you, it's not without its moral setbacks. Blood tech!" Thian warned.

The pair chatted until it was time to close out the evening call.

"Right, buddy, well don't forget, learn all you can! Ask a lot of questions. Bye for now!"

***

A few days later, Flax sat with Borak in the tinkering lab, doing just that—learning all he could. While he still had simple jobs in the shop, like stacking shelves, even these small tasks proved useful. He soaked up everything he could about the objects he was putting away, including variation and kind.

"Let's try not to break a horn this time. We'll need your wind balance undimmed for the sake of the work." He opened a drawer and brought out a copper sheet spool. "Come." Flax leaned in as he coiled the flat wiring around Flax's horns. "Here, this should help. A protective layer. Like goggles for your horns. Speaking of, put on your goggles, boy!"

Flax could feel it innately when his horn had been cut by the glass on his first week. Like a sense of balance at sensing the wind was off, a little on the left side where the horn was missing. He had learned in school that as punishment and in war, many Warix cut off the horns of their enemies to disable their connection to the wind element. Without them, one cannot sense the wind until they regrow—full amputation would mean two full days disabled, about a week before full recovery. Flax had only chipped his, but could imagine what it would be like to lose it all, just awful.

Borak was a patient instructor, and together, as promised, they took apart the motorbike one afternoon. Flax stared at the tubes and parts, wrench in hand, goggles over his eyes, loving every minute. Borak even revealed the flying machine he had been working on, and ideas spread into inspiration as the flying machine and motorbike merged into a new thing of their combined creation.

Maybe after his spy mission, he could just become an engineer in Sen'Prin City with all the knowledge he was accumulating. Even the nagging, "*Who am I?*" feeling dissipated when he and Borak were in the tinkering shop.

Although he was learning a lot about engineering, Borak didn't like to talk much, especially about personal details. Flax was starting to wonder if he even had a story to tell, or was just in this shop since birth—but he waved off that ridiculous thought. He hadn't stopped thinking about Yulah's version of the Great Split, and was extremely curious to ask what Borak's opinions were.

Every attempt to take up talk of politics, like where Borak was during the Great Split, and how much he knew of where his raw materials came from, was met with grunts and wave offs. While Flax admired Borak's engineering skills, he had mixed emotions and confusing feelings, and constantly pondered what kind of man Borak truly was.

As Flax got used to the daily routine, life became marginally less exhausting, to the point where in whatever infrequent spare time Flax had between reports and work, he managed to take walks around the city.

The next time Yulah came to the stop, Flax asked if she would take a walk with him when his shift was off.

"If you could show me around town once the crowds are gone, it would be helpful to my adjustment here." It was summer, and the sun wouldn't set until late.

"Sure, why not." Yulah shrugged, but smiled, then left with her usual crate pickup.

She returned around ten, just as he and Borak finished cleaning up in the tinkering room. A knock on the door, and she appeared, beaming at them.

"Nice evening, you two!"

"G'night Flax." Borak winked at Flax, who blushed.

"It's not like that…" he started.

"I'll lead the way," she said, "after all, I should make sure you don't get lost around the big city." Leading Flax by the crook of his arm out the shop, they sauntered into the warm evening streets. She led him up and they weaved through the hilly neighborhoods of Sen'Drorn. Flax, overwhelmed by so much, took along his engineering notebook to scribble maps 'for himself.' They traversed a bridge with a brook below, where a young couple canoodled.

Then the clouds descended and the thunderstorms began, causing a flash summer storm. Flax and Yulah ran to take cover under the eaves of a building from the sudden downpour, laughing at their soaked clothes.

"I know where we can go to dry off," Yulah said.

She led him up the winding streets of volcanic stone, Flax's legs burning as they ascended and the arches of Sen'Drorn fortress rose ahead. It would be rude to use wind energy here, unless perhaps they held hands first, and coordinated to move in sync. No way their romance was at that stage yet.

The building set they ended up at bordered outer walls of the fortress. Yulah led him up stone stairs, shaded by tall trees, to a porch with a view of the pine trees at a remnant forest within the city walls. It was a tranquil corner away from the city center. If her place had been at a different angle, it would have had a view of the rooftops from a hill of this height.

"Wait here, I'll get you a towel," she said.

Flax stood on the porch gazing at the trees. His clumsy, masculine step creaked the floorboards, causing him to cringe in disruption of such a serene night, especially as Yulah returned from inside and tossed him a towel.

"So, Flax. How do you like working with Borak? I've known him many years," she said, toweling herself off. He assumed they would be leaving in a moment, but instead she took seat in a chair by a table set. Her soft grin bade him to sit.

Flax sat down and said, "I find him…er. He's not much of a talker. But he's fair. And a decent teacher."

"How about where you came from, you parents must be pretty proud of you for coming out to the big city and putting farm life behind."

"Yeah." Flax played with his hands under the fragile table between them. "And you? How did you grow up?" he answered, steering the conversation away from himself.

"My parents weren't really there for me, they ran off when I was young. Uncle Mal basically raised me. But I think he did fine."

"Sounds like a good man, I would like to meet him some day," said Flax.

She looked out into the trees. Silence fell. The sun was setting, turning the sky gold, and the spaces between the trees to grow denser and blacker, and the thick forest to seem impenetrable.

"I'm not so sure," she answered finally.

They sat in silence for a time, before Yulah said, "Well, it's getting late."

"Yeah," he agreed, getting up. She got up too.

"Your hair is so funny when it's wet. Come inside so I can dry it properly."

Taking his hand, she led him inside. His heart beat rapidly.

Flax rolled over to face her, she lay silhouetted by the lamp behind her. "Am I your first?"

"I'd be lying if I said you were. Why? You ask as if…"

Flax blushed and squirmed. "No, it's not! Just, um." He was lying though, and not doing a great job of it. She smirked but stared to her other hand, gliding over the bedsheets.

"You're like my age!" he blurted. "How many other guys…?"

"I dunno. Doesn't matter does it?"

Shockwaves of jealousy stiffened him.

His expression must have betrayed him, as a moment later she rolled away. Before he could lean after her, she took a graceful exit to the bathroom.

"I'm sorry…" he moaned.

While she was out of sight, he waited, looking around her place. His ears perked up and he kept one directed to the bathroom, while he slid open her wooden drawer. He froze, holding his breath as his heart nearly stopped. He closed the drawer. A badge bearing the logo of the Sen'Drorn military lay inside.

CHAPTER THIRTEEN

Meleena and Deem sat on the ground, panting. They had made it out of the forest of stampeding trees.

"What kind of trees were those, anyway!" Meleena breathed, still exhausted from having the wind knocked out of her.

"I tried to warn you before we got separated," Deem said softly, looking over his shoulder. "They aren't trees. They are a herd of animals. It was their grazing we heard earlier, not cattle. And the vangrots hang out on their horns, eating their droppings."

"How did you know all that?" Meleena asked.

"I sensed it, I dunno."

"Brilliant! Be proud. You're the only one of us that paid detailed attention to your surroundings."

Inspecting their form, she realized it. Their shallow churning roots resembled long pointed hooves, the dead branches more like horns to the touch, and their trunks pulsed as if breathing like heavy warm bodies.

Meleena tried to stand, her legs shaking. Open cuts and fresh bruises stung as she helped Deem hoist the unconscious Talla onto Pinchy's carapace. He would carry her as they continued into the valley, hopefully into civilization.

The leg she had fallen on ached, and her bruised face winced at every step as they hobbled away from the moving forest in the trim grass. But that wasn't as bad as the sinking feeling in the pit of her stomach. Poor Peela, where was she now? Was she hurt in the stampede, or had she made it out safely?

She stared back at the moving forest…She couldn't go back in there. She must have been staring back a while, as Deem turned back too.

"I know…but we can't go back now. We need to get help," he said softly.

Meleena tried to say, "Yeah," but only a sad utterance squeaked out when she tried to speak. Tears blurred the vision already impaired by her broken glasses. She blinked them away, cleared her throat.

Finally, she said, "Yeah. We should get cleaned up, and drop off Talla anyway."

"I'm sure the locals who know this place better can help us find your kelpies," Deem said with a strange perkiness, his best attempt to sound hopeful.

They continued in silence from the herd and into the narrowing valley, where the trampled grasslands eventually gave way to a cleared earthen path, and finally to a dirt road.

Deem cheered as they tread on this first clear sign of civilization.

As the surrounding hills corralled the landscape into a narrow valley, so the air did change. It was noticeably thicker, a hot and humid air that labored their breathing, yet turned the walls of the valley lush and green.

"We must be in a tropical microclimate," Deem panted. "See, look at all the fruit trees!"

On the hillside, fruit trees blossomed. At each step, their arrangement switched between a dense mass and empty rows: a planted orchard. The dirt road changed to cobblestone. The largest span of the wilderness for their journal was finally over. Through the forking cracks in her glasses, Meleena was overcome with the beauty of the orchards on spiraling terraces through the valley way, with an occasional stone structure nestled between them. Properties stretched to border the road.

"I've never seen fruit like these before," Meleena remarked, struck by the diversity.

There were narrow stalks with heaping fruit, which caused the whole plant to droop, contrasting fat, wide trunks with tiny, spiked leaves and tiny orange fruit, winding trees with strangely shaped fruit protruding from bushels between broad leaves.

A crop of swirling blue vines brought the sweet-pungent scent of Blue Root tea, transporting her momentarily. She longed to be home, with all the comforts she had left behind.

The creaking of wooden wheels popped her daydream, and she looked ahead to see a cart piled high with fruit coming at them. She gasped—a thin Meruyan sat atop, and a hulking creature she had never seen before pulled the cart with two tree-like legs. Its face bore familiarity, with enormous round eyes like a squid and six tentacles drooping from its face, each as wide as one of Meleena's thighs. The cart wasn't the only thing it hauled, most of the beast's body was covered by a hard hump, which she could see as it passed was actually a spiraling shell gliding on a smooth snail tail behind the effort steps of the hulking webbed feet.

Meleena and Deem exchanged amazed glances.

The Meruyan nodded as he passed, dressed in baggy linens. It seemed strange, off, for a Meruyan to not wear water-compatible clothing. They also seemed thinner than the residents of Pontai'Desa, and kept their green hair flowing long... it was as if more of their nutrition needed to come from their hair absorbing the sun's nutrients.

As they came in from the outskirts, they saw Meruyans toiling in the fields. Some picked fruit, others hauled large baskets to carts, which had more of those squid beasts of burden strapped in. Occasional figures stood much taller among the various Meruyans, dotting a couple per field. Meleena couldn't make out what they were.

Feeling off about the puzzling sight, Meleena noted, "Amazing how different it is here, and how many types of orchards and farms there are."

"Yeah, can't wait to try some exotic fruit!" Deem licked his lips, missing her point entirely. Pinchy gurgled, perhaps in agreement, or perhaps just adjusting the weight of Talla's body on his back.

"Too bad Talla is missing all this." Meleena glanced at Pinchy. "I do almost feel sorry for her." Meleena's mind buzzed, trying to take it all in. Her hand moved with the compulsion to reach for her journal. Then a painful flinch as she realized it was gone and she could no longer record the new plants and fruit she had seen.

They again exchanged wonderstruck glances as the road led them under a stone archway and into a village. At least that part appeared to be normal. Familiar symbols carved into the stone arch read in Meruyan: "Village of Gebuk'Desa."

Gebuk'Desa didn't appear much different from Pontai'Desa at first glance. Wooden posts with signs pointed the way to named fields and locations. 'Backlak's Frim-Fruit Farmstead,' 'Caralan Copper Mines,' 'Iron welding factory,' 'Lake bungalows.' Meruyans scooted around the streets, running errands in their kelpweave tunics and robes. Some were wet, with fins protruding from wide sleeves. Carts traversed the streets, pulled by the huge squid-beasts, loaded high with fruit or small metal objects Meleena didn't recognize. A cart passed in front of her face, nearly knocking her off her feet, loaded high with star-shaped fruit she had never seen before. The side of the crate was stamped Property of Quail Egg Cafe. She had also never heard of such a cafe, though she knew a quail was a small, woodland creature she'd seen only in the forest. A shiver went up her spine, but she didn't know why.

It was all so familiar, yet off. Some Meruyan men walking by carried wooden crates, some open with similar metal gadgets inside. They were often accompanied by more of those tall figures. Their skin and hair colors were woodsy, brown and tan, ears pointed, and Meleena now realized they were Warix. Their clothing moved on their frames differently: it was clearly made from a plant-based fabric. They wore uniforms with shoulder patches, featuring the flower-maned lion in gold on a deep green background. She'd never seen a real lion, but it was known even among her people as a Warix symbol for nobility and strength.

The Meruyan driving the cart earlier had been wearing the same fabric rather than Kelpweave; now she knew why he had also struck her as off. Startling as it was to see Warix, she was in no mood to explore the town at this moment.

A great heaviness pulled at her, traumatic throttling from unfamiliar monsters aside, she had still done enough camping and trekking for a lifetime. She longed to see the indoors again, even fantasizing about sinking into a pile of pillows.

Meleena glanced over again and was surprised that nobody took any notice of Pinchy, a giant lobster with a passed-out girl on his back. A crinkling of paper got her attention. She turned to see Deem taking out his map. "Hey, Meleena, I think we go this way...Woah!"

He stopped as he noticed two Warix pass by. He gasped and dropped his voice low, "What kind of Meruyans are those? Or, are they...?" He trailed off.

"Warix, a forest people. Just as we are a sea people. I'll tell you about it later," answered Meleena. Her leg throbbed with pain, and she was starting to get annoyed. "Where are we going again?"

Deem pointed to a sign on the post and read, "Meruyan Town Hall"— it led up a steep road that spiraled into the inland mountains.

They kept an eye on Talla's body as they ascended into the lush green hills. Ferns and great tropical leaves surrounded them, and the stone road again became dirt paved.

Up the hilltop, many thatched-roofed bungalow homes lined the road, a neighborhood connected with roads disappearing into lakes, presumably leading to underwater homes.

Meleena pointed to a familiar stone building among the houses, which looked much like Pontai'Desa's own government building.

Meleena again felt strange, inquiring if Deem shared in her feelings about the town hall standing among the homes, instead of in the center of town.

"Yeah, even in the underwater community, it's central," he said as they approached the stone courtyard outside the Town Hall.

"Welcome, future leaders!"

They jumped as voice startled them, and an elderly Meruyan man stood up from a bench in the courtyard.

It was Professor Levlos, the Council member who had introduced himself on their day of departure. He swirled his hands in a spin of greeting, to which they repaid, but stopped halfway through when he noticed Talla laying atop Pinchy, and hurried closer.

"Oh my! What happened to your face? And what have you got there?" Putting a hand to her forehead, he said severely, "Come with me to the healer's. Right away."

He brought them a few homes down the path to a small flowering garden of purple wildflowers and knocked on the straw door.

The straw inverted and was replaced in the doorway by a plump Meruyan woman, beaming under her coif of purple hair.

"Why, hello! Oh my, the Future Leaders are here!" She had a mousy, nurturing voice. She spun her hand in the twist to greet them. They did the same in reply.

"I am Saru, your host! Come in! You must be starving!" she said.

Then, noticing the ragged state they were in, and the lobster carrying Talla. "Oh my! Let's get you cleaned up and tended to!"

Deem whispered to Meleena, "Host? I thought she was the village healer?"

Professor Levlos, right behind them, chuckled and said, "She is both!"

"And for good reason!" she belted out. "Future Leaders are sent to me half the time straight away anyway in abysmal shape. It was easier for me to just become official host." Noticing Talla, she changed focus. "Oh my, let's see to her first."

She scuttled inside, leaving them at the open door, heading right into a kitchen on the far side of a hallway.

"Feet!" reminded Professor Levlos, taking his shoes off outside and washing them in a bucket before going inside. Meleena shoved off her boots. The water felt great on her feet, but when her toes came down on the rug, the softness rushed up and through her like warm tendrils hugging her heart. Finally, civilization.

Three small children rushed into the halls, and without saying anything, guided them into a room with large pillows atop woven reed furniture. The older two were girls, the youngest, a boy. They placed warm water buckets under their feet and platters of prepared snacks and water to drink onto tables around them. Saru came back in shortly.

"My children." She beamed, patting the head of the smallest child. "They're very helpful around here while their father is in the factories for many hours every day." Meleena took a seat on the thatched woven furniture.

A low, bubbly whining sound made her turn. Pinchy had stopped halfway through the doorway, unable to enter, seemingly reminding them of his cargo. His tall eyestalks danced.

Saru and Professor Levlos lifted Talla off his back and onto a couch in the den. Her children brought her wraps and ointments, and she dressed her wounds. Talla stirred but did not open her eyes, as if in a restless dream.

"Dear, will you bring the lobster to the stables out back?" She beckoned to her eldest daughter, who quickly led Pinchy away. Saru turned to Deem. "He'll have fresh fish guts and a place to sleep there…We usually get kelpies."

She continued with inspecting Talla, turning her head in hand. "It looks like your friend hit her head, but I got her patched up now. She'll be alright, she just needs some time to rest."

Saru next looked at Meleena's leg, rubbed healing ointment onto the bruises which immediately soothed the throbbing. One daughter ran and brought her mother pieces of round glass, and she popped them into Meleena's broken glasses frame.

"I can see again, thank you!" Meleena applauded the daughter, who beamed and nodded. Her blue eyes peered through large round spectacles too.

"So how did y'all get so banged up coming out here?" Saru asked.

"I was just about to ask you about something related to that," Meleena started. "We lost track of the path at some point. There was this forest, but the trees didn't seem like trees, and vangrots ambushed us, then the trees seemed to move, even attack us! Our kelpies and all our supplies are gone." At that she turned away, trying to hide the tears encroaching on her vision. "I just hope Peela is safe, how can we ever get them back?"

"Oh, dear!" Saru waddled over and hugged her tight and said, "It sounds like you were in the Moving Forest. Those dreadful trees! It isn't supposed to be on the path!"

Saru and Professor Levlos exchanged looks of concern. Then, Saru leaned back and pointed to the red scarf around Meleena's neck.

Saru's turquoise cheeks went ghost white. "That scarf...where did you get it?"

Meleena had forgotten she still wore it. She pulled it off her neck. "I found it in the moving forest. After climbing a tree. That's where I saw my and Talla's kelpies run off and out the other side of the forest."

"Oh my! We call them Gommwoods. Because of the eerie sound their chewing makes. It's unlike any other in a forest. After the rain, the odor of wet grass brings them in...I'm so sorry you had to deal with them. You really climbed one? Many have been lost in the Moving Forest forever. You are lucky to have made it out. The boy that scarf belonged to was not."

"You know whose scarf it is?"

"Yes, a long while back. A local farmer's boy. He disappeared one day, nobody knew what came of him. I can return it to him for closure."

"Of course!" Meleena blushed and handed it over.

"Concerning your kelpies, if they made it out, they probably went to the sea. kelpies naturally gravitate to large bodies of water."

"I can send someone to search for them," said Professor Levlos. "In the meantime, rest and gain your energy. Then, we can go for a short walking tour."

**

After comfort and nourishment, Meleena and Deem felt up to walking again. Although sore and exhausted, they were energized by the idea of having their first official lesson of the Journey. Leaving Saru and the children to watch over Pinchy and Talla, Professor Levlos led them into the front garden and through the neighborhood of thatched Meruyan bungalows, down a back road into the farmland.

"Here we grow, as you might have seen, many different sorts of fruit..."

"Why have I never tried any?" Meleena inquired.

"They are more for the Warix."

"Oh! I have a question," Deem eagerly called out. "I've known about Warix from school lessons, but have never seen one before. Will we meet one?"

"The Warix are here to work and probably won't like to be disturbed."

"Why are they here?" asked Meleena causally, as they passed through the bustling center of the main village again. Her question was cut off by the din and chaos, the acrid tang of dung, the occasional trumpeting from the immense squid creatures pulling loaded carts about the cobblestone.

"And what are those?" pointed Deem.

"Neutolyths! Don't worry, they are tame. Marine beasts of burden native to the coasts in this region. Much better for pulling heavy carts than kelpies."

"They have soulful, intelligent eyes," Deem said softy. "I hope they are treated well…"

Meleena nodded in agreement, she too had noticed this and other strangeness. She said, "And I haven't seen many kelpies around here, either."

Professor Levlos answered matter-of-factly, as if it was normal, "Kelpies are more for riding. You won't find any around here—no reason for a Meruyan to be taller and faster than a Warix here, it can be intimidating." He chuckled. "The Warix can't ride kelpies, as their body language isn't compatible to forming such bonds. They can only be tamed by a Meruyan. Yes, the slow-moving neutolyths have a much more even temperament."

Meleena asked again, this time more impatiently, "And why exactly do we have Warix all around here?"

"They oversee our productions." Again, Professor Levlos spoke as if this was a basic, given fact of existence. "They help us mine important materials for living, for both peoples. In exchange, they also provide their own materials for us."

"Like what?" asked Deem.

"Fine clothing, wood from trees for building materials, and power generators that they refill regularly, which provide superior indoor lighting, heating, cooling, fire for cooking," Professor Levlos listed.

Meleena recalled that her town, Pontai'Desa, did not have such technology. They used candles for lighting, fire for cooking. Then again, they weren't serving the Warix so closely.

"What's wrong with Meruyan kelpweave or rock lobster carapace?" Deem asked, taken aback. "We hand-make it in my village."

Professor Levlos said, "Oh, it's nothing like these woodland materials the Warix have shown us. Have you heard of linen, wool, or silk? So much to educate! The fine Warix have invented a way to make these into clothes and fabric, with machines!" He beamed proudly as he said so.

"But Kelpweave can get wet...it is better suited to marine life! Going and coming from underwater!" said Deem, crestfallen, trying to argue. "My mother weaves it...we all do. For generations..."

"Living under the water is outdated, ancient ways. The higher-class Meruyans don't want to get wet daily anymore. That's why we live inland and farm on Warix land. Did you see the lakes around the main village?" Professor Levlos moved his hands out as if to show off the village.

Deem slumped. Meleena felt for him. She too knew the ominous discomfort of this place, strange and different.

"Modernizing is the future!" Professor Levlos belted proudly as they passed buildings with stone and wood, sturdier, fancier...Is this was what a Warix city might look like? Some buildings were like this in Dlawn'Edo's crescent island.

"Why, they've also taught us how to mine the hills for precious metals which can be used for all kinds of technology they have developed. That is where we will tour today—a factory which makes copper widgets, instrumental in Warix tech and inventive design."

Professor Levlos continued to educate as they strolled down the streets, passing more Meruyan hard at work, as they went to a very different part of town. On the hills, caves with manufactured entries and windings dirt roads replaced the farms, and large barn-like structures cluttered the valley. They reminded Meleena of the kelpie stables in shape, but these barns were much larger, and had black stone columns, belching fumes above into the cloudy sky. As they came close to the giant barns, Professor

Levlos issued them forward. "These are factories where we turn raw materials from the mines into gadgets for the Warix." They tread up a wooden ramp into the interior, following Professor Levlos up clanking metal stairs, and into the rafters overlooking a large open warehouse. Levlos explained the scene before them, "Here, Meruyans weld the metal into gears and intricate shapes for use in our cities. The Warix export a lot of what we make, where their brilliant minds, called researchers and engineers, work to invent new technology to share with us. So, everyone wins!"

Everyone, or some, was just one of the questions that spun in Meleena's mind. She watched as raw metal entered one side of the building by neutolyth cart, and was unloaded via Meruyan men into large funnels. Hot sizzling sounds wretched forth, as it came out the other side in liquid form for further deviation and processing on long belts, to be handled by gaunt Meruyans wearing thick gloves and tongs. Each step was overseen by pacing, uniformed Warix. Warix up on rafters at the upper edges of the building moved in repetitive, methodological manors, like a dance, with strange pipes at their sides. On the ceiling, spinning fans hummed, and strange orbs fixed to wires dangled. The glow seemed to be encased in the same material as her glasses. It was a lot for the young Meruyan to take in.

On the long, moving table belts, she watched the metals of different colors move and split up at various stages, mixed with other metals, until the final products that came out in different areas in all sorts of exotic shapes. All the Meruyan workers had dark rings under their eyes and often straightened up only after some barked words from the Warix managers, words Meleena couldn't quite make out.

Professor Levlos beamed proudly at the sight below went on, "The Warix develop technology with these parts, combining them in new ways, and then they share with the Meruyans whatever they make. Hand-wound timekeepers, machines for cooking, cleaning, all that stuff. Their developers are called engineers. We also have factories that assemble parts into established machines."

They went around back and watched the finished products get loaded into crates and then the crates onto fat cargo-holding machines, which were some distance away so they couldn't get a good look at them. Surrounded by groups of Warix, these machines went launching off and flew into the air, then sailed through the sky until they were out of sight. Meleena's mouth dropped open.

"Woah! What was that?" She hadn't been impressed by technology in her life until this moment. This was nothing like the fancy gadget her brother had on, the "gift from the Warix." She shivered, just like earlier when they entered the town.

Deem said, "I never saw something swim on land before."

Professor Levlos explained, "Warix transport. They use inventions of theirs which swim through the air. They call it flying, and those are 'flying machines.'"

Meleena furrowed her brow. "Is that really fair? It looks like they are taking everything."

"Oh yes, it's fair for quality of life. As I said, they bring the technology back to us later, so it's worth working hard for it."

Professor Levlos, hands on his hips, continued to beam with pride.

CHAPTER FOURTEEN

The next weeks went by quickly for Flax and with a similar routine: he continued to go out with Yulah, report his findings back to Thian, and learn engineering from Borak without much personal progress. In an attempt to find his father, Flax requested that Yulah take him to meet the various shopkeepers around Fleeg Street. He told her it was to become aquatinted with the people.

He knew dating her was wrong on some level, that such ties with "the enemy" put everyone at risk, but Flax had a way of mental blocking, a bout of denial and living for the moment. That time when it would all end seemed no nearer day-to-day, so he could always postpone worrying.

Plus, Yulah was an excellent guide in the quest he had shared to find his father.

It seemed to be part of her job to know everybody. Was this related to whatever it was she did for the military? So far, there was one coffee shop owner with similar eyes, hair, and horns to himself, but since his fair brown features were not uncommon, that didn't mean much. Plus, he seemed a little too old for his mother. Another man, who ran a furniture shop, laughed similarly to himself, but he didn't see any other resemblances in the sharp-chinned, curly haired man. That one had been Yulah's idea, but Flax merely shook his head.

In his spare lunch breaks, if he didn't have plans with Yulah, he would return to some location Yulah had shown him, taking it in fully and without her to hurry him along.

Yulah also invited him back to her loft sometimes, where they got much more acquainted, and Flax forgot all about the mission or his place in the order of things. With Yulah, at her loft, he was just a boy losing track of time with an amazing girl.

Late at night, he returned to his place to the sound of Borak's snores. He went to his room and climbed out the window onto the roof with his wrist-com, that he kept stuffed under his mattress. He wound the battery with wind shot into small chambers, then switched it on and tweaked the signal for a call to Sen'Prin headquarters.

"Hey, buddy! How goes it this evening?" Thian's voice came through on low volume. "Got anything to report?"

In all the business, Flax had neglected to prepare anything. He'd left the general checklist, unread, under his bed, and was not about to climb down and get it now.

"I, uh. Yeah. Sorry, man. I can tell you about the, er, roof tiles they have here…"

A laugh came through. "This is so unlike you, Flax! You're usually the responsible one!" Thian laughed. "I have a general stuff checklist. We could use some details to build a map of the city layout. Or if you got some time later to wander the sewer systems."

Flax stared up at the stars. "I don't have time for anything. But I will try to be better."

He still felt frustrated and distracted that he had failed up until this point to track down his father. Why did he think this would be easy?

But maybe Thian knew some of quirks that Flax didn't realize about himself, which Flax could then compare against the potential fathers. Nyshenyu forbid Thian knowing what it was for: Flax had never disclosed such details even to his friend about his parentage. Having a personal connection to someone in Sen'Drorn would have jeopardized everything, let alone dismissal from his current role.

"Hey, Thian, what are some of my quirks?" he began, thinking of a reasonable excuse. "I, uh, wanted to make sure not to embarrass myself in front of Yulah on our next date."

"Hah! Yeah, sure, Buddy. Oh, you mean the way you sometimes scratch at your left horn and close your left eye when you are thinking? It's a weird thing I've always noticed you do."

"What! I don't do that! Something else!"

"Sure, you do! Just try not to do that on your next date. Okay, you also chew on pencils when you are concentrating. You get pretty serious and bossy too, like a drill sergeant. Even though we were the same rank. Like when we were tailing those Hyish, and you ordered me to find out where they take their—"

"Come on!" he interrupted. "That was useful info for us to blend in with the Hyish. You can't blame me for that!" Flax cried, lamenting his inability to carry out the urge to throw something playfully at his friend.

Thian's tone softened on the line. "But you have endearing qualities, too. When you are concerned about someone, you get this puppy look, like your eyes are going to drop off the sides of your head like runny eggs. It's sincere, and it makes me forgive you every time for your bossy mood. Do that one with Yulah, and she will fall for you."

"Thanks, Thian." Flax picked at the roof tiles with his clawed fingers.

"It did almost get us caught that time I tripped on my Hyish robes and landed face down in the sand! You were too concerned. No Hyish would behave like that!" He barked a laugh, helping the mood return from the brinks of sentimental.

As usual, they chuckled, and the conversation soon turned and devolved into their common reminiscing of adventures past. Flax felt a bond and appreciation for his friend, which he had never stopped to notice before. How much they had been through and how strange it was to be chasing new relationships with strangers in the enemy city. It plagued his dreams that night, but by the morning, the feeling had passed, replaced by a new determination. It came with the realization that Thian was his only real friend. It's not like he was unpopular growing up, he had friends from the years in school and early Sen'Prin service days, but none that stuck through the busy times. They all parted ways when they received military assignments.

He wanted something like that with his father too—he had to expand his social circle. As if there was time for that.

The next evening, Flax sat in the tinkering room with Borak and tried to apply what he learned. If only he could get Borak to banter about his past, like so easily happened with Thian. But his relationship with the wizened old man wasn't the same. It took time to get to know Borak—he wasn't the type to come of his shell all at once.

He watched Borak pick up a spanner and explain his reasoning for the prototype of their flying machine. "This could work, if we could get the energy strong enough into a small enough funnel on the side…"

But Flax was distracted, rattling his brain about his mother's description of his father, from the years past. It was only in the last year she even told Flax the truth, that his father had not died in the Great Split, escaping this oppressive empire, but had, in fact, never left Sen'Drorn.

Why haven't I come up with an answer to all this? Why is this so hard? Maybe I could ask some Warix in town if they had girlfriends that left them during the Great Split? No, that would be ridiculous. It'd probably cause a fight and get me kicked out of here.

"Flax?" He tried to hand Flax a wrench, waving it in his face.

"Uh-huh." Flax had been drifting into space. He now lowered his left hand to take the wrench and realized it had been scratching at his horn. "Huh." *I guess I do that.*

"You seem mighty distracted today," Borak said, puzzled, leaning on his knees into the flying machine's core motor. Flax put the wrench down on a nearby work table, next to a tin of pencils that were all chewed at the ends.

"Oh, I was expecting yer to twist some screws in here." Borak scooted back from the guts of the flying machine, a look of concern flashed on his face. "Are ye alright?"

Flax looked up in time to see Borak ask this while scratching his own left horn in puzzlement.

Flax, eyes wide, looked into Borak's concerned eyes… Those eyes, the same shade of blue as his own. He all at once began to see it… Despite his balding and greying, the remaining flakes of brown in Borak's hair were the same shade of brown as his own. His skin, much less tanned from the sun, but similar bronze to that of Flax's in winter, when he got less sun. And Borak *did* tend to spend all his time indoors, whereas Flax had just blown in from the deserts... so that could account for differences... Maybe, one could even argue bone structure, square jaw, eyes sloping downward, giving them an inherently soft look.

Flax's eyes widened as a new suspicion gripped him. A bead of sweat crept down his forehead. He couldn't unsee the likeness now. Was this only his imagination?

"What's yer problem, son? Busy place here, we gotta keep things moving if yer not in the mood for our pet project..."

Flax choked at the word 'son' and its possible irony. He couldn't speak.

"We can pick this up later if yer' too tired," Borak reasoned.

"Yeah, I just got in a little fight with Yulah and am distracted." One upside of dating, it provided a good cover story for where he went and his torrid emotions. But for now, Flax needed to devise a way he could know for sure: could Borak be his father? Now, knowing where Borak was in the Great Split was more important than pure curiosity.

CHAPTER FIFTEEN

The sun was beginning to set as Meleena, Deem, and Professor Levlos left the Meruyan factory, and dark by the time they reached Saru's dwelling.

She had prepared a large dinner of spiced fish and rice. Tasty, though Meleena found the meal contained a curious lack of vegetables for a region farming so many of these crops.

Meleena had asked for a pencil and paper. She couldn't sleep without recording some of her observations and sketching the neutolyth and Gommwoods. Deem rested on his bed nearby in the shared guest room. Talla, still unconscious, had been moved to the third bed. Saru blew the candle lights out, and Meleena's eyelids dropped, and she gratefully eased into the comfort of a warm bed after all that nature.

Her head spun from the intensity of the day, and a world of intense dreams sucked her in. She saw stampedes of Gommwoods coming at her, with red scarves whipping around their horns. Laughing Warix faces appeared on their trunks. Deep purple vortexes revealed slumping factory worker Meruyans, who left an assembly line of metal gadget work to ask for food in Saru's kitchen. She beamed, but her shoulders slumped.

Brightness warmed her face, causing Meleena's eyes to flutter open. It was morning. Bright sunlight streamed in through the thin curtains, like fingers stretching over the floor.

Deem was already awake, his nose in a book. *He really puts us to shame.*

"What are you reading?" asked Meleena.

Deem startled, causing his hand to jerk, and the front of his book to tilt forward and bonk him on the nose.

"Oh, hey, you're up!" He rubbed his nose and checked the front cover. "Oh, it's nothing, just a brief history of mining in this region. It's ideal for orchards, but also rich in minerals, like copper, a golden-red-colored metal that is instrumental in technology development. Boy, I'd love to see that in action on our tours."

"Somehow, I think we just produce the parts, not the design and research part," Meleena answered gravely.

"Why do you say that?" He looked puzzled.

Meleena shook her head, and kept her voice low, "The Meruyans seem so unhappy and overworked in those orchards and in those factories. We haven't seen the mines yet, but I assume it could only be worse there."

Deem thought for a moment before answering, carefully setting down his book. "Yeah, I don't get why people would want to trade their lives for working inside like that. Just for some fancy tech? We don't even have those things underwater, and we do just fine."

"Professor Levlos acted like everything was normal. How could it be? Something seems fishy to me."

Deem took off his glasses and set them on his bedside table. "Well, let's not go jumping to conclusions. I'm sure it's making them happy, just not my personal preference. I mean, I'd rather live without any of those things in the sea."

"That flying machine was just so unlike anything I've ever seen. How does it work? Why don't Meruyans have those, like in the Southern Villages?"

"I bet it's your fault somehow, Meleena," came a raspy voice from the corner.

"What?" Meleena turned to see Talla rolling over, still apparently sleeping.

"You provoke the worst in people." Talla's eyes opened weakly.

Meleena shot up from the bed. "You're nonsensical! When did you even wake up?! And how can you blame me when you don't even know what we are talking about!"

"I know you best of everyone." Her eyes closed again.

Meleena looked at Deem, shaking her head and trying not to lose her temper. "All she does it blame, and judge me, can you believe her?"

"She's sleep talking," Deem murmured.

"Clover!" cried Talla, thrashing in her covers. "Where is he!? You lost him, I know it!"

"I knew it!" cried Meleena, throwing her arms up. "You mudfish!" She couldn't take it anymore, the dam she had kept against Talla's constant steady abuse had finally burst.

"You are always blaming me!"

"Stop it right now!" Deem cried. They stopped momentarily. He trembled and Meleena guessed he had never shouted in his life. "Meleena, how can you possibly be arguing with her right now? You two are unbelievable! Just when I thought things were finally getting better between all of us. Dare I think we had become friends, even!"

Tears streamed down Meleena's cheeks. "Don't you get it, Deem? We saved her life, and she won't even acknowledge it, the only thing in her subconscious is blaming me for the disaster with the moving forest!" She turned back to Talla. "Well, Talla, it's all on you for bringing food and shouting at them!"

Talla's body didn't move as she grumbled again, almost peacefully in slumber, "Meleena cheated her way in. She doesn't deserve to be here. That's why bad things happen to us."

Meleena fumed, compelled to leave the room to end this unbearable situation. She couldn't help her pounding head, but when she stormed out of the room, she crashed into something hard blocking the doorway.

"Children! Please stop fighting!" Saru wailed, pounding a wooden spoon against the doorway with a jolting whack. Meleena backed up, and Deem froze.

"Sorry, I have three children," Saru added, entering the room.

Meleena's muscles tightened, but she knew she couldn't leave or lose her temper in front of Saru. "I'm going for a walk!" she tried to say casually, drifting out the doorway.

Saru's voice called, "But the next lesson, and breakfast?"

But Meleena took off running as soon as she was out of sight, fleeing the cottage, only yelling back from the front garden, "I'm not hungry!" wincing at her failing to conceal her mood.

At least they couldn't see her bright cheeks or face. She did a quick sun surrender before stomping down the lane towards town but turned when she heard thumping footsteps from behind. Deem was running down the lane after her, his straw sandals slapping against the stone and resonating off the buildings.

"Wait, Meleena! I want to come!"

Meleena stopped and waited and shook her head as he came close. "Okay, Deem…I guess, I owe you…For saving my life and all."

He beamed and did an awkward, gracious bow.

She blushed. "Don't get used to it." Maybe it wasn't so bad, making the journey with others.

"Now, what is all this drama about between you two?" Deem asked as they headed down the path away from Saru's house.

"I dunno." Meleena shrugged. She didn't really know why she was so frustrated. "I try to ignore her, but sometimes the anger builds up, and I just lose it in an attempt to defend myself. I shouldn't have blown up like that. I'm just frustrated. She's a distraction from something else I'm trying to figure out."

She had moved to a more critical issue at hand, bigger than their squabbles. "It's those Meruyans. Working in the gadget factory, and on the farms. They look gaunt and wear their hair long, probably supplement their nutrients from the sun, because they are underfed. Their whole village seems so busy all the time. Notice how Saru's husband is never home?"

"Oh yeah, he came back early in the morning last night. It woke me up, so I just started reading." Deem shrugged.

"See! How is that a way to live? They are nothing more than a factory, for themselves, or the Warix."

"Maybe you're upset because Peela is still missing…" he said softly, putting a hand on her shoulder. His big blue eyes made it hard to be mad,

Meleena only gaped. She couldn't argue there. She felt out of control, unable to even go searching.

A cloud of frustrated thoughts was interrupted by a frantic thudding from behind, making Meleena and Deem turn. It was Talla, running down the lane. "You can't just go and do things without me!" she yelled, stopping once she reached them, and panting to catch her breath. "I already missed the first tour!"

Meleena furrowed her brow. "We're not on any tour, we're investigating...It's mischief."

Talla crossed her arms. "Well, I want to be part of it." She put a hand to her head and rubbed it. "Even if my head still hurts."

Deem shrugged. "Let her stay, could be good bonding..." He stopped as Meleena shot him a look.

"Fine, I don't care. I just want to get to understand what's really going on in this town." Meleena sighed, catching them up on her observations.

"Look, I'm sorry." Talla sighed. "I didn't mean to yell at you. I was in a dizzy haze. I'm actually..." She rubbed her arm and looked down. "I'm very grateful to you two. You saved my life."

"Oh, well..." Meleena stuttered. She had never gotten anything like an apology from Talla. It filled her with a feeling like sinking into a warm bath, extremely satisfying.

"Alright," she softened her tone, ready to get back to the point at hand, explained for Talla's benefit. "We took a factory tour earlier, to Professor Levlos's utter pride, but I was just explaining to Deem that it seems off to me. The Meruyans work long, tough hours. What is it really like here, without Professor Levlos to make it all sound normal?"

"Or are we looking at it through a biased lens of an alternate culture?" Deem said thoughtfully, looking at the sky.

"Uh, yeah," Meleena puzzled. The three of them continued walking. "Just listen for a moment. Last year, I went to a Council meeting, and met a Warix named Governess Arenay. Her group is at war with another group of Warix. Since she is our ally, I assume we are working for her side here. Working hard to fight against the other Warix, the bad ones who wrecked our village last year."

"Oh, when you shore dwellers crowded our underwater community? I remember that," Deem said.

"What are you on about, that was a storm," Talla argued.

"These bad Warix manufactured some kind of storm, to trick us into fleeing so they could search for some ancient thing, a pendant, they thought was hidden with us. A weapon. But I don't know enough about that yet. More to learn."

"What about Professor Levlos?" Talla continued. "Wouldn't he have told us? Do you really think he would be keeping something from us?"

Meleena shook her head. "He speaks on behalf of the Council, but I don't know their motives. They might not want us knowing the truth until we're officially on the Council. There are no guarantees we'll pass Aldrok's Journey."

CHAPTER SIXTEEN

Several months had passed since Flax had started his assignment in Sen'Drorn City.

One night he came to Yulah's loft on his own to meet her, and she made an unusual suggestion. "I'm taking you someplace special tonight."

"What?" Flax never could guess what she was up to.

"Just come with me." She took his hand and led him into her kitchen. Behind the bright yellow wallpaper, a clay animal head hung on the wall and she pulled on the decorative piece. Flax's mouth hung open as a cave-like hole opened into a dark tunnel.

She led him by the hand and they climbed through the porthole. It led down a hall that smelled of sweet wellspring water. Its carpeted floors allowed their steps to stay silent, though their shadows stretched long behind them in the dim electric lighting. The hall lead to a spiral staircase.

"Where are we—" Flax tried to ask, but she responded with only a knowing look.

With only trees on one side of this place, we must be going—could only be going—towards Sen'Drorn Castle, thought Flax.

They wandered more corridors, more stairs, but Flax paid careful attention to every turn. He gulped. Maybe this wasn't romantic at all, had she found out he was a spy?

They entered through a chamber door, and she pulled it shut behind them. Bookshelves lined the walls and a large ornate desk stood in the center. There was an empty cage for a large bird. The only light came from high windows, which, when Flax's eyes adjusted, gave way to a breathtaking view of the city.

Yulah set a stack of papers from the desk onto the floor. "So they don't fall."

Her fingers traced the surface of the table. He watched the rise and fall of her shoulders with her breath, behind the veil of gossamer hair. Then she approached and starting kissing Flax on the neck. He stood, dumbfounded, heart pounding, and tenderly put his hands on her waist.

They backed their way into the bookshelves and tumbled towards the desk, removing clothes. They didn't get as far as he'd hoped when Flax tripped on a stack of papers beside the desk.

"Oh no!" they both cried, as the collection of papers fluttered everywhere. Flax was on his back, but Yulah, who had kept her balance, was now scampering to recapture the flying papers.

"Oh! This was a mistake! What was I thinking?" Her face turned beat red. She was so flustered that a fluttering uneasiness appeared in Flax's stomach.

He grabbed at the papers, trying to restack them, but Yulah howled and stopped him from helping. "No, I will clean this up. What was I thinking! He is away, but still…"

Flax had no idea what she was talking about, but his skin crawled with the realization that this might be the chamber of her superior. Certainly, only someone important would have a view like that from Sen'Drorn fortress.

"Just stand in the corner and don't touch or look at anything." She sighed in frustration, trying to organize the papers. One flew off from her grasp and landed by Flax's feet. He couldn't help but pick it up.

It was a photograph of two Warix. Flax recognized the bushy hair and steer-like horns as none other than a young General Malotus, right hand of the Emperor of Sen'Drorn. He stood against a lush background, a young Warix woman by his side. Flax's blood froze in his veins…

"Give me that!" Yulah grabbed it away, but upon seeing Flax's face, looked as well.

Round face, red mohawk. A young Arenay. In low-ranking Sen'Drorn military uniform, matching Malotus. They must have been teenagers no older than Flax when this was taken. Not only that, they were holding hands.

"Is he...? That's your superior? General Malotus?" Flax breathed.

"I thought we could have some fun in here. You can't tell anyone what you saw here." Now Yulah looked genuinely scared.

"Do you know who *this* woman is?" Flax urged. *Governess Arenay and General Malotus knew each other? And used to date? This is too much to process right now.*

"Huh? No. Some military buddy of his?" She turned it over to find words, scratched out but still legible. *Arenay, love of my life.*

Flax shrugged, trying to act cool, but inside he was reeling. His heart thudded more than during their make-out session.

He pulled his clothes on while Yulah shoved the letter back into the stack of papers.

"I saw nothing, let's just get out of here," Flax said, and they hurried back to Yulah's flat to hold each other in the safety of her room.

Later, Flax paced his room, lost in thought. *Arenay and Malotus? What is the significance? Could this be why Malotus fights the Sen'Prin, because it's personal? This information could prove useful later. I just don't know how, yet. But worse than that—my girlfriend works for Malotus. How can I still date Yulah, knowing this? Is it right to date her now that I know all this?*

Yes, it's best to keep going. It will look suspicious if I stop seeing her now that I have learned all this about her position. And I do have feelings for her! I don't need to report what she tells me.

The decision didn't comfort him the next day, when Flax sat across from Yulah at their usual lunch hangout, the Quail Egg Cafe.

Yulah spoke in vague terms about work. She was clearly embarrassed, which Flax guessed since "Uncle Mal" turned out to be General Malotus.

"About last night… I guess now you know," she started, then broke off. She lifted a small piece of starkfruit from a saucer and popped it into her mouth.

"What?" Flax bit into the juicy fruit, enjoying every moment of the nectar running down his cheeks. Intellectually he knew it was wrong, but he couldn't help it, he just didn't feel guilty about indulging in the exotics of Sen'Drorn, so disconnected from the truth of its origin here.

She swallowed the fruit and took a swig of tea.

"Do you believe in the Pendant of the Wind Goddess?" asked Flax. "You know, the legend where her soul is trapped in it, and she will grant powers to those who unlock her from it, or something."

"I'm… afraid I can't talk about this, Flax. It's not that I don't trust you…"

"Just curious, it's a famous legend, and you know, I thought since you are close to the top of Sen'Drorn and all…"

"I don't know anything." She leaned in close to him, dropping her voice to a whisper. "Okay, well, mostly nothing. There was a war meeting about it, once. About a year ago, we had a Meruyan with a possible lead." She leaned back. "But it was just that, legend, and nothing came of it."

Flax knew exactly. That man, tortured and killed in their dungeons and the resulting Meruyan raid. Of course, he knew more than Yulah even, since Flax had been at the Meruyan–Sen'Prin follow-up meeting. Of course, a 'civilian' like himself ought to know nothing of any of this, so he feigned a standard level of outsider interest. What Yulah's response proved, however, was that Sen'Drorn had no new leads, which came as a relief.

"Yeah, of course," he sneered. "So, do you know about any other legends? Big city Sen'Drorn things, that we don't know about in the farm?" Innocent enough and along the same vein.

Yulah picked up a fruit and turned it, her slender cheekbones puffing in a spooky impression. "Only that in the city there was once some talk of a mysterious fruit, just like the ones here, from the Meruyan trade routes, but that it was poison, and corrupted the minds of those who ate it. They say they went insane. I hope none of those get served to us here!"

He gave a lighthearted laugh, but inside his stomach felt uneasy. It was strange enough that the Sen'Drorn had a legend of a poisonous fruit coming back, when the Sen'Prin had another legend, of a lost fruit that only brought empathy. He hated that this was not *really* his life. He couldn't just sit with this fine girl, and laugh, and leave it at that. It would have to end somehow, someday. He reminded himself why he did this, because nice people can be on the wrong side.

"Those poor Meruyans, don't you feel bad, though?" Flax let slip, thoughts melting onto his tongue.

"Well, yes, a little I suppose… but, they need us too! They would starve if not for our interference. You know they agreed to this in a contract with us."

"That can't be true!"

"Yeah! They did."

"Well just because it's a raw deal doesn't make it fair…" he started to say, but his voice faded to an inaudible murmur. "Forget it." He smiled, deciding not to go down that road. Better to just enjoy the moment with her and forget his mounting problems for now.

Flax saved his moral quandaries for that night, with Borak in the workshop fixing orders from the day. Flax had been trying to get Borak to open up more about his personal history. He had thought finding his father would be the hard part, but it proved to be the easier challenge. Though they spent a lot of time together, Borak was not the kind to let anyone in quickly. All Flax really wanted was to learn more about his father, yet Borak deflected personal questions, piling on the workload, and keeping himself at arm's length. Flax tried clever workarounds to get information from Borak, like talking about himself, then asking Borak if he ever had anything like that happen to him. Flax worried about sounding too eager in Borak's life. *Nushenyu forbid* he'd come off sounding weird or nosey.

But that evening, now some weeks after Flax figured out Borak must be his father, an unexpected thing happened. Borak, leaning over the seat of their flying machine and adjusting its carburetor, said, "Flax, I noticed you've been going out with that Yulah girl a lot. I've known her a long time, she used to come in here with her father when she was a child. He was a military man himself, now passed. Good luck to yeh with her, I applaud that you've found the time to balance the datin' world with my trainin'."

Flax thought this an excellent opportunity. "So, what about you then, Master Borak? Have you been glued to this job all your life, or have you ever ventured out and found the time to entertain a woman?"

Borak chuckled, but flushed as he looked Flax in the eyes. "Ah right Flax, yeh been good, I will tell ye a story." Borak proceeded to come out from under the flying machine and sat down on a steel chair by the workbench.

Flax was intrigued that Borak actually stopped working for this moment, and took it as a sign to start flooding out more questions. "Were you ever married? Do you have any children? What's life like for you outside the shop?"

Borak lifted an eyebrow. "Do yeh want me to tell yeh a story er not?" Flax shut his mouth in devastation at the near-miss. He bowed his head in silence toward Borak. To his relief, Borak continued.

"Anyway. Sad truth is, I never really had a lasting girl. I basically been married to my shop all my life. Very many years ago, when I was myself just an apprentice, I had one serious relationship with a very memorable woman. She and I had some political differences, see."

Flax stared, fixated. The moment of truth was upon him. "How so?" He sweated in his work jumper.

Borak shrugged. "She was into it, and I couldn't care less."

"What?"

"I dunno. I was just an apprentice, worked hard same as you, spent all me time with my master, the previous shop owner. He told me to ignore all the political unrest, sayin' it would pass and be nothing. We kept focused on the workshop." Borak rustled about in the old iron chair, shifting his weight to get more comfortable.

Flax listened intensely.

"This girlfriend of mine, though. She was always gettin' frustrated with my avoidance. She was active with what she thought were these important issues. To make a long story short, we split up over it. That was about eighteen years ago by now. I never heard from her again. She, well…she doesn't live in Sen'Drorn City anymore."

"She left in the Great Split, didn't she?" Flax said gravely.

Borak ignored the question. "Looking back, I guess I was just a coward and chose my work above everything else. I was never strong enough, in my feelings that is, for any woman to pull me away from my love for this place…" He looked around the dusty old workshop and sighed at it with affection. "Well, best get back to work now."

"Please, can you tell me more about it?" Flax begged.

"Maybe later, boy. We got work to do! This stuffs painful for me to speak 'bout if yeh will understand…Makes me wonder about my life choices, and think that maybe someday I should retire, before it's too late, and find a woman to grow old with. Well, growing even older than I am now, heh."

With that, Borak changed the topic to the gadgets and gizmos which he loved so much. He opened a cabinet and pulled out some drawers full of backup widgets he had made. "I have designed so many of my own parts for existing products…An' this one here, this one fits into the little pendulum you find in the traverse counter machine…And this one, as you may have guessed, is a screw and pivot that fits into the tailpipe, so it can turn in the little personal flying machines. Of course, all of these fancy devices we have and fix really aren't as complicated as one might think. I mean, you have already been working here for weeks now, you know what it's like to fix these sorta things.

"Yeh see, boy, things we have seem high tech on the surface, but we actually just use our own wind energy as the power source. We have not advanced to real propulsion systems for generations. This makes us seem to have a highly advanced technology, but is largely not advanced at all when yeh look at how the source all goes back to our innate wind power. But as yeh may or may not know, the Warix are in a position of power over the other races because of this, because the other races can't use it.

Hence, the Meruyans remain in the dark ages of technology and under our thumb. New tech is invented also specifically with this in mind I'm afraid, specifically capitalizing on the fact that non-Warix cannot access it."

"Borak, I had no idea you were so worldly and knew about the Meruyans. Or cared!" Flax commented, holding his tongue from adding *for a Sen'Drorn living in denial of their crimes.*

"Well. I don't like what we, the Sen'Drorn that is, do," replied Borak, removing his heavy workman's gloves, smudged with black oil at the fingertips. He washed his rough hands in the industrial-sized sink.

After shutting down the lights and machines, the two headed upstairs from the workshop as Flax anticipated, restarting the conversation in the flat above the shop. Borak's living room had a fireplace and two leather armchairs, each angled toward the fire. Borak had altered the chairs himself, of course, fixed with little springs for leaning back, adjustable wooden table flaps, and all kinds of hidden pockets.

Flax slipped into the soft armchair, engulfing his body in decadent comfort after a long day on his feet serving customers and working the shop. By now he finally did more than just use a wrench to tighten bolts and learn what every little doohickey was for. Borak stood over the fire, building and stoking it, before dropping into to his chair as well.

"Wind power, meh boy!" Borak said, gazing into the crackling fire from his armchair. "That is an innate privilege we Warix all possess, and it is quite easy to come up with new technology that uses it. I feel for the Meruyans, I do. Without it, they can't wind up automated machines to keep track of things for themselves. Sometimes I wish I hadn't been a coward back then, and had stood up for them, and gone away with Odella. Who knows who or where I'd be today."

Flax held back the smile at the mention of his mother's name.

Borak was silent for a time. The two of them sat there pondering and taking in the night, staring at the fireplace as it crackled. Borak went over and opened a window. He sank down into his armchair once again, reaching into a pouch and pulling out an old wooden pipe and matches.

He started on another topic, as he often did. "I got this idea for another machine, which can hoist objects up to the second story. It involves ropes and a spinning wheel under a basket, of course powered by wind. Needs recalibrating though, on a test I sent a cake up, and it splattered right into the ceiling! Heh…an apprentice would have been nice back then!"

Then, something strange happened. Borak turned to Flax and said, "Ya know, it's nice to have yeh here, Flax. Yeh are a good assistant, and like a son to me. I never had a family of me own before. What I mean is, it's nice ter have yeh around…"

"Thanks, Borak." Flax's heart raced, he didn't know what to say. "You are like a father to me, too."

Borak said, "Anyway, perhaps it is time to get some rest."

After they parted from the lounge, Flax retired to his room. He stared at the ceiling from his bed, contemplating what Borak had said. A warm wave washed over him—Borak had not willingly abandoned his mother, nor stayed for reason of lacking morality. He was a good person.

He longed to tell Borak the truth about their relationship, but how could he ever? How much longer could he keep the secret, while still living here? The truth pained him until he drifted into sleep.

CHAPTER SEVENTEEN

Meleena, Deem, and Talla arrived at the center of Gebuk'Desa, the town in the Northern Villages, where busy Warix and Meruyans loaded and moved crates piled high with copper widgets. Another busy day. Meleena was determined to find out more about the working life of the Meruyan here. The dust swirled around her feet, and she glanced up to see flying machines passing overhead, carrying sacks of fruit that dangled below underneath.

"This way." Meleena pointed to signs for the copper mines.

They walked along a wide dirt road on one of the hillsides. A grassy hill with a farmhouse on it stood on the left, up the hill. Wooden beams held up a cave-like opening in the hill, flanked by boulders on each side. A steady stream of Meruyan men pushed wheelbarrows full of shining lumps of glittering reddish ore, which Meleena supposed was copper, from the dark opening out into the field, behind the small farmhouse where one of those flying machines was parked.

Deciding to approach, Meleena waved Deem and Talla forward. She pointed to a thick tree they could hide behind at the corner of an adjacent fruit orchard. The orchard was unattended, and gazing up into the leaves, Meleena could see it bore fruit that was still green and not yet ready for harvest. With Deem and Talla on her heels, they could inspect the open-topped flying machine. It roosted in the clearing, long spindles of tan cloth flanked its sides, and it had grated floors with handles jutting up. What was the function of all of this?

A dozen Meruyans bustled throughout the area, coming and going from inside the mine, depositing copper ore onto the flying machine's open back, while the few Warix mainly directed the process. Other Warix stood around, munching on fruit and socializing. Some played cards at a table in the shade of a large tree.

"Be careful, filthy pond scum!" one Warix barked at the Meruyan, who loaded the full crates onto the flying machine. Meleena was close enough to see their arms wobble from the weight. When the flying machine's cargo was packed, the socializing Warix finally started stirring. What a windy day, thought Meleena, rubbing her chilly forearms as the wind picked up again.

From this distance, they could finally make out more details of the flying machine and how it operated. Several of the Warix who previously stood around stopped leaning against the trees and stepped onto the machine, as the Meruyans scattered a good distance. They held onto the handles with one arm and stretched their other down a wide tube at the shoulders of the machine. Then something happened that made Meleena's jaw drop. Gusts of wind seemed to burst from their hands and flow through the tubes, and down the channels in the cloth, which spun, quicker and quicker, until the machine became dislodged from the ground, and as the Warix kept energizing it, the rotating fabric turned faster, and the machine became airborne.

The carrier lifted straight up off the ground, launching a backdraft of wind onto the ground below.

Meleena and Deem exchanged amazed glances.

About twenty paces away, one of the Meruyan men who had lifted the cart into the flying machine, had wandered off. Panting, he leaned against an orchard tree.

"You're right, Meleena, Professor Levlos would never let us get near to this kind of action," Talla said sarcastically.

"Don't you see?" Meleena pointed to the machine. "That! How is that thing flying?"

Talla crunched her face but came up with nothing.

Deem shrugged. "I mean, we do that all the time underwater, swim all over the place, up, down, wherever. Is it that hard to do on land?"

"Yes!" Meleena burst out. "I forget you aren't used to living on the shore. But it's not like underwater. Meruyans don't have stuff like that. Did you see how they made it fly? They were manipulating the wind with their hands!"

Deem shook his head. "Hmm, Professor Levlos said the Warix share their technology with us. That machine looks like all it does is carry loads off, who knows where."

"...To their cities," Meleena finished. "They clearly take almost all of what we produce! And"—Meleena lifted her hands—"we can't manipulate wind. How much other technology do they have, but can't and don't share with us, because it runs on wind power?"

He pondered a moment. "I dunno, this is still a lot of conclusions to draw."

Talla chimed in. "I say, whoever is smart enough or strong enough to impose a system like that, should be able to keep it. It's just superior powers being successful."

"Except the Meruyans are at the bottom," Meleena growled.

"You there!" barked a voice in their direction, causing the trio to jump. Meleena had forgotten in all the excitement to stay quiet, but to her surprise, it wasn't directed at them.

A stray Meruyan mine worker, his face and linen pants full of dusty earth, had wandered away from the mines and into the orchard, just a few trees away. He had picked a fruit to eat, slumping behind a tree facing away from his workplace, though not inconspicuously enough, as the shouts continued. A grey-skinned Warix of advanced age with thinning black hair and twisting horns came stomping into the orchard to wrangle the Meruyan man.

"His uniform looks fancier than the other Warix. He's probably their supervisor," Meleena whispered to Deem as they rotated undercover behind the tree to watch. On his shoulder, she saw a sigil of a flower-maned lion on a green backdrop.

"Get back to work!" the Warix barked again. The Meruyan man winced and scurried further into the orchard with his apple, but the Warix cracked a long object, which made a thunderous sound before wrapping around the Meruyan's leg, flipping him onto the ground. Then the Warix turned and shouted at a group of Warix socializing nearby. "What are you doing standing around? There are Meruyans slacking all around here! There is one right there! You are all useless!"

Then he marched closer to the Meruyan worker, still tangled in the whip, and blasted him with a wind burst, knocking him over to one side. The socializing Warix took little notice of their supervisor—they were still chatting away among themselves.

"Get back into that mine and stop eating our produce!"

The Meruyan stammered to his feet, now free from the whip, and ran off with a fearful expression.

"You three!" the supervisor turned his fierce eyes toward Meleena, Deem, and Talla, who shuddered, realizing too late they were not as hidden as they thought.

"What are you doing there? Shouldn't you be in the mine?"

He marched up to them, getting very close. He was somewhat muscular but quite short for a Warix, not much taller than Talla. Deem stood behind her, gripping her shoulders, causing her to shake. Meleena's heart pounded, but although taken aback, a wave of courage overtook her after witnessing all this. The other Warix now took notice, yet instead of backing up their leader, they only giggled among themselves, interested to see what would happen next.

"We do not work in any field, or for any Warix master!" Meleena huffed, staring into his eyes, which sent a shiver down her spine. They were more like voids, white and without pupils.

"The Meruyans are a proud people!" Deem said, gulping, nervously and adding the awkward statement.

"Who do you think you are talking to like that? I am Thowler, overseer of these mines!"

His lower lip twitched, and a pulsing vein became clear in his broad forehead. His blank eyes glowed silver as he summoned a swirling mini tornado to his upturned palm, his other hand cracking the thunderous whip.

Meleena ground her teeth and removed her new glasses. Everyone became a blur of shapes and colors, reducing her fear. Meleena took a deep breath. "I am a Champion of Aldrok's Journey, a future leader of the Meruyan people, and you have no right to harm me!"

Overseer Thowler puffed his chest, but the whip dropped from his hand as he huffed, "Who taught you to speak like that to a Warix!? You clearly don't know your place here!"

Just as Meleena shrank away, Talla took over, staring into his pupilless eyes, and shouted, "I don't like your brand of abusive work!"

Talla backing her up? A new strength rose from inside Meleena, and she scowled alongside Talla. Deem, who had been hiding behind, merely winced and shrank further. "What are you two doing?" she heard him urgently whisper.

Overseer Thowler's face turned bright red. He gaped at her and then lifted his wrist, which held a mechanical device around it, not unlike the one Meleena had seen her brother wear. He shouted into it, "It's Overseer Thowler—I need support at Copper Mine Jensen!" A static buzzing sound replied.

Meleena recalled her brother's wrist gadget. Standard Warix tech that was barely reaching the privileged rungs of Meruyan society—a gift from their brother on the Council, in their case.

Thowler smirked at her. "Let's see how big-headed you are now! I may not be allowed to touch you, but the General will surely know what to do! It is your good fortune he is in town, and you can take your concerns up with him."

Thowler crossed his arms, a smirk on his ugly face, as Meleena and the others waited for what would happen next. She didn't know what to do, where to go, only folded her arms and scowled back at him.

The wind picked up again. Without moving her head, Meleena saw from the corners of her eyes a tornado blowing over the path on the hill beside them, coming closer. She gazed at its core, where two glistening sparks caught her eye, which held firm until the tornado dulled in power on the gravel outside the mine.

With a sudden whip and lash of pressure, the tornado subsided in a barrel of wind, and the sparks of two glowing eyes fixed on them, now in the face of a tall, leanly muscular Warix. Steer horns protruded from a shaggy, black mane, dark against his ashen skin tone. His features cast a ferocious, wild appearance, yet his dignified posture portrayed quite the opposite. His hands locked behind his back as he approached with poise.

Something about his contrasting features, natural beastly wrath, held back by self-restraint, struck Meleena with awe. As he came up behind Thowler, he gave a half-smile, Thowler's height reaching only to the badges on the dark Warix's decorated uniform.

He cast his face down on them. Deem quivered, Meleena gulped, Talla's hands slid limp from her hips.

"I am General Malotus, supervising these operations. What seems to be the problem?" he spoke quite softly, though his pointed ears twitched.

Thowler threw a fit, his clenched hands in the air, trying to explain that this girl was in the way and disrespecting them, but the man was hearing none of it and quickly shushed him, turning instead to Meleena.

"No, I believe I asked this girl. What has happened here?" He smiled, bearing sharp pearly whites. It was not a warm smile, but one to intimidate.

Meleena stepped back.

Overseer Thowler's smirked. In a sudden gust of wind, the usual pressure of ground beneath her feet disappeared as Malotus lifted her off the ground.

She managed to utter, "We are future leaders from the Southern Villages, here to learn about all that's going on here!"

"Ah, so that explains the...unusual behavior."

The wind died and Meleena's feet returned to the ground.

"What a bold girl you are..." Malotus cocked his head in intrigue. "A couple of passersby come to see how we run our operations. And here I was under the presumption you had a guide to show you around."

"Your operations are…oppressive…" Meleena again realized, for some reason, they couldn't harm her. "Stealing products and exploiting the Meruyans who live here! Arenay would not like this!"

"Arenay!?" Malotus belted out a chill laugh. "My my… we don't want you getting the wrong impression of the Sen'Drorn."

"Sen'Drorn?" gasped Meleena. "You…"

"I beg your pardon?"

Her mouth fell open. "How is that possible…?"

Deem, and Talla exchanged puzzled looks.

Malotus looked down at Meleena, his sharp eyes now dark green, penetrating. "We are simply operating a business, trading goods for services. The Warix provide the Meruyans with technology, so they themselves can enjoy life on land. All the Sen'Drorn ask is to have a couple of shipments sent to them as well. That is the contract we have signed with the Meruyan Council. It is, therefore, impossible to be unethical. Pardon me."

Catching them off guard and without another word, he stepped aside, whipped up a small tornado for himself, kicking up dirt as it went over the path. The Warix underlings seized Deem, Talla, and Meleena. Their clawed fingers dug into their shoulders.

"Oo, he'll get you now," Overseer Thowler cackled.

After a tense pause, Malotus's tornado returned and dissipated with a Meruyan in his outstretched arms. Professor Levlos struggled until he was set down and slid onto the ground. He got up, dusting himself off, looked confused and alarmed, then indignant.

"Councilman Professor Levlos, I have found your little fishies far from their roost. Stick to schedule as agreed, and don't make them my problem again, or I will make myself yours and theirs, with less restraint than I am kind enough to offer you at this moment." He tried to sound polite, but his eyes glistened with an insane fiery madness. Meleena could hardly look. Overseer Thowler cracked his whip.

"Yes…sir," Professor Levlos squeaked and cleared his throat, changing tone as he addressed Meleena and Deem now. "Come along with me. You are in serious trouble for sneaking around on your own like this! You could have disturbed production or hurt yourselves!"

Meleena shook her head in disbelief. This guy was still playing right into Malotus.

"Is it true, Professor Levlos? We're under a contract with the Sen'Drorn?"

"Yes, of course! We only work with the Sen'Drorn!" Levlos chuckled, tense, and wringing his hands. "Would never dream of breaking that alliance!"

Meleena said no more. She could merely watch the situation unfold.

Professor Levlos put his hands together. "We are sorry to cause you trouble, sir!"

Malotus sneered. "I must get back to business now."

He disappeared in another tornado and was gone. Talla passed out, clutching her head.

Once Talla came to, the three followed Professor Levlos up the dusty path in silence. Levlos marched them straight back to Saru's place, demanding they would wait out the rest of the day at the house. "You will stay there, supervised, and no more talk of this or outings until Talla is fully healed."

Meleena figured it was just an excuse. Professor Levlos was mad, embarrassed, and needed some time to cool down. It got worse at dinner that night when Levlos extended his punishment. "You youths will not be allowed to wander the streets in free time anymore."

To Meleena's surprise, it was Talla who came to their defense. She batted her eyes and cast a bright smile, tilting her head. "But, sir, how will we learn? We promise not to cause more trouble. You have my honor."

He grumbled, "I simply cannot have you disturbing production or obstructing the daily life of citizens."

Confident and yet soft, she mewed, "Come now. We will behave."

Meleena stared in disbelief, how could that work? Yet Professor Levlos was disarmed. He scoffed. "Alright, fine. But if I get called away or hear one word of any of you disturbing the peace again—and be sure I will be asking around town—those involved will fail and be expelled from The Journey and barred from ever joining the Council."

"Yes, sir." Talla nodded in calm agreement. "We accept your terms graciously."

Meleena had heard Talla speak like that to teachers, bargaining for better grades with charm and reason. It always amazed her how she could be so blatant in such demands, though never could imagine it used in her favor. She realized at that moment that maybe she had something to learn from Talla, after all.

At light's out, they could finally fill Talla in on what she missed. Meleena tried to convince the others of her theories about the Warix. It was clear enough to her that Warix had wind power, and used it to power machines, which Meruyans couldn't.

"I mean, Malotus didn't hurt us, plus he said it himself, there is a contract," Deem had reasoned. It was hard for them to believe her about these unconfirmed "other Warix" at war with these apparent allies. And so, they remained unconvinced.

Meleena, though still frustrated, dropped the topic over the next few days of tours, as it wasn't worth it without any new evidence. Without her journal, the pressure built up inside her. She was unable to organize her thoughts or put her observations on paper. On tours, they watched the Meruyan production and continued to hear all about the great history and modern production techniques.

After nearly a month of studying in the Northern Villages, Professor Levlos announced some good news one evening over dinner. Some farmers by the shore had located Peela and Clover. They were safe, found grazing on algae and kelp not too far offshore.

"I was going to wait two weeks for our overnight trip to the underwater villages, but since your kelpie companions have been located, I suggest we get an early start tomorrow and ride them to the underwater villages. Since they are halfway there already, and we will need them to ride underwater anyway. I shall go ahead and meet you at the edge of town tomorrow morning. It is a short walk, and I trust you three not to get lost."

That night, Meleena dreamed about a skeletal kelpie rising from the sea in a cold mist, coming at her in a rage. She pleaded that she was going to try to find her, that she would get her back safely, but the skeletal kelpie huffed and launched itself at her, while pages scattered the ground from her destroyed journal. Her parents' shocked and disappointed faces floated around her, sending a cold ice chill down her spine. The tall Warix, Malotus, appeared. She asked if he was friend or foe. He said he was there to help her but then stepped aside for the kelpie to slash her to death. She awoke in a cold sweat, and it was dawn.

In the morning, they rose to find a tropical storm had rolled in and it poured all night and morning. The capital shipped supplies for their overnight trip, including a rucksack, first aid kit, clothes, and a day's rations of Warix bread, cheese, and Meruyan seafood.

Standing by the front door, looking out at the dewy pasture and bright fruit trees, Meleena's heart was heavy. Was Peela safe? Her new journal unshredded? She longed to be united with them both, soon.

CHAPTER EIGHTEEN

Flax stood at the service counter of Borak's shop, daydreaming on the nice evening he had with Borak. He wasn't even bothered by a screaming child in the store, whose parents browsed the products, ignoring the cries. Any minute now, his shift would end, and there would be no more taking orders from crazy clients, causing a commotion, no more mundane questions, whether their trinkets were actually broken or not.

Flax thought about his time working here, that his father was a decent man all along and the lavender-haired angel who walked into his life, both of whom he constantly had to lie to about who he was. He was exhausted. And such was his complicated life, trying to balance the people he had come to care about with the inevitability that it would all end one day, one way or another. To choose between them and his loyalty to the Sen'Prin was harder each day he stayed in this life.

Yulah came through the creaking shop doors. "Hey Flax!" She leaned over the desk and kissed him on the cheek.

"Why don't we come to my house tonight? After a nice dinner out, that is!" Yulah winked at Flax. He blushed. She was so irresistibly sensual.

After a few minutes, and a nod and wink from Borak, they headed into town for dinner, followed by the walk to her house.

As they made the uphill hike to Yulah's loft, she slipped her hand daintily into Flax's.

"I want to show you someplace new." She led him around the back of her building to a mossy wall with a ladder embedded into the green web.

"This will take us to the roof. It's very romantic." She winked. "And, I have some important good news, 'military VIP exclusive' news to tell!"

She read his doubtful expression. He'd hoped instead for some nice, indoor relaxation. Cuddling, perhaps. Yulah gave him a look of playful pleading as she held the ladder. "Come on, up, up!"

With a small wind burst, she flew up, the ladder serving as mere guidance, and poked her head down at him from above. Now he had no choice but to follow her up.

The view was mesmerizing from up there. She was right about that. From the rooftop, one could see above the whole city nestled in the middle between curtains of pine trees, with the spires of the fortress off to the left. A dark, clear sky dotted with stars loomed over the glittering city lights, forming a spherical landscape. The two sat there for a while, lost admiring it, and each other, in the enveloping peace and tranquility of the night. Yulah sat so elegantly, with her hands together over her upper thighs, leaning against his body. Her head rested upon his shoulder. Flax was beside her sitting sideways, bodyweight leaning on his arm for support, the other around her waist.

For a while, Yulah spoke not of any news, but of their general lives in the city, and how happy they were to have found each other. The conversation sidetracked onto the topic of Borak and how nice it is that she frequented the shop. Flax agreed and gave a happy sigh. He was not feeling so talkative, enjoying relaxing in the balmy night.

"Since I am on the job until so late most days, working with Borak long past business hours, it has been great that you can visit me so often," Flax spoke softly, his words flowing out into the sweet night.

Yulah let out a gasp at the sentiment of Borak. The name had reminded her of something important. She cut in, "Borak certainly is a skilled engineer and gifted inventor. His work has not gone unnoticed within the fortress walls." Flax looked intrigued.

Yulah continued, "This is top secret information, though. Officially, there will be a message delivered to the shop sometime tomorrow…I just wanted to tell you the good news myself."

"Oh?" Flax stared.

Yulah beamed. "The Emperor wants someone to create top-secret new technology. Developing engineering products large scale, for military use. They have begun training soldiers already and soon will need high-tech gear to match. Like things that Borak makes, which enhances wind powers. He's a great inventor, you know."

Flax looked stunned. "Borak?"

"Yeah, he's a genius, your mentor, you know. He invented a clever new technique to enhance wind energy on lighter gear. High surface area copper chambers scale up wind energy exponentially, developed and used exclusively for gear for us."

Flax shook his head. He had no clue what she was talking about.

Seeing his puzzled expression, she added, "Yeah, you know. He was under contract from us not to even tell any apprentices about it, but surely you might have wondered what was in the boxes I collect twice a week?"

Borak has been making supplies for soldiers? His heart fluttered. I...even made some of this stuff...

"Is the Emperor planning to march troops against the Sen'Prin sometime soon?" Flax asked.

"Well, they haven't decided on when exactly, but they have to prepare for the future and the inevitable destruction of those Sen'Prin traitors. Anyway, Borak's fine work was mentioned by name at the recent war meeting. He will be honored by Sen'Drorn. He has been chosen to move to the fortress to work full time for us and scale up to military engineering operations."

"Ah yeah?" He smiled weakly, head feeling faint. "What about Borak's shop?"

"It gets even better!" Yulah giggled. "Don't worry about the shop! His shop on Fleeg Street can remain open, thanks to his apprentice...That is, you! Borak has instilled his knowledge in you, Flax. You could take over as owner and new engineering master on Fleeg Street. You can hire an apprentice of your own! This is a huge promotion for you both! Aren't you excited?"

Flax was still absorbing it all, like shockwaves electrocuting him to the bone. Yulah fell on him in a warm embrace. Worse still, Flax knew he had a duty to report this information to the Sen'Prin. They would not take this well. Maybe he could hide it from them. But for how long?

When they descended from the rooftop, Yulah invited him into her loft.

"I...I can't tonight," he stuttered. "All this is a lot to think about. It's a big change. I think I'll call it early."

He leaned over and gave her cheek a kiss before turning to leave.

"I understand, you want to tell Borak the good news. Just don't go telling anyone else, it's a huge military secret!" She blew him a kiss as he tried not to stumble on his flight down the dark hills and stone paths towards town.

CHAPTER NINETEEN

The rain beat down, obscuring the view of the hills as Meleena, Deem, and Talla headed down the lane, Pinchy scampering beside them. They passed sprawling fields freshly shorn, lined with wildflowers and ferns, dripping wet from the rain. The sun rose over the glorious landscape, accenting ancient palm trees which bent, drenched in the thickening rain.

They passed fields and small wood-dome huts, becoming less dense as the fields expanded onto the hills over the horizon. The forest lay beyond the cultured orchard filled lands, dense and lush and still undisturbed.

After following a muddy track leading out of town, they came to a fork, with a moldy wooden sign directing from above. Tall grass slumped in the overgrown fields along the road, and water ran off the roadsides into little streams.

"Can either of you see where we should go?" asked Talla, pouting. Her sprouted arm fins pushed her dripping hair from her face.

Meleena tried to read the sign, also holding her hands above her eyes and squinting from the rain. Her arms were heavy. As much as Meruyans were accustomed to being wet, that mainly applied to being in the water. They really didn't like the rain. It was a big inconvenience of their kind when living on land.

"This way says, 'The Sea,'" she called. Odd, the ocean, just an afterthought. *How far the Meruyans had come from their roots, so they need a sign to tell them where the ocean was!*

The other direction's sign wasn't easily legible. While both were green with moss and wear, this one looked particularly damaged, even scratched out.

"I just can't wait to be back home underwater," Deem said.

"Let's just go," said Talla. "One step closer to victory."

"Wait, what about this other way?" asked Meleena. Her stomach twisted into knots at the warped letters of the moldy sign. The aroma of wet wood, mud, and the stench of neutolyth dung was mingled with something else—a hint of burned wood. In that rain, it seemed impossible.

"It looks like just more villages that way."

"Can we take a quick detour and have a look?" asked Meleena. Her curiosity seemed to be pulling her that way. She sensed something was odd about it. She wanted to know more.

"I need to know more. I don't care if you guys follow me or not. I need to see more of that place, without their eyes on us."

Deem nodded. "Yeah, I guess I'm also curious…but only a quick look, and that's it."

"Agreed." Meleena smiled.

Talla folded her arms. "I'd really rather not."

"Open your eyes, Talla! Something bigger is going on here! Don't you want to be the best Council member one day? The more you know, the better chance you have," Meleena argued.

Talla raised her eyebrows.

"This is the edge you need! They wouldn't even know how you know these things. You'll just look smarter than everyone."

"What things?"

"Whatever is being hidden behind that path. But you will never know if we don't go take a look."

Just then, Meleena turned. The sound of rain beating was disrupted by splashing mud. A farmer driving a neutolyth-pulled cart was heading their way along the path.

"We need to decide quickly. They won't like us snooping around."

Talla shrugged. "Okay, fair."

Meleena's heart was already racing, and she darted into a dip off the side of the road to crouch behind tall reeds. Deem jumped too and pulled Talla in. Pinchy scuttled behind among them. Ducking together, they watched through the grass curtain as the cart rolled past. The trio grinned at each other, visible steam coming from their breath.

What a rush! This was even better than those mischievous days she had ditched school for the forest alone. Now she had friends to enjoy sneaking around with. Yes, she dared to entertain the odd notion.

Never would she have thought it could be these two.

"I think it's safe now, let's hurry," she whispered, straightening up. Talla, Deem, and Pinchy followed as she snuck up the steep path.

They didn't stop until they were over the hill and out of sight of the main road. The rain lightened into mist, and the aroma of burnt wood intensified, replacing the sweet scent of damp grass. Meleena was relieved when her arm fins shrank back down.

The rucksacks bounced on their backs as they crossed the dip in the hill, which led down into an adjacent valley. On all sides, the hills were abandoned and devoid of plant life. The trees were nothing but black nubs. A sense of dread washed over Meleena. She wiped the moisture from her forehead, wrung out her hair, and rubbed her glasses on her tunic.

"Meruyans were just not meant to be out in the rain," she muttered, feeling exhausted and grumpy.

She looked around to gain her bearing. The forest had been cleared. Clearly, the farmland which replaced the jungle was burnt away. Remnants of wooden houses were collapsed around, in the rough form of a village.

"Woah…what is this place?"

Meleena looked over at Talla, who looked perplexed, frowning at the site, and Deem's eyes, which had grown wide behind his large frames. Meleena figured her face looked like a combination of the two as she gulped.

They walked further, stepping over charred wooden beams and iron parts. Broken ox carts and skeletal remains of animals sat on barren farmland. Pinchy gave a whimpering hiss.

"Yeah, it looks like a fire," whispered Deem.

"Do fish have fins?" said Talla sarcastically.

The path sloped so that they could see another hill. This one was not as empty. Meleena could make out some sort of shadowy grey figures on the hillside. Pinchy made an urgent bubbling sound again.

"Not now, Pinchy," Deem whispered to him.

"Look! Is that Malotus?" asked Meleena, pointing. She could now see the grey military clothing of the Sen'Drorn, lined up in successive rows. A Warix stood facing them in emerald-green uniforms. She could make out General Malotus's wild black mane and protruding steer horns. Her heart raced.

"So that's where he spends his free time," she gulped.

"This place is awful."

Malotus's face turned, and he looked up the hill.

"Oh, crab-claw! He's looking at us!"

"It's too late to hide!"

In a coordinated motion, Meleena, Deem, and Talla turned and rushed back down a hill, trying to get out of sight.

There was a whirl as the wind picked up, sending ash and damp mist into their faces.

"Pinchy!" Deem called, as they ducked again. Pinchy scuttled away so fast. He was over the hills and out of sight before Meleena could catch her breath.

"He's run off back to town!"

"That can't be a good sign," gulped Meleena. Having failed to convince them to return, he apparently took the initiative for himself. Perhaps his age had brought him wisdom.

"Oh, how lovely," came a deeper voice. "Seems we have guests."

Meleena spun around to see a mouthful of pearly teeth grinning at her. In the distance, she could hear the soldiers chanting in sync. Malotus and two guards at his sides stood behind them. Malotus brushed his black bangs from his eyes as he glared down at them.

"What are young Meruyans doing here?" his velvety voice cooed. "You are disrupting my training session."

Meleena choked for words. "I...we..."

"What is this place?" asked Talla.

"This is the burnt lands."

"Accidents happened," said a guard.

"Please, let us educate our guests. They are here, aren't they? Though you know you have no right to be here. But since you know about it now, maybe we can make examples of you."

His guards grabbed Deem and Talla. Malotus continued to lock eyes with Meleena.

Meleena gulped and removed her glasses. He became a blur of ashen color. Now confidence returned, and no fear, she shouted right at him, "I don't care if you do have some sort of deal with the Meruyan, I think it's corrupt! If you are enemies of Arenay, that makes you the Warix who attacked my village!"

Malotus looked taken aback. "You're from that village...with the pendant...How could you possibly have guessed?"

Her eyes widened. Thunder boomed in the distance. "You!"

"Oh, me." A smile returned, as did his pearly, sharp teeth. Damn that smile.

"It really was you." Her eyes widened, and she took a step back. He stepped forward on those ashen, wolf-like clawed feet, clasped in steel above and below the open boots.

His guards' gloves sparked.

"I can do what I want with you," he purred. "You are here at my discretion, and I want to have some fun."

"I uhh..." she said hesitantly.

His eyes widened.

The guards held her friends firmly.

"Oh, you know something, do you? I believe I am going to keep this one..." He flared a smile that cut deep. *How are his smiles so creepy?* She became transfixed, trying to anticipate his next action.

"Well, let's say I had to destroy everything to enforce the rules. You see, one of the secrets of the Sen'Drorn is, we taught your people valuable technology, but in the end, you can't use most of it, because you can't manipulate wind or fire. Our wind goddess blessed us above your water gods…"

Then she saw it, much too fast to respond. His piercing green eyes clouded with silver, like smoke running through and filling them. They shined with it, illuminated. Before she could dodge it, his hand lifted and shot a burst of wind, throwing her backward onto the ground. The wind picked up around them, and Malotus's feet lifted from off the ground. "This will be fun. No witnesses."

Deem, Meleena, and Talla, all shouting, were rolled into the wind gust with Malotus, and they lifted high into the air. The force of the wind beat continuously, her clothes whipping around. Meleena grew dizzy, the corners of her sight black. Bits of ash stung her eyes. Rain and pebbles slapped her with moisture and cuts. Just as the world disappeared from view, the speed changed in the great storm. The forces weakened. Another dust cloud was forcing its way in, interrupting the flow, like a cloud hitting another and merging, neutralizing. They felt themselves lowering back to the ground.

Calling above the wind, Meleena heard a silky woman's voice as they tumbled to the ground. A beautiful Warix, probably only a couple years older than Meleena, stood over them. Her wispy violet hair settled as she stood next to Malotus, her eyes glowing silver.

"Mal, you can't just kill these kids! How many times do I have to beg you not to be so destructive!"

"Yulah! What are you doing here?" Malotus snapped, his shining silver eyes narrowing and returning to green.

"I have an urgent message from Emperor Ryogrim, sir! Oh my! Are these the troublesome Meruyans you mentioned in your transmission?"

"Never mind them. What did Emperor Ryogrim want?"

"Since the Pendant hasn't turned up, we have to develop new weapons and a new strategy. The Emperor needs you back for another war meeting. Now let these Meruyans go!"

"But, Yulah, they shouldn't be here. I can do what I want with them."

"For storm's sake. I'll escort them back to town."

"Yulah…I didn't raise you to disobey me."

Yulah turned to Meleena, Deem, and Talla. "Come with me, young Meruyans."

Malotus shook his head, his stare penetrating, though he didn't make any move to stop her.

"Hold onto me and each other for stability." The purple-haired girl created a gentler tornado. Instead of being caught up, twisting in it, they held into a tight hug, which felt much smoother.

Meleena's feet tingled with the unnatural state of being so far from the ground, but the rush in her head became wonder: these wind abilities of the Warix were really quite fantastic—especially when not being used to torment. Meleena wished she could control a tornado.

"Oh, fishbones!" Deem gasped, looking down. Talla was silent with terror.

Meleena tried to picture Governess Arenay commanding a tornado. She watched the landscape change from blackened back to lush green.

Meleena spotted a small, robed figure that could only be Professor Levlos. He ran towards them as they descended. Closer to the ground, Yulah's hands lowered, and the group loosened their grip. They landed softly on their feet.

Professor Levlos had a kelpie at one side. Pinchy scuttled at his other.

"Pinchy!" exclaimed Deem, running to his pet.

"Where have you kids been? You weren't at the meeting place!"

Yulah spoke first. "I believe I found your wards. They are safe now, but they really shouldn't have been in the Burnt Lands…"

"Oh my…they went *where?*" Professor Levlos appeared flustered.

"We almost died!" Meleena shouted, her legs still wobbling in protest. "This is Yulah. She works for Malotus. You know him. This time he tried to kill us."

"Well!" protested Levlos. "I hardly think…"

Yulah said, "I have to go now. But, Meruyan, I need to warn you. You got on General Malotus's bad side today. You need to be far away from here before he returns. He holds a grudge. Is there a way they can go north sooner?"

Professor Levlos crinkled his brow, considering. "I will alert Mayor Tegushi in the Arctic City and see if she can accommodate an early arrival." He pulled a conch shell from his pocket and spoke into its opening. He set it down on the ground, where spindly legs emerged, and a hermit crab unfolded and scuttled quickly out of sight.

Yulah's eyes widened.

"We Meruyans still have some tricks of our own." He smiled.

She bowed and waved goodbye to them all, then backed away before starting a tornado that flew over the horizon.

Professor Levlos looked at Deem, Meleena, and Talla, about to scold them. At that moment, in their own words, they turned on him first.

"Meruyan life is not what you have told us! What are the Burnt Lands? What is really going on here?" Meleena demanded.

"We want answers! *Now!*" Talla stomped.

"...Or we won't follow you another step!" Deem chimed in, shaking.

Professor Levlos's eyes widened. He was at a loss of words.

Meleena wasn't done. "The Meruyan people aren't working for the Sen'Prin nation! The Northern Villages are on *Sen'Drorn* land! The same Warix nation who destroyed my village last year. General Malotus says he's overseeing lawful work. How can the Meruyan Council exploit its own people like this?"

Professor Levlos regained control of his voice. "Alright. At this point, I guess you have a right to know. As you've learned in school, Warix explorers first made contact with Meruyan. But here, things were different. The Northern Villages bear the brunt of the debt for our technology."

"But we learned it was about cultural sharing..." Deem said.

"At first, yes. The Northern Villages started growing crops, but more and more Meruyan began moving to this area from underwater, to supply Warix labor demands, and for the promise of a better life than in the sea. As you saw, the entire valley system is now farmed for the Sen'Drorn."

Meleena crossed her arms. "They look overworked and underfed."

He sighed, his eyelids sagged. "Well, maybe they do rely a *little* more on the sun's rays in their hair to be effective workers. But now you know as much as I do. No secrets. There is no easy solution here."

He went on, "I am sorry to have deceived you. I am proud of what they do. They work hard. The Council has agreed to these terms. They don't see another way we can benefit otherwise. I should have been honest about it earlier."

"The Council, living in the protected mountain city benefits more than these average working Meruyans do!" Meleena stomped.

"Sure, they live better on average. But what can we do? We need the Warix, and they can demand whatever price they want for their technology. The shore is their world. Even your glasses were provided by the Warix. Most Meruyans can't even see, couldn't live here, without the Warix. If the Meruyans want to live on land, they have to do what the dominant Warix nation wants."

Meleena unfolded her arms and removed her glasses, like a cage upon her face. Just two pieces of glass and wire, yet they allowed her to view and draw the wondrous plants and animals of this world above the sea. This was the world she grew up in, called home —more than the sea.

"Why don't the Meruyans just return to the sea and avoid the Warix altogether?" Deem suggested.

Meleena looked at him. She knew the answer for herself and suspected it was the same for other Meruyans.

Professor Levlos said, "It's not a simple fix. Now that we Meruyans have known life on land, we're addicted to the technology. You can't simply return to life underwater, knowing what great things you are missing. Never to taste cooked food again, the comfort of bedsheets, nor tell the time of day. I will show you on our next leg of the tour, The Underwater City. It's the last true Meruyan city, for those who opt out of technology and stay in the wet ages. They live a simple life that would bore us to tears."

Deem knitted his brow. "I live underwater. It's not so bad."

"You're unusual, then. The population of The Underwater City declines each year as their youth goes ashore to see what they've been missing. Those who leave don't often return. I'll show you this city, and the history with your own eyes. Please, let me be your honest guide going forth. We still must retrieve your pets from the seashore. I hope to arrive at your inn tonight before dark."

Meleena gasped, she had forgotten all about her kelpie in a mess. *Peela.* Her pulse quickened with anticipation: a mix of sorrow and excitement.

Though they followed him without protest, Meleena turned to the others, hoping they got the hint to hang back. They took her lead, slowly falling out of earshot of Professor Levlos.

"We have to do something. Those poor Meruyans are suffering, and our government won't even help them!"

Deem and Talla exchanged nervous glances.

"I'd love to help them, but what could we do?" Deem pouted.

"I don't know, but it has to be something," Meleena said.

Talla rolled her eyes. "We'll be kicked out of the Journey for sure if we stir up any more trouble."

***

Yulah pushed open the door to Malotus's chambers with a heavy heart. She knew she was in trouble for standing up to him. For freeing those Meruyans.

Malotus stood by the window. She froze, watching the obsidian waterfall of hair and steer horns stretching from either side. He stroked the plumage of a sleek moss-maned falcon sitting like a statue beside him, its long, thorned tail swishing.

"You know what I like about animals?"

"What, Uncle?"

He tossed a dead mouse, and the bird caught it and gulped it down. She knew this falcon. He had been a gift from Emperor Ryogrim.

"The best thing about an animal is, you can always tell when it's loyal, and when it's hiding something."

The bird gave a striking shriek and took off out the window. Malotus turned around and studied her. A jagged bolt of electricity shot up her spine. What did he know? *Was this just about the Meruyans, or could he possibly know something about what I let slip to Flax? Or that we were in*

here that one time and found the picture of him and Arenay...It wasn't my
fault he saw that!

"I would never disobey you, Malotus! You know I only intervene during the worst of your destructive moods, as agreed. I had to save those Meruyans, it was only right!" Her knees wanted to buckle, but she resisted, rushing towards him to counter their shaking, and interlocking her hands in a desperate plea before falling into his arms in a snug embrace.

"Yulah, you mean the world to me. You know it." His voice was so soft, strained, she knew it took everything for him to say so. Though he could never utter the word 'love,' it was the closest he could get.

"And I am grateful to you, Uncle. You have always been there for me. I would never hurt you!" Her vision went blurry with tears, and she sobbed in his arms, leaning into him, knowing she couldn't pull away even if she had wanted to.

"Don't get close to that apprentice boy. Remember, you cannot trust anyone. People will let you let yourself be vulnerable to them."

Malotus's grip tightened, he held her as if she were an insect caught in a flytrap. No, a child with his blanket. Yulah simultaneously believed it was both. Thoughts raced through her mind, as she doubted and retraced the past few days' events. *I'm sure I can trust Flax, he's different.*

Yulah's wristcom buzzed between them, whirling as a message came in. Malotus's arms loosened, so she could check it. It spat out a tiny message: "Order up at Borak's Gears n' Gadgets."

She left him, arms at his sides, weak like spent charcoal.

Out in the starry night, the cold air bit her cheeks, and she shuddered. Above all else, as she left the fortress, a sense of general unsettling overtook her. Everything felt surreal. Despite the cold, heat built up in her chest, and she broke into a run. Passing a whiff of night-blooming jasmines, she thanked the night under her breath, as her feet pounded the pavement, carrying her magnetically to where she knew she had to go.

CHAPTER TWENTY

The news from Yulah weighed on him heavily, but Flax had some duty to attend to before heading home to Borak. And Borak! What would he think about all this? Surely the Sen'Prin wouldn't like this, either. What would it mean for his position and life here?

If he was caught, the punishment would be having the horns cut off—unable to sense the wind or connect with its energy until they grew back about a week later.

Flax queasily lifted his wristcom and called home base from a quiet back street. He knew he couldn't keep this from Sen'Prin. The situation would unfold quickly and spin out of his control without some backup. Maybe Thian would know what to do about this.

He sat on a crate. The acrid odor of rotting fish singed his nostrils, but then, it seemed fitting to the nature of his message. A pang of pain hit when he thought about using Yulah, his own girlfriend, for knowledge to report to the Sen'Prin. Despite her position in the government, it was very unusual for her to give him any information he could actually tell them. His reporting had mostly been about the daily life of the people, including what kinds of things their stores were stocked with. Food markets displayed the quality of what the Sen'Drorn truly had in terms of resources. All this, of course, granted to the people via their Meruyan-abusing government.

"Yes? Flax? Can you hear me?" a voice came quietly from his wristcom.

"Thian? Thank goodness…" Flax explained everything, how the Sen'Drorn military planned to promote Borak for their weapons-making, including their plan to keep Flax on as shop owner.

"What can we do, Thian? I am lost here!"

"It's gone too far, buddy, I'm sorry. I have to turn this over to a higher rank."

"No, Thian, don't!" It was too late. A click and Thian was gone. He sat alone in the alley, watching his breath, then a moment struck. His wrist-com buzzed again.

He answered, and an unfamiliar voice came. "*Agent 043*, your position is destabilized, soon compromised. Borak is now a threat to our empire and must be assassinated. Do it and leave the city as soon as possible. We cannot let him into their custody to get a chance to make weapons for their army…"

"What? How can I?" Flax sputtered into the other end.

"Your position is compromised, you will be a fugitive, but as you are a Sen'Prin spy, it doesn't matter, you will be back in the safety of the Sen'Prin by then," explained the operative on the other line, again as if his hysterics required it.

"Borak is a good man!" Flax shouted in a panicked and flurried state of mind. Lights came on in the windows upstairs, and he fled from the alley in the cover of darkness.

"He works and lives in Sen'Drorn, the enemy nation. Put your new relationships aside. It is not real. The master engineer is no longer your master, he will soon become a threat to us all. From what you have reported, he is a genius inventor. The Sen'Prin won't stand a chance against their army if they harness his expertise. You must end him, tonight. You mustn't forget where your loyalties lie!"

Begrudgingly, Flax whispered, "Okay, I will get back to you soon," before hanging upon them. There must be another way. He'd never kill his own father. Not that the Sen'Prin knew who he really was.

After wandering the dark streets in his panicked state, he at long last arrived at Borak's flat late in the night. He tiptoed in, closing the door slowly, moving upstairs to the flat above the shop.

Flax found Borak sitting by the fireplace, a small gadget in his lap, slowly turning it with a wrench.

"Have a nice date with Yulah? I bet she's a great—"

"Borak!" shouted Flax, face flashing hot.

"I was going to say, cook. I figured she cooked for yeh, since yeh were gone so late. She has brought some pastries to me before. Ah mighty…"

"Listen, sir…It's good you're up so late. I have some news from Yulah actually that I need to tell you about…"

"Sure, my boy, what is it?" Borak put down the wrench and looked up. Though it was his normal way of speaking, being referred to as "my boy" all the time only stung more.

Flax excused himself for a moment and got some water to choke down, which gave him enough of a voice to continue speaking despite the big lump in his throat forming as he looked into Borak's eyes.

He sat down in the other armchair by the fire, and explained the promotion, everything Yulah had told him.

In an unmistakably miserable and biased tone, he spun the description of the promotion to sound bad as possible. Flax uttered, "They will force you to work for them at the Sen'Drorn fortress."

Borak was both stunned and confused at the end of the explanation. "Doesn't seem so bad. I mean, I'm sure the pay is good, and I'll be living in the fancy fortress. Flax, what's this really about?"

"It would mean the end of our apprenticeship. I'd take over your shop. Me! Is that what you want? You built it up all your life! You don't want to help the military agenda develop ways to murder innocent others!"

"Yes, well, what choice do I have?" he sighed, turning over the gadget in his hand. "It is sad, Flax, but you know…I think the shop would be in fine hands with you in charge. It's not like it's closing down or nothin'! And we all get pay raises, your girlfriend is right about that…I don't understand why you are so down in the dumps…isn't this good news? Even if I don't support the war, it is my duty to serve if needed."

Flax couldn't believe what he was hearing. He was desperate to convince Borak further. "I can't believe you have been making supplies for them this whole time! It's an unjust war! What about that girlfriend you had in the Sen'Prin?! The closest thing to love you have ever known...She lives in that city, just like other innocent people. Families! You will be making weapons to kill..."

Borak rubbed his grease-stained hands together. "That's the far forgotten past! Before the likes of you was even born! And, I'm not directly hurting anybody by conceiving of gadgets and building them armor...err."

"I can't let you go!" Then Flax let out a strange piece of information. "It is my *job* not to let you go!"

His heart throbbed. He covered his mouth with his hands.

"Well, I know you would no longer be my apprentice then, but that still seems like a far exaggeration...and we could still visit each other—" mumbled Borak in between Flax's speech.

"No, no!" Flax thrust his arms up and held his head in his palms. Flax tried to get a grip on himself. "I would sooner have to kill you, Borak. My...my own mother lives in the Sen'Prin city!"

Borak lifted one eyebrow and eyed his apprentice. "What are you on about, boy? Calm down! That doesn't make sense. Aren't you from some small Sen'Drorn outpost town?"

Flax's chest was heaving, the nerves in his fingers tingled painfully. He tried to sound calm. He spoke dryly. "I'm going to be busted one way or the other soon, I might as well tell you..."

Borak tilted his head in confusion.

Flax sighed heavily. "I was sent here by the Sen'Prin...and I took on this mission working under you not knowing you were my father...even the Sen'Prin don't know. I am registered as not having one, or else dead somewhere...I guess you never knew this, but, your old girlfriend is my mother."

"That's ridiculous! How is that even possible?! She left with the Sen'Prin during the split...and...How old are you exactly?"

"I am almost eighteen years old. My birth was almost a year after the Great Split…"

"Well, the dates add up…But, how could she not tell me…unless she didn't know herself until after the split…" His old wrinkled eyes grew wide.

"How exactly did you end it with her, again…?"

"I was such a selfish coward, but I never knew by *how* much …All this time I have had a son, in the Sen'Prin city…"

"Yes, I never knew about you growing up. When I found out I had a father who lived here, in Sen'Drorn, I became a spy for the Sen'Prin military, in the hopes of getting assigned a position where I could meet you. I never intended for things to go like this, or the serendipity that I would end up working for you, and loving it so much…"

"Well, mah boy…" Borak started, before tears welled up in his eyes for the first time Flax had ever seen. "I…You really are mah boy!" He started wailing at that moment, unable to speak anymore, and in one swift motion stood and scooped up Flax into a tight bear hug. Flax's heart was beating wildly, and he could feel the same from Borak in the heartfelt embrace.

Then out, holding him by the shoulders at arm's length, Borak gaped at Flax, eyes searching his. "So, it's possible that yeh are my son. And yeh grew up to become a Sen'Prin spy… Who knew!" Borak looked Flax up and down as if seeing him for the first time. "Boy, all those times I called yeh 'son' or 'boy'… I mean, that's just how I talk, but all this time, it was actually true!"

Flax looked down, avoiding eye contact. It was true how hard that had been for him.

Borak continued, "Well, I am happy to know yeh and have yeh as an actual son! I produced such a fine boy, that is, yeh are very enjoyable to be around. Smart, muscular, handsome. And a mighty competent engineer! Of course, I see now why that's the case, yeh got my blood in yeh!"

"That's all very sweet, and I'm happy to hear you say that, but—" Flax said.

Borak interrupted, "Well I've bonded with yeh lad, what can I say? What more could I ask for? For my apprentice, who is like a son to me, actually be my son!"

"Yes, yes..." Flax begged him. "But now that you are being promoted to this weapons master, my mission has changed. They want me to assassinate you! Now you see that I cannot let you take that job! You would be hurting my people. And with your technology in their hands, the Sen'Drorn will leave them in ruin!"

"Yes...Now I see...Tell me, son! Is your mother still around?"

Flax responded, "She is doing well, she owns a flower shop in Sen'Prin."

Borak beamed, tears again welling in his droopy eyes.

Flax continued to blurt out everything he had been holding in until now. "But can you tell me about how you came to live here, in Sen'Drorn capital? Why didn't you join the Sen'Prin? Especially since your own partner was involved in it...How did things come to be this way!? I have been so curious about this my whole life. Do you have any idea how hard it has been to keep this from you? To not ask you every one of my curiosities?!"

"I'm sorry. I just avoided politics at Gruul's side. Now I see my neutral position wasn't such a victimless crime after all. But you know my life was and has always been here, in this shop. It's is all I know. I am sorry if you expected a worldlier father, but..."

Flax corrected softly, "No, Father, are you joking? You are so much more than I ever thought my father would turn out to be."

Borak smiled at him, but it soon melted into a look of concern, droopy eyes and all, as he said sadly, "It seems things are on the cusp of changing, though. Our shop days are coming to an end. Old Malotus will come to collect what he wants. His master weapons maker. I realize now that I cannot accept my post by the Sen'Drorn blindly, as I once did. But what can we do to resist?"

Borak stared into the fire.

Flax spoke up. "Well, you could join me. I'm leaving here."

Borak said nothing. The crackling fire was the only sound now.

Finally, he said, his voice cracking, "I…I cannot just leave my shop, my home, this life, Flax…"

"But…" Flax tried to argue, but he was cut off by a jolt from the wrist-com.

"What is that?" Borak sat up.

"The Sen'Prin are calling…" There was a long silence as Flax didn't pick up, and they both stared at the gadget on his wrist. Not a moment after the buzzing halted, just like that day in the Jade desert, the line of green text summoned him a new coordination. His hands tingled with pain again. His heart skipped a beat.

"I will be right back," He gulped. "I'm sorry, Father."

CHAPTER TWENTY-ONE

Meleena, Deem, Talla, and Professor Levlos arrived at the oceanside, on the far outskirts of the Northern Village territories, on the way to Underwater City. They hoped to find the farmer who had promised to secure Meleena and Talla's kelpies, Peela and Clover.

Dark clouds huddled over the sea, promising a storm. Fog obscured visibility at the beach. Even stepping onto the sand, the sea blended into the sky. Waves crashed so loudly they had to shout. Meleena held her hair together with her hands to keep it from whipping around.

"Does anyone see the Meruyan or kelpies?" asked Professor Levlos.

A trumpeting bellow echoed through the fog. *Buluuuuu!*

"A wild neutolyth herd," Professor Levlos shouted. "They beach here sometimes. Stay close! They are wild and can be unpredictable if they feel threatened."

Meleena gazed at the fog. The outline of giant shells and tentacles of varying sizes were just barely visible. There were calves among them, which meant protective mothers.

"Over here!" shouted a Meruyan voice. A cry rang out among the trumpeting sounds, this one distinct and unmistakable. Peela. The kelpies broke into a run and reached Meleena and her group long before the farmer.

"Clover!" squealed Talla, hugging the neck of her pet.

Peela's tentacle mouth licked Meleena's hands affectionately. She seemed okay, aside from the shock of things. Meleena touched her scaled hide. She looked healthy, no visible cuts.

The Meruyan fisherman caught up. "This fog is a nuisance! I would go underwater quickly if I were you, before you run right into this pod of neutolyths!"

Meleena inspected what remained of Peela's saddlebags. They were torn up, almost nothing remaining inside. Raided by the vangrots. The journal was gone, which meant so were all her new wildlife notes from the trip.

Peela squirmed. "It's okay now, Peela." They touched foreheads, as Meleena tried to sooth the sensitive beast. But how could she, when she didn't feel soothed herself?

Thunder cracked as lightening rippled through the clouds. Another neutolyth trumpeting cry rang out. Meleena turned to see the bounding shell as a neutolyth charged towards where the group stood on the beach.

The beast reared up onto its hind legs. Its many trunks and leafy webbed front feet towered over them, about to trample Peela. Meleena jumped in front of Peela and threw her arms to look bigger, crying out her own mimicking trumpet. "*Ahooo!! Bulluuu!!!*"

The other Meruyan, caught off guard, gasped in horror as the rearing neutolyth sprayed a cascade of water on Meleena, still at the forefront of the group. The drenching over her limbs caused her arm fins to spring outward, startling the beast. The neutolyth stumbled backward, the weight of its giant shell toppling it onto its back.

Meleena still frozen, face wincing and fins standing in display, opened her eyes and slowly dropped the posture. The others tried to get over the shock, shouting words of encouragement, shock, and relief.

The neutolyth, stuck on its back, trumpeted for help.

"Quickly! We need to submerge! It will be safer in the sea," Professor Levlos called over another crack of thunder. The farmer bade them farewell and galloped off to the shore villages on his own kelpie.

More huge, round figures began to emerge from the fog. The pod of neutolyths were coming. Meleena and the others huddled close and made a dash for the sea. Meleena had just enough time to toss her glasses into a waterproof case, snatching Deem's as well. She figured he'd never have remembered to do this on his own, nor easily buy another pair. Fighting harder than ever against the powerful waves to submerge, they clung to their mounts, who dragged them underwater and propelled them away from the angry neutolyths.

The seafloor dropped quickly, which aided in the getaway. Meleena's heart thudded as the water knocked at her, her icy hands grasping Peela's mane for dear life.

***

They came barreling down the sand dunes, their fathers shouting to them from over the hills.

"Let'sss get a move on!" they hissed in the reptilian language. The Hyish children didn't care, they rolled until they were dizzy. "Before the floodsss begin!"

The ocean pounded beside them, dimming their calls. The Mayfee clan caravan would be leaving soon.

One Hyish boy rolled the other way, finding his scaly body wrapped in cool wet sand. He rolled to get up, when something hard smacked the small of his back. He dislodged it from the wet sand while exposed and squirming sand crabs dug back into the muck around it. An oblong teardrop shaped object with a carved face in it stared up at him from silver eyeholes.

"Let'sss get a move on!" This time it came blaring from the Chieftess herself. Her electric pink hair and lavish silky garments blew in the wind, as colorful feathers splayed from her bent elbows and jangling piercings announced her presence as she galloped atop the dunes on her Netic. Its obsidian scales and her stately form struck the boy with awe as she rounded up the caravans nearby.

The other children over the hill hissed in retreat to their kin, so too the boy ran up the dunes to join them, clutching his discovery tight in his hands. They left a mosaic of footsteps in the sand as they wobbled over the dunes to the collapsing tents packed by their parents, who scooped up the children and tossed them into the caravan along with the cookware.

"What'ss thisss?"

The boy looked up as Mayfee and her Netics stared down at him. With a sense of duty, he bowed and held it out for her to take. He knew to respect the Chieftess.

More Netics, the slithering beasts of burden, with their prickly spines and bloated neck-sacks hauled caravans forward by the hundreds.

As he sat atop his family's caravan, the boy whispered, "Goodbye blue sea, I will miss you," and held back the tears from the loss of his ocean treasure.

***

For Meleena, the sense of panic from escaping the neutolyths took a while to recede. Finally, when they were safe in the sea depths and a distance from shore, they could stop and climb onto their kelpies and ride properly. Deem transferred from Pinchy's claws to his back.

They rode through the open ocean, so deep and vast as Meleena had never experienced. It made her shiver with unease. Black-and-yellow spotted eels passed beneath them. Off in the distance, hundreds of manta rays undulated across the vast blueness, their forms obscured by dust. The sea was murkier than back home. She wondered if it could be runoff from the Warix mining operations.

Once they felt safer, Meleena had more questions for Professor Levlos. Now that they were underwater, they had to switch to the first Meruyan language, a series of echolocating clicks.

"You must know the Warix can manipulate the wind, right?" she asked, riding close to him.

He said nothing, only a bubble left his lips with the last air. They'd be breathing through their skin now.

Meleena clicked in simplified speech, "Of course, you know. You were not shocked when that Warix girl brought us to you!" Her range of vocabulary was limited in the less-used language.

Pinchy uttered a deep hiss.

Meleena continued. "We can't use half of the Warix tech. It's wind-based. So why that crummy deal?"

Professor Levlos didn't look at her when he clicked in reply. "I already told you. Even without wind power-based technology, it's enough to keep the Meruyan hooked. Paper for books to educate our young, lumber for building, many household appliances. You can't even speak efficiently here. You have grown up speaking a Warix language all your life."

Meleena was taken aback. It had never occurred to her before—but if Meruyans had adapted to life on land because of Warix contact, they must have learned to speak from the Warix.

Deem chimed in, in perfect Meruyan-tongue, "I still think it's better to live underwater. The Northern Valley Meruyans should return to the sea where Warix can't touch us."

"You will learn more tomorrow on our tour of the biodome. The Meruyan researchers will tell you about Meruyan attempts to adapt Warix tech to underwater living. Meanwhile, we will soon arrive in the Under-water City, and for you shore-dwellers, experience what it is to live like them, without technology."

They rode deeper, entering a sheltered valley. The markings carved into the inner valley walls noted Meruyan dwellings. Safe from predators, to be read by intelligent life only. Kelp, intentionally planted, grew to form fences and property lines. This included farmland, with rows of planted sea vegetation extending outward from the valley in swirling shapes along the cliffs. Kelpies and neutolyths dotted the settlement, alongside Meruyan going about their business.

Meleena and the others entered a neighborhood with almost-buildings. These were structures of compacted mud and plant, some several stories tall, with sea plants growing atop. This felt more city-like than her own underwater community. Still, Meleena had expected more civilization than this.

At least the city was in harmony with the surrounding nature.

They passed an open marketplace. Signs advertised: "Fresh Lobster! Still got quite a pinch in 'em!" "Mollusks! Just plucked from their sea beds today!" "Sea slugs! Get 'em while they're still slimy!"

The Meruyans seemed at ease, far from a life being rushed around by Warix.

Professor Levlos waved for Meleena, Deem, and Talla to follow as their kelpies swam up to a rocky landing spot. Levlos dismounted and hitched his kelpie to a stalagmite. "Here you will find your room for tonight. Below is the main entrance for the Council's Underwater Town Hall. You can find breakfast there in the morning, and I will meet you just after dawn."

Meleena dismounted from Peela, watching schools of little fish and rays swim by. Visibility was clearer at these depths, though silt particles clouded the sea above. Like all underwater Meruyan territories, this was the deepest that allowed for their hair to still absorb the sun's rays for nutrients. If there hadn't been a storm out, Meleena would have enjoyed that—she was ready for a break after such a long day.

Professor Levlos said, "I used to be able to see much further out into the tranquil blue sea from here. But visibility has gotten worse with each passing year. Now, youths, get some rest after this long day."

He opened their room with carved out bed holes, tethered kelpweave nests inside.

There was another cave room with a hole for a bathroom, no sink obviously, underwater. Hard stone surfaces in place of wood for furniture.

"I'll find out more info tomorrow about your earlier-than-planned departure for the Arctic City after this. Sorry about the change in plans, though you shouldn't have snuck off, really."

Professor Levlos left them to rest for the evening.

Meleena and the others hung out on the porch with the view, rather than in the stark room.

At twilight, everything under the waves shimmered. Meleena sat on the porch and watched the city change. Colorful fish swam, the city traffic of Meruyan riding kelpies peaked and waned, and a calmness descended. Bioluminescence lit the city. Meruyans carried sticks tipped with bright, squishy balls. Glowing algae adorned and lit doorways and streets. It seemed like the primary function of the light was for the Meruyan to find their way back to a safe shelter to overnight in. It didn't seem adequate for staying out and socializing.

They swam back into the sparse room and floated into their kelpweave bed-nests. There'd be no writing in a journal tonight. All writing here was laboriously carved in stone. It put Meleena in a state of unease.

The night was long. Meleena hadn't slept in underwater bedding since the stormy night the Sen'Drorn had attacked their village. It felt eerily familiar, as she recalled Malotus's eyes in the storm this same day.

Talla also stirred around a lot, uttering troubled noises, which didn't help.

Deem snored away.

In the morning, Meleena crawled out of the nest, eyes burning.

***

As planned, Professor Levlos arrived shortly after breakfast to bring them to the biodome.

Meleena, Deem, and Talla met him in the sand dunes outside the inn, mounted their kelpies and lobster, and ascended. They drew up to the open ocean. Meleena's heart soared as she sat atop her reunited companion, patting Peela's neck as they glided through the refreshing underwater currents.

Professor Levlos explained more as they passed over undersea Meruyan suburbs, which didn't look like much more than stone building markers from above.

Meleena had spent all night wondering about ways to solve the Meruyan's troubles. She asked Levlos at first the opportunity. "So, why do we contract for the Sen'Drorn, not the Sen'Prin?"

"It has been this way for generations, when there was just one Warix nation. The Sen'Prin was formed only eighteen years ago by Arenay, a noble Warix who stood against our oppression."

"How did it happen?"

"Governess Arenay was once just a young soldier, stationed in the Meruyan production lands, with a distaste for it. She told the truth to the Warix people and gained enough followers in the Warix nation to start a rebellion and break off into the Sen'Prin. However, they have been fighting for their survival ever since they broke away from Sen'Drorn. And it never resolved our problems—we remained under the same contract and control, by the Sen'Drorn. The Council roots for Arenay in private, never officially. We have to continue working on Sen'Drorn land, to keep the resources flowing. We don't want them to lash out, either...Like the burnt lands you saw."

They drew up to the shallows. The sun's energy hummed in Meleena's hair follicles. They rode to a sand barge housing a huge bubble-like structure made from some kind of translucent webbing. They dismounted their kelpies outside as Meruyan researchers in kelpweave robes came out to greet them.

The bubble let in as much sunlight as possible, and no water. Meleena was thankful for the comfort of speaking again. Even if, for the first time, she realized it was actually the Warix's language, which she'd been speaking all her life. The Meruyan never had one for land.

The biodome chamber was full of old Warix technology, in fact. Repurposed for experiments, Meruyan researchers tinkered with various strange contraptions.

"What's this structure?" Deem asked.

"It's called a boat. Something the Warix produced to sail across the sea."

Meleena, Deem, and Talla exchanged perplexed glances.

A researcher showed them some rusted copper products. "We can use certain Warix wind power objects underwater, by redesigning them. By moving our fins and muscles, we can power it with the water currents, replacing the wind power. There is no energy storage underwater, however. So it is still inferior in some ways."

"Why so rusty?" asked Talla, touching a paddle-wheeled contraption.

"It's hard to get products under here. We can't produce these gadgets or parts ourselves, and are still designing replacements."

"So, it's basically a very expensive and impractical way to use their tech underwater?" Meleena shrugged.

The researcher sighed. "Yes. We can use our fins to guide water currents through the nodes that usually use wind energy, but not those that use electrical currents."

"We're better off inventing natural solutions, like glowing animals and stuffing them into globes," another researcher said.

"We also experiment with growing land crops," the first said brightly. "On small islands above the waves, near the sand barge."

A researcher said, "An earlier civilization that doesn't exist anymore. Ancient Warix came on boats a thousand years ago, seeking a Pendant said to contain their Wind Goddess's spirit. It is said that they stayed, and lived in harmony with the Meruyan on the islands around here. They survived because of the Meruyan food traditions, plants and fish. Legend mentions in particular some delicious fruit, now extinct."

"What happened?" asked Meleena.

"This golden age lasted hundreds of years, until a new Warix ship arrived and destroyed them. This happened on the mainland too, with the same outcome. Every time a Warix group ate the Meruyan fruit, they would become peaceful, and always, another Warix tribe would eventually come, refuse to share in their offerings, and conquer, wiping out the civilization."

Meleena felt this was all very strange. If only there was some way to change things, make life more equal for the Meruyans on land.

A third researcher came over and spun her hands in greeting. "Councilman Professor Levlos, two messages have come in for you."

"You mastered long-distance communication underwater?" Meleena asked, amazed. Even with all their attempts at development, they were so far from making life underwater anything like Meleena had come to need.

The researcher held out two hermit crabs. "They carry bubble messages."

"Oh, right."

Professor Levlos held the shell holes to his ear, one by one, and listened. "Well, kids. You're all set to continue to the Arctic City tonight."

"What was the second message?" asked Meleena, still not ready to trust Professor Levlos.

"Uh…The situation at the Northern Villages has become…tenser. General Malotus was not amused by your peak at the burned lands."

Meleena crossed her arms. "In other words, we're not allowed back in the Northern Villages."

Levlos nodded gravely, and that was that.

***

Yulah entered to find Malotus leaning over his desk in the candle-lit room.

"Sir, Emperor Ryogrim is restless," she gulped. "He said we should prepare to attack the Sen'Prin soon. And to forget about the Pendant. That it's gone without a trace."

"Yulah, look at this," Malotus said, ignoring her statements. "Do you have any inkling to whom it might belong?"

A journal lay open on the table in front of him, flattened leaves and other feathers scattered the table beside it. He plucked a striped feather from its pages. He showed her the front cover, clay inlaid with shells and pearls.

"My men recovered it from a field in the Northern Hills. Obviously, Meruyan made. And there are drawings in here. Unmistakably of the Ram's head pendant. Look at these."

He turned it to show her the small teardrop-shaped doodles in the margins of the writing. "They do look like the ram's head…" she said with unease. "May I?" She flipped through a couple of pages to find sketches of birds, leaves, seeds, various trees and animals, and some scribblings of thoughts and descriptions.

Malotus said, "She also has the insignia of Sen'Prin drawn in here." He pointed to sketches of scarlet nectar-sprigs. One was even drinking nectar from the flower-maned lion. He knew full well the Lion was the Sen'Drorn symbol, never to be depicted alongside that pesky thorn in its side.

Malotus continued, "There are more sketches of plants and beasts, but these Sen'Prin insignias are redrawn in many places. Like a memory its author couldn't shake. It must be that Meruyan girl."

Yulah looked up from the page.

"Yes," Malotus continued. "The one you saved from snooping in the Burnt Lands the other day. I'm grateful you stopped me from killing her."

Yulah gaped. "But how do you know it was her?"

"When that girl confronted me in the fields, she mentioned she was on that silly Council Journey, which is also written about in here. I also had my officers pay the Council hosts in the Northern Villages a visit—they recovered similar loose-leaf pages."

He held up loose-leaf papers. There was a sketch of a neutolyth among hand-written entries. "They were made by *that* girl. The hosts said she is called *Meleena*." He breathed her name with the breathy excitement of a wolf about to chase a deer through a snowy forest. "She knows about the Pendant. She is probably the last person to have seen it. And she may still have it hidden in her hometown. We will need to pull together a team for another raid on her village."

She lowered the journal to look at him, and Malotus met her with an expectant grin.

Her heart sank. It was obviously Meleena's. "Or, um. Maybe she keeps it on her? Maybe we don't need to tear that poor village apart again? I believe they were heading to the Arctic City soon. I could go inquire more—"

"Good point." He stood up. "We will do both. Once again, I'm glad you didn't let me kill her earlier, Yulah. Thank you, now go deliver a message for me to the Emperor regarding the next raid. I will go and find that girl."

Yulah gulped. He went to the window, a glint in his eye as he nodded her farewell, and then took off on a gust of wind.

CHAPTER TWENTY-TWO

Flax retreated to his bedroom to catch the call from Sen'Prin headquarters, leaving Borak in the chair, teary-eyed, staring into the fire.

"What is the report?"

Flax admitted everything to his superiors, full of angst. He thought he might be sick when he received his orders.

Kill his own father? No way.

"Have you carried out your task?" the wristcom asked.

Flax tensed, the unfamiliar voice was not Thian's. "You should have completed your mission, and disposed of the old engineer by now, you are being summoned back to Sen'Prin."

"Already?" Flax's heart beat wildly.

"Go to headquarters immediately, once you have completed this task. This assignment is considered complete. We expect you back tonight."

Flax scratched his left horn and winced. He wondered if they'd have his horns for this.

"What?! No, I haven't killed him!"

"Why not? It is your loyal duty as a spy to the Sen'Prin!"

It was already very late, past bedtime, though Flax would not have an early workday tomorrow.

He gaped at the voice on the other line, "I...I cannot kill Borak. He is not guilty of any crime yet...He will refuse the task by the Sen'Drorn."

"You cannot know that..."

"Yes, he will, because I told him the truth...That I am a spy for the Sen'Prin, and that he is my true father."

"Your father? What? Impossible, your record has you as…" There was a pause on the other line, then the quiet voice returned. "No father listed…So, are you siding with the Sen'Drorn then, are you corrupted?"

"How dare you accuse me of that! I am coming back to Sen'Prin and taking Borak with me! Did you ever think, instead of killing him, he might be of use to our cause? I explained everything. He'll be loyal to us now!" Flax didn't know if Borak would come with him, but he had to argue something.

"Kill him now and return, or you will be marked a traitor."

"No! I will not! Please!" Flax yelled.

"You are not thinking straight about this mission, nor were you ever, because of this undisclosed family complication. It would be too difficult. Do not risk your safe return for him. If he isn't loyal to them as you say, he will surely die by their hands at this point. But you never should have been placed on this case at all. Now return to the Sen'Prin immediately for disciplinary action or face treason charges." It was followed by a click and long buzz. The stranger on the other side had hung up.

A new wave of urgency overtook him. *I have to get Borak and I out of here and clear this up as soon as possible.*

Yesterday he had just been living his life here, dating a nice girl, working a nice job with his father as his teacher. Things were great. But he always kept it in the back of his mind that this was a mission, something that could not last. It was never really his life, and it would have to end at some point. He just couldn't predict how or when, or that it would be so soon. He thought it could be years even. Hoped maybe.

"I…uh…spoke to my superiors. They said I need to leave right away. My position is compromised. We have to go, tonight. With the new Sen'Drorn orders, I have to take you with me to the Sen'Prin. That is the only way to avoid the original plan of assassinating you, and you know I could never do that…"

Borak looked up at Flax. He appeared to be quite tired. "I er…Tonight? I couldn't just leave this place now. I'm not ready," he stammered. "Plus, it would look bad if I left tonight, since Yulah already knows the orders. And who will carry on my legacy here? The store? My name that

I have built up…All my gadgets. No, I'd need a chance at least to pack up some of my most guarded plans and patterns…"

"Borak, I'm sorry. It's too risky…"

"Call them back, tell them the two of us will go, er, even tomorrow night. I would be of much greater use to the Sen'Prin if I at least had my patterns…it's my life's work."

"Alright, I'll try…" That was a good enough possibility. He climbed to the roof and called with his wristcom.

The superior barked, "Do you know how hard it is to infiltrate the Sen'Drorn? Why do you think your position was so unique and so long in the making? Sorry, Agent Flax, but we cannot just send somebody to pick him up. Meanwhile, your cover is blown. Return to the Sen'Prin *immediately*!"

Click. It hung up again.

He returned to the living room again, but this time Borak was back in the armchair with one hand over his face.

"Borak, they are still demanding that I return tonight. If you cannot leave with me, then you must leave on your own."

Borak looked up again. Fighting back the tears, he said quietly and defeated, "Alright, boy." He did not give much more explanation. "I don't know I have it in me to leave just now."

"Only Yulah and the government know about this. You might have a day or two before they come for you…I guess this is goodbye until then."

"Flax, there's a windboard from a client here you can take, that youth who keeps crashing his. I were just fixin' it tonight upstairs, take it. Since yer motorbike has become our pet experiment an' all."

"Thanks, Dad." Saying it for the first time under such circumstances felt like his heart was bleeding. "Be safe and discreet—get out of town as soon as you can."

They hugged one more time, then Flax went into his bedroom and gave it one last look. It was now or never. He would have liked a more definite answer from Borak, but now only time would tell. He was only glad the Sen'Prin operative had not again ordered Flax to kill Borak, perhaps he forgot now that the variables were more complicated.

There was no looking back now. Windboard under this arm, he packed what little personal affairs he had—change of clothes, an apple, and his fake documents—into his rucksack, and dove out the window. He felt assured that he would soon be home in Sen'Prin City, and his father would have the strength to get out of Sen'Drorn City safely. His father no longer would have a death sentence, and they would be reunited—this time as a family.

It will only be a couple days at most.

Flax's mind displayed the image of the warm living room where his father sat, playing on repeat the scenarios they had just lived together. At least now his father knew who he really was.

When he got to the stone pavement behind the shop, Flax pushed off down the winding streets on the windboard, realizing as he fought to maintain balance, that he had never ridden one before, and it was a lot harder than it looked. At this late hour, the streets were empty.

When Flax arrived at the Sen'Drorn city gates, he easily made up an excuse to the guard—an engineer's apprentice, going out on a late-night pickup for materials from another town. Since this had been true on some prior occasions, the guard let him pass. Thanks to the early news from Yulah, they would not yet be looking for strange behavior.

Flax rode along the same road he had arrived on. He went slow so as not to fall as he got used to the windboard. Once out of sight of the guards, he blasted away in a cloud of dust. The pulse of wind extended from his core and channeled through little holes in the surface of the board, amplifying it through copper turbines underneath, which directed the air to add thrust to the wheels.

It might not have been the safest speed to go down those roads, but his pounding heart and the ecstatic adrenaline rush, his fear, his anxiety, threw his wind power into a frenzied and uncontrollable state. Getting there faster would help him get over the anxiety sooner, should he find clear passage. At every turn, he expected to find that loose rock which would send him skidding to his doom, shooting along crooked stones on rubber wheels, moving at an absurd momentum in the darkest hours of the night.

Flax hoped to return to the small farm town, Vendengire, where his Sen'Drorn assignment had begun. There, under the safety of Sen'Prin, he could return to the home city. But as he drew nearer, he let out a gasp. The green and gold flower-maned lion flag waved from unfamiliar wooden watchtowers. The Sen'Drorn military must have recaptured the city.

Thinking on his feet, he came up with a backup plan. Avoiding the center of town, he drew near a peripheral farmhouse on the windward side, then sharply jerked the direction and spun out of control, diving off before the board, skidding along the road, and smashed into a barn, exploding in a burst of fire and crunching metal. Bramble-sheep groaned, dogs barked, lights came on as the village inhabitants rustled from their beds. They would not find the owner of the board in that wreckage, and maybe presume him dead.

Flax had summoned a small wind updraft to soften the blow as he tumbled headlong into the dirt. Still moving fast, his cheek and right side of his body took the brunt of the impact. He groaned in agony, lifted a hand to his burning cheek—it was streaked with blood. Trembling to his feet, his right arm and leg panged.

He dusted himself off, and limped towards the woods, using his hands for minimal propulsion, as uneven wind energy from his legs would not have boded well for staying upright.

He would follow close to the woods toward the Sen'Prin capital, still very far away. It would still be hours before he reached home, and in his state, he could not pass over difficult terrain. Not over mountains, nor forests. He would have to take it slow, go in stealth.

***

Borak slumped in his living-room chair, watching the glowing coals fade to black in the crackling fire. The night was half over already. What had he done, staying here all those years? Thoughts swam through his mind, plaguing him, rotting away while his heart pounded in his chest, his blood burning him beneath his skin. He could hardly take it anymore. He had to do something.

There was a knock at the door. The bulky engineer stood up from his seat by the fire and lumbered in a daze. Who would be here at this hour? He dreadfully hoped it wasn't some official to give him news of his 'great promotion.'

Yulah stood in the open doorway. "Is Flax here? He seemed upset earlier about something, and I wanted to know if he was okay."

Borak stared, his heartbeat thumping in his eardrums. *Come up with something to say to her. Flax is sleeping. No, he...* "He's gone out somewhere," he blurted out.

"Out alone at this hour? How strange!" She furrowed her brows.

I hope that boy doesn't break her heart...She has powerful friends.

"Er, I mean, sleeping. We are both tired. G'night."

"Borak, are you alright?"

"Yes darlin', I guess the years are catching up to me. I need to start turning in earlier!"

"Okay, well, I guess I'll see you guys tomorrow then." She waved awkwardly but turned to go.

"You too, yes." Borak smiled sleepily and shut the door.

Finding himself alone again, he found he could not stand still. The last thing he needed was Yulah suspicious of them. Another thought occurred to him. He had to get out of here before Yulah gave him the news, or things would look much worse if he left.

I'm not going to be a coward this time. I'm done sitting by while the world spins my fate around me. I need to be there with them. With my son.

Now was the time to act. Not tomorrow...he didn't have tomorrow. He could hardly live with himself now.

He threw his possessions in a pile and realized he had no idea where he was going to go. He had no notion of the landscape outside of Sen'Drorn City, nor did he have the faintest notion where Sen'Prin City was. Just getting out of here, someplace they couldn't find him, that would be a start. He walked away from the pile. There was nothing to bring. He stomped down to his workshop and lifted the white curtain on the contraption he and Flax had been experimenting with. The first personal-sized machine made from Flax's old motorbike. It still resembled the original motorbike, they had just replaced the wind-channeling copper tubes that had run along the side and connected them to the motor with larger, artisan crafted ones. The finer detail granted more surface area and higher energy synergy, much like the tech in Borak's specialty armor-craft. Triangular sails along its sides allowed for better control of airflow while steering in the air.

He knew exactly *how* it should work, this flying motorbike prototype, but not *if* it actually would.

Grasping it by the handles, he wheeled it from the shop to the deserted street, where the wheels silently rolled over the uneven stones. A triangular flag waved between the handlebar, indicating natural wind direction, so he arranged himself accordingly, though there wasn't much wind tonight from ground level. He mounted and kicked with one foot, casting bursts of wind energy into copper tubes streaking from handlebar to wheel. Now to get it airborne. Building momentum and speed, he bumped along the cobblestones, knuckles white and cursing that he had not installed better shock absorbers—yet lengthy Fleeg Street made for the perfect runway, and the machine lifted in an updraft created by his own power. He zoomed past doors, locked down for the night, past second-story windows decorated with flower boxes. He passed wind-landing sills and grey shingled rooftop slabs, until he was high into the night's sky, above the jumble of buildings and sloping rooftops.

He turned the wheel this way and that, in a rush around jutting spires of building tops, while keeping his wind energy conducting through his copper-toed boots to keep aloft. Finally, he launched in an updraft and landed atop a high building. In the distance, gray clouds spun just beyond the outer stone walls. Though he couldn't see them, the Wind Guards who kept the everlasting storm moving stood at nodes along the walls. If he got closer, he might be able to spot their glowing silver eyes—those eyes that glowed more hours per day than any other Warix and led to early blindness in the name of duty. If he could disable a guard, and weaken the storm in their node, perhaps he could pass through.

Borak heaved a breath of the cold, night air. How would he get past all of that?

His palms sweated. How would this machine fare in such a storm? The flapping triangular flag guided his aim. He concentrated his wind energy through his legs and kicked off, laughing into an updraft as he flew upward at the wind's best angle. He aimed the bike towards the outer city walls.

This is insanity! He dug his left hand into his pocket, feeling among the cold metal scraps he always kept on hand. He pulled out a small device, used for jumpstarting small machines. Careful not to drop it, he shot wind energy through his palm, which lit the spark on the taser end. He steered the motorbike with one hand and gripped the crackling taser with the other.

As he sailed towards the stone wall, the fog enveloped him.

He searched for the glistening eyes.

There, a shadowy outline of a head pitched upward, with raised arms channeling the storm.

Borak waited for the perfect moment as he sailed over, then he released the taser, and it fell, its warm glow shrinking into the fog.

With a loud crackle, the warm light flashed as it met its target. The silver eyes vanished, but a shocking yowl made Borak flinch as he sailed into the spinning grey ahead.

It wasn't clear if the downed Wind-Guard made any difference in the swirling winds ahead.

Borak felt weightless. He tried to keep the bike steady just a moment longer as the wind slammed him like an uppercut punch to the chin. He jerked the wheel counter to the storm's spin just as it caught him. He pitched forward and was thrown from the flying motorbike, but as he tumbled helplessly down, he knew he had cleared the wall and would be landing somewhere on the other side. He only hoped the landing would be soft.

CHAPTER TWENTY-THREE

Professor Levlos spoke to Meleena, Talla, and Deem outside the Biodome. "It was nice teaching you, teens. Please be safe on the next stages of your journey. I hope you have learned something in our time together. To find your way, ask about the Arctic City town hall. You will stay in guest housing there as well, and the Mayor will meet you."

"You are not coming with us?" Deem asked.

"Praise the waves!" The click-version of the utterance by Meleena and Talla was accompanied by their rolling eyes—they chuckled, Meleena remained amazed she was getting along with Talla.

"You will be in better hands there, with the Mayor as your local guide. Now..." He leaned in. "You can embarrass me about life in the Northern Villages, but do not utter a word of disrespect about your views of her city to her, or you will all be disqualified!"

These were his final words as the distance between them grew further apart in the open ocean.

After some time, the water temperature dropped and became chilly on Meleena's arms. "We must be getting close." She signaled to the others. Her heart raced. Would she be ready to take her place in society after this? Would Arenay accept her? Without her botanical journal, she felt as if a bleeding darkness oozed from her heart—empty, worthless—all her hard work and recordings, gone. She was nothing without them.

The ocean shelf became visible in the distance. Meleena looked up to see in the distance a lighter patch, where the seafloor shallowed, and curved into a large ring—The bay of the Arctic City.

They swam closer atop their mounts. Meruyan pictographs etched into the rocks welcomed them to Arctic City.

"Well, this is much better than those Gommwoods," Talla joked. Meleena kept silent. She wasn't in a talking mood.

They swam between double rows of wooden beams that guided their way to civilization.

"But what is this structure?" asked Deem, reaching out to feel a wooden beam. They broke the surface, and a burst of sound erupted into a scene full of life. Children's laughter, ambient chatting, merchants barking—Meruyans, young and old strolled along boardwalks, ate treats, children ran across grassy parks and splashed in the sea. It looked like an ongoing festival; the city lights behind sparkled even in the day, the backdrop of buildings painted in stunning colors—pastel pinks, oranges, and blues. Though it was late, the only sign of sunset was a thin orange tinge on the horizon, a halo for the snowy mountain backdrop.

The air was crisp and fresh, like the mountain itself breathed life from its icicles—it was nothing like the steamy jungle air of the other Meruyan lands. Meleena couldn't help but forget her fears and woes to take in the beauty.

Professor Levlos had arranged for them to meet with the Mayor upon arrival for a tour. Perhaps it was the brisk air, but Meleena found herself actually excited for once.

Water dripped from their hair and off their eyelashes. Meleena brushed it away and put her glasses on. They dismounted and walked their pets onto the beach, and onto the boardwalk. Deem paused, looking around, until Meleena pointed to her face, and in a moment of recognition, brightly retrieved his glasses as well. He also pulled out the kelp-weave parchment map of the Arctic City streets to lead them. Meleena chuckled, hers was long-lost by now.

As they walked inland, they realized the citizens, talking, laughing, hanging out, were not just Meruyans—there were Warix among them. Warix wearing Meruyan fashion, sitting together at benches, eating unusual summer foods. Meleena even saw her first Warix children! One small boy ran in front of her path, chasing after a Meruyan girl.

"Not more of this. What's their scheme?" she groaned to her friends. Talla frowned in agreement, Deem grunted but focused on the map, carefully tracing the streets with his pointer finger.

He led them deep into a web of fantastic buildings—tall, crafted of both stone and wood, and well maintained. Shop windows read, "Horn re-shaping: get Meruyan engravings here! No loss to wind sensitivity!" Teenage Warix loitered in packs by the entrances.

Bronze lampposts already on lined the smooth stone avenues, as Warix strolled alongside Meruyans. It was the nicest city Meleena had ever seen, or been lost in.

"Er, I don't know how I messed this up..." Deem apologized, still squinting at the map.

They looked to Talla, who rolled her eyes. "Am I the only one not scared of asking for directions?" and so she did, approaching a Meruyan woman with a baby stroller asking how to find the Mayor's office, and soon they were back on track, in another direction.

They walked their mounts towards an elaborate building, flanked by statues of fanged woodland creatures standing guard and lighting the building from inside their mouths. Roofed stalls lined the wall around the corner, where kelpies stood hitched to posts draped in bronze light, some drinking from a large trough in front. A Warix woman in fin, furry clothes was standing by the beasts, staring at them.

They led Clover, Nashi, and Pinchy to the stalls, Pinchy hissing his complaints at the domestic arrangement. "It's okay, Pinchy, you are with me always," Deem said, holding up his prized carapace. Talla shook her head.

Meleena turned to see the Warix woman following them.

"What do you want?" Meleena turned, intercepting her approach.

The Warix startled, and her face flushed with color. "Hello, young Meruyan, sorry if I startled you. Are you the future leaders on Aldrok's Journey?" Meleena eyed her suspiciously, and the Warix bowed, her long silver hair spilling over her shoulders. "I am the Mayor's assistant. I was sent to show you your rooms. You must be exhausted from a full day of travel. Please, I will send someone to stable your mounts overnight. This area is just for short stops." She lifted her hand graciously, indicating the stables.

A Warix, greeting them on the journey? Meleena felt it more than strange, downright unsettling after everything they had been through. But she was exhausted, and they agreed to follow this woman inside, upstairs to the guest quarters of the governmental building. Meleena dropped her bags on the floor and fell asleep on top of the floral bedding.

"Meleena?"

"Huh?" She awoke with a snap, her muscles stiff.

Deem stood over her, already dressed in his day tunic. "The Warix lady is here. It's time for breakfast, then Mayor Tegushi will take us on our tour. Talla is already downstairs."

They joined Talla in the breakfast room, a grand place with high ceilings that smelled of sweet cakes, with pastel yellow wallpaper. Meleena took a seat by the tall window, where the streets were already alive with the daily bustle. How odd to see both Meruyans and Warix mingling together. Even the occasional Meruyan clopped by on a kelpie.

On the marble floors, steps echoed. "Young Meruyan," came a voice behind them, the Warix assistant, and beside her, a well-dressed Meruyan woman.

"Welcome, young leaders! I am Mayor Tegushi, are you ready to start the tour?" The Meruyan beamed. She had a stack of scarves draped over her arms, and she handed one to each of them. "In case you find it a bit chilly here."

"As long as anyone can remember…" Tegushi said, walking between them, black shoes clacking on the stone, "Warix and Meruyans have lived together peacefully, in a free exchange of culture and technology from both sides. This is an ancient city. Soon we will celebrate its three-hundred-year anniversary."

They passed shops and people as the bustle of the day was in full swing. The smell of salt and strange foods wafted in the crisp mountain air.

"There are shops where one can buy Meruyan craftwork and art. In fact, Warix often get their horns engraved."

Teenage Warix walked by with elaborate markings on their horns. Meleena thought back to the artifacts in her father's study: to that engraved Warix horn she had held so long ago. It must have come from here. She asked, "What do you think about the Sen'Drorn and the Sen'Prin Warix? How they split off over the Meruyan exploitation?"

"Yes, it is terrible, if only they could see that domination is pointless, and all creatures are equal. But sadly, it is impossible. The Sen'Prin will fall to the Sen'Drorn. It's best to ignore their situation and keep your head low, and obey the Sen'Drorn contract, young Meruyans. When you join the Council of Elders, you must accept this truth."

Meleena, Deem, and Talla looked up at her, shocked.

"What?!" Meleena gasped. "How could you say that?"

Meleena stopped walking.

Tegushi cleared her throat and said, "Even though the Sen'Prin's intentions are pure, they are only the latest split faction in a long repeating history. I am sorry for the harsh news."

Meleena's eyes welled with tears. "Don't you care? Don't you want to stop it or come up with a solution? What about the legendary Pendant the Warix are searching for?"

"Perhaps the Pendant is only for war, I don't know, but it sounds like only the most brutal seek it out. Do you know why it is this way?"

They followed her to the edge of town, and a wide space opened to the mountainous horizon. The wind blew softly on their faces.

Tegushi continued, "Let me explain. Here, we have a legend of a mysterious fruit of empathy. They say, the Warix who made first contact ate this lotus fruit, and its electricity flowed in them, thus they could see the equality of all peoples. You see, Warix are naturally ruthless. Before civilizations, there were only Warix tribes, and those who didn't eat the fruit continued on their path of domination, declaring those who ate it and made peace with the Meruyans to be poisoned in the mind. How could they live together and not take advantage of the weak? And so, they laid ruin to any civilization they could. An enlightenment, splitting, destruction cycle repeated until the fruit were destroyed forever by Sen'Drorn, a hundred years ago."

"But the Sen'Prin split was eighteen years ago, by governess Arenay, she must have been enlightened!"

"Then her ancestor must have been one of the last to have eaten it. What can I tell you? The stronger, ruthless Warix always dominate in the end, perhaps with this legendary Pendant you speak of."

Meleena wasn't ready to give up. "There has to be a way to free the Meruyans from Sen'Drorn oppression. Can't we get the world to be more like this place?"

Tegushi shook her head. "I told you the Arctic City is three hundred years old. It was founded by enlightened Warix refugees, fleeing the domination of a previous split. If the Sen'Prin are smart, they best go into hiding someplace barren at the edge of the world, like we have. We are small and have nothing they want, but we have forged our own little paradise here. The Sen'Prin have picked a fight with the Sen'Drorn in an attempt to change the powers that be. And for this, sadly, their nation will be defeated. Do you understand? You must let things be."

There was nothing more to argue over. The cold that pulsed in Meleena's veins was not from the outside chill. Tegushi's prophecy for the Sen'Prin could not pass.

Later, Meleena, Deem, and Talla had free time to wander the city and parklands. The carved stone bridges shimmered with flecks of ice and plentiful moss, reveling in the dampness. This added an earthy aroma to the fresh mountain air, while a babbling brook added a tranquil calmness.

"It's all fine here, but nobody has any hopes for making life better for the Northern Hill Villages!" Meleena said, frustrated.

"So, wait, this extinct fruit was first in use by Meruyans, and then destroyed by the Warix ancestors of Sen'Drorn? Then they made us dependent on them and basically enslaved us. They destroyed anyone who stood up against it," Deem said.

Meleena scowled. "That about sums it up."

"But what can we do about it?" Talla posed the question on all their minds. "You heard her, it's a long history of this. We have to accept our place in the system, try to negotiate small victories where we can, serving on the Council."

"But that doesn't solve anything!" Meleena argued.

Deem looked down, his boot scratching at the frozen earth. Geese waddled by, picking at the grass. A falcon circled overhead, its long tail trailing behind.

"Come with me…" Meleena pulled them under a willow tree, its long draping tendrils providing some secrecy. "Remember back in the Northern Hills when I told you about that Pendant? If only there were some way we could find it before the Sen'Drorn, it's the only hope I can imagine." Meleena sighed.

"What does it do, exactly?" Deem asked.

"I don't know. We just need a plan to find it before them, if we are to save the Sen'Prin."

Talla crossed her arms. "But all we know is, it was last seen underw—"

Her words were cut off by a whistling wind through the garden, followed by a frosty shiver as all three huddled into their borrowed scarves and rubbed their arms for warmth, puffs of frozen air blew from their breath. The winds of the Arctic City brought a chill like nothing they had ever felt.

"My you three have traveled far…" a familiar voice whispered, breaking the sound of their shivering breath. Somewhere distant, a falcon screeched.

They all jumped as Malotus's wild green eyes and broad horns peeked through the willow veil. He stepped inside, tiny icicles strewn throughout his beastly black mane, spilling onto his shoulders. In black regalia, he contrasted starkly with the natural surroundings. He smiled eerily, which sent a chill through Meleena equal to that of the icy wind.

"Why are you here?" She stood up, and her friends did the same behind her.

His tone was flat and steady. "I heard you talking about the Pendant. Where did you last see it?"

Meleena crinkled her face.

"Oh, come now, girl. I found your little journal…" He took a step forward. Meleena felt a cold bead of sweat on her forehead. Her teeth chattered from the cold.

Her journal had survived after all, that much lifted her spirits even beyond this horrid moment. "How did you find it——" Her voice caught in her throat.

"Your father instructed you to hide it from us, didn't he?" His voice betrayed his rising temper.

She clenched her fists, but felt hot despite the biting cold. "I'm not telling you anything!"

Deem and Talla shivered and drew closer together. Meleena stood her ground and looked him directly in the eyes.

"Have it your way," he said as an afterthought. "If you won't tell me here, I'll extract what I need like last time, from Councilman, what was his name, Lock?"

Malotus lunged forward, but Meleena dodged, and Talla tossed her a decorative garden spear. Meleena caught it and held the tip to Malotus. "Not another step!"

Malotus howled with laughter. "Oh, that is something, isn't it!" He made a gesture, a backhanded slap in the air. A gust of wind sent the spear flying. He leaped forward, taking Meleena by the front of her shirt in his clawed hands.

He brought her up close to his eyes, bright, they turned from green to silver, and in one strong kickoff, he whisked them off the ground, the gust knocking Deem and Talla on their backs.

"Meleena!" Deem shouted.

Talla screeched indecipherably as their images blurred with the raging snowy wind, and they shrank away from view. Malotus held Meleena tightly in the flurry of the tornado. She could only squint her eyes to keep pieces of ice out, as hail and snow blasted at her. He was carrying her away from the Arctic City.

CHAPTER TWENTY-FOUR

Yulah couldn't sleep. Flax had been acting strangely. Borak too.

No, I'll go to the shop first thing in the morning when they open. I'm sure it's all okay. But I should have never chosen between Malotus and Flax, I should have just kept my mouth shut.

First thing in the morning, she checked the shop. She looked up at the swinging sign on Borak's Gears n' Gadgets, but the lights were off, and the door remained locked as she waited. Other shops opened around Fleeg Street, and the early shoppers speckled the streets. She ran upstairs and knocked, then banged on the door to their flat until a cold shiver ran down her spine. *This can't be...*

She ran off to do the only thing she knew of, find Malotus in his chambers. He'd have just returned from his mission to find that Meruyan girl.

She burst through the door to his chambers. "What...Um. Did you find the Pendant?"

He looked up from his desk, head tilting to the side as she struggled to catch her breath.

"Morning, Yulah. No luck with the Pendant, but she knows something. I have her captive for further questioning." He eyed her. "Something else is on your mind."

Stay calm. She shivered.

"Malotus, yes. Um, I was just a little concerned about Flax. He and Borak didn't open their shop today." She scratched the back of her horn.

"Curious," he said. There was silence for a moment. "You didn't say anything to him about our plan, did you?"

"I er…" His piercing green eyes were too much, her tears welled up, and the room became the inside of a fishbowl.

"Yulah, what have you done?" he whispered as she burst into a fit of sobs—the room filled with the sound of her crying and a loud scratch from Malotus's claw ruining his desk's veneer, and his wooden chair sliding back against the stone.

She felt him wrap his arms around her. "Shhh, child," he soothed. "I knew you could not trust him. I told you heartbreak was inevitable, but this…"

Her throat was tight in fear and panic. She could not speak, then Malotus pulled away. "Where did we find this boy again, when we selected an apprentice for Borak? Outside the city walls…Vendengire…the village that we recently recaptured from the Sen'Prin?"

Malotus's arms locked on the corners of his oak desk, and he flung it like a rag against the wall with an earsplitting snap.

Then he spoke the very thought that strangled her.

"He is a spy for the Sen'Prin."

Yulah cowered and cried, "That's absurd!"

"Yes. He is, and he has killed Borak."

"Why would you say that?"

Malotus shouted over her sobs, "That's the order I'd have given under these circumstances! That's what *I* would have done in his position. You, Yulah, have killed Borak. The greatest engineer we have ever known. And vital for this war effort."

Yulah's cheeks flushed, hot and madder than Malotus now. She wailed, "I will hunt him down! We will send our best men, and I will capture him before he gets away! We will have his head on a spike by the day's end."

Malotus's face softened, surprised by her show of wrath, though she took no mind. It scared him, the flare in her eyes that reminded him of himself—that she was now becoming as embittered as he.

He said in his levelheaded demeanor, now with a hint of sorrow, "I will order the guards."

***

Swamplands shimmered with the dawn light outside the towering Sen'Drorn walls. Insects screamed their chorus through the web of rotting trees and bubbling green compost waters. The sludge spewed from hollow husks and covered every entangling root, as one Warix man slogged over and through it all up to his waist.

Borak wore workman's clothes, splattered with the swamp's messy offerings. A crashed machine lay in pieces nearby, having ripped through a line of moist, rotting trees. He had been thrown straight into the bog.

Who would guess that last night, this man had been selected to serve the Sen'Drorn in a highly honorable position of Chief Military Engineer Borak? Had he accepted, he would have received new laboratory facilities, wealth, the freedom to invent, and a legion of engineers to serve under him. No, that was never an option. Not since his apprentice had come out as his only earthly kin.

It was hard to think with the constant buzzing and croaking. Was there even a way out of here? He was utterly lost and had been wandering for a while now. Possibly in circles.

As long as Borak breathed and could keep moving, he had hope. Then a bubble of noxious goo grew in front of him and popped in his face.

" *Yyaaakk*!" he cried, wiping the slush from his eyes.

Up ahead, a small figure appeared among the gnarled trees. Borak pondered if he should remain hidden. Then again, maybe they could point him towards a village. He'd act natural and escape properly, once he made it to the town.

"Who is out there? Hello?" Borak called, straining to see the figure, which was small, like a child. "I need help! I'm lost!" He shuffled towards it, losing it in a murky haze.

A Warix girl of about six poked her head out from a tree in front of him, making him jump. "Little girl, are yeh okay?" he called.

How did she get in here? She must live nearby.

Her hair came down at her shoulders in two circular braid loops, and she wore a villager's smock. Both were green and wet from playing in the swamp.

"Are yeh lost here, child?" he inquired, approaching. "Do you know the way back home?"

The girl eyed him warily, unsure what to make of this man. "It's okay. I won't harm yeh, I'm actually lost here myself."

She dashed off, leaping over curling tree roots and grazing her hand on tree trunks for balance. Borak scampered after her, trying to follow the direction in case he lost her. He coughed and wheezed from the thick air and spat out some insects; in his rush he had run through a swarm.

Then the girl, almost out of sight, a speck in the distance, stopped shrinking. He caught up to find she'd tripped on a root, and now stood there, hands raised, her body full of green mud. Then came the fearful cries, drowning out the burbling, buzzing swamp sounds.

Borak bent on one knee. "It will all be okay." She nodded, blinking her eyes dry as a trail mixed with the mud. He scooped her up and wiped the mud from her face with his sleeve. "Which way is your village?"

She pointed and led him onward.

He maneuvered over the obstacles with more care now, through the swamp, until finally, radiant light beamed from the line of trees ahead, leading them into an open grass field.

They passed sheep grazing in the morning haze, then a stone well to wash off in, where he set the girl down. She ran off again, and he followed to where a small village peaked over the hill.

With a heavy sigh of exhaustion, he buckled to his knees. He still needed to get out of his clothes, wet and slimy.

Cautiously, he made his way into the cobblestone streets. This close to Sen'Drorn City, this could only be one of their towns.

He edged along smaller streets, avoiding the central square. Locating a clothing shop, he dawdled by the entrance until it opened.

The bell rang, and a Warix man dressed in fine purple garments greeted him. "*Nushenyu's blessings*! You look like you're having quite a rough morning. Have you been in the swamp? Let me offer you something!" The man ushered him behind a curtain so he could change. "Do you have any coinage on you?"

"I er, yes." He plucked a few metal coins from the sloshy pocket, where they clanked on the wooden floor.

"Hey!"

"Don't worry! I'll find you something nice." The hand returned and deposited a folded stack of tweed clothes into the booth. "We got all sizes, even for someone as bulky as you! Let me know how they fit."

Leaving the shop, Borak felt infinitely better in his crisp, clean clothes, despite the lack of sleep and all the stress. He had left the wet workman's clothes with the merchant to dispose of, and nobody would suspect him as an outsider now. Maybe he could even find an inn to sleep a few hours with the coins he had left.

Meandering the rest of the streets in this small village in search of one, he froze: several Warix in military uniform passed at the end of the street, the sigil of the flower-maned lion on a green background visible on their shoulders. Surely, they were only guards. Just to be safe, he turned a corner and went another way.

It wasn't long before more were at the end of that lane. He turned on his heels and walked right into a tavern, just opening its doors.

He barely got the words out to order a pint when a hand rested on his shoulder, making him jump.

He wheeled around. "Where'd you get these clothes?" a Sen'Drorn soldier asked, his grip tight. Three more soldiers blocked the doorway.

"I, uh, paid for these fairly. What crime have I committed?"

The soldiers moved, making way for another uniformed Warix, tall with wild black hair. General Malotus, and he was forcing another man through the door. It was the salesman whom Borak had bought the new clothes from.

Borak tried to act calm.

"Yes, sir. That's the man who came in wearing the muddy swamp clothes," he stammered. "I sold him those new."

His captor shoved him to the floor.

"Thank you. You may go," he said in a smooth voice.

Borak had never met General Malotus, but he knew of him. The famous Sen'Drorn General and his unsettling demeanor was known by all.

"Borak, having a pint outside of town? I'm surprised you're not with Flax. Tell me—where is he?"

"I don't know what you mean, I was…just out to buy things for the shop, and next minute I'm being, accused of, what exactly?"

"Odd, I find you here just hours before the announcement of your new assignment. And your apprentice, why is he not manning the shop?"

Borak shrugged, trying to play it cool.

"A guard at our walls informed he was hit from above…by a taser that fell from an unknown flying contraption. Both are the sort of contraptions one might find in an engineer's workshop. I'd expect nothing less from you, Borak. The Great Engineer of Fleeg Street."

Borak's face became hot. There was no use denying it now.

"Be proud. Not many have ever successfully traversed the Sen'Drorn wind wall. Now come with me. You have some answers to give."

"I ain't telling you anythin'!" he snarled and turned, ready to fight his way out of this bar, but four soldiers sprang to action. Kicking tables out of the way, they got him off his feet and pinned him to the floor.

Malotus put his face close to Borak's, such that if he turned his head, his horn could poke an eye out. "Flax. He's a spy for Sen'Prin, isn't he?"

Borak felt it better to keep his mouth shut at this point.

Malotus shrugged. He turned away and let the guards muscle him off his feet. "That's alright. I'm sure Yulah will track him down soon. I'm just happy to see you are alive."

Borak tried to plead. "I'm not with him, I ran off on my own! I will no longer participate in your tyranny!"

Malotus crossed his arms and snarled, "Well, that's not up to you. You *will* keep working, if not for glory, then for duty. You owe a debt to your nation. We have been good to you. Because of our service, you have been prosperous all your life."

He struggled against the soldier's grip with all his last strength, until something heavy struck him from behind, and everything went black.

CHAPTER TWENTY-FIVE

Borak awoke in a dusty cell, empty except for a floor and cot inside stone walls and bars. He rubbed his pounding head. His hands found the bump.

A strange girl with blue hair lay in the middle cell across from him.

He startled as a voice from down the hall, which he could not see, shouted, "He's awake!"

A distant flickering torchlight bounced with quick echoing footsteps— several guests approaching his cell.

General Malotus led the pack, Yulah behind him, and several uniformed Sen'Drorn soldiers, the flower-maned lion sigil almost appeared to growl from their shoulders.

"Borak, the famous engineer of Fleeg Street," Malotus said, looking proud and well-groomed. "Committing treason."

Borak, covered in dirt, merely scowled.

"I don't need to know how Flax turned you to disloyalty. I just need his whereabouts. Before you begin your work from the dungeons."

Borak spat on the ground.

Yulah appeared behind him, dark and puffy-eyed. She looked like she hadn't slept in days. Her cheeks stained with tears.

Malotus shot out his hands, and a burst of wind slammed Borak backward against the far cell wall. He slid down to the floor but retained the strength to look at Malotus.

Malotus opened the cell door; Borak got to his feet and raised his fists. Malotus lunged, his black hair swinging with him, as he punched Borak in the jaw before Borak could take a swing.

Borak reached for the rusty bedpan from the floor, threw it at Malotus, who batted it away, but shook his hand in pain. Malotus lifted his arms and a gust of wind threw Borak sideways against the far cell wall.

"I will tell you nothing," Borak said again, taking a long watery blink.

Malotus's mountainous black mane and wide horns loomed over him like death come for him. But then something odd happened. He glanced sideways at Yulah, who only scowled at the floor. Malotus's expression suddenly changed: it softened, to Borak's astonishment. He stepped back. "You are no use to us dead." Malotus sighed.

He took an audible breath and locked the cell. Just before he and Yulah disappeared down the hallway, Malotus turned back and said, "We *will* find Flax. And execute him."

Borak sank to the floor of his cell.

What have I done? He put his hands in his lap, calloused and worn from a lifetime of service.

***

Meleena woke up shivering. She lay on cold stone as the musty stench of standing water and rotting fungus filled the small room. An animalistic instinct bade her not to move.

"You're awake."

It was the echoing voice of a Warix guard. She could see him from the corner of her eye behind iron bars. "You will enjoy your stay here. And maybe you will even remember where you last saw the Pendant before Malotus makes a special trip to bring your parents in for questioning too."

Another heavy figure somewhere laughed.

Meleena held back from crying, as if a ball of seaweed were wedged in her throat.

She said nothing, staying on her side until the patrolling guard's feet betrayed their motion away from her.

She looked over her body—at the scars accumulated on this trip. From the Gommwoods and the river crossing. Her new journal, gone. She only endured the Council's journey as far as she had because of the others.

Deem's kindness and preparedness, Talla's bright, outgoing nature. How could she, Meleena, think she could do it all by herself? She was captured because of herself: her own mistakes, losing the Pendant, and keeping up that foolish nature-journaling hobby.

"Are ye alright there, girl?" came a soft voice from nearby.

Meleena held her breath and listened.

In the cell across from her sat an older, muscular Warix man. His clothes were tattered, his frown deep behind a blackened eye and bloody limbs. He looked like he had been through a lot.

"Why would they capture a sweet Meruyan girl? Now I've seen it all. Things ain't turning out to be as I had thought around here, and somehow it has taken me a lifetime to realize what's been around me all along." He sighed, though Meleena had no idea what he was talking about, she felt bad for him.

"I'm here because of these Warix, the Sen'Drorn. They are terrible, tormenting my people, and trying to get secrets from me to make life even worse for them. I'd rather die than tell them anything," she huffed, word vomiting her frustrations. "Sorry, this was a lot for me." She couldn't help the swelling wave of sorrow inside her.

"I have a son your age," he said sadly.

Meleena smiled at him. He exuded calming energy. It was contagious.

They spoke about their lives, bonding over their dreams and interests if they were ever to see the outside world again to do them. Clinging to her love of nature, and his of engineering, the two kept sane for those long next few hours.

***

Flax limped along the tree line, under the forest canopy but with the farmland on his right to keep from getting lost. His leg was busted. He couldn't use any wind power safely, off-balance like this.

Thoughts swirled in his mind like the updrafts that blew in the orange and red fallen leaves. About Borak, and Yulah, his broken life, everyone he had hurt. *What if Borak doesn't come? I've messed up his life enough.*

He shouldn't have to. But I love him. But would he really go work for them? And Yulah? She's certainly better off without having met me.

The wind blew in circles around him, rattling the trees and stirring a carpet of leaves into a sound like crumpled paper. It wasn't simply the natural tranquility of an autumn forest, but a sign that Warix were coming.

He turned to see that several individuals had landed in tornados at the nearby farm. He ducked behind a hefty, mossy log, but the wind blew stronger, it was coming towards him. Sweating, he ran, but the fallen leaves crunched and gave him away. There was nowhere to run. He turned, but the descending soldiers appeared on every side, and Yulah dropped through the canopy, eyes bright silver, knocking back trees.

"How did you find me?" he gasped.

"Please, I know you, Flax. Even though Borak wouldn't give anything away. Knowing you, you would make a romantic escape. Stop by Vendengire. When I saw the crashed windboard, I knew I was on the right track. We just searched the surrounding area until we spotted movement. It wasn't hard."

Flax's cheeks burned as Yulah's tone changed from angry to desperate. "Tell me you are not a spy, Flax. Maybe you were just against the war? Got scared, fled?" she shouted as the wind around her dissipated, and she stood before him. "We have captured Borak."

"Yulah! What? Where is Borak?" He said, anxiously.

"He is in our jail! You told him something!" she cried out.

"He…" It was hard for Flax to believe. "He fled?" He felt touched.

"You didn't know?"

"Hear me out." Flax knew this would be his only chance to try to explain himself. "I never meant to hurt you. It was selfish, and wrong. Just like my taking this mission. Yes, I am a spy, but I did it to find my real father, who lives in your city. He turned out to be Borak. If he left, it was because he had morals, and I got through to him. We couldn't work for you. I'm sorry."

He fell to his knees. There was nothing to do but surrender without a struggle.

Yulah's face became harsh, furious, and sent a kick right at his stomach. "I trusted you! And you were spying the whole time. Malotus always taught me never to trust anyone, now I see he was right."

"For what it's worth, Yulah, I never betrayed your trust to the Sen'Prin, I never used our relationship to our advantage..."

What he really wanted to say, though didn't think it would go over so well was, "Yulah, listen. Remember that time we were in Malotus's office and we learned about Malotus and Arenay's past together? You told me Malotus doesn't even like The Emperor. He's only doing that terrible job for personal reasons. For revenge. Maybe you can persuade him, somehow, to leave his post. The two of you could join us and start over somewhere else."

She wouldn't understand.

Tears streaming down her cheeks. Yulah turned away and shouted to the soldiers, "He must face his fate at the capital!" Then to Flax, "You will hang for this."

The soldiers bound him in chains. They pulled his wristcom from his arm and smashed it on a rock. Pieces of metal flew everywhere. Two soldiers bound him in rope, including his eyes. The world went dark as the soldier's hands gripped tight onto his shoulders. Soon, his feet lost contact with the ground in the familiar whirl of wind as they launched a tornado for his transport.

***

The Sen'Drorn soldiers marched Flax down winding steps. His eyes still blindfolded, he relied on sound. From the way their steps echoed, it was clear they were heading into an underground, stone tunnel.

"Flax!" came a familiar voice, small but tender.

A guard sniggered, and the rope fell loose around Flax's neck, returning his sight. His father, bloodied and bruised, was being marched the other way up the hallway.

"Flax!" Borak shouted again as they passed in the corridor, both muscled forward by guards. "I want to apologize for everything!"

"Shut up, old man!" a guard barked.

"Borak, no! I am the one who is sorry!" Flax called.

Their eyes met, for one brilliant second, and Flax stared deep into Borak's stone-brown eyes, which mirrored his own, in color and muted tears. And then Borak was gone, thrust out of sight. Flax could not turn around, but shouted with all he could muster, "I will save you, somehow!"

And that was it.

The two guards shoved Flax, sending him crashing to the ground. The blunt pain returned as he met the stone, followed by the jagged sound of the metal gate closing behind him. Lock clicking, boots shuffling, pivoting, growing more distant until they were gone. Yulah had not even entered the dungeon with them. Flax clenched his teeth. The sound of those grinding iron bars continued to reverberate through his skull long after they'd gone.

But he was not alone in this cell. To his surprise, there was a small, blue-skinned girl sitting in the corner. Her flowing blue hair danced though she didn't move.

"Are you a spy?" she said, staring at him with wide eyes.

The sparsely lit dungeon flickered.

The guards didn't bother to keep it energized with wind power when unmanned. So when the turbines had stopped, it grew dark. A small window cast a dim strip of light in.

"Er. Long story," Flax answered. He didn't feel like talking right now. The memory of Yulah's scorn made his skin crawl and choked him. He stared at his hands, clenched into fists. They appeared to be made of stone in the eerie light.

He felt utterly rotten. *Being on the "good" team means nothing if you destroy the trust of those you love, regardless of what lies they seem to believe.*

His injured leg throbbed as he adjusted his posture, but was nothing next to the doubts swirling in his mind. Borak, Yulah, and Thian. He had made things worse for them all. First, when he requested the mission change, leaving Thian stuck in the desert, alone on the tedious mission.

Dating Yulah, toying with her heart and betraying her trust. Even getting close to his father was only to make himself feel better. Borak was fine before Flax had shown up. Now his life had been ruined.

Selfish. Flax hadn't cared enough about the Sen'Prin mission or righteous cause of helping the Meruyan. Indulging in the exotic delicacies of the oppressive city as if he was a local. What a terrible spy he made, losing himself among the Sen'Drorn people. Now he wanted to tear himself apart with his own claws to end the guilt.

It was time to change his priorities.

The light returned as the guards came to toss down dinner trays with an unsettling clank.

The Meruyan girl moved to sit on a straw bed, the dinner tray on her lap. "Wait, I know you," she said, not eating. "You were taking notes with Arenay at a meeting, in Dlawn'Edo, the Meruyan city. About a year ago."

Flax could only vaguely recall. It felt like a lifetime ago. So much had happened since then. "Who are you? And what did a Meruyan teenager do to get herself locked in here?"

"My name is Meleena. I was at that Meruyan Council meeting with my father. It's a long story why I'm here. Malotus…" She broke off, looking unsure where to continue from there.

"Oh," Flax muttered knowingly. He looked up at her from his seat on the floor. It made as much sense to him as anything else Malotus would do—why not add kidnaping Meruyan youth to the list. "I'm Flax. I work for the Sen'Prin resistance nation. I was spying in Sen'Drorn City. Until I blew it, as you can see."

Meleena jumped to her feet, setting the food tray aside untouched. "I want to be a spy too."

"What?" He almost laughed despite his mood. "A Meruyan spy? How would you even travel without—?"

"Without wind powers?" She furrowed her brow. "I used to observe nature, thinking the wild contained valuable lessons people could learn from. When I met Arenay, I wanted to bring my knowledge to the Warix. I only recently discovered there are two nations, both at odds with one another. I want to join the Sen'Prin, Arenay's people, to stop the Sen'Drorn from exploiting the Meruyan."

"Well, a good spy is resourceful. Look, if you can get us out of here, I'll tell Arenay to take you in."

Meleena nodded.

Flax's stomach grumbled. "I guess we should eat. Looks like wheat mush and mixed seeds." The Meruyan girl picked through the mess with her fingers as Flax picked up his spoon, ready to chow down.

"Wait, stop!" she dove towards him, slapping the spoon away. "Don't eat it!" She plunged her hands into his dinner and started picking through the wheat mush.

"Are you feral?! I'm starving!" *Nature girl, indeed.*

"Look, these could be our way out!" She held out her open palm, where she had picked out a number of large, lumpy seeds. "These are seeds."

"I can see that…Uh, I was planning to eat them."

"Specifically, these are Tumbumble seeds. They grow quickly and have strong roots. Maybe they can grow in the cell." She examined the windows. "They can probably even break these stones around the window. We can plant them in the stone crevices in the light of the window, so they can grow."

"Can I at least eat the mush?"

"I'll need the mush for fertilizer."

Flax's stomach grumbled again. "You've got to be joking…how are you not starving?"

She rubbed her arm. "I am hungry. But a Meruyan's hair brings us some nourishment from the sun. Just like all moss-furred animals, and these seeds. We plant them in the mush, anchor them in a moist, muddy spot in the wall, mimicking their natural habitat. They grow in cracks of rocks and trees, and need minimal sunlight."

Flax stared dumbfounded in the seeds. "How do you know all that?"

Meleena shrugged. "You just have to observe. I used to keep a journal before it was taken by the Sen'Drorn. It was a stupid interest."

"Well, not if it gets us out of here."

"We will need to wait for the morning and see if it grows."

So they pressed the seeds into a mud-rich wall between the stones and went to sleep.

Flax awakened to a horrible sound, like the world being ripped asunder. Green roots snaked along the wall, opening cracks and weakening their foundation. They split at the core as the root sought space to grow. The plant had also sprouted a drill-like seed pod, which burst open at Meleena's touch and busted open the weakened wall with a crash.

CHAPTER TWENTY-SIX

The window burst open with a loud crack and sunshine spilled in, filling the cell with light. Squinting into the light, Meleena peered over the rubble, entangled with vines. Flax followed her as they climbed the vines like a ladder.

They found themselves standing just off the fortress at street level. Now they just had to escape Sen'Drorn City.

Down in the prison, they heard shouting and echoing footsteps. The guards would soon discover them. There was only one direction in which to head.

"Great work! But let's keep running!" He held onto her hand and tugged on it as he continued sprinting. Meleena was pulled after him, blushing slightly. She regained her balance and spun by his side as they ran. She noticed he was limping along, one of his legs injured.

"Hey, you!" A guard was already climbing through the hole in the gate. He shouted into a device on his wrist. "We need guards! Guards to the prison!"

"Stay with me, I know where we are," Flax shouted to Meleena.

"Really, where is that?" She was struck with awe at the towering city around her as she ran beside him down the street. They cross-crossed and made crazy turns down various narrow alleyways and jumped over staircases. These buildings were twice as high as the ones even in the Meruyan city of Dlawn'Edo, forming intricate mazes. Meleena felt as turned around as when she was among the Gommwoods, but did her best to keep up.

Something caught her eye that almost made her stop running. She glimpsed blue skin. A Meruyan? They were in an alley, hauling away barrels of trash. She recognized a boy, a few years older than herself, and a wave of shock hit her. Sen'Drorn City was where the Meruyan council was sending apprentice rejects. They must have made some deal with the Sen'Drorn to use them for city maintenance. Her heart sank. They were stuck here, in this life against their will. How close she had come to being sent here…to sharing their fate.

But now was not the time to dwell. Meleena would have to find some way to help them later. If she made it out herself.

Guards swarmed in from flanking streets, as they attempted to cut-off the escape.

"Where are you leading us?"

"To another side of the fortress."

"What!? I thought we were escaping?! How do we get out of here?"

"I told you. I need to rescue my father. They have him!"

"Now?!" Meleena's heart thumped. Flax seemed to have lost his mind. Maybe she would end up like those poor Meruyan after all.

The screams of townspeople and guards blazed behind them at a constant din, letting them know they were close, and could not slow down for any moment.

"Can't you call for help on your wrist gadget?"

"Wristcom. No, they destroyed mine upon my capture."

Flax tossed some boxes aside as they ran through an alleyway. Meleena could see a more populated area at the end of it.

"Yulah's flat is up the hill, ahead. We can hide there. I know of secret tunnels nearby that can get us into the fortress."

"Well, fish-nugget." Meleena was out of ideas. She only knew going back to the fortress seemed like the opposite of a good idea.

Meleena was already panting as they ran through another square, through more alleys and up winding stone paths until they reached a forested trail. The shouting of guards let her know the distance was closing between them.

"Just a bit further!" Flax shouted, pointing to the forest glade within the city. Meleena felt a sinking feeling in the pit of her stomach as she turned around to check for guards, then she ran straight into a tree. No, not a tree. Meleena realized with a shock, as she bounced off a large brass chest plate. The armored Warix guard grabbed her by the neck and arm, twisting her so she fell to her knees choking. Flax, out of sight somewhere to her left, croaked and fell to his knees beside her as they exchanged horrified glances.

The trees were within spitting distance.

"We knew where you would go, master Flax. We have our shortcuts," came the voice of the head guard. "Malotus gave us special orders to watch for you by Yulah's flat."

"Oh gusts," he squeaked.

This time their hands were bound, necks put in iron clamps, and they were led away. The guard's eyes glimmered, Meleena winced for she knew it meant he was about to issue wind power and take off in a whirlwind.

"Stop!" Shouted an echo from the direction of town.

"I'm here for you, buddy!" Footsteps raced up the pavement, and wind bursts slammed, knocking Meleena, Flax, and the guards off their feet in a tumble of wind, like a washing wave of the tides.

Standing before them was a Warix with shaggy brown hair and a copper cone around his left arm.

"Thian!" gasped Flax.

Meleena realized he was the other young Warix at the Meruyan Dlawn'Edo meeting last year.

The guards stood up, and one of them called, "Wind blast usage is forbidden inside the city!"

The guards lunged at Thian, providing a short window for Meleena and Flax to take off. They ran in different directions.

A city guard yelled to Thian, "What are you doing? These are dangerous criminals! We have no choice but to arrest you for attacking the guards!"

He thinks Thian is one of them! Meleena thought as she ran. Maybe this could provide backup in the confusion. Then someone cast a wind burst, knocking Flax back, and Flax retaliated as best he could with his injured leg, shuffling to the side.

Some of the guards had wind enhanced gauntlets to knock them back. The intricate copper wires twinkled off the sun into Meleena's eyes, making it hard to see clearly and leaving sun-stains on her vision. Then a thrust on her arm launched her into a side corridor. She slammed hard against the stone wall, and looked up. Flax was staring at her, holding her away from the commotion, though she heard yelling and the sound of destruction. Meleena struggled to catch her breath

Thian ducked beside them a moment later.

Flax laughed and slapped Thian on the back. "Thian! Great to see you, buddy. How did you get here?"

Thian panted and spoke through a broad grin. "I came to save you! With all that intel you sent me, we made maps, outlined sewer systems, a bunch of things!"

"Well, much appreciated!" The two embraced in a strange hug that involved a lot of back-patting.

Then Thian bent to grip a porthole of iron bars in the ground and cast the heavy thing aside with a clang. He made a gesture for them to follow. Meleena had never seen anything like it before. She hesitated. Flax jumped first, so she followed, landing on her feet in the dark pit. Thian jumped in after them, closing the lid above their heads. The only illumination came from a glowing light source on Thian's forehead.

"How did you even know to come and rescue me?" Flax asked as they crept through the sewers.

"After we last spoke, and things went south, and you didn't come back, I assumed something was wrong. Except you didn't seem to need my help busting out!"

"It was all her, believe it or not!" He smiled at Meleena, who waved.

"Right on." Thian beamed.

They turned various corners among dark passages lit by Thian's head torch, which dimmed and had to be wound every few minutes. Thian held hand-drawn maps, scratching his chin as Flax looked over his shoulder.

While the pair decided which forks to take, Meleena stayed quiet, just following, though she could tell they were headed in one direction over long stretches.

"Impressive! All I gave you were the utility hole locations, and you put all this together down here?"

"Well, me and the team back at base. You'll see them again shortly."

Flax stopped. "Wait, where are you leading us?" He turned right at the next fork. "We want to go to the fortress!"

"What? Are you crazy?" Thian ran after him.

"They have my father!"

"They're looking for you! You'll just get captured too!"

"I don't care, I need to save him."

"No, we need to regroup and form a plan!"

Meleena sighed. "I don't want to go either, for what it's worth."

"I promise I will help you." Thian turned to Flax and put an arm on Flax's shoulder, partly in support, partly to prevent him from walking off farther. "But we need to regroup and form a proper plan with Sen'Prin first."

Flax grunted, his body pointing in the direction of the fortress. Meleena shot him an exhausted look. Her knees trembled. She just wanted to be out of this stinky place and far from that Warix prison.

"I promise I will help you return here and break in and rescue Borak. But let's not go back to jail, or get ourselves killed."

Flax sighed. "Fine, I guess there's no other way."

They followed Thian and his map in the direction leading to the edge of the city walls until a bright light was visible at the end. They crawled from an opening to find themselves in a sewer runoff leading into some woods. A thick sewage river traversed their exit portal below.

"No wind powers!" Meleena warned before they took off down the cascade without her.

"Oh, right." Flax turned to her, and she held tight onto his chest, and he pushed off in a burst. They flew over the swampy river, landing on soft grassy earth.

"This way, I have an airship waiting." Thian led them onward into the dry woodlands with trees heavy with bristly leaves. Their fallen, brown matchsticks covered the ground she trod over, dampening their gaits and emitting a sharp, earthy fragrance. Meleena found it purely tantalizing.

A group of four-legged animals bounced across the deeper woods, as Meleena turned to glimpse them. If only she'd still had her journal. Maybe she'd never get it back from Malotus. But was she really going to see Arenay again? At the center of their world? That was enticing enough to offset the pain. *Who knew it would take losing my journal to eventually lead me here?*

They made it to a clearing, where several trees had been felled among the rigid forest. Three Warix dressed in Sen'Prin military colors revealed themselves, with a flying machine like the ones Meleena knew from the Hill Villages. "We will carry you to Sen'Prin. Hop on." They wore thick goggles and helmets so Meleena couldn't see much of their faces.

The soldiers took their places by the copper shafts, while one went to the helm, his feet ready to press on small plates sticking up, his arms gripping a T-shaped structure jutting out.

Meleena, Flax, and Thian climbed onto the platform, the place where the cargo crates were normally loaded at the farms. Thian said, "Hold on tight." Meleena felt uneasy, clenching her jaw and clutching the side rails until her knuckles turned white. She wasn't a fan of this flying thing. Her stomach sank as they lifted off and traversed the tree canopy.

"Ah, gusts!" Flax shouted, and Meleena turned to see they weren't the only thing flying by the pointy treetops. Behind them, several airships followed, but Meleena could tell they weren't friendly, the green uniforms gave away that they were Sen'Drorn military. Theirs were equipped with spiraling copper horns and extra solders, aiming their hands at the ready. Projectiles flew at them full force, propelled by wind power and amplified from the mechanisms they used.

"Damn!"

He and Thian lifted their arms and called forth a counter wind, deflecting the projectiles, which turned out to be jagged stones, which bounced away from their airship. Meleena hoped the forest animals were safe down there. The other three Sen'Prin had to keep powering and steering the airship, scrunching their faces to hold form. Meleena felt utterly useless.

She darted her attention around the forest. Maybe she could find something helpful around here, her own way. Different heights of trees; curling vines; a sunbathing reptile on a branch; large birds flying overhead. What could be advantageous here?

Thian and Flax were already panting. They were exhausting themselves and the enemy airships were drawing near. Then, she saw it. Some of the trees among the pointy ones. Different tree varieties? No, they were jutting branches bare of leaves poking through. Gommwoods.

"That!" Meleena shouted, turning to the Sen'Prin manning the helm, turning the copper T-jangle every which way, presumably connected to a series of copper shafts under the floor from the other two providing the power sources.

"Fly lower!" She pointed to the barren trees and shouted to the driver, "If we could fly low over there, or better yet, startle them into a frenzy, perhaps they could snag the copper undercarriage of the Sen'Drorn airships."

A buzzing rang out. Thian answered his wristcom, sparing the other hand to bat a stone. "Arenay?"

"Thian! The current spies say the Pendant has been found. Where are you?"

"The Pendant!? I er...I'm not at Sen'Prin City. I sorta...went to rescue Flax..."

"What!?"

"Yes, we're on our way in an airship."

"No trouble!? How did you get in there!?"

With Meleena's guidance, the airship dipped and passed over a patch of Gommwood horns, and the Sen'Drorn airship followed, trying to keep aim with their shots. A rock hit the side of the airship with a wrenching crash.

"Well, we are currently under chase by Sen'Drorn, but we are coming!" Thian roared.

"No, Thian, there's no time! Ditch the guards and fly south to the Hyish lands. You two are our experts on Hyish customs. We need you and Flax to negotiate with the Mayfee clan before the Sen'Drorn find out. We will send coordinates."

"Eh, sure. One thing is, well. We have a Meruyan girl with us."

"What?!"

They dipped again, dragging along the Gommwoods, clanking the bottom of their own airship.

"Careful!" Meleena shouted above the din. "Arenay! I want to join you and be a spy! I can help!"

They lifted again and the Sen'Drorn airship struggled to pull out of the sharp turn, dipping also along the Gommwood patch, only their ship failed to rise, their copper wiring looped on the boney horns of the trees like an anchor.

"There's no time to drop her off anyway. But please, stay out of this," Thian snapped at Meleena.

"She just saved us all by leading the Sen'Drorn airship to crash into some trees. That was all her idea," Flax answered defendsively.

"They're called Gommwoods," Meleena said.

"She...wow. Do what you can, then..." Arenay hung up.

A string of green coordinates appeared on Thian's wristcom screen. The distance grew as the pursuing airship lagged, and soon they were out of sight. Everyone onboard the Sen'Prin airship cheered, and Flax clapped Meleena on the back.

"Alright, boys, I'll lead the way!" Thian grinned.

Where were Deem and Talla now? Were they still on the journey, in Arctic City? Or had they gone home sooner as a consequence of her capture? Would they keep Peela safe to return to her father?

A stabbing in her heart crippled as she thought about how worried her parents must be. No Meruyan knew if she was even alive. They sailed on through the air, over the mountains, towards lands Meleena had never seen.

CHAPTER TWENTY-SEVEN

Meleena, Flax, Thian, and the Sen'Prin soldiers steering the airship flew over vast landscapes. It was too high for Meleena to make out in much detail, except the land changing from one biome to the next. From forest to farmland to open green plains, and finally, to arid foothills with jutting mountains to the west. Meleena vaguely recognized the crest shapes of those mountains from when she first set off on Aldrok's journey.

"Are those...the Meruyan mountains, where Dlawn'Edo falls are?" she asked, pointing to the spires.

Flax pitched his head up, then grabbed Thian's wristcom for a look. "Yes, the coordinates are leading us to the foothills on the inland side. That must be where the Hyish are."

"It sure beats the desert," said Thian.

As the airship descended, a colorful sprawl of tents came into view.

The conductors guided the airship over an outlying hill, shielded from view of the encampment by its steeper angle and a wall of scrubby trees. The airship landed, and Meleena jumped off first, happy to touch the ground again. Thian and Flax followed, directing the Sen'Prin guards to stay back and guard the airship and watch for Sen'Drorn approach.

"How are we going to get in there without Hyish clothes?" Thian asked.

"We'll need to barter for some," Flax said.

"Why do we need new clothes? Aren't we welcome to trade here?" Meleena asked. The three of them made their way up a grassy knoll as they discussed this.

Thian and Flax looked at each other. Flax explained first. "Yes, and any foreigners walking in the open through Hyish markets would draw too much attention. Every fur trader, emerald dealer, and spice mixer will be drawn to our side, trying to trade with us."

Thian added, "With Warix, they assume we all come with some rare treasure, and the Hyish are drawn to what they perceive to be rare things. They are less familiar with Meruyans, but let's assume the treatment will be the same." He smiled, his goofy grin reminding Meleena of Deem, sending a sad pang to her heart that her friends were not with her now.

"Lucky we parked near the garment market. I'll get them," said Flax, pointing over the hill to the south as the three of them reached the top.

Thian slipped some coins into his hand before he wandered off into the valley. "Good luck."

Meleena inspected the landscape, leaning her hand on the trunk of a tree as she struggled against vertigo. Thian offered her a look at his wrist-com, which contained a compass, to help her get her bearings. The green, rugged hills became steeper to the west nearer the mountain, growing softer into fine waves as they tapered into the sweeping eastern horizon. In the valleys between, a sprawl of Hyish tents dominated the landscape, forming clusters of dwelling tents interspersed with open spaces. Judging by the higher volume of people, this had to be the marketplace.

Flax returned shortly with brightly colored robes folded over his arms. Meleena pulled hers over her head and observed the group of hooded figures around her. The hot sun cast no shadows, and Meleena wiped a bead of sweat from her brow.

Meleena followed Thian and Flax down the hill, into the maze of tents. The area was abuzz with the hissing language of the Hyish going about their day. The sweet aroma of cooking fires and smoke rose as lunch commenced. Hyish women carried clay pots, and children ran through the chaos. Meleena's eyes widened as some Hyish, particularly children, spat fire freely to start cooking fires, to warm sitting rocks, even as part of socializing. Then, even more, she saw them using the fire for glassblowing. A stack of rough-cut glass sat by a Hyish, and Meleena realized something.

The lenses in her glasses were produced by Hyish...That info could come in handy.

Each tent was a patchwork of linen weave and leather, some decorated with bells, small animal bones, seeds, shells, or other small, natural trinkets. The decor seemed to match with the symbols on triangular flags waving atop their central stake.

As they rounded a corner, Meleena jumped—she had brushed against some large beast, who had been sleeping by the entrance to a tent. Its long, scaly limbs coiled tenderly around plump, bristly torsos. The scaled head uncoiled and blinked at her. Meleena stopped. She was so close she saw herself reflected in its black eyes. A long tongue whipped out and in, tasting the air, and the bristles from its body stood up, like hundreds of cactus needles. Meleena extended a trembling finger for it to sniff. It turned and curled its snake-neck back around its body, whose needles dropped flat again, tail twitching as it returned to its slumber. Meleena sighed in great relief and tiptoed off to catch up with the others. This time, she'd pay more attention to her surroundings.

"Stay close," Flax said as she caught up with them, trying to see where he was indicating while shielding her eyes against the bright midday sun. The scent of spices and cooking wafted through the area. Meleena's stomach growled. She realized she hadn't eaten all day. They meandered through groups of tents, entering from one cluster to the next, avoiding crowded paths that led into crowded market pockets. "We're edging around the central market. We need to find someone from the Mayfee clan who can direct us towards her tent."

"How do you know this 'Mayfee' has it?" Meleena asked.

"If the Pendant was found, she would get her hands on it. The Hyish have a saying, 'be it black tea or mead or silver key, all treasures flow, towards Chieftess Mayfee.'"

They passed a Hyish man holding a pair of woven shoes, and Flax spoke to him. "Arash'sha, ne Mayfee na lang?"

Meleena's eyes widened as she heard him speak the Hyish tongue.

"Na ga sshhek," the man responded, pointing his scaly hand.

"H'th'kaya." Flax bowed. He motioned for Thian and Meleena to follow.

"That's about all he knows." Thian chuckled to Meleena.

They wove through more tents, from one cluster to another, until they arrived at a group of tents whose tabard bore the snake-hawk skull. They arrived at a central tent, much larger than the others, with the bones of a winged snake running across the top.

"This must be it. The skull of the snake-hawk," Flax whispered, then approached two hooded Hyish guards who blocked the entrance.

Flax pulled back his hood to address the guards.

"Do you speak the common tongue? We are here to see Mayfee. We hear she has something to trade us."

"Desh'ju, Warix? Sssen'Drorn?" the guard answered in his harsh tongue.

"Desh'ja Warix, we are...Uh. Yes, ready to make an offer," Flax said, keeping his voice low.

"Uhn, ghha." The guards nodded, and one slipped his flexible serpentine torso inside the tent, while the other didn't remove his gaze from them. The upper half of the first guard slipped back out after a moment, then the guards pulled back the braided tassels to reveal the inside of the tent.

They entered to find Mayfee sitting atop a jeweled golden armchair, looking down at them from below her spiked purple hair and jangling piercings. Her feathered elbows splayed atop the chair arms, leaving her clawed hands to dangle freely, granting her a regal, yet easy sensibility. Two more guards stood with their bulky arms crossed at her side, like interwoven pythons.

She stood up at their entrance, her sash dress cascading. "Warm sands welcome," she hissed, in a broad smile, slit eyes glistening with intelligence. "I'm surprised to hear you have come to me before I have even had the chancccee to pay you a visit. You mussst have eyess everywhere to know I have something for you. And you mussst really want it, to pursue me with such haste." Her reptilian slit eyes, pin needles, darted between them.

Flax and Thian nodded, but strangely, their heads bounced in rapid pulses. Meleena copied the movement, trying to follow along with Hyish custom. Mayfee responded with the same, which then permitted them to stop.

Then Flax spoke to her. "We came to obtain it personally. We will give you all the riches we have."

"You are Sssen'Drorn?"

"We, uh, we are Sen'Prin, but we will pay you more than Sen'Drorn."

"Sssorry. Sen'Drorn richer than Sen'Prin. That means they have more to offfer. I wait, sell to them for the higher price."

"Please," Flax offered gently. "You don't want to sell to them! Better to sell to us. They are a bad cause, and we will pay more over time, because we will be more grateful, and take care of Hyish needs."

"Hmm...I don't understand how this makes sense. Sen'Drorn more established, more shiny gems, gold, and grains in their vaults. Hyish do not care about your Warix politics."

Meleena didn't like how this was going. Negotiation made her think of Talla, fighting for their rights against the Northern Village curfews. This gave her an idea. Since her time in jail, she had resolved it was okay to ask for help.

"Okay, you go now. I sell to Sen'Drorn. Please, go about and enjoy our markettsss. We have other nice things you can trade for. We welcome rare Warix treasures."

And just like that, they were swept from the tent by the guards, and stood again among the tents, this time without a plan.

"What do we do now?" Flax bore his teeth and wrung the hem of his robe into a twisted mass.

"I have an idea," Meleena said. "Call me crazy but, I actually know a good negotiator and someone so kind they'd have to agree." It was the only hope they had, so they decided to give it a chance. After her kidnap, Deem and Talla were more likely back at Dlawn'Edo.

They called Sen'Prin on Thian's wristcom and explained what had happened, and their idea to regroup. After some time, Arenay called them back.

"I'm sorry to hear it," she responded. "I have spoken to Councilman Ives. Your friends are safe." Meleena was surprised the Meruyan Council even had tech that connected them to Arenay, but was not surprised they would withhold that. That must be how Arenay knew in the first place to come after her village's attack.

"Meleena, your friends have completed their journey and are safe in the capital city, resting and awaiting final interviews with the elders. The Meruyan Council are relieved to know you are alive and safe with Sen'Prin and have sent word to your family. They want you to know that you are not disqualified from joining the Council when you get back."

"I don't want to join the Council. I want to join Sen'Prin and be a spy. Er, but that's not the point right now. Is it possible to send the others, Deem and Talla, here? Please, it's important in obtaining the Pendant."

"What good will that do?" Arenay asked.

"They have acquired skills during Aldrok's journey that will make them integral. Please trust me. You're out of other options."

The line went silent for a moment. She could hear only muffled whispers as a discussion amongst those on the other line ensued. Flax grabbed Thian's wrist and memorized their exact coordinates, those of Mayfee's tent, off his wristcom.

Then, Arenay's voice retuned. "I'll send a ship for them. Dlawn'Edo is just over the mountains. You have permission to send your airship to pick them up. It shouldn't take them long." She hung up.

As Thian, Meleena, and Flax dashed back to the airship landing site, Thian's Wristcom buzzed again. It was one of their Sen'Prin airship riders. "Agent Thian, tornados were spotted to the north on the horizon, heading straight for the Hyish encampments. It must be the Sen'Drorn coming for the Pendant. Have you secured it?"

"Thanks for the tip. We were about to call you—we haven't secured the Pendant, but we need you to go to Dlawn'Edo and pick up two Meruyans. Meet at the landing coordinates when you return," said Thian.

The airship was well on its way by the time they arrived at the site. Meleena spotted what they had reported on over the horizon. A shiver ran down her spine as the distant dust devil drew near. There was nothing to do but wait and hope the airship carrying Deem and Talla arrived before the Sen'Drorn could get the Pendant.

Just as the tornado's force descended, she saw the airship returning. "They can't land under that tornado!" Thian cried.

"Even if they could, the Sen'Drorn must not see a Sen'Prin airship!"

Meleena's heart sank as the airship flew right by. But then, she saw small figures drifting down, inconspicuously, but at Warix-assisted speed.

Deem's beaming face greeted her from under a leather-bound helmet before he touched the ground, strapped to a Sen'Prin soldier. Talla came screaming behind, her pearl necklace flapping in the wind, parachutes streaming behind like beetle wings, as the Sen'Prin soldiers stood up and released their passengers.

The tornado ceased, and the enemy Warix landed on the next hill over, thus far unaware of them, but Meleena and the group didn't wait around to give them a chance.

"Talla, Deem, it's great to see you! Sorry for the rushed greeting, but we need you to go negotiate for the Pendant. Flax will lead you there," Meleena cried. "I will stay back to hold them off!"

Deem caught her arm. "Peela is safe, all our pets are being cared for back at Dlawn'Edo."

"Thanks." Meleena breathed a sigh of relief, rare good news in all the mayhem. But no time to dwell on that now.

Flax, Talla, and Deem disappeared over the hill towards the tents just as the wind around them pressurized from the impending energy.

Meleena smeared her face with paint from a split gourd sitting by a nearby tent, so it appeared green and scaly over her blue complexion. She pulled her hood up and ran to a hitching post with a beast like the one she had bumped into earlier.

Thian shouted after her, "Wait, where are you going? Only a Hyish can mount a Netic. Their backs are packed with needles!"

She ignored him and approached a beast.

Thian danced about and yelped, "They are coming!"

She met the Netic's eyes, keeping still and extending her hand again to meet its forked, probing, tongue. Its mouth parted to reveal rows of needlelike teeth to match those sticking out from its limbs and body, but Meleena didn't flinch. To her, this was just like any other animal she had met. Not to be feared, but to be understood. She looked at the floor, blinking heavily. Her hand cautiously made way to the Netic's emerald scaled forehead, and she rested her hand there, on the cold, smooth scales. It let out a low rumble, and its spikes retracted to flatten on its back.

Meleena climbed atop its back, just below the shoulder blades, just as she had seen the Hyish sit. Its flesh felt cold and leathery on her thighs as it slithered forward on broad feet towards the Sen'Drorn Warix.

The Netic trampled into their path, blocking them, her heart pounding wildly.

She had expected to see Malotus or Yulah. Perhaps they were busy answering for the jailbreak of Flax and herself, for she did not recognize the four Warix in front of her, clay-gray skinned and muscular, bodies heavily laden with satchels jangling at their sides. Lavish necklaces adorned their necks, gold and gemstone loops around arms, waists, fingers, and yet they walked as though unburdened.

Meleena gulped. *Why hadn't we thought to bring anything shiny to trade with?*

She mimicked her best Hyish accent. "Sssen'Drorn. I am your guide to Mayfee. Please, come with me. I'll lead you to her."

They looked at each other in confusion. "Did they know we were coming?" The others shrugged.

"Yeesss," she hissed knowingly.

To her amazement, they followed her. Meleena rocked side to side as the Netic slithered along, the Warix beside her as they entered the peripheral tent maze, moving in the opposite direction from Mayfee's clan. The Sen'Drorn negotiator looked up at her, narrowing his eyes. She patted the side of the netic, allowing it to relax and unflatten the spikes on its sides. The Warix sprang away with a yelp, keeping a safe distance between them and any good views of her face. She held back her excitement, having had no clue it could do that.

After a few minutes, they came to a market clearing, where the scent of mixed cinnamon, cardamom, and other powdered scents made her sneeze.

One of the Warix said, "Wait, these are the spice markets. According to my instructions, her encampment is usually over by the gem market."

"Er, it'sss different thisss time…" Meleena hissed.

"But the location of the marketplaces reflects each clan's trade crafts. They don't produce spices."

"What'd her flag look like again?" another asked.

Meleena gulped.

"I thought it was a hawk-snake skull!"

They stopped following her and looked up. One of them shot a wind burst, knocking her hood back to reveal her hair.

"That's no Hyish! It's a Mer—"

Meleena's heart pounded. She didn't wait for him to finish his sentence before she clicked her heels; the Netic released a deep rumble and slithered on at full speed, leaving the Warix shouting and shoving their way through the crowded spice market. Meleena turned around long enough to see the throng of Hyish descend on them with interest, only to be knocked back in puffs of wind, and the Warix turned on their heels and headed in the opposite direction.

Flax sat in on the negotiations with Deem and Talla. He had led them in Hyish apparel, and they were graciously readmitted to Mayfee's tent on the notion of new grounds to trade with.

Talla first tried the moral argument. "What I know about the Sen'Drorn, is that the Sen'Drorn nearly destroyed my village and have been exploiting my people for years. And they say it's their right to do so because they are powerful or smart or whatever. But if you give them that pendant, they will use it to conquer and kill more innocents."

Mayfee only listened, still except for the vibration of her round drum-like ears and the occasional blinks of her large eyes. A bead of sweat ran down Talla's forehead. Flax didn't think this argument would work on them.

Talla continued, "And why wouldn't they use it to dominate the Hyish? To take all their riches away once they conquer the Sen'Prin? Nobody is safe. It's not worth the greater price you will be paying later. You're better off long-term to sell this pendant to Sen'Prin."

Flax thought that would get a rise from Mayfee, but she merely continued staring.

Talla hissed at Flax, "You gotta help me here. I know nothing about Hyish culture."

He whispered in her ear, "Right, sorry. Do a long blink to let them know when you are done speaking. Also, they love rare things, so appeal to that…" Flax urged.

Before she had a chance to continue, a raspy voice came from behind them. "What a lovely speech." The tent curtain parted, and four Sen'Drorn negotiators stepped inside, panting and short of breath. Their leader announced, "We come on behalf of Sen'Drorn to purchase the Pendant."

While Talla paused, stunned, Deem tried to continue her point. "What's the worth of anything if we live in an unsafe world of hate and misery?"

The Sen'Drorn negotiator pushed them aside and barked, "Who do you think you are? Don't listen to these Sen'Prin deviants, Mayfee. Best not get involved in our politics. We bring rare gems!" He and his men unpacked satchels. Gems of all colors spilled out: rubies, sapphires, and emeralds tumbled onto the floor in front of Mayfee, followed by gold and silver coins.

"You see? They have nothing but threats," Talla barked right back. She gave the long blink, and Mayfee snapped to life again. She pointed straight at the pile of riches on the floor.

"I sssaid I don't care about your politics. The Hyish are ssstrong, the most numerous. The Sen'Drorn know they could never overtake us."

Deem whispered something to Talla, and they removed their hoods to reveal themselves, as Meruyans with floating hair.

Mayfee leaned forward on her chair.

"You are blue!" Mayfee said with a flickering of her tongue.

Talla said, "We are Meruyans. We have vast riches of our own, so *rare* and exotic to land-dwellers."

"*Rare?*" Mayfee repeated.

"*Rarer* than anything a Warix could ever trade you," Talla said.

The Sen'Drorn negotiator barked, "What, that's ridiculous! They have just a bunch of fishy junk!"

Mayfee addressed only Deem and Talla, eyes fixed: "Go on…"

Deem said, "Y-yes! We have amazing things!" Deem brought a handful of sea glass out from his pockets and held it out. "This is one form of Meruyan currency."

Flax looked on in amazement as much as Mayfee herself. Talla did the same, adding her own small heap of shimmering sea glass, and the Sen'Drorn negotiator cried, "That has no real value!"

Deem removed something from his pocket: a gleaming scale shaped like a fingernail, about the size of a hand. "The carapace from a giant lobster. Toughest material on land or sea."

"You will be the envy of all the other Hyish," Talla said, removing a concealed pearl necklace from around her neck, a lavish design of silver and black pearls.

***

Meleena, atop the Netic, galloped back to the airship site.

Flax, Deem, and Talla came running up a hill. "Meleena! Let's go!" Flax shouted and pulled her from the atop the Netic with a huff of wind.

"What happened?" Meleena cried, stunned, and collapsing onto the airship.

"Mayfee went for the Meruyan riches, to be delivered by the Council," Flax said.

"Her mouth was practically watering when I gave her my pearl necklace, and Deem handed over his prized carapace," Talla explained.

"And the rest?"

"The Council and Sen'Prin will soon send a caravan of pearls and scales to the Mayfee clan to settle the rest," Flax said. "Even I'll admit it's sad that this worked…but I guess you have to play the right game."

Meleena thought about the Hyish fire-made lenses. With this new trade, perhaps the Meruyan might be able to buy from the Hyish directly, cut the Warix out, and weaken their grip on the farmers.

A scream rang out. In a thunderous burst of wind, the four Sen'Drorn Warix burst forth from the encampments, tens of Hyish rushing in tow.

Thian waved to them, arms in the air, as the soldiers fired up the airship for liftoff.

"Hurry!" Flax urged, and they all jumped onto the flying machine, which took off, leaving a cloud of dust to beat back the coughing pursuers.

CHAPTER TWENTY-EIGHT

The airship took off to the east, a vast mountain range to their left, and a patchwork of farmland and forest on the other side. Meleena, Deem, Talla, Flax, Thian, and the Sen'Prin forces finally came to what appeared to be a large crack in the mountains. Elevating towards the peak, Meleena saw layers of the canyon, sheltered by a steeply growing forest with buildings nestled under the towering trees.

So, this is how the Sen'Prin nation survives. Their city is a natural fortress.

She could make out raised platforms, interlaced with bridges between buildings. A tumbling, rocky riverway fed patches of terraced farmland.

How Meleena wished she could explore it. Maybe she'd get to when things settled down. Except, the city looked even more challenging for a Meruyan to get around than Sen'Drorn. A city built for wind power users.

As Meleena looked to the distance, she couldn't help but wonder what else was out there. Past the strifes of Warix and Meruyan. What other lands, peoples, or creatures, lived there? Other nations, with their own problems, or a whole lot of nothing to be explored? There wasn't time to dwell on such thoughts now.

At the highest point of the canyon, the airship shifted and came to land on a stone rampart between large trees. Meleena gazed up at the nondescript stone and glass walls built, like an extended cave, from the canyon. It could only be Sen'Prin government's headquarters.

"Not as elaborate as Sen'Drorn, but far more secure," Flax said. He limped off the ship, dragging his bandaged leg, and held a hand out to help her step off. She swayed as she regained her land-legs, managing not to fall over.

A dozen Sen'Prin and even some Meruyan in Council robes came out to greet them, talking over each other and helping everyone off the airship.

"Welcome!"

"*Hurrah!*"

"Do they really have the Pendant?"

Governess Arenay stepped onto the landing pad. She was just as Meleena had remembered her, with striking amber features like an autumn's day.

She greeted them, "We are thrilled you made it back safely! You three Meruyan are truly honorary members of the Sen'Prin nation. We could not be more grateful. I also heard you have secured the pendant. We will alert the Meruyan Council and your families right away of your safe return."

Meleena presented The Pendant from her pocket. *Luckily, this time, it did not fall out,* she thought, recalling the first time she held The Pendant in her father's study, one year ago.

Governess Arenay guided everyone inside, where the landing platform led into a large, round chamber with a dome ceiling. The Sen'Prin flag of the purple nectar sprig on a white background decorated the main wall.

The entry hall branched, with the lower walls of stone and the uppers made of glass. This created a wide-visibility effect, so the spotted conference rooms, work chambers, and engineering facilities were all visible from the center. Winding stairs leading to higher and lower levels followed the room's curve. Meleena figured down was where the non-flying entrance, to and from the city, must be.

She also spotted a row of wooden fighting dummies with floating pegs built for sustaining practice wind attacks.

There were all kinds of seating areas, where some Warix and the Meruyan Council sat down. Meleena and her friends remained standing, close to Arenay.

"We need to figure out how to activate the Pendant," Arenay said, turning it over in her hands. She brought it close to her eye and tapped it. She focused her hands to pump wind energy inside. Her amber pupils clouded to silver orbs. As she did so, the Pendant did the same. The tiny eyeholes in the ram carving, which had already a similar inner light, began to glow with striking radiance. When Arenay opened her hands it dimmed again and everyone gasped.

"Can someone get me a cord?"

Someone brought Arenay a copper cord, looped the Pendant, and fastened it around her neck. The copper conductor caused the eyes to glow even stronger. The inhabitants of the room held their collective breath.

Nothing more happened.

Arenay looped The Pendant around a wooden dummy and hurled wind at it. The dummy whirled around from the stunning blow, but nothing else happened.

"Meleena?"

"Your grace? I mean, Governess."

"Call me Arenay. Meleena, you were the last person to possess it. Do you recall anything unusual about it, any unique properties? Or perhaps any information listed in your father's study about it?"

Meleena thought for a moment. *What do I know?* "There wasn't any information on it in the study."

Arenay plopped The Pendant into Meleena's hand. She stared into its strange silver eyes, glowing from within, and bubbled with anxiety thinking about Malotus's eyes, always about to strike.

"They say the spirit of The Wind Goddess is in there," said Arenay. "She is the source of the Warix's wind power."

Meleena needed to concentrate. She took a deep breath and closed her eyes to perform the sun surrender. Her hair drank up the sun's rays, and an energizing warmth pulsed through her. She concentrated on the last time she had seen The Pendant. How it seemed to float underwater, drifting when she had let go.

Drifting. Very unlike a stone.

More like wood. Very much like…

"A seed!" Meleena blurted out.

Flax gave her a curious look.

Meleena explained, "Fine, give me a hard time for always seeing plants in everything. But it floats in water and has some life force from inside. And look at the shape —the top where the loop is—it's pointed like a seed. Let's plant it, water it, see if it grows."

Now everyone gave her a curious look.

Meleena shrugged. "If I'm wrong the worst is, it gets muddy, I look silly, and we try something else."

Thian laughed and crossed his arms in amusement. Deem and Talla nodded, while others shook their heads.

Arenay looked thoughtful. "What do you need to test this theory?"

Soon they were standing in a garden off the main room, where herbs and small trees grew between two walkways. Fish swam in a shallow fountain under bright green lily pads. The shadow of the mountain protected this inner garden, perfectly protected from the eyes of outsiders.

Meleena dipped The Pendant in the fountain, then covered it in the soil. Nothing happened.

"Arenay, try using concentrated wind on it again."

Arenay crouched beside it, cupping her hands over the buried Pendant. The spot began to glow that familiar, wispy silver from between her fingers, and she jumped back.

"It's hot!" she whispered. With a pop, the silver seemed to hatch as a bright green stalk stretched from the soil, unfurling two floppy leaves, then four. Then it stalled.

"I think the wind energy is like fertilizer to it," Meleena suggested.

Arenay supplied more wind to the earth around the new plant. Beneath her fingers, it stretched into a vine in all directions.

Flax's jaw dropped. "It...it *is* a plant."

Thian's eyes widened. "Too bad. I would have liked to see some kind of mega-wind weapon."

"Or the gifts of the Goddess acting as something other than fertilizer," added Talla. Thian nodded at her, grinning at the remark. Her blueish skin blushed white.

Meleena turned to focus on the plant. She inspected bumpy bobbles along the surface—they pulsed with electric blue bioluminescence, reminding her of those she'd seen lighting the underwater cities.

Arenay declared, "Surely, these fruits are the source of improved wind power."

"Wait!" said Flax. "In Sen'Drorn City, they have a myth about a fabled fruit that poisons the mind, makes one go insane. Are we sure it's not that one?"

Meleena said, "In the Arctic City, they told us about a fabled fruit that enlightened the mind. It could be that one."

"Well someone has to volunteer to try it…" Arenay said. Everyone eyed each other and the pulsing bobbles.

Arenay, after a long pause, said. "Surely, someone will step up."

Deem stepped forward and plucked a bobble but couldn't bring himself to bite it.

"*Oysters on crackers.*" Talla shook her head and stabbed another bobble with a twig. It burst open, and she drizzled some of the goopy insides onto her tongue. "It tastes…sweet." Her eyes narrowed, and she stared at everyone.

"How do you feel?" asked Arenay.

"It's like…I can see the silver glow everywhere. It's connecting everyone, like a life-force ribbon. It makes sense of things somehow."

At this, Meleena took the second try. She gulped down the sweet juice. A peaceful calm washed over her like an ocean current. All the plants and people, Warix and Meruyan alike, emitted the soft silver glow, and when she reached out and touched Flax's hand, she could feel his life force pulsing through with their same energy. After a moment, she asked, "Flax, can you use some wind energy?"

Flax sent a blast upwards, and Meleena could see the silver wisps coming from his core, pulling more from the wind, and concentrating it outward. It was the underlying force in everything, made visible.

"It's all from the same source. The wind goddess energy, it is a form of life energy that pulses through us all. It's as if the Warix can send a part of themselves out into the world."

She could see the silver wisp in the plants, and in The Pendant plant's Fruit.

After a few moments, the ability to see the silver wisps faded, but the knowledge, the new sense of understanding and connection lingered.

After Flax tasted a fruit, he said, "It's the same fruit! To the Sen'Drorn nation, it's poisonous. The knowledge of the interconnectedness turns people away from the path of domination for prosperity. If only we can get the Sen'Drorn leaders to eat this fruit, maybe they would stop exploiting the Meruyan and trying to destroy the Sen'Prin nation."

"Then, we will just have to infiltrate Sen'Drorn, bring the plant to them," said Arenay.

Meanwhile, Meleena attempted to plant the seeds from the fruit, to grow more plants, but it didn't work. From this, she concluded, "The seeds must be immature, and need some other conditions to develop, like the original mother seed." She dug up the Pendant Seed from the ground. Within seconds, the entire plant shriveled.

"What are you doing?" asked Flax.

"When we infiltrate Sen'Drorn, they'd never agree to eat the fruit if we brought it to them. Not with their poison fruit myth: which is based on this same situation, historically, by the way. They need to see the real 'Pendant' and plant it themselves to believe the fruit came from it. Like we did here today. We must convince them that eating it will enhance their soldier's powers in battle."

Everyone agreed, and Meleena beamed with pride. She finally felt understood—her nature skills valuable.

Flax turned to Arenay. "Governess, how do you propose the logistics? Also, I would like to rescue Borak. He's an important engineer. We could use him on our side."

"I've been told he is your father."

Flax blushed. "That's not important. He is the most valuable weapon in the kingdoms, after the Pendant. Maybe we can try trading Borak for the Pendant?"

Arenay considered for a moment. "No. Malotus is too clever, he would suspect something was up if we tried to trade the Pendant away, even for a great engineer. But I have another idea. Flax, you will pose as a defector, since you now have a history with them. You and Meleena have escaped their prison already, I'm confident you can do it again."

Flax turned red, his eyes at the floor.

Arenay continued. "You will go to Yulah, say you want to join them, bringing Meleena as your hostage and the 'stolen' Pendant as proof of your loyalty. Somehow get them to eat the fruit. You will leave first thing in the morning. Tonight, rest up. Surely we won't send you back to jail twice in one day."

Arenay turned at Deem and Talla. "I'll need you two, and some of my spies, for another mission. You will spread the fruit in the Sen'Drorn Northern Village lands. To Warix and Meruyan alike. They're used to eating exotic fruit. It shouldn't be too hard to convince them to try it. Let's see what mayhem we can stir up there."

"But what can we do to help the underwater Meruyan communities?" Deem asked.

Talla said, "Fitting in with the Warix on land is the future. Meruyan have established themselves on land now. For most of us, there is no going back to the sea."

Deem sighed. "I understand. I learned from Aldrok's Journey that there is a lot more to the world than my previous life underwater. I can't imagine just staying underwater after that, either."

Arenay said, "Progress can only be made when we realize we must re-design the system from within, not fight it directly in war. What you can do is help the Northern Villages, and cut off Sen'Drorn supplies. Help the Meruyan people understand and rise up for themselves. Our spies will wear stolen Sen'Drorn military uniforms, and pretend to have caught some 'farmers,' Deem and Talla, eating a delicious fruit. They will pretend to confiscate it, eat it, and offer it to all the soldiers and workers."

That night, in a borrowed bed in the Sen'Prin headquarters, Meleena struggled to get to sleep. There was too much on her mind. Deem and Talla would be putting their lives at risk too. They would depart by airship to the Northern Villages, with a satchel full of the vibrant fruit. Her own mission with Flax to Sen'Drorn Fortress would be even trickier. There was too much that could go wrong.

CHAPTER TWENTY-NINE

In the morning, Meleena, Flax, and Thian, and a small wind crew set out on an airship heading for Sen'Drorn. As they landed in the pine forest a short hike from the outer wall storm, Thian reiterated the plan. "The woods are too dense here for scouts. Head up that way towards the sewer line, like before. We will be waiting here when you get back, and if we don't hear from you soon, we're coming to rescue you."

Meleena felt the weight of her pockets, packed with fruit from the Pendant. The Pendant itself hung around Flax's neck. He had a taser in his pocket, borrowed from the Sen'Prin tech lab. They snuck around to the sewer system where they'd made the escape.

Climbing back through the sewer system, they retraced their steps.

Is this really a good idea? Meleena followed Flax as they crept up to the forest patch inside the walls, to a low wall and balcony. He bound her hands in rope.

"This is Yulah's flat." He threw a rock.

"What are you doing?" Meleena whispered through gritted teeth.

"Trust me."

Yulah appeared on the balcony dressed in military regalia.

"Flax!?" Her eyes flared. "How could you be here?" She looked panicked and angry.

"Yulah! Listen to me! I'm on your side! Look what I brought you as proof."

"Flax, I need to know this is not a trick!" Tears streamed down her face, clasping her hands together in desperation.

"It really is the Pendant!" He held up the Pendant to her. "This Meruyan can even show you how to use it."

Meleena stepped out and presented her tied hands. Flax continued, "I needed her to show me where it was first. Once she led me to it, I double-crossed her."

Yulah's face turned red. But she let them inside and took Meleena by the arm. Meleena burst into tears, knowing it would be better to play the part of accepting defeat. Flax pulled the Pendant from his neck to present to Yulah. She didn't guess at the fruit stowed in their pockets.

"Meruyan, I will take you to Emperor Ryogrim. If you will show us how to use it, we will spare your life. Flax, don't leave this spot," she warned, her eyes locked on him for a long time.

Meleena wrinkled her nose. "For the good of my people, I will go with you, but I am *not* your prisoner."

Yulah nodded. "I'm sorry. I will see to it that you are released unharmed when this is over. Just like last time." She winked, referring to the time when she saved them in the Burnt lands. Yulah turned to Flax, a glow in her eyes. "Flax, I mean it. Wait for me here so we can talk when I'm done. I need to know I can trust you."

Meleena gulped, looking to Flax, who kept his eyes on Yulah and gave her a nod. Meleena's stomach churned at how well he was pulling off the insincerity.

Yulah took the Pendant and led Meleena into the kitchen, where a cave-like hole in the wall was open. They went into the dark, damp smelling passageway with walls lit by flickering torches.

***

Flax, standing in Yulah's flat, felt heavy with guilt at what he had to do next. The moments ticked by. Perhaps he should listen to Yulah. What if he just stayed here, and professed his love to her? His desire to hold her grew, to give up on all this other nonsense, thinking that maybe if he stayed he could see Borak freed, that Yulah could pull some strings

And then what? Would things be back to normal? His false life? This was never his life. Borak would still be making weapons for a dishonorable nation, built on the backs of the Meruyan people. They were off somewhere, living in squalor while citizens of Sen'Drorn sat in cute cafes and built gadgets from their copper mines. No, he needed to stick to his principles, even if it meant losing Yulah.

His legs shook, but he willed himself to take a step. Stop thinking, just run. Several minutes had passed since Yulah and Meleena had left. It was enough time to continue down the corridor unseen.

As he crossed the threshold from her apartment into the dark passageway, his stomach flipped with sorrow at what his action would mean to Yulah.

It was time to think strategically, not emotionally. Get a grip! He knew from his prior experience of Sen'Drorn layout, that wherever they kept Borak, it would be in or near the dungeon block.

Flax ran down clockwise spiraling stairs to the fortress bedrock. The stairs opened to various cells, some with prisoners, some with stairs leading who knew where. There, a grate in the ceiling. *If I follow the ventilation pipes, I will certainly find the labs.* Exhaust from engineering machinery needs to go somewhere.

Flax sprang up and caught the hatch. Another jump, and he was up. Returning the hatch, he crawled around until the scent of electrified copper carried the first clue he was on the right track. As he neared, he felt lightheaded from the density of fumes, rising and thickening the air—the exhaust from machinery warping and cutting materials. Dizzily, he listened and followed the sound—an echo of clanking steel and shuffling of chained feet, the whir of the machinery, and the barking of orders. Looking down at each grate opening, he finally came upon the prison laboratory.

He had a bird's-eye view of long laboratory counters, littered with tools and gadgets. The shelved walls were packed with equipment and machines. Flax took solace in the fact that Borak was probably enjoying the toys in a facility like this, an upgrade even from his own. Minus the freedom to make what he wanted, of course.

Sen'Drorn guards lined the walls.

"If you need a device tested, we are making rounds soon," announced a guard. "And if you need a tool or part, we will attempt to provide it."

Then he spotted Borak. He was tinkering with some gadget, but without his usual grace. He kept dropping things—how unlike him—and Flax knew he was resisting.

***

Meleena followed Yulah through the winding hallways, copper wall turbines rotated, which Meleena could only guess were pumping fresh air inside for wind power use.

They paused, Yulah knocked on a chamber door. Heavy metal hinges creaked as the wooden slabs parted, as a cold shiver ran down Meleena's spine when Malotus stepped out.

Behind him, a falcon screeched and landed on the window, eying Meleena like she was lunch. She both feared and admired its trailing tail of barbed thorns and handsome folds of moss on his chest and neck.

"What is it, Yulah?"

"You won't believe it. I was right! Flax is defecting. He really was trustworthy! He brought us proof. He came through for our love!" Yulah's tear-stained eyes flared with madness. Meleena's stomach clenched. It just didn't seem right to trick her like this, even for the greater good.

Even Malotus looked concerned when he saw Yulah's disposition. There was a glint of sorrow and pain in his face that Meleena could empathize deeply with.

Yulah continued, "Look! Flax brought us *the Pendant!* And this Meruyan girl who led him right to it. She knows the secret to unlock its power." She handed the Pendant mother seed to Malotus. He turned to study Meleena's face, she had a sense that he was looking for deception in hers, before taking a moment to turn the seed over in his hands.

"It...it really *looks* just like the legend." His eyes widened. He shot Meleena a corrosive look. "How did you escape my prison, girl?!"

"I told you, Flax let her out, so she'd lead us to the Pendant?"

"Hogwash! I wouldn't trust that boy if…!"

"If he led us to the Pendant and brought us back your prisoner?" Yulah's eyebrows lifted in hope.

Malotus looked tense.

"And why do we want her?"

Meleena squeaked. "It's true, sir. Only I know the secret to unlocking its power." She hoped volunteering would keep her alive.

"Oh, *is that so*?" he spat. "I've never met such an insubordinate Meruyan in all my years."

"Yes, you will not be able to figure it out without me. That…is why they captured me." Meleena could tell she was slouching, cringing from him, and battled to keep her spine straight.

Malotus cast a nervous glance at Yulah. "I will show the elders and call a meeting with the Emperor to discuss further." Malotus kept the Pendant and disappeared down the hall. "Take her to the throne room shortly."

Pendant tight in his hands, Malotus disappeared down the corridor. It went against every fiber in Meleena's being, watching him leave with it.

***

Flax stopped to think. Studying the room from above, he attempted to locate the door to the engineering lab prison. Then with a clanking sound, followed by a guard stepping into his view, he had his answer.

Flax crawled through the exhaust system towards the spot, until he arrived at a grate to kick down and lowered himself into the nearby corridor.

A Warix in an apron came out and gasped. Flax lunged at him with the taser, shocking him and knocking him out, barely catching the tray of snacks he carried before they could clatter to the floor.

He was outside the guard's break room. He went inside and closed the door, his chest heaving from the sudden action. Central tables contained trays prepared with snacks for the guards: crackers, jam, and fruit. He pulled his Pendant fruit out and crushed it into a paste, and replaced it for the jam.

He riffled through a cabinet and came up with a disguise to look like the other guards: apron and hat. Stepping over the chef's unconscious body by the door, he was ready.

He pulled in a deep breath and got himself into the mindset. He was just bringing snacks to his fellow guards. Flax kicked through the door and announced, "Snack time!"

It didn't take long for the guards to drop their posts and rush to the trays. They devoured the crackers and jam, despite some complaints. "Where's the variety?" Soon, the guards looking around in a dizzy confusion, then their eyes transfixed on the prisoners.

"I'm...so sorry," they were saying. "It's painful to see them in chains! How can we enforce this cruelty to other Warix?"

Flax's heart beat wildly as he watched the guards unchain the prisoners.

Prisoners, unchained, looked around, confused. Some ran for the exits. Flax rushed into the mess, trying to reach Borak across the room, and in doing so, attracted attention from some of the prisoners. One elderly Warix approached him. His long red hair and delicate face reminded him of an arrowhead.

"You brought the fruit. *The* fruit!"

Flax, startled, blinked at him. "Who *are* you? And how do you...?"

He looked tired from years of imprisonment, with sad, sunken eyes. "I'd recognize the effects anywhere. I am Plymore—they imprisoned me for finding the Pendant last time. But for forty years, I've been a tester for tech in development. More interestingly, who are you?"

"Last time?" Flax echoed. "I'm nobody special. Just here to bust you out."

Plymore followed Flax, stumbling between tables towards Borak. Borak was wading over and came into Flax's arms in a heavy embrace. His eyes wet, he choked, "Flax! How did ye find me? I'm so sorry, my boy! For everythin'! Hesitating! I should have gone with ye' right away!"

Flax was also choked by tears. "No, Borak, it's okay! Let's just get out of here."

More guards streamed in, and Flax had no choice but to taser them. Borak grabbed a similar tech off the table, and a bulging-eyed prisoner with curling red hair climbing his horns like vines joined their side. He was wearing a copper-infused jacket. Plymore strapped on a belt of copper tubing. Flax guessed these gadgets all helped in some way with enhancing wind energy thrust. That would be especially useful in these indoor chambers with poor circulation.

***

Meleena waited with Yulah in the corridor after Malotus had gone.

Yulah rubbed her arm and asked, "So, have you ever seen indoor plumbing?"

Meleena's expression dropped. "Uh, we have regular toilets in my village, and plumbing. We are not that primitive."

Yulah looked surprised. She smiled awkwardly. "Ah, okay. Heh, uh sorry."

Yulah led Meleena through the hallways until they reached a balcony with black volcanic columns casting an intermittent shadow on the inner wall, lined with portraits. Meleena realized they told a history. Small Warix tribes across a wild landscape sharing, trading, and warring. Warix tribes finding the Pendant, eating the fruit. Small blue figures emerging from the sea, Meruyan, trading crops. Later, town and city street scenes, then killings like a plague, battles depicting storms and tornados, and after battle scenes, portraits of the top generals who became emperors for destroying those afflicted, who had cut down the poisoned opposition and reunified them. Great splits and unions. Clearly, they told a story like the Arctic City, but more gruesome and told from a perspective of the victors, by those who felt their cause just.

How fascinating, I wish there was more time to study these.

Yulah guided her through a chamber door and out of the hall. The light burned her eyes as the double doors parted. Two guards stood at the entrance to the room, and more awaited just inside.

Inside, the tall stone arches formed an impressive room, with high vaults and an open ceiling with tilted copper bands to let in and trap wind in the ceiling areas.

Trumpets resounded, making her jump. "Announcing Emperor Ryogrim!" the Warix soldiers shouted.

Meleena's first glimpse of Emperor Ryogrim was through the mass of her tangled blue hair as she shuffled into his presence. He entered and sat on a black-rock throne atop a semicircle of padded stairs. His Council followed and sat down on the amphitheater stairs. Behind the throne, a large silken banner, gold and green, depicted the flower-maned lion, just like the symbol on the airships and uniforms on Warix in the Northern Hilly villages. At this size, the creature seemed only ferocious, not noble.

"So, the Meruyan fortune has bought the Pendant from the Hyish?" asked Emperor Ryogrim in his deep, booming voice. "What a shame that the fates have brought you here. Did you expect less than to be double-crossed by those Sen'Prin anarchists?" He let out a burbling laugh.

"Yes..." Meleena shrank back. She thought it best to wait until she could prove herself, Pendant in hand. Except Malotus had it, and he wasn't here.

"So, how do you activate it?" Ryogrim leaned forward, eyes hungry for information.

"Obviously wind power," said another. "Our blessed wind Goddess no less."

"But why would a Meruyan know the secret?"

"Yes, previous emperors have found it and failed to unlock the power," said Emperor Ryogrim.

"Maybe by tossing herself into the river, *Nushenyu be praised*, she intended for Meruyan to find it? Maybe we need one to unlock it?" one councilman theorized.

"I don't know if I believe *that*..." spat Emperor Ryogrim.

Meleena shuffled her feet, trying to figure out when she could have a word. "Most excellent Emperor and advisors. You must submerge it in water. It's a seed, actually. A fruit that grows from it will enhance your wind powers. I am a naturalist." She made up the title at that moment, trying to sound official, and decided to go with it.

"What is that?" He eyed her with wonder and suspicion alike.

Meleena bowed. "Your excellency, Naturalists are trained Meruyan experts in animals and plants, who unlock secrets like this."

Gasps and chattering, they looked at her severely, eyes bulging.

"Are you aware, girl, that here in Sen'Drorn City, we have a legend of a poison fruit?" said another.

"Yes, who do you think you are, making claims like that?"

"Maybe it's a fake! Who brought her here, anyway?"

"It was the Gods!"

"No! It was that traitor who escaped our prisons!"

"How can we trust him?"

"We certainly can't blindly do what *she* says!"

The advisors nodded in agreement. Meleena's heart thudded, and her blood rushed to her face. This was not going as expected.

***

Flax, Borak, the elder Plymore, and a few others ran down the hallways, their feet making a racket on the stone cobbles. Many carried prototypes they had been working on or had snatched from the tables. Flax didn't have time to inspect them, but tantalized by the thought of looking over this tech later.

It hadn't been more than a few minutes before they passed several guards from other parts of the fortress who began the chase, shouting a cacophony of indignations.

"Where are we going?" asked Borak as they ran around a corner.

"Meleena is here, probably the throne room. I want to bring you outside to safety, and then I will go back in and try to extract her...if they believe I'm still on their side."

He turned the corner ahead of them, trying to figure out which way to go. He'd not been through here, and it was confusing. At the start of a corridor leading to spiral stairs, he said, "Hold on, I'll go ahead and check that it's clear, or that this is the proper stairwell."

They waited back in the shadows while he climbed. It wasn't lit, his arms against the walls helped propel him quicker, eager to see where it led.

At the top, he bumped into something heavy in the darkness. Feeling around for the door, it opened for him and burst into light. "My, my…" General Malotus stood in the passageway. A spike of pure terror ran through Flax.

"Hey…I uh, was just looking for Yulah…" He tried to sound collected, but his heavy breathing was hard to mask.

"Flax." Malotus stared. "Coming from the dungeons, I see."

Flax blinked at him.

Malotus's eyes narrowed. His sharp green eyes conveyed more pain than hatred. "I knew you would hurt her again. And now you have broken her. You will regret your actions towards my ward."

It was then that Flax noticed Malotus wore a glove, intricate with branching copper tubes—the work of Borak. "You like my toy? You like gadgets…let's test this out, shall we?"

Malotus aimed his hand at Flax, which launched a burst of wind so strong it knocked him back against the wall. Flax was outmatched in tight, indoor quarters. His horns sensed such little wind, he'd barely channel anything without enhancement here. Even the taser wouldn't spark.

He could only fight back physically. He grabbed Malotus by his broad horns, wrestling his head down.

The shaggy maned general barked, "Oh, you like to fight with your hands, do you? I'll see to it that you don't use any wind for a while."

Malotus punched Flax in the stomach, so strongly with the enhanced wind glove that shockwaves pulsed through him. He doubled over, knees coming down hard on the stone. Malotus grabbed him by his small horns, flung him, and the pulsing wind hand sent him flying down a new corridor.

Malotus dragged him, choking and dizzy and losing consciousness.

***

Inside the throne room, Meleena stood with Yulah, surrounded by the ring of advisors and Emperor in the middle, deciding her fate and the Pendant's.

One advisor with clouded eyes spoke up, stroking a long grey beard. "When we got word of a Pendant sighting from the Hyish traders, the men we sent to secure it came back empty-handed. They are in the dungeons now, of course. So as far as we know, the Sen'Prin have it. Maybe what the Meruyan has brought us is not this same Pendant, but a trick—to weaken or poison us! The Sen'Prin may still have the true Pendant. We should remain cautious, for we cannot attack them if they do—if this is indeed a fraud."

They bickered among themselves.

"Yes...Why should we listen to her?" said Emperor Ryogrim, and with a flick of his hand, added, "Let's just toss her in the dungeons, do some tests on it ourselves."

A shiver of terror bubbled through Meleena, spreading from her throat down to the tingling ends of her fingers and toes.

Ryogrim stood. "So that's it. We treat this with utmost caution. Where is the Pendant, anyway? Ranfaf the Third, fetch General Malotus. He should have brought it to us by now."

"I'm sure he's busy doing something repugnant..." she mumbled under her breath. Yulah, still by her side, shot her a look of surprise.

"No need." Malotus strode into the room with his usual air of confidence, and Meleena flinched. His hands were stained red, residue dropping onto the floor from one hand's clawed fingertips. The other hand, balled into a fist, clutched the Pendant. He approached the Council, and the Pendant plopped from his fist into Emperor Ryogrim's fat hand.

Emperor Ryogrim turned it over, inspecting it closely, as Malotus backed away into the center court alongside Yulah, his red hands now locked behind his back. The red was unmistakably blood.

"While you were off cavorting with that bird of yours, or Wind-Goddess knows what, we have come to a decision about the Pendant. We don't need this Meruyan girl right now," Ryogrim commanded. "Take her to the dungeons and prepare the interrogation chamber."

Malotus bowed. "Right away."

"What!?" Yulah combed her hair nervously. "That's not what we agreed on. I promised I'd keep her safe!"

"It must be so, Yulah." He wore a look of impenitence. "She is working with Flax to conspire against you."

"No! He would never!" Yulah crumpled to the floor.

"I caught him snooping around the fortress."

The Emperor waved a hand. "Get that Meruyan out of here."

Malotus curled his hand around Meleena's forearm. She whiffed the dried blood on them and struggled to shake him off. "NO!"

She wriggled free, her heart beating so fast it might leap from her mouth onto the floor as she tried to take off running towards the door. She looked around for Yulah. "You promised I'd be safe!" Yulah didn't answer. She had beat her to the act of fleeing the room.

Malotus didn't miss a beat—he kept pace and grabbed Meleena, holding her so she could not escape. But before he could drag her from the room, Yulah let out a wild scream.

Everyone looked up to see that she was by the door, caught by the wrist. She struggled as a Warix held her, his birch-white skin contrasting her mauve complexion. He had mad, bulging eyes under flaming hair that twirled all the way up his sticklike horns—Meleena hoped he was on her side.

"What in *Nushenyu's Storms* is going on here?" Emperor Ryogrim cut into the silence, standing up from his chair.

Guards lunged towards the door as the mysterious Warix shifted Yulah to face outward. A half dozen other Warix appeared behind him, brandishing strange gadgets on their arms, legs, hips, that Meleena didn't recognize, but they shined with Meruyan-made materials: tanned leather, metals, and intricate copper tubing. "You don't want me to hurt her!" he shouted.

Meleena smiled: Borak was among them. They all looked quite disheveled, with sunken eyes, matted hair, baggy clothes overlaid with leather aprons. But where was Flax? A cold chill hit her: he was not among them.

Malotus let go of Meleena and put up his claws, in order that the engineering slave would do the same. He did so and sent a shot of wind power at Malotus. This was just long enough for Yulah to continue fleeing from the room. Meleena could sense the blow to Malotus, whose fists tightened. He stepped one foot forward and caught himself. He wanted to follow Yulah. But of course, he couldn't. Not with a bunch of freed slaves blocking the exit.

And then, just like that, they were at each other—the engineers and guards, kicking and knocking each other back. Muscular guards with heavy bladed gloves, backed up by Malotus, who rushed in, blasting engineers with a wind force to rival theirs.

As for the panel of elders, some jumped behind their seats to cower. Others tried to escape via wind energy out the open ceiling. Timid and scared, they tried to flee, but the engineers had a power greater than their own. Their gadgets channeled the wind and pushed it out stronger on the other side. Some stored it up and shot it in great bursts.

Emperor Ryogrim, old as he was, did not shy from the fight. Meleena knew from the picture outside that he got to this position for being a war leader. He got up, the grey-haired and flabby mass of him, eyes shone silver as he summoned great energy to the fight. He flooded into a tornado, ripped a bench from its nails, and threw it towards the engineers.

One of them was caught across the face, and he collapsed to the floor.

Meleena was determined to get to the Pendant and secure it in the chaos.

Several guards were defending themselves against the engineers, some were on the ground, unconscious. She tried to look inconspicuous, but there was still the odd one out who, in spite of the chaos, attacked her.

Meleena defended herself the only way she knew how. Reaching into her pockets, she got out some of the spare fruit, partially smooshed, and rubbed it in the eyes and mouth of the guard lunging at her. Then she waited for more guards to attack her, and rubbed it in their faces as well. It wasn't hard. She was the Meruyan they wanted to secure and perhaps kill.

They struggled, blinded from the fruit in their eyes, spitting from the fruit in their mouths. After a moment, they would go passive and stop. Soon after, they would be beaten or slashed into unconsciousness by engineers who'd commandeered their blades.

The open sky filled with a torrent of clouds. Then angry weather took hold, and roaring thunder drowned out the clamor of blades and shouting. The crazy-looking prisoner with flaming red hair cackled as a strange weapon shot smoke towards the sky. Intermittent lightning cracked like a whip, illuminating the room and destroying parts of the exposed walls.

Meleena ascended The Emperor's stage and spotted it. Emperor Ryogrim had forgotten the Pendant in his assault and had left it on the armchair of his throne. A crack of lightning hit the wall behind her, setting fire to the tapestry bearing the royal Sen'Drorn emblem. The storm and wind on silk decorations stood no chance against the real element. Meleena scooped the Pendant into her hand, but before she could secure it in her pocket, a bark caught her off guard.

"Girl!"

Malotus, some paces away, pointed at her. She shuddered but didn't expect a falcon, like the ones she'd sketched in the wild, which screeched and flew down from between the widely spaced copper rafters right at her. Meleena ducked, narrowly avoiding his thorny tail as the beast landed on her and slashed her hands, prying the Pendant loose from her grip. She pinched its moss-covered neck, and it let out a yelp and stopped flailing at her. She proceeded to scratch its neck, grooming the moss folds. It rolled backwards onto the throne in submission as she once-more retrieved the Pendant.

Cursing, Malotus leaped forward on wind-powered strides. He lunged at her, knocking her to the ground behind the throne. The scent of the burning tapestry and waves of heat from the fire threatened. The Pendant knocked away and skidded close to the flaming banner. Malotus shouted, but the thunder was too loud, and she couldn't hear what he said as he stepped over her and saved the rolling Pendant from the edge of the flames.

She fumbled, holding herself up enough to just catch him by the hair, pulling Malotus backward by his thick black mane. Pulled to the ground, he growled and turned, bending and grasping at her hands, trying to shove her off with one hand still grasping the Pendant. As his head flailed, he gored her cheek with his horn, and she screamed, but this was her one chance to get the Pendant out of his hands where he'd likely only wrestle it back, or...

This was also the only chance. Releasing his hair with one hand, hanging on for dear life with the other, reminding her of the bucking Gommwoods, she slid her hand into her pocket, flinching at the cool, sticky goop, and shoved a piece of slimy fruit into his mouth before he could buck her off.

He certainly was not expecting that. Meleena didn't have time to linger on the thought as Malotus spit it out, eyes widening in momentary disbelief.

Did he swallow any?

Angry and disoriented, Malotus stumbled backward into the burning banner and shouted like a singed animal. The Pendant dropped from his clutches and rolled. This time, Meleena was unable to stop it before it reached the flames.

"No!" Meleena shouted, watching it blacken, crinkle, and pop, oozing and burning.

CHAPTER THIRTY

A gust of wind whisked out of the fire. Meleena's eyes widened as the storm swirling above was sucked into the spot where the Pendant had been, leaving clear skies and ending the thunderous commotion. A large transparent creature with curling horns and silver eyes floated there, made of wind pressure incarnate.

Weapons dropped to the ground with the clank of metal on stone. Mouths hung open, everyone stopped what they were doing, mid-action, and stared at the spirit that hung in the air, as if their voices were taken in the gust. As if all air had been sucked from the room.

A voice, gentle like the rustle of weeping willows, spoke. "I'm free…"

Gasps filled the room, but nobody moved. As some kneeled or bowed, others did the same until they were all doing so.

"You…Warix. There is no need to bow, creatures. I am at fault for your plight. I trapped myself in a moment of passion and regret, and now I can finally get out of here. I will never again dwell in the realm of mortals, nor meddle in your affairs."

"Storm and thunder! It really was *the Pendant*," choked Emperor Ryogrim, gaining his voice back. "Wind Spirit…the Pendant is destroyed?" A tone of sorrow for the loss of his potential weapon.

Meleena glanced at Malotus, bowing, a state of utter shock worse than when he was force-fed the fruit some minutes prior.

"There is much more than this in the elemental realm. They grow from the backs of navanax beasts, another creation in the lands of my sisters. I'm sorry for all the trouble that I've caused. If it is of any consolation, you may keep your wind powers."

"Wait!" Meleena cried out. "I am not a Warix! You have tipped the scales away from the Meruyan people! I demand you make it right!"

"What about *us*? Wind Goddess Nushenyu…We're your devoted servants, who worshipped you all these generations! You must reward us by destroying our enemies!" Emperor Ryogrim pleaded.

"I am not a Goddess. Merely a creature. Like you, but of another nature."

"How can I find the Water Spirit?" Meleena yelled alongside him, feeling more indigent than afraid.

Wind Spirit Nushenyu looked at her. With a shrug, she floated up and away and was gone.

"Arrg! The Pendant is destroyed…" Emperor Ryogrim stomped his feet. "And she never even helped us…"

Meleena crumpled to the floor, feeling the same way.

"It never was an avenue of destruction, nor any kind of weapon!" cried the elderly Warix prisoner with long ears and tired eyes. "It produced a fruit to show you peace! My exploration brought it to you, Sen'Drorn leaders, on your orders, almost a hundred years ago, and you had me locked up for it! You never believed me!"

"Noo!" shouted Meleena, crying. "After all that! And now, the source of peace is destroyed!"

"It's not over, girl." Malotus grabbed Meleena, and with one long wind-enhanced stride, pulled her off the ground towards the chamber exit. Her glasses shattered, and crisp images blurred into fuzzier shapes.

Malotus, grasping Meleena, forced her through the stone corridors of the fortress, down several hallways and winding stairs. The dungeon would be close now. The sound of dripping water didn't lie. They were heading to the gloomy underbelly of the fortress.

He brought her into a room, but it was worse than a prison cell. She gasped as she saw a figure inside, hanging from the wall. Another body lay in the corner. Blue skinned, with the ragged remnants of a kelpweave robe, intricately stitched.

"Councilman Lock…" whispered Meleena, a lump in her throat. Her head throbbing, she could only stand in shock, though Malotus had relinquished his grip.

The body on the wall was a Warix with nut-brown hair. The blood drained from her face as she realized it was Flax. He looked different. Something was missing. Her stomach lurched: his horns had been removed, and his head was bleeding.

Meleena trembled, she was sure she'd be next. Malotus had taken a seat at his desk, where a large ornate glove sat beside him. He turned it over and ran a finger over the swirling copper handiwork.

"I couldn't believe him…I had to know the truth…" Malotus murmured almost inaudibly, his voice hollow. "Yulah…who has she become? I fear…" Malotus didn't sit with his usual, confident military posture, but slumped. Meleena's eyes widened as she understood.

"Here. This is yours." Malotus pulled open his desk drawer and held out a thick book.

Meleena's heart raced. "My Journal…" It had frayed bindings, and much of the original decor—pearls and shells, once inlaid—were gone. Flipping through the pages, it was missing all the samples she'd collected, and many pages had been torn out. Her heart sank—all that work, that love, now returned broken and bruised. She put it in her pocket.

Meanwhile, Malotus stood up, his bloodstained hands shaking. He went over and untied Flax, letting him plop to the floor. Flax got up slowly, tears streaming down his cheeks.

"I always hated the Emperor," Malotus said gruffly. "Your wind energy will be disabled for about a week until your horns regrow." He waved a hand at Flax, then opened the door to the chamber. "What are you waiting for? Get out before I change my mind…"

"Bullspit! What's your game, you crazy goat?" Flax stood, shaking all over, but prepared to lunge at Malotus even in his weakened state. Meleena got between them to hold him back.

"Stop, it's the fruit…" she whispered.

"I don't care! You're a monster!" Flax pushed passed her and bore his teeth in Malotus's face. "Did you recapture my father too?"

"I saw him and the others in the throne room!" Meleena cried. Flax turned to her, his eyes widened.

Malotus brushed away his black mane, his teeth also bared. "GET. OUT."

They ran without another look back.

***

Yulah sat alone in her flat in the dark. She couldn't stop her head from spinning. She was going to pieces. How could Flax have turned out like this? After everything they went through, tricking her. Could he even love her?

When you think you can trust someone and awful thoughts swarm your mind, and it stings with rejection, and you can't imagine where you went wrong. Or how you could love someone like that? Was it a lie all along? Did he ever have any feelings for me?

Adrenaline filled her. Cold shivers, despite the blanket. She had to move.

She couldn't bear the sight of Malotus. She stung with pain at the thought of his condescending comfort.

And then, footsteps and clamor above—both smashing and shouting. The blanket gave a shock, static electricity. A pop from above.

Was that lightning?

What is going on in this place?

She remembered the Meruyan girl she'd abandoned in the Emperor's chamber. A slight pang of guilt. She'd saved her once before, but it sounded like more than the simple ordeal she'd fled.

She dashed out her door and through the corridors, back to the throne room, heart tearing at her, only to find it in utter disarray. Guards and prisoners scattered the floor, dead or unconscious. Silken banners were on fire. She looked up, drawing herself up through the partially destroyed copper ceiling gaps, and saw over the skyline.

Borak, in a wind storm, with Flax clinging to his shoulders, and the Meruyan girl grasping the back of an elder escaped prisoner, alongside several others in tornados. The one with the bulging eyes who had grabbed her earlier grinned over his shoulder at her now, which made the hairs on her arms to stand on end—vile beast.

It looked like they were heading over to attack the wall protectors, the wind-guards, who were much more vulnerable from inside the wall.

Flax reached out and held the girl's hand. They sure seemed happy to get away together. Was it only comfort, or something more?

So that was it. Flax had left her here, without a word to her face—holding the hand of the Meruyan girl. Rage bubbled in her, with a rush that made her head pound sickeningly. The deceit stung like burning rain, flooding her body with waves of heat.

She'd have her revenge on those savages—Sen'Prin and Meruyan be damned. Malotus had been right all along.

A noise snapped her from it. Emperor Ryogrim crawled out from behind his throne, startling her.

"Sir!" she called to attention. She was fully devoted. She vowed allegiance—for her empire, or maybe for revenge. She only knew that nothing and nobody would toy with her heart like Flax had, ever again.

***

Flax was relieved when the airships touched down in Sen'Prin City.

How had they managed an escape like that? Bursting over the walls in the wind, Flax had held tight in Borak's arms. He was unable to summon wind of his own without his horns. They managed to get to the Sen'Prin airships that awaited them deep in the nearby forest.

His head throbbed. It was odd not to be able to use his wind energy. He'd been cut off from one of his basic senses. He couldn't feel the direction of the wind. It no longer ran through him.

So this is how Meruyans must feel, at the mercy of others with wind power. Meleena had stayed close with the elder Warix, Plymore. There was an endearing energy about the old Warix. He seemed like someone Flax might have known his whole life. Though Flax had to admit it was nice to be carried in his father's arms, to need him. If only he could have when he was a boy.

The new engineering inventions they brought had done the rest of the job, providing the strength to break through the wind-guards at the storm wall. He knew this was much easier from the inside going out. Even with that tech, it would have been impossible in the other direction.

And then there was Yulah. He caught her looking back at the top of Sen'Drorn fortress, there, watching them go—a thin figure with flowing hair. His heart stung at the sight of leaving her, no explanation, hurt once again. He didn't have a chance to tell her how he really felt, and she wouldn't have believed him anyway. Today's victory seemed almost unworthy in the face of this sacrifice. *How could he do that to Yulah?* He had feelings for her, were they love? His cheeks were hot with shame. It hurt more than the bruises from Malotus's torture. He deserved it for his treatment and betrayal.

As the airship steered into the landing base, Arenay came out, at the helm of the welcoming party comprised of Sen'Prin and Meruyan alike, soldiers, scholars, and family. They helped the freed Warix prisoners off the airship, pleased to hear about who they were and what gadgets they had brought.

"Flax! What happened to you? You look hurt!" His mother charged out of the crowd. He had almost forgotten he was being held up by Borak, who set him down as his mother rushed to inspect the wounds. "Your horns! Oh, *gusts*, I'd like to smack 'em hard!" Her lips pursed as if she'd sucked a lemon, cheeks flaring red on her tan face.

His parents, meeting again—he'd hardly believed it possible.

Borak shifted his feet. "Odella...do you recognize an old fool like me?" he asked softly.

Her eyes sparkled with recognition. "My, oh my...is that Borak?"

"I should have done right by us all those years ago!" Tears filled his eyes. "How could you not tell me I had a son?!"

Odella shrugged. "I had to choose—the fugitives of the rebellion were on the move. It was chaos, you know I couldn't wait for you anymore. But you two seem to have met anyway, somehow." She smirked, tears in her eyes as she looked between them.

Flax smiled. They had a lot to catch up on.

*****

When The elder Warix, known as Plymore, set Meleena down, Arenay hurried over to greet the group. "Meleena! What happened?"

Meleena hung her head. "They didn't even plant it. I thought they'd at least hear me out, but they were too suspicious. The Pendant was burned up, and the Wind Spirit herself came out." Her eyes glistened at the memory.

Arenay's eyes grew wide. "Nushenyu…"

"Yes. Nushenyu said there were others, like the mother seed, growing in the elemental realm on the backs of some beast, she called a Navanax."

Arenay's amber eyes drifted to the sky. "Fascinating. Nobody knows where the elementals live, but we will have to investigate this further. You've given me much to think about."

Plymore added, "Of course they wouldn't let anyone utilize the Pendant. They are too paranoid about the poison fruit."

Arenay bowed to Plymore. "Welcome to Sen'Prin. I see Flax rescued more than just his father from Sen'Drorn fortress. Tell me about yourself."

Plymore introduced himself. "I was an explorer the last time around, nearly forty years ago, sent by Sen'Drorn to find the Pendant. We found it, but when I showed it to them, they too did not believe The Pendant was real. Since it didn't enhance wind power, it was deemed poison for the mind, and a trick. Those who did try it only wanted to better wages for the Meruyan. So, I was imprisoned, and have been a test subject for their tech development all these years. Until young Flax here rescued me."

"What happened to The Pendant after that?" asked Meleena.

Plymore shrugged. "Tossed into the sea, where the Meruyan found it. And the cycle continued."

Arenay's hand covered her mouth while she listened. "Well, that is enlightening."

"Wait, I know you: scarlet hair, fierce eyes. You are the daughter of my comrades. I recognize the resemblance. You stood against your own nation to help the Meruyan."

"My parents always taught me to value all life." Arenay took his hands, and a single tear appeared on her face.

Meleena said, "Even if The Pendant surfaced many times, this is the only time it's been destroyed. The cycle of Warix factions, peace and war, that it has created for generations is broken. What hope do we have now?"

Arenay smiled, "I guess we never have to worry about racing the Sen'Drorn to find the Pendant anymore. And it seems we have their best wind-tech engineers on our side now. Perhaps we can assert some pressure on them, soon. For now, they are weakened. They won't be ready to launch an attack against us for quite some time."

Meleena looked to Flax and the engineers he had rescued from the Sen'Prin laboratory. There was Bruce, Plymore, a handful of other middle-aged Warix men, and that crazy-eyed Warix with flaming red hair who had launched a storm with his gadgets. They certainly were an interesting bunch.

Meleena added, "Speaking of loss, I got General Malotus to eat the Pendant fruit. Then he let Flax and me go. Do you think it will change him permanently?"

Flax responded, "His grudge against Arenay motivated Malotus as General of Sen'Drorn. He had no loyalty for their Emperor. The fruit helped him let go of the anger, and see how his life was spent hurting others for nothing. He'll have to quit now."

"Indeed." Arenay nodded, her auburn cheeks turning crimson. "That old fool."

Flax blushed too, and looked to his feet when he asked, "I saw a photo of you two. *Together.*"

Arenay sighed. "He kept the picture. Yes, we were once in love. But he mistook my interest in activism as a choice over him, since it took up all my attention, rather than something we could do together. But that's a story for another day." She turned to Meleena. "Young Meleena. You have helped us so much. I would be honored for you to join the ranks of

Sen'Prin. Your title can be *Naturalist*, for all your useful knowledge about the natural world."

"Thanks, I'm honored to accept the position." Meleena bowed. She pulled out the journal that Malotus had returned to her. "I never expected to see this journal again when I recovered it from Sen'Drorn Fortress. I'll have to spend some time rewriting everything from memory."

"You will have some time. You shall return to your hometown in the meantime, to await your first assignment."

Meleena nodded, still clutching her journal. Then Arenay politely excused herself to help the newcomers find a place to settle in. She bowed to Plymore. "Thank you, Plymore, it has been enlightening to meet you. Go with my people and I will have them set you up in your own cottage in the city. You have a permanent place among us, in our council, if you wish it."

Plymore nodded, his leaflike ears swishing humbly.

Another airship landed on the deck, and some Meruyan hopped off. It was Councilman Ives and Meleena's family. She was grateful they had brought her a new pair of glasses.

She hugged her parents, Tomiyan, and even Kelrick. Unlike the rest of her family, who seemed delighted to be there, Kelrick looked cross. "You embarrassed us all. Running away from Aldrok's Journey and starting a mess!"

"What!" Meleena protested. "That's not what happened!"

"Ah, don't worry about him." Her father waved it off.

"It's good to see you too. But, there is something I need to know. Did either of you call in a favor to get me into Aldrok's Journey? Back when…"

Kelrick looked insulted. "As if I would ever!"

Her father hugged her again. "Meleena, you earned it yourself."

Meleena laughed. "Well, I am going to work for the Sen'Prin, as a naturalist."

Another airship came in for a landing. Deem and Talla hopped off and came running over to Meleena.

"Meleena!" Deem shouted, catching her eye. "We did it! We got some guards to eat the fruit, and Meruyan productions will be stalled there for a while!"

Talla shook her head. "It's not that simple. Some Meruyan workers were injured in the chaos. There's been a crackdown on labor. The Meruyan recognized their poor situation, but not how to get out of it. Sen'Drorn grip on them is still strong, and they will crack down when a new cycle of guards rolls in."

Deem added, "The Meruyan are still on their land, bound by contract and will be kept in place by violence if not loyalty."

Meleena explained her own mission and outcome. Governess Arenay and Councilman Ives went over to them.

Arenay said graciously, "I'm sorry to hear your problem persists, Meruyan. We will continue to ally in secret and fight the Sen'drorn. One thing we can do is help Meruyan get fair trade for their glasses. Instead of Sen'Drorn made, maybe we can buy and assemble glass from the Hyish directly. It's a start."

"Now that we know they like Meruyan treasures, I've convinced them to extend their trade route to our lands," smirked Talla.

Councilman Ives said, "Arenay of Sen'Prin, we are in your debt, you have proven to be on our side in our time of need."

Arenay blushed. "It wasn't me, it was your three youths. You picked good Champions this year!"

Councilman Ives turned to Meleena, Deem, and Talla. "You are all welcome to join the Council, naturally."

Deem and Talla both agreed.

Deem said, "The system may not be perfect, but being in a position to influence policy is better than running away from it."

"Everyone deserves a fair shot at a good life." Talla shrugged.

Councilman Ives declared, "Then you shall join me in the capital, Dlawn'Edo, to begin in your junior positions."

Meleena thought about their futures: Talla would make an exceptional negotiator for trade deals, be it with Hyish or Warix.

Deem could join the department for underwater community resources, to make sure they get what they need. Perhaps he could train giant lobsters as mounts.

Meleena politely declined the Council's offer. Councilman Ives bowed and wished her best wishes as Naturalist of Sen'Prin.

After an evening together with everyone in Sen'Prin headquarters, celebrating their victory, Meleena rode with her family and friends on an airship bound for her hometown, Pontai'Desa.

From the air, Meleena spotted a view of the glorious Meruyan capital, its cascading waterfall and mountainous lake a speck on the vast green mountain landscape as they flew south. Before long, the familiar hills of The Southern Villages rolled before them—then the onion cottages of Pontai'Desa by the sea. Her home. In context with the rest of the world, it seemed even smaller than when she had longed to leave. Meleena knew her stay would be short and sweet, this time around.

ABOUT THE AUTHOR

J.B. Lesel is a fantasy writer living in California and sometimes in the forests of Germany. When she's not writing or lounging like a cat, she has an unusual hobby of volunteering abroad with strange wildlife. She has a Master of Science in Psychology, working in content writing and data analytics. BORN OF WIND is her debut novel.